LOVE IN THE MAKING

LOVE IN THE MAKING

ROISIN MEANEY

LARGE PRINT
Oxford

First published in Great Britain 2010
by
Hachette Books Ireland

Published in Large Print 2011 by ISIS Publishing Ltd.,
7 Centremead, Osney Mead, Oxford OX2 0ES
by arrangement with
Hachette Books Ireland
An Hachette UK Company

British Library Cataloguing in Publication Data
Meaney, Roisin.
    Love in the making.
    1. Friendship - - Fiction.
    2. Bakeries - - Fiction.
    3. New business enterprises - - Fiction.
    4. Large type books.
    I. Title
    823.9'2–dc22

ISBN 978–0–7531–8818–7 (hb)
ISBN 978–0–7531–8819–4 (pb)

Printed and bound in Great Britain by
T. J. International Ltd., Padstow, Cornwall

For Mags, who came up with the title, and Orla, who should be running her own cupcake shop

January

"Hang on," he said. "Just . . . hold on a minute, would you?"

They were already late, Hannah struggling into the hurriedly bought black dress that was beginning to look horribly like a mistake. Too stiff to sit comfortably, too long to feel sexy, too short to hide her knees. Too young, dammit, for a thirty-two-year-old to get away with.

Why had she listened to a shop assistant who was paid to tell everyone how great they looked, no matter what ridiculous thing they put on? But Hannah had listened, because the shop was about to close and she had to buy something. And now she was a hundred and forty euro worse off, and she hated the dress.

And they were going to be late, and it was her party. And she'd cut the damn tags off.

"I hate this dress," she said, doing up the three oversized buttons that for some reason had seemed charming in the shop. At least Patrick would tell her she looked lovely, and she'd pretend he wasn't lying, and try to convince herself that it wasn't that bad. How could a dress that cost a hundred and forty euro not be lovely? At least it had to be well cut, didn't it, at that price? And the fabric must be halfway decent.

"Isn't it awful?" she asked. "Don't know what possessed me — I could easily have worn my blue." She waited for him to say all the right things.

But he didn't.

"Hang on," he repeated. "Hannah, there's something I need to talk to you about."

She swung away and began rummaging through the biscuit tin that held her jewellery. "Great. Now I've gone and lost one of my good earrings." Cross with him for not reassuring her, but where was the point in starting a row when they were halfway out the door? The last thing she needed was for him to be in a sulk for the night. "Patrick, come on," she said, still bent over the tin, "the taxi will be here any minute. Where's your clean shirt?"

He took the three steps that were needed to reach her, and put a hand on her bare forearm. "Hannah, will you please stop doing that a minute," he said evenly, "and listen to me? Will you, please?"

Hannah stepped sideways, leaving his hand behind. At least she loved her deep red shoes with the shiny silver heels that Geraldine, knowing her daughter's taste so well, had set aside for her the minute they'd come into the shop.

"Patrick, we haven't time, it's nearly ten to." She slid her feet into the soft leather, admiring how much thinner her ankles immediately became — how did a high heel manage that? "Please will you get changed?"

"I'm not going." So softly that she nearly missed it.

"You're what? What?" Turning too quickly, her hand catching the edge of the biscuit tin, knocking it off the dressing-table, sending it flying. It tumbled onto the wooden floor with a clang, earrings and bangles and necklaces skidding and rolling and clattering everywhere as she turned back to him.

"What do you mean, you're not going?" She searched his face. "Patrick, what's up? Are you sick?"

He shook his head, but she saw now that he did look a bit pale. He must be coming down with something, and she'd been in too much of a hurry to notice it.

"I've met someone," he said rapidly, his eyes skidding away from hers. "I'm really sorry, Han — honest to God, I never meant it to happen. I swear, I . . ."

Hannah's head felt as if it was emptying, everything inside it draining out as fast as it could. The sudden feeling of lightness made her sway; she grabbed the edge of the dressing-table and held on. "You've . . . what? You've met someone?"

A year and three months they'd been together. He'd taken her to Paris; he'd said "I love you", in all kinds of weather. You didn't take someone to Paris and then meet someone else. It just wasn't done. It was plain bad manners, if nothing else.

"I'm so sorry."

His face was terribly pale, she realised now. A little lilac vein thudded gently in his temple. Two deep grooves ran the length of his forehead. A faint grey circular stain the size of a two-euro piece sat on the shoulder of the white shirt he'd been wearing all day.

She wondered what could possibly have caused a stain like that in that place.

"Han. Say something."

His voice brought her back. She noticed that breathing was becoming something of an issue. She moved towards the bed and lowered herself heavily onto it. She leant forward, resting her head on her black nylon knees, and inhaled deeply, feeling the air shuddering into her.

"Are you OK? Han?"

His voice sounded thick. Maybe he was crying. She hoped he was crying. Her knees smelt of lavender.

A horn sounded outside. She lifted her head carefully. "There's the taxi," she said. "Come on, you need to get ready."

Her words sounded breathless, as well they might. Patrick was standing in the same position, not crying but looking as if he might be thinking about it. Her head felt so light, with nothing left inside.

"I'm sorry," he said again. "I can't go. I can't . . . pretend any more."

Pretend? She clutched handfuls of the duvet. Her palms were damp. "Don't be silly," she said. "Of course you're coming — it's all arranged." She squeezed the cotton-covered feathers as she curled her toes inside the red shoes.

"Hannah," Patrick said, "I feel terrible about this, honestly. It wasn't planned. I never meant to hurt you."

The horn sounded again. Hannah let go of the duvet and stood up. "Come on," she said. "You still haven't changed your shirt."

He shook his head. "Han, I'm leaving. I'm moving out tonight."

"No you're not," she said. She picked her way across the floor, avoiding the spilt jewellery, and took her bag from the chair by the wardrobe. "I'll wait for you in the taxi," she told him. "Don't be too long, will you?"

She lifted her coat from its hanger, pulled her blue wrap from the shelf. "You've got five minutes." There was a tiny buzzing in her ears. Something was lodged in her throat. She pushed her arms into her coat sleeves. "Don't bother picking up that stuff — I can do it when we get home."

She walked downstairs, her hand squeezing the banister. She opened the front door and closed it gently behind her. The evening air was knife sharp. She pulled her coat around her as her silver heels clacked on the cement path that was already whitening with frost. The taxi looked black in the streetlights, but it could have been any dark colour.

She opened the back door and slid in, murmuring a greeting to the driver.

"Just yourself?" he asked. He wore a woolly hat and smelt of mints. The car was warm. The radio was on, some trumpet music playing softly.

"Yes," she said, not looking back at the house. It occurred to her suddenly that she hadn't asked Patrick who he'd met. How had she not asked? What if it was someone she knew? What if everyone knew about this other woman except Hannah?

"Where to?"

"Oh . . . The Cookery."

She'd booked for eight people. She'd have to look at his empty seat all night; it would keep reminding her that he wasn't there. She dipped into her bag and fished out a crumpled tissue, and pressed it to her eyes. Her mascara wasn't waterproof: she had to catch the tears before they did damage.

Was he packing a bag right now? Were his suits laid out on the bed? Had he taken his orange toothbrush from the glass in the bathroom? Or was he on the phone to the woman, telling her he'd done it?

Hannah took it badly, he might be saying. *She wouldn't listen, she kept telling me to get ready for the restaurant. I felt rotten.*

Saying he'd see her soon, saying he couldn't wait.

She was frightened at the thought of going home and finding all the empty spaces he was going to leave behind, all the places he'd filled with his books and CDs and clothes and golf clubs when he'd moved in. His empty hangers rattling in the wardrobe. Maybe he'd spread out her clothes so it wouldn't look so bare when she slid open the wardrobe door. But she knew he wouldn't think of doing that.

And what about the things he'd forget, because there was always something you forgot? Clothes in the laundry basket, books out of sight on top shelves, socks at the back of a drawer. What of the letters that would still come addressed to him? What of a voice on the phone asking for Patrick, someone he'd forgotten to tell?

And of course his smell would still be there, in the bed and on the towels, draped along the couch, seeped

8

into the cushions, waiting to ambush her around the house. What was she to do with his smell?

She hadn't asked if he loved the other woman. She couldn't bear the thought of that, of the love he'd had for Hannah being gathered up and transferred to someone else. Maybe he'd never — but she stopped that thought before it could go any further. Of course he had — you knew when somebody genuinely loved you.

Didn't you?

She was glad the driver didn't try to talk. He probably knew there was no point, seeing her in his rear-view mirror all hunched up. She was glad of the music, glad not to be sitting in a silent car with a stranger who might have felt obliged to say something.

They were getting near the restaurant. She found her little handbag mirror and dabbed with a corner of her tissue at the black smudges that had formed after all under her eyes. The driver turned on the overhead light.

"Thanks," she said. It didn't help much, such a watery wash of yellow, but another driver wouldn't have thought of it. She brushed on lipstick and ran her fingers through hair she hadn't had time to dry properly. Not that it would have made much difference — all the blow-drying in the world wouldn't take the kinks out, just like all the colour rinses in existence didn't make the slightest difference to the boring mid-brown colour she'd been cursed with.

She tried smiling at herself in the little mirror. She'd have to smile for the next two hours at least. There'd be champagne. They'd all be toasting her, wishing her well in her new business.

"Patrick is sick," she said, smiling at the face that smiled back at her.

"Sorry?"

She looked up and met the driver's eyes for an instant in his rear-view mirror. Had she really said it out loud? "Nothing. Just talking to myself."

They pulled up in front of The Cookery and Hannah paid and got out. She moved towards the restaurant, practising her smile.

"Hang on." She turned. The driver was holding her blue wrap out the window. "You forgot this."

"Thanks." She draped it around her shoulders as he drove off in his woolly hat. Then she walked into the restaurant, her heart sinking as Adam spotted her from the corner table and stood up, as the others turned, smiling, towards her. As her mother began to applaud.

Patrick dropped the last of his cases onto the pale green carpet. "That's it."

"You're sweating." Leah reached up on tiptoe and ran her little finger across his forehead. "Ugh. Big sweaty man in my nice ladylike apartment."

He grabbed her wrist. "Hey, I've just lugged practically everything I own up two flights of stairs. You should be glad I'm not stretched out on your nice ladylike carpet with a coronary."

Leah laughed. "God, imagine that — after waiting for months to get you to myself, you go and die on me."

10

"Well, it's not going to happen tonight." Bringing her hand down and pressing it to his groin, holding it there until she felt a reaction. "Does that seem dead to you?"

"Oh darling, you're so romantic." She wriggled out of his grasp and moved towards the bathroom. "Come on, I need to scrub you clean before I can take advantage of you."

Hannah's face, when he'd told her, when she'd finally realised what he was telling her. Everything changing in it, the colour draining away, even while she was still telling him to get a move on.

Saying she'd wait for him in the taxi, like some part of her refused to hear what he was telling her — Christ, he hadn't expected that. He'd been waiting for tears, or maybe a few things pelted at him, some kind of unpleasant scene certainly, but not that.

Leah undid his shirt buttons as the bath filled, as the air became warm and moist and scented. She unbuckled his belt and unzipped his trousers, and eased off his shorts. She pulled out of his embrace, catching his hand as he tried to untie her wrap — "Not yet, you animal" — and he stepped over the side of the bath and lowered himself slowly into the foaming water.

"What are you thinking?" She reached for a pink sponge.

"Nothing — I'm too tired." Leaning his head back and closing his eyes, inhaling the musky scent of whatever she used to make the bubbles.

The meal in the restaurant would be over by now — they'd have moved on to a bar probably. He wondered what Hannah had told them when they'd asked where he was. Of course they'd be all sympathy for her. They'd hate him for dumping her, despise him for his timing, so close to the shop opening. He imagined her mother's reaction, and his heart sank. He'd always liked Geraldine, and he knew the feeling had been mutual.

"Happy?" Leah soaped his chest, his shoulders, the length of his arms, squeezing foam and warm water onto his skin. "No regrets?"

"No regrets." He opened his eyes. "Why don't you get naked and join me?"

She shook her head, smiling. "Bath's too small, babe."

But it wasn't too small, he was too big. Six foot four and wide as a rugby player. Beside him Leah was a nymphet, a five-foot-two slip of a thing with boy-short blonde hair and the palest skin, weighing just over half his fifteen stone.

In bed once she'd fallen asleep on top of him, one of the few times they'd managed to spend a whole night together, and the weight of her hadn't bothered him at all.

Hannah was more solidly built, edging always towards a plumpness she battled against, but that Patrick had never objected to. He'd loved the small ripples of flesh around her waist, the heaviness of her breasts, the generous curves of her buttocks, the comfortable dimply softness of her thighs.

Hannah's bath was bigger too, an old cast-iron affair, stained and mottled with spidery cracks but roomy enough for both of them at a pinch. He had some fond memories of that bath — and what harm were memories?

"Right, I think you're clean enough." Leah squeezed out the sponge. "Up you get."

"Are you going to bath me every night?" Standing on the blue mat drying his hair briskly as Leah wrapped another towel around his waist.

"Maybe. Depends on how you behave yourself." She turned towards the door. "Follow me in."

Patrick wiped steam from the mirror and checked his reflection. He raked fingers through the thick, almost black hair, rasped a hand across the stubble on his jaw. He should have shaved before he'd left Hannah's — Leah didn't appreciate the he-man look — but he'd been anxious to be off, nervous of Hannah coming home early from the restaurant maybe, to plead with him to stay. He brushed his teeth with Leah's toothbrush and dropped the towels into her pale blue wicker basket.

In the bedroom she'd lit candles and spread a fresh bath sheet on the fawn carpet. "Lie on your stomach," she ordered, and Patrick lowered himself to the floor. Leah undid the belt of her robe and knelt and straddled him, and he closed his eyes as he felt the warm massage oil trickling onto his back, as her hands began to spread it over his skin, as the scent of eucalyptus wrapped itself around him.

"I could really get used to this," he murmured.

"No talking."

Her fingertips drummed down his vertebrae, the sides of her hands chopped across his shoulder-blades.

She'd put one of her salon CDs on, all breathy Pan pipes and swishing waves, and he thought of the CDs arranged alphabetically on Hannah's bookshelves — Iris DeMent and John Lee Hooker and Willie Nelson and James Taylor. He thought of the two of them sprawled on Hannah's deep red couch reading the Sunday papers, with Willie Nelson singing about gypsies who wore golden earrings.

Hannah's bookshelves. Hannah's couch. Even after sharing it with her for more than a year, he'd never regarded the house as theirs, always hers. It was officially hers, of course: she'd bought it three years before they'd met, and she'd taken in a tenant to share the costs. When Patrick replaced the tenant they'd split the bills and mortgage repayments, and he'd repainted the entire downstairs, sorted out the garden and bought the patio furniture she'd never got around to, but it was always Hannah's house. Maybe on some level he'd known it wasn't his final destination.

"Roll over."

It had been Hannah who'd led him to Leah. He'd complained of aches and pains after a longer than usual bout in the garden, digging up her ancient box hedge and replacing it with willow fencing, and Hannah had called into Leah's salon the following day and bought him a back-massage voucher.

She hadn't asked him about the woman he'd met, the woman he was leaving her for. He'd expected her to, he'd been ready to tell her the truth — it was the least she deserved — but she hadn't asked. She'd find out soon enough, of course: Clongarvin was too small, and he was too well known. How would she feel when she heard Leah's name, knowing that she herself had been the one who'd brought them together?

Leah moved from his chest to his legs, stroking from knee to thigh in strong upward movements. For such a petite creature, her massage was deep and satisfying. She eased his legs gently apart and began to knead his inner thighs, using slow, circular movements with her knuckles. As she inched towards his groin he felt himself stiffening pleasantly in response.

"Why, hello there." She smiled, and Patrick reached for her, sliding the robe off her shoulders, and Hannah was forgotten.

It was the longest two hours of her life, but she got through it with nobody guessing. She thanked them all for their help — her parents and Adam, and Adam's two cousins, and one of their girlfriends who she'd met for the first time a week ago — and she drank the champagne when they toasted her success, and she ate enough Dover sole not to arouse anyone's interest, although every mouthful of her favourite fish was an effort.

She told them that Patrick was in bed with food poisoning, and they all accepted it — why wouldn't they?

"Oh, the poor thing," her mother said. "I'll never forget how awful I felt after those prawns that time — remember, Stephen?"

"I certainly do," Stephen answered, winking at Hannah.

"Still can't look at them. What did Patrick eat?"

"Er, sausages, I think." Hannah pushed her glass across the table towards Adam. "Could I have a top-up?"

Towards the end of the meal, when she was doing her best with a slice of lemon cheesecake, Adam leant across and said quietly, "You OK? Anything up?"

She shook her head. "Just a bit stressed about the opening, that's all." Her face was rigid from smiling.

She'd have to tell him, she'd have to tell her parents. But not tonight, when she'd hardly taken it in herself. Maybe it was good that she had this distraction while Patrick's bombshell was still so fresh and raw. Maybe by the time she got home the first shock waves would be receding, and the urge to smash something, or have serious hysterics, would have passed.

But the thought of the empty dark house waiting for her, the thought of going home to nobody, the thought of all the unanswered questions caused a new stab of despair. She lifted her glass and drank too quickly, causing a little red wine to splash onto the front of her horrible black dress. No matter, she wasn't planning to wear it again. She hated it, and now it was the dress she'd been wearing when Patrick had broken up with her. It was the break-up dress. How could she ever look at it and not remember?

He's gone. She said the words in her head, and a dart of pain shot through her. She pushed her glass towards the wine bottle. "More," she said to Adam. "Just a bit." Not too much, or the truth might come out, and the night would be ruined for everyone.

She shared a taxi home with her parents, having truthfully pleaded a headache when the others began talking about a nightclub. The driver with the woolly hat was still on duty, the same soft jazzy music still wafting from his speakers. Hannah sat beside her mother in the back, afraid suddenly that Patrick would still be in the house.

"I must say I really like that restaurant," Geraldine said. "The food is just right, and they don't give you huge portions like other places."

"Mmm."

How long did it take to pack up your half of a relationship? What if he was just leaving now? What if they met him on the doorstep, surrounded by cases? She should have stayed out longer, ignored her pounding head and gone on smiling for another hour or two.

"And that waitress couldn't have been more helpful."

"No."

The house was dark, and there was no sign of a suitcase outside. Hannah's heart sank as she opened the taxi door, wanting him there now as fervently as she'd dreaded it moments earlier.

"We'll wait till you get inside," her mother said. "Have you your key out?"

The hall was warm. Patrick's leather jacket was missing from its usual hook. His golf umbrella was gone. She kept her coat on as she walked slowly through the house. His laptop, his books, his CDs, all gone. His toothbrush, his pyjamas, his slippers, his clothes. His aftershave, his razor. His tortoiseshell comb. The bathrobe she'd given him for Christmas, less than two weeks ago.

She crunched on something as she crossed the bedroom and bent to pick up an earring. She remembered the biscuit tin falling to the floor earlier, and saw it now sitting back on the dressing-table with her jewellery inside. She dropped in the stray earring and sat on the bed, feeling bereft.

He was gone. He'd left her and he was gone. He'd met someone else and he'd packed everything up and left her. They were over: there was no "they" any more. After fifteen months, Hannah was alone again.

She kicked off her shoes and pulled back the duvet and climbed into bed in her clothes. In her new black dress and black coat and blue wrap, in her foundation and mascara and eye-shadow and blusher and lipstick. She curled into a ball and closed her eyes. She wrapped her arms tightly around herself, yearning for his. Wanting the warm weight of him on top of her, wanting his mouth tasting hers. Wanting to pull his pillow towards her, but afraid of what that might do to her.

She wished she'd had more to drink.

Patrick lay on his back in the dark, wide awake. Leah was facing away from him, a faint asthmatic wheeze to her breathing. He moved his head and read 2:35, as it blinked redly on the bedside locker. The room was brighter than Hannah's bedroom at night, the cream curtains no barrier against a streetlight directly outside. There was more traffic here too, on Clongarvin's second busiest street. He'd get used to it.

He was going to have to get used to a lot of things. He turned onto his side and reached towards Leah, stroking the line of warm naked skin from hip to ribcage. She made a soft sound as he moved his hand to rest on her breast. He suddenly found himself remembering Hannah's breasts, how much fuller they were. He pushed the image away and ran a thumb slowly across Leah's nipple, backwards and forwards, feeling it respond to his touch. Leah stirred again, her breathing lengthening, and pressed her body back into his, her hand sliding onto his thigh. He reached past her stomach and found his way between her already opening legs.

Hannah was sweating when she woke. The clock beside the bed read 3:11. There was a tightness around her throat, something was bunched uncomfortably at her waist. She pushed the duvet back and groped for the lamp switch. As the room flooded with light, as she took in the empty space beside her, as she looked down at her crumpled clothes, it all came flooding back.

She swung her legs out and stood on the floor. She unwound her wrap and pulled off her coat, and let them both fall. She tugged at the black dress until the three giant buttons popped, one by one, and clattered across the wooden boards. She stepped out of the dress and yanked off her tights and knickers, and unhooked her bra. She threw everything in the vague direction of the laundry hamper and reached under her pillow and pulled out her grey tartan pyjamas.

He was gone. He was in another woman's bed now. He was gone. She pattered out of the room and into the bathroom, hardly aware of the cold tiles under her bare feet, oblivious to the tears that were trailing blackly down her face.

"I can't believe it," Alice said. "He walked out on her, just like that?"

"Just like that, no warning whatsoever." Geraldine pressed buttons on the calculator. "I don't know how she kept it up at the restaurant." She turned the wine-coloured stilettos upside down and crossed out €150 on the sticker and wrote €105 beside it in blue marker. "She said he'd got food poisoning — nobody suspected a thing."

"Well, why would you? It's the last thing you'd be expecting . . .tPoor Hannah, though. How's she coping?"

Geraldine replaced the stilettos and picked up a pair of chunky black platforms. "Badly. She's very upset, naturally." She used the calculator again. "Less thirty per cent is forty-eight ninety-nine. Will I round it up to fifty?"

"Do." Alice watched as Geraldine made the change. "But how could he leave her now, when she's just about to open the shop? Talk about bad timing. Is there someone else, is that it?"

Geraldine's mouth twisted as she turned the shoes right side up. "Apparently. He wouldn't say who."

"God, that's awful."

"Of course, I never trusted him," Geraldine said.

It wasn't true. They *had* trusted him, with his big job at the paper and his flowers every time he and Hannah called round, and going golfing with Stephen just like a real son-in-law would have done. But it felt good to say it now. "He never appealed to me, there was always something underhand about him."

"Mmm," Alice said. "Well, there must have been."

"Oh there was. I mean, who's to say that this woman was the first? If he strayed once, you can bet he did it other times. Poor Hannah's well rid of him." Geraldine replaced the shoes. "Have we the bottom row done?"

"I think so. What about the ones over there?"

"Anyway," Geraldine said, taking her stool across, "there's plenty more fish in the sea."

"There is, of course — and a nice girl like Hannah won't be waiting long, you can be sure."

Alice hadn't been at the dinner in The Cookery, and neither had her husband Tom. Hannah had suggested inviting them, but Geraldine had discouraged it. *You know what Tom's like after a few drinks.*

But Alice is your boss, Hannah had said, *and Tom works with Dad, and they've both been hearing about the shop for ever — and they got me the clock. They might expect to be invited.*

Why would they? They didn't help get the place ready. They weren't up a ladder with a paintbrush, or sanding and varnishing floors like the rest of us were.

And that had been that, and Alice hadn't been a bit put out, as Geraldine had known she wouldn't. Alice would be the first to admit that while Tom was great company he could be a bit of a trial after one drink too many. He'd have taken over Hannah's night, and Geraldine wasn't having that.

"I think it might be time for tea," she said now, putting her blue marker on the counter.

"Absolutely," Alice said.

Neither of her parents had noticed anything strange about Hannah in the restaurant. Both had observed that she hadn't eaten very much, but Geraldine had put it down to nerves at the thought of the shop opening at last, and Stephen had assumed it was yet another of his daughter's inexplicable attempts to shed a few pounds.

So when Hannah had called around the following evening and told them what had happened, in between sobbing on Geraldine's shoulder and eating five chocolate Kimberleys from the pack she'd brought them, it had come as a complete surprise.

He's met someone else, she'd wept. *He didn't say who.*

I hate to admit it, Geraldine had said when Hannah had finally left, *but it's probably a good thing they didn't get married after all.*

Stephen had given her the look over his glasses that always reminded her of a professor.

Don't say it, she'd ordered. *I know what you're thinking. You wanted them to get married too — it wasn't just me. You hated them living together without being married just as much as I did. I'm only saying, the way things have turned out, maybe it's as well they weren't married.*

22

It mightn't have happened if they'd been married, Stephen had pointed out mildly. *He might have thought twice about running around then.*

Or he might still have done it, which would make Hannah a deserted wife now. At least this way she can make a clean break. She's well rid, if you ask me.

Stephen had rattled his newspaper. *I thought you liked him. You always said you did.*

Well, I don't any more, Geraldine had answered crossly. *Whose side are you on?*

Ours, of course, Stephen had said from behind the paper.

Well then, stop defending him.

I'm not defending anyone. I was just saying you liked him. We both did.

Well, now he's gone, so we don't like him any more, she'd said, and Stephen had wisely allowed her to have the last word.

Except, of course, that it wasn't the last word.

How dare he walk out just like that? She'd taken a chocolate Kimberley and unwrapped it angrily. *Hannah's devastated. How'll she be able to open that shop after this? It's less than a week away.*

Of course she'll open the shop: it's just what she needs to take her mind off it. And won't you be there anyway to help out? She'll be fine.

Her heart won't be in it, though.

Maybe not — but that won't stop customers coming in.

Geraldine had sighed. *She's nearly thirty-three — most of the men her age are married.* She'd glared at

23

the biscuit. *She'll have to get a new tenant in — she can't afford that house on her own, especially now with the shop.* She'd rewrapped the Kimberley and laid it back on the plate. *I could kill that man.*

After several seconds of silence Stephen had risked lifting his newspaper again, and Geraldine had thrown him an exasperated glance before turning to stare gloomily into the fire.

Hannah held up her glass and Adam emptied the last of the wine into it. "Should I open another?"

"No." She swirled the glass and watched the red trails snaking back down the sides. "Not on my account. Mornings are miserable enough these days without a headache."

She rested her head on his shoulder. It wasn't getting easier to do without Patrick, but she was getting more used to feeling horrible all the time. Maybe that was some kind of progress.

"I've nearly phoned him," she said. "Loads of times. And I've typed loads of text messages, but I haven't sent any of them."

"Good," Adam said. "Don't."

"I won't." She swirled the glass again. "I'll try not to. But there's so much I want to know."

"Why? What good would it do? Just let him off."

She drained the glass and reached forward to set it on the coffee-table.

"Two days to go," he said.

She burrowed her head into his shoulder and groaned. "Don't remind me — I'm petrified."

24

"Now cut that out." He found her hand and squeezed it. "You'll be great. This is what you've always wanted, remember? Your very own shop, selling all your own stuff."

"I'm still petrified," she said, her words muffled. "What if nobody comes in?"

"Of course they'll come in." He lifted her hand and counted on her fingers. "One, you're new. Two, it's the first dedicated cupcake shop in Clongarvin. Three, it looks fantastic — no small thanks to me — and the location is perfect. Four, nobody bakes cupcakes like you do. Five, you're giving them away free."

She turned her face to look at him. "One complimentary cupcake with every order is hardly giving them away free. And anyway, that's only on the first day." She nibbled a nail. "What if nobody comes back for more? Or what if someone says they got food poisoning? What if —"

"Stop that," Adam said. "I'm living proof that your cupcakes are impossible to resist, and not at all poisonous. You'll be the talk of Clongarvin within a week."

Hannah smiled faintly. "We'll see."

"A word of advice," he said.

"What's that?"

"Don't try selling leftovers the day after. They won't keep."

She slapped his arm half-heartedly. "Nice try. You know very well they're good for at least three days. Leftovers will be half price, and that's that. For the last time, you will not be getting a steady supply."

"That's what I'm afraid of," he said gloomily. "You'll be so busy baking for the shop, I'll never get to taste them again."

"You could try buying a few, like everyone else. I'll see about giving you a small discount. Although I feel I should point out, darling" — patting his generously proportioned stomach — "that you could do worse than laying off the cupcakes for a while."

He grinned. "That's better — you're beginning to sound like your old bitchy self."

"I'm going to be baking all night and selling all day — I'll be too wrecked to be a bitch." She put her head into her hands and groaned again. "God, what possessed me to think of opening a cupcake shop? Why didn't you stop me?"

"Yeah, like you'd have listened to me for a second. Anyway, the one to blame is your granddad — it's all his fault for leaving you that money. But like I keep pointing out, you don't have to do it all on your own — you can take someone on part time."

"And like I keep saying, pay them with what? Granddad's money bought the lease, and most of the paraphernalia, and not much else. You know I'm already up to my neck in debt . . ." She trailed off. "Did I tell you that the new food processor cost almost eight hundred euro — and that was in a sale?"

"Yes, I've heard that more than once. You'll remember I nearly fainted the first time." He shot her a stern look. "And I'm sorry, but I have no sympathy with you being broke when you still haven't put that ad in."

When Hannah said nothing, he added, "You haven't, have you?"

She reached for the TV remote control and turned up the volume. "Stop nagging."

"Turn that down. I haven't mentioned it in two whole days. When are you going to do it?"

She pressed the mute button and dropped the remote. "I don't know . . . next week, maybe."

Too soon, too painful. *Person wanted to share house* meant accepting that Patrick was definitely gone, like bundling a dead person's clothes into black plastic bags for the charity shop, like taking someone's name off the roster when they found another job. Six days without him felt like six years, but still it was much too soon for a tenant.

There was a short silence. Adam stretched his arms above his head. They watched a man in a white coat mouthing something to a woman on a hospital trolley, but Hannah's thoughts were far from *ER*.

She'd lost count of the times she'd found Patrick's name in her phone and almost pressed *call*. Who is she? she wanted to demand. When did you meet her? How long was it going on? How could you do this to me?

But lying alone in the middle of the night, the silent questions changed. When are you coming back? Don't you know I'll forgive you? When did you stop loving me?

"I suppose," she said sadly, "I'll survive. At least I'll be too busy to mope." She reached for her scarf and hung it around her neck. "Right, I'd better be off. I'm trying to get to bed early these nights, so the new schedule won't be too much of a shock. You don't have to come," she added, as Adam took his feet off the coffee-table and reached for the leather jacket slung across the arm of the couch.

"Right — and when you're mugged your father won't string me up for letting you walk home alone." He zipped up the jacket and shepherded her towards the door.

"Come on Kirby," he said, and the black Labrador lying in front of the fire raised his head and looked at him. "Come on," Adam repeated, and Kirby hauled himself to his feet and plodded after them.

It wasn't raining. The evening was clear, stars studding the sky. Hannah tucked her arm into Adam's as they walked the streets towards her house, Kirby padding along behind.

Anyone looking at them would think lovers, or at least boyfriend and girlfriend, a couple of some kind anyway. It had taken Patrick, and most of Hannah's other boyfriends, quite a while to feel comfortable with her having a male best friend.

"You know what's just occurred to me?" Adam asked as they walked.

"What?"

"Today's the eleventh, so you're opening on the thirteenth, right?"

"Mm-hmm."

"And my birthday's on the thirteenth of August."

She looked at him. "So?"

"So it's exactly seven months from the day you open."

"And your point is?"

"My birthday," he said, "can be your deadline. Whatever happens in the meantime, give yourself at least seven months to make a go of it."

"Even if I go broke in the first week?"

"Yes. Even if you have to sell your house to keep it going."

She stopped dead and looked at him in horror. "Sell my house? You're kidding, aren't you?"

"Of course I am." He nudged her along. "I just think it would be good if you had that date as your watershed."

"My watershed?"

"You know what I mean. The date that you can finally say 'I've made it.' The date that you renew your lease for another decade."

She laughed. "The lease is for a year."

"You know what I mean. You agree not to give up before then? Promise?"

"I . . . suppose so." She hesitated, and then added, "Yes, I mean yes. I won't give up before your birthday."

"You promise?"

"I promise."

"Good. We'll have the mother of all parties then, two things to celebrate." They approached her house. "I told you to leave a light on," Adam said, frowning at the darkness beyond the glass panes in the front door.

"I know — I forgot."

They were almost exactly the same height. They'd been friends for more than twenty years, since they'd signed up for the same swimming class at the local pool. Hannah still swam as often as she could, and while Adam's interest had waned around the time he discovered girls, he'd migrated by then to Hannah's circle of friends, and over the years the two of them had grown closer.

Funny how they'd never been drawn towards one another romantically. Hannah loved Adam, but the thought of being in a physical relationship with him had simply never been an option for her, and she was quite sure it had never occurred to him either, thankfully. If they were both romantically involved at the same time they might go out as a foursome, but other than that their love lives didn't intersect.

"You busy this week?" she asked.

"A meeting tomorrow, hopefully some new business. Other bits and pieces to finish off." He designed websites, working from the small flat he'd invested in around the time Hannah had bought her house. "I'll call in on Wednesday," he said, "to collect my free cupcake."

"Only if you buy some," she reminded him.

"God, you're hard. You'll go far."

They reached the door and he put his hands on her shoulders. "Best of luck — not that you need it. You'll be great, I know you will."

She smiled. "Thanks Adam."

He hugged her, enveloping her in the leathery scent of his jacket, kissing her cheek loudly. "Night-night. Put the chain on the door."

The house was cold. Now that the heating bill was Hannah's alone, she had to economise. She filled a hot-water bottle and set her alarm for eight. The next couple of days would be busy, shopping for ingredients, organising her kitchen, setting everything in place for Wednesday morning when her new regime would begin. When she'd rise at three in the morning to make and ice one hundred and forty-four cupcakes for the first time.

She'd practised, she'd timed everything. Four trays into the big oven at a time, forty-eight cupcakes baking for twenty minutes while she put the next lot of mixtures together. The first lot cool enough to ice by the time she'd filled the last of the second batch of paper cups and made up the various icings. Eight varieties each day, fifteen different tastes rotating as the week went on.

Five hours max from start to finish every morning, breakfast grabbed somewhere along the way, as soon as she was awake enough to feel hungry.

Load the van, drive to the shop and unload. Fill the cupcake tree that sat on the counter with one of each variety. Arrange the hundred and thirty-six others in the display cases. Open at nine, close at five. Bag the leftovers in threes, drive home, eat dinner and get to bed by nine at the latest. Up again at three to start all over again.

Was six hours enough sleep? It would have to be. Could she keep that up for seven months, six days a week? What had possessed her?

She undressed quickly. This was the worst time, going to bed by herself — and waking up alone came a close second. Maybe she should get a cat, or a small dog that would curl up at the end of the bed and help her to feel less unwanted.

She burrowed under the duvet, trying to think positively. Wasn't this what she'd always wanted, since she'd begun working in Joseph Finnegan's bakery twelve years ago? She used to imagine running her own place, selling exactly what she wanted to sell, answerable to nobody. If only she had the money.

And then Granddad had died, three years ago last August, and his house had been put on the market a few months later, and had sold just before prices had begun to fall. And Hannah, his only granddaughter, had been given enough from the proceeds to realise her dream.

Last November the little corner unit on the main street had become vacant. After dithering for a few weeks she'd finally taken the plunge and signed the lease, and told Joseph Finnegan she'd be leaving at the end of the year.

She'd invested in a cooker that took up twice the space of the old one — forcing a complete reshuffle of her other kitchen appliances, during which the tumble-dryer had migrated to the shed — and she'd bought the frighteningly expensive food processor, along with the thousand other bits and pieces she hadn't realised she'd need.

Adam and his cousins had rallied, and the little shop had gradually been scrubbed and sanded, and painted and fitted with display cases and shelves. And last week a man had painted "Cupcakes on the Corner" in bright blue letters on the yellow strip of wall above the front window.

The shop was tiny — not much room for more than three customers at a time — but there was space around the back to pull up with the van. Adam had set up a website and designed stationery and printed off leaflets that they'd pushed through letterboxes, stuck on telegraph poles and supermarket notice-boards, and slipped under car windscreen wipers.

And just after Christmas Hannah's kitchen had been inspected by a health inspector and deemed a suitable place in which to produce the cupcakes.

So everything was set. She was poised at last to make her dream come true — and the one person she wanted by her side had left.

She reached out in the darkness and found her phone on the bedside table. She opened a new text message and inserted Patrick's name on the recipient line, then typed *I miss you*. She held her thumb above *send* — and slowly moved it across to press *exit*.

Save message? the phone asked.

No, she replied with her thumb, and the words vanished.

She replaced her phone, closed her eyes and forced herself to begin measuring flour, sugar and butter. For some reason, mental baking usually sent her right to sleep.

"Mum?"

"Hello."

Leah's heart sank at the cool tone. Her mother hadn't come round yet. "I'm just ringing to see how you are," she said as brightly as she could manage.

"He's moved in, has he?"

Leah could picture her face, pinched with disapproval. "Yes, he's moved in — and his name is Patrick," she added before she could stop herself, having vowed that they wouldn't have another row. "Mum," she said quickly, "please don't be like this."

"Easy for you to say," her mother answered, "when you don't have to face Geraldine Robinson at bridge every Friday night."

"She can't possibly blame you —"

"And who else would she blame, when it's my daughter who stole her daughter's boyfriend? You should have seen how upset she looked last Friday — I dread to think what she'll say when she finds out who's responsible for all this."

Leah closed her eyes and took a breath. "Mum, let's not get into this. Just please try to understand. Nobody planned it; I didn't set out to —"

"You knew he was involved with someone else — you should have had some self-restraint."

"It wasn't like that; It's not something —"

"Imagine what that poor girl is going through right now," her mother went on, "and her just about to open up a shop. Geraldine was telling us all only a couple of weeks ago how nervous she was about it. Remember how tough it was for you when you opened your salon? How would you have liked to be landed with something like that on top of it?"

34

With an effort, Leah held her tongue. No point in arguing: nothing she could possibly say would make a difference. Not when her mother had been in Hannah's very situation thirty years earlier — only worse, because Leah's father had walked out on his wife and small daughter. At least Patrick hadn't been married to Hannah, and no children were involved — not that there was anything to be gained by pointing that out, of course.

And it was definitely not the right moment to break her other news — although time was running out for keeping quiet about it.

"Can we meet for lunch?" she asked instead. "My treat. Maybe Wednesday?"

Her mother's sniff was perfectly audible over the mobile network. "I might be busy — I'll have to check my diary."

Leah dug her nails into her palm. "Well, give me a ring," she said lightly. "I'll keep one o'clock free. Let me know, OK?"

Hanging up, she opened the appointments book, took a pencil from the jar and wrote *lunch with Mum* in the one o'clock slot on Wednesday. She lifted the phone again and made a booking at Giovanni's — her mother liked it there.

And Leah would wait until after the pasta to tell her what had to be told.

And her mother would rant and rage all over again, and probably not talk to her for another month.

She lowered her head into her hands and groaned quietly. It wasn't as if she'd set out to lure any man away from another woman — that had never been her intention. Not that she hadn't been attracted, right from the first time they'd met, when he'd walked into the salon to claim his massage. She remembered admiring the broad chest, the muscular arms. She remembered him flirting with her, warning her to leave his towel alone.

She'd been disappointed when he mentioned a girlfriend, but not surprised — the gift of a massage generally came from a woman. And that had been it, as far as she was concerned. He was with someone else, no point in going there. Even after he'd made it plain that he was interested, she'd resisted him for as long as she could, insisting over and over that she didn't want an affair.

But in the end he'd charmed his way into her bed. He said all the things she wanted to hear, convinced her that it was over between him and Hannah in all but name. *She means nothing to me*, he insisted. *I just have to find the right time to leave her. I will leave her, I swear.*

Was it so bad then, that Leah had finally given him the incentive he needed to do just that?

The doorbell rang. She lifted her head and pasted on a smile, and crossed the room to let Martina Hennessy in for her Indian head massage.

Alice spooned more peas onto her husband's plate as he lifted the wine bottle and refilled their glasses. She wouldn't finish hers — one glass was all she could manage comfortably — but if it was in her glass it meant he couldn't drink it.

They never used to have wine with dinner — this was a new thing. Tom had got a case for Christmas from a patient he'd picked up during the year who worked in the off-licence trade, and they'd got into the habit of a glass or two in the evening. Alice could have lived without it quite happily — she'd never taken a drink until well into her thirties, apart from the odd brandy — but now it was a given. A bottle opened half an hour before dinnertime, and more often than not, gone by the end of the meal.

"There's more potatoes," she said.

"I'm alright, thanks."

He was well able to drink; he'd always been well able. There'd been times, mercifully few, when she'd had to put him to bed. But up to now he'd only drunk when they were out, and most of the time he managed to stop before it went too far, when he was still the life and soul of the party.

And it wasn't much, she supposed, a bottle of wine between two people. Where was the harm in him relaxing after his day's work? Except that he drank at least two-thirds of the bottle each night, and sometimes she noticed a slur in his words, and she worried about his condition the following morning — because who wanted a dentist with unsteady hands, or who smelt of drink as he bent over you?

"You heard about Hannah," she said. "I presume Stephen mentioned it."

Tom cut into his steak. "Mentioned what?"

"Her boyfriend left her."

"You're joking. The fellow from the newspaper?"

Of course Stephen wouldn't have told Tom: men didn't talk about things like that the way women did. They probably discussed the latest match results or political shenanigans when they had a break in the clinic.

"Just walked out on her," she said. "About a week ago now."

"That's too bad." Tom chewed his meat and lifted his glass. "They were together a good while, weren't they?"

"Over a year. Geraldine was convinced he'd propose at Christmas."

"So where's he gone?"

Alice made a face. "Some other woman, apparently. Moved in with her, I suppose."

"Mmm."

His wine glass was almost empty, hers practically untouched. In a minute or two he'd raise the bottle and hold it out to her, and she'd shake her head and he'd empty it into his glass.

Six whites and six reds they'd got, all French. She wouldn't know one wine from another — they all tasted the same to her. By the time the case was gone it had become a habit. Now he brought home two or three bottles any time he went to Lidl for the cheese he liked. "Six ninety-nine," he'd tell her. "Couldn't leave them behind at that price."

"Are you busy tomorrow?" she asked.

"Kept going. The usual."

"Will you have time to call into the cupcake shop?" she asked. "I thought it would be nice to show our support on the first day, and I won't get a chance, with Geraldine gone."

"Right."

"Get half a dozen of whatever she has, a mixture. And don't let her give them to you for nothing."

"OK."

He reached for the wine bottle. She put a hand over the top of her glass, and he emptied what was left into his own.

He was only relaxing. There was no harm in it.

A hundred and forty-four, twelve trays of twelve. Were a hundred and forty-four cupcakes enough for one day? There was no way of knowing. What if she'd made too many chocolate orange and not enough lemon and lime? What if everyone wanted vanilla coconut and nobody looked at the mocha? What if people hated the cream cheese icing and only went for the ones topped with buttercream? Was Clongarvin ready for mascarpone frosting?

"Stop."

Hannah looked at her mother. "Stop what? I'm not doing anything."

"You're worrying. It's as plain as the nose on your face."

"I can't help it — my stomach's in a knot. I feel like I've been up for hours."

"That's because you have. Did you get any sleep last night?"

"Not much. And the kitchen is like a bomb hit it."

"Don't mind the kitchen — I'll give you a hand to tidy up later. I hope you had some breakfast."

She shook her head. "Couldn't — I'd have thrown up. I'll run out for something later." She tweaked one of the cupcakes on the display stand. "Does this look OK?"

They sat in individual wire circles that curled upwards from the central branch. Each cupcake was labelled with a brightly coloured tag attached to a cocktail stick.

"They look great. All those lovely colours."

"I was sure I'd never get them all iced — it took much longer than I thought. Just as well I gave myself plenty of time." She darted a glance at the clock on the wall. "Mam, it's five to nine already."

Geraldine turned towards the door that led to the back room. "Which means we have five minutes. I'm putting on the kettle."

Hannah stared at her. "It's five to nine."

"And the place looks great, and it smells wonderful, and we're all set. And you need a cup of tea, whether you want it or not. And so do I." She disappeared.

Hannah looked out through the plate-glass window. "There's nobody waiting outside."

Her mother's voice drifted back. "Why would there be? You're open all day, aren't you? People don't normally have cupcakes for breakfast."

Hannah pushed a cocktail stick a fraction further into the top cupcake on the stand. "These labels are too small. I told Adam they were too small."

40

Geraldine reappeared. "They are not too small; I can read them fine without my glasses. And I love that writing — it's so cheery-looking."

"Font."

"Pardon?"

"It's not called writing on a computer, it's called a font. And that font is called Mufferaw. We couldn't decide for ages between that and Sybil Green. I wanted Sybil Green but Adam persuaded me that this one is easier to read —" She broke off. "What? What are you smiling at?"

Geraldine stepped closer and put her arms around her daughter. "Relax, my darling — it'll be great. Your cupcakes will be famous in no time. You'll have such fun with this — wait and see."

Hannah nodded against her shoulder. "I know I will."

But she knew she wouldn't. She knew she'd made the biggest mistake of her life, taking her grandfather's money and putting it into this liability, this tiny little cubby-hole on a corner that nobody else had been interested in renting. Why hadn't somebody stopped her? Why were they all letting her make this colossal, expensive mistake?

Geraldine moved towards the back again. "There's the kettle now. Are you tea or coffee?"

"Tea." She didn't want tea, she wanted to go home. She glanced up again at the big orange wall clock in the shape of a sun that Alice and Tom had given her as an opening present. "It's a minute to nine," she called.

"Deep breaths," Geraldine called back, and Hannah inhaled shakily. She must be the only idiot opening a shop in the middle of a recession, signing a twelve-month lease when she could be out of business in a week. It wasn't as if cupcakes were basic foodstuffs that people would keep on buying no matter how tough times got. They were one of the luxuries everyone was cutting back on. She shouldn't have set the prices so high — who on earth was going to pay €1.75 for a bun, no matter how fancy it looked?

Geraldine returned with two steaming mugs. "I think we're all set." She smiled. "Why don't you open your shop for the very first time?"

Hannah walked to the door. She stopped, her hand on the key, and turned back to her mother. "Mam, what if nobody comes in?"

"And what if you open the door," her mother replied, "so at least they have a choice?"

Hannah smiled and turned the key. "There." She switched the sign that Adam had printed from *Sorry, fresh out of cupcakes* to *Come in — you know you want to*. "We're officially open," she said. "I'm officially running my own business." She paused. "For however long it lasts."

"You'll be here for years — you'll become an institution." Geraldine blew on her tea as Hannah came back behind the counter. "People will travel from all over for Hannah Robinson's cupcakes."

"I don't know about that, but I'm here for seven months anyway — Adam made me promise to stick it out till his birthday in August."

"You'll be flying by then, I'd bet anything."

They watched the steady stream of pedestrians passing the window.

"Drink your tea," Geraldine ordered, and Hannah lifted her mug obediently. A minute went by. Geraldine rubbed with her sleeve at a smudge on the glass-topped counter. Hannah tweaked another label on the cupcake stand, then undid and retied her apron strings.

"I don't know about that chair on the wall," she said. "I'm not sure about it."

"Just you wait," Geraldine said. "It'll be a real talking point."

It was Granddad's rocking chair. They'd painted it bright blue to match the sign above the shop, and they'd got a man to hang it on the yellow wall to the left of the counter, since there was no room for it on the floor.

"What if it falls off and kills someone?" Hannah asked.

"Don't be silly dear," her mother answered placidly. "The man said a hurricane wouldn't knock it off that wall."

Another minute went by, and another. The orange clock ticked steadily.

"I should have got a computerised cash register," Hannah said. "Nobody uses a drawer for money any more. It's ridiculous."

"It's quaint, and people will be charmed by it. And the bell over the door too, lovely and old-fashioned, really characterful."

"Mmm." Hannah wondered if there was such a word as "characterful", and decided that she didn't care.

At eight minutes past nine a man's head appeared around the door. "You open?"

"Yes." A twin chorus.

"Nice bell. Blast from the past." He spotted the rocking chair on the wall. "Now that makes a change from a picture."

Geraldine laughed, catching Hannah's eye triumphantly. "We wanted to be original."

"Well, you're certainly that." He approached the counter. "I believe it's your first day."

"It is — and you're our very first customer," Geraldine told him.

"Am I really?" He peered at the cupcakes on the stand. "In that case, I'd better buy something. What's good?"

"Everything," Geraldine told him, resting her mug on the shelf behind her. "And I'm sure you saw our sign telling you about our opening offer of a free cupcake with every order, but since you're the first customer, we'll give you two free." She turned to Hannah. "That OK, love?"

Hannah smiled and nodded, because what on earth else could she do? "That's fine."

Two free cupcakes, and he might only buy one. She willed herself to relax. Who cared if he only bought one? It was still her first sale, wasn't it? And if he liked the one he bought, not to mention the other two, he'd surely be back for more. And it wasn't even ten past nine.

So what if she was so tired she could sleep standing up? So what if she still felt miserable whenever she found the time to feel anything? She'd just opened her own shop. Maybe people didn't give up eating cupcakes just because there was a recession. Maybe they still needed treats — now more than ever.

The man grinned. "Two free? Excellent, many thanks. In that case, I'll take two chocolate, or my wife will never forgive me, and two of those coconut ones."

"Good choice — the coconut are my favourite," Geraldine said, reaching for a yellow box and almost knocking her tea off the shelf. "My daughter made them all, you know, earlier today. They're as fresh as they could possibly be."

"Excellent," the man said again, pulling a wallet from his jacket. "Tell you what, why don't you throw in a couple of those lemon and lime too? Since it's the first day. And I'll leave the free ones up to you."

Six. He was buying six. Hannah watched as Geraldine arranged his purchases carefully in the box. Maybe it wouldn't be a complete disaster. Maybe she'd actually make a small amount of money before her mother bankrupted her.

The horror bloomed on Fiona's face. "Tell me you're not serious."

Leah tightened her grip on her water glass. "Mum, I'd hardly joke about something like that."

"When?"

"June."

Her mother closed her eyes briefly. "You're four months gone."

"Thereabouts, yes."

"And . . . you're obviously keeping it."

Leah looked sharply across the table. "Obviously."

"I assume," her mother said coldly, "that it's the newspaper man's child."

Leah's knuckles were white around the glass. "Of course it is."

Their plates sat between them, the remaining pasta cooling, the sauces just beginning to congeal. Leah's two twenty-euro notes were tucked into the bill wallet, waiting to be collected.

"And I suppose he's delighted," Fiona said.

Leah met her mother's eyes steadily. "Yes, of course he is. We both are."

Fiona's smile was bitter. "Well, isn't that nice? A happy couple, and a baby on the way. Just what I always hoped for my only daughter."

Leah stood up abruptly, almost knocking over her chair. Forget the fifteen euro change: nothing was worth this. She grabbed her bag and pulled her jacket from the chair back. "I have to go now. I hope you enjoyed your lunch."

She didn't look back as she strode towards the door. Once again she'd let her mother get under her skin. She always swore it wouldn't happen, and it always did. It was unfortunate that Fiona played bridge with Hannah's mother, but it was hardly the end of the world. Relationships broke up all the time, Geraldine Robinson knew that as well as anyone, but Leah's mother was determined to make a song and dance about it.

The pregnancy of course had been a gamble, and Leah had hated lying to Patrick about the Pill not working, but it had paid off. He was with her now — and he *was* happy about the baby. He kept telling her how happy he was. Nothing her mother could say would change that, and in time she'd have to come round to the idea of being a grandmother.

Leah walked quickly through Clongarvin's busy lunchtime streets until she reached the pretty lavender-painted window-boxed frontage of Indulgence, She let herself in and leant against the door, breathing in the subtly scented air, her hands coming to rest on the stomach that was just beginning to swell.

At ten minutes to five Hannah untied her yellow apron and hung it on the blue star-shaped hook behind the counter. She leant wearily against the display cases as her mother counted the unsold cupcakes.

"Twenty-seven," Geraldine announced. "How many did you say you started with?"

"A hundred and forty-four."

"So that's . . . a hundred and seventeen gone on the first day. That's wonderful."

Hannah smiled tiredly. "Not bad, I suppose." Not all sold, some given away — a fair few given away — but still, not a bad day's work.

Geraldine indicated the leftovers. "What do you want me to do with these?"

"Bag them in assorted sixes, and put them in that basket. Leave out the extra three, and we'll bring them home."

Hannah emptied the money drawer — a few had remarked on it and there had been lots of comments too about the chair on the wall — and bundled the cash into her satchel. Geraldine arranged the bags of leftovers in a green basket that announced, on another of Adam's signs, *Yesterday's bake — almost as nice, half the price.*

They mopped the floor and wiped down the shelves. They unplugged the kettle and switched the door sign back to *Sorry, fresh out of cupcakes.* They loaded the van with the trays and turned off the lights, and locked the front door before sliding down the security grille.

And as they rounded the corner to get back to the van, they came face to face with Patrick Dunne, editor of the *Clongarvin Voice.*

It was the first time Hannah had seen him since he'd walked out, just over a week ago. His pale green tie was new. Her heart thudded as she took him in. She looked a mess — she must look a mess after the long day, in her flat black shoes and wide grey trousers and black top. The outfit she'd chosen so carefully for her first day in the shop felt so dowdy now.

Her old brown satchel was slung across her body, not matching anything. No hint left, probably, of the lipstick she'd slicked on hours ago — it had no doubt been chewed off by nine o'clock. Her hair must be lying flat on her head, with no time to do more than aim the dryer at it for half a minute this morning. And the skin under her eyes would be bagging, she was sure, with tiredness.

Her cheeks prickled with heat. Great — a big red face was all she needed. She heard her mother's indrawn breath beside her.

"Hannah." Patrick's smile was forced. "And Geraldine. How are you both?"

He carried the briefcase she'd given him for his last birthday. He smelt the same. He was horribly hearty. He was nervous. They'd shared hundreds of nights — she'd lain in his arms so many times. They'd made each other laugh and cry. She'd thrown a bowl at him once. He'd switched to boxers for her, and taught her to play chess. And now he was nervous, and hearty.

"Fine," she told him. "We had a good day." She was surprised at how normal she sounded.

"Hannah's shop opened today," Geraldine said, her voice icy.

"Yes," he said immediately, "of course it did. It went well, I hope?"

He'd forgotten. Hannah had been planning this for months, he'd heard her talking about it forever, and he'd forgotten. She didn't matter to him any more. Nothing she did mattered to him.

She turned to her mother. "Let's go."

"You're in a hurry," Patrick said, moving off. "Good to see you both. Take care." And he was gone, his aftershave lingering.

"Well," Geraldine began, "he's got some —"

"Don't," Hannah begged, and her mother was silent.

She drove to her parents' house, where her father, who'd left work an hour early, was under orders to have the shepherd's pie heated up by half past five.

And all the way home, she thought about the fact that Patrick had forgotten.

"Best seller so far?"

"Chocolate vanilla, easily."

"So you have those every day, as a staple. Worst seller?" She thought. "Not sure . . . maybe forest fruits, or apple and cinnamon."

"So you do those once a week. Write it down."

They were in Hannah's kitchen. It was half past seven on a Friday evening, and pitch black beyond the big latticed window. Cupcakes on the Corner had been open for three days. Adam was making coffee, Hannah was scribbling in a notebook. Some woman was singing "Famous Blue Raincoat" on the radio.

"Mam's been brilliant," Hannah said. "I don't know how I'm going to manage on Monday when she goes back to the shoe shop and I'm on my own. She welcomes everyone who comes in, makes sure they know I'm just starting off, and that I bake everything myself. She practically forces them to promise to come back."

"Good. That's our Geraldine." Adam lifted the kettle off its base and poured water into mugs. "Now, are you making any money?"

Hannah shook her head. "Hard to say for sure — I haven't done a proper breakdown of outgoings and incomings yet — but I'd suspect I'm just about breaking even, if that."

Adam brought the coffee to the table. "Breaking even is fantastic. Time enough for profits; what you want to do now is keep your head above water."

"Well, I suppose I'm doing that, just barely. Nothing's been disconnected yet, and no sign of a bailiff, and I haven't got a bill in at least two days." She closed the notebook and lowered her head onto the table. "But boy, I sure am tired."

"Poor you." Adam ruffled her hair. "I'd offer to help, but my cupcakes would close you down in a week."

"I've been making them in my sleep," she said. "Did I tell you? Every bloody night, as soon as I nod off. You'd think I'd get a bit of a break in my sleep. If I never saw another cupcake I'd be happy."

"Well, don't look at this then." Adam peeled the paper from a chocolate peanut butter cupcake, one of the half-dozen he'd bought on Wednesday. "I'm delighted to report that I'm still a big fan." He bit into the soft beige sponge and coffee-coloured icing. "By the way," he said, "I don't think I told you — Nora and Jackson are officially over."

Hannah lifted her head. "Oh Adam, you're not serious?" She picked up her mug. "I remember you saying they were having problems, but I didn't think it was that bad."

He shrugged. "I wasn't too surprised myself. Nora's been hinting that things weren't going well for a good while now." He and his twin sister talked several times a week, computer to computer.

"So they're definitely splitting up?"

"Yeah — she's going to come home for a while." He took another bite of his cupcake. "Pity, I liked Jackson."

Hannah sipped her coffee. "Another relationship gone. Is she terribly upset?" She wondered if Nora had been the one to end the marriage, and guessed that she had.

"Doesn't seem too bad. She hasn't said anything to the folks yet."

Since their retirement, Adam's parents had moved fifty miles away from Clongarvin, back to the tiny village where they'd both grown up, and where Adam and Nora had spent all their childhood summers.

"D'you think Nora will settle back in Ireland?"

He shrugged again. "Dunno . . . hard to say. You never know with Nora."

"I forget how long were they married."

"Just over four years." He drank coffee. "Ah, she'll bounce back. My sister is nothing if not resourceful."

Hannah could think of plenty of words to describe Nora O'Connor — or Nora Paluzzi: wasn't that her married name? — and "resourceful" wouldn't have been the first to spring to mind. Adam's sister had been a year behind Hannah at school, and had hung around with girls who didn't look twice at the likes of Hannah Robinson — she wasn't pretty or slim enough to interest them.

Nora had Adam's green eyes and russet hair, and there the similarity ended. She'd been spared his freckles, her nose was smaller and her lips fuller. She was also half a head taller — and the last time Hannah checked, at least two stone lighter — than her twin.

While Adam was perfectly presentable, not even Hannah could call him handsome, but Nora had always been striking — and blessed with the confidence to make the most of her looks. She'd moved to the States a week after her eighteenth birthday, much against the wishes of her parents, and without a single qualification apart from a mediocre Leaving Cert. In fourteen years she'd been back just a handful of times.

Jackson Paluzzi, a paediatrician, was her second husband; her first marriage, to an older university professor, had ended after less than a year. Whether by design or accident, neither relationship had produced children. Hannah imagined that the news of a second divorce wouldn't go down too well with Adam and Nora's parents.

Adam drained his mug and stood up. "Better get off and let you make tracks for bed. You'll be looking forward to a lie-in on Sunday."

"I sure will."

"What about coming out for an hour tomorrow night? A jar somewhere, just to relax you?"

Hannah shook her head. "Sorry, but I already have a plan — hot bath, face pack, good book. If I have a drink it'll be in the bath."

"Just an hour," he said. "Why don't we check out that new wine bar?"

"What new wine bar?"

"Vintage, down by the quays. It's only been open a couple of weeks, where Delaney's hardware used to be. Someone said there's live music at the weekends."

"Delaney's is gone?"

Adam smiled. "You definitely need to get out more."

"Maybe . . . I'll see how I feel tomorrow night." She pushed her chair away from the table. "There's something I haven't told you," she said, getting up.

Adam was pulling on his leather jacket. "What?"

"I met Patrick on Wednesday, on the way home from the shop." She took their two mugs over to the sink.

"You did? You never said. How was it?"

"Not good. Awkward." She turned on the tap. "He was so . . . formal, as if he hardly knew me. He'd forgotten about the shop opening that day, can you believe it?"

"Bastard," Adam said lightly.

"My mother was there, which I suppose was just as well." She rinsed the mugs and put them on the draining-board. "I cried my eyes out later."

"You know what?" Adam said. "That's the worst over. The first time you meet them is the worst."

She took the tea-towel from its hook. "I know . . . There'd been flowers delivered to the shop in the morning, and the first thing I thought when I saw them was that he was having second thoughts and wanted to come back." She tried to laugh. "How pathetic is that?"

"Who were they from?"

"Alice and Tom, sweet of them." *All the very best with your new venture*, Alice had written, and Hannah had buried her face in the hothouse roses that smelt of nothing, and swallowed her disappointment. "I try not to think about him, honestly, but it's easier said than done."

Much easier said than done when she kept bumping into reminders around the house. Yesterday she'd thrown his half-full jar of Marmite into the bin. Last week it had been his prawns from the freezer. The Nicholas Mosse mug she'd brought him back from a trip to Bennetsbridge would be harder to let go.

She took the unsalted butter from the fridge and left it to soften. She set her utensils and baking trays on the worktop, all ready for the early hours. "You know, I thought his timing was horrible — when he finished it, I mean, just before the shop opened, but imagine how much worse I'd feel if I wasn't so busy now. Maybe he planned it that way." Up to her eyes in recipes and vanilla essence and poppy seeds and dried cranberries and chocolate chunks. No time to think about what he might be doing, or whether he missed her at all. Asleep, whatever about the dreams, as soon as her head hit the pillow — which she'd moved to the middle of the bed.

"I deleted his number," she said quietly, "from my phone."

That had been hard. She didn't want to think about that, about his name disappearing. She searched for something different to say. "I'm thinking of getting a cat," she told Adam, filling the kettle again for her hot-water bottle, "to keep me company."

"What about getting a tenant," he asked sternly, "to keep you solvent?"

She sighed. "I know, I know. I must put in the ad. I will, honest. Next week."

"Swear?"

"I swear." Apart from all the negative connotations of replacing Patrick, she still balked at the idea of sharing her house with a stranger. But financially it was unavoidable.

Adam crossed the kitchen and kissed her cheek. "Right, I'm off. I'll call you tomorrow to see if I can drag you out."

"Don't hold your breath — I probably won't go."

When he'd left she took the hot-water bottle from its drawer and filled it. Not even eight o'clock and she was off to bed. At least it was dark — what would it be like in the summer, when she was going upstairs in broad daylight?

Time enough to worry about that. She switched off the light and left the room.

"It's Leah Bradshaw." Geraldine's voice floated in from the hall as she hung up her coat.

Stephen didn't turn from the computer. "What is?" he called back.

Geraldine walked into the sitting room, rubbing her hands together. "God, it's chilly out tonight. Leah Bradshaw is the girl Patrick left Hannah for."

Stephen's fingers stilled on the keyboard. He looked across the room at his wife. "Who is she? Do we know her?"

Geraldine poked the fire before tipping in coal from the scuttle. "I wish you'd keep this going when I'm out.

She's Fiona Bradshaw's daughter." And, seeing his blank expression, she added impatiently, "Fiona Bradshaw, who I play bridge with. You know her — she has some environment job with the council. You met her at Aoife's cocktail party in November. Tall, dyed red hair. Too thin. She brought those orchids when I did the Alzheimer's tea thing here last month. I remember you asking her about them."

"Oh yes," Stephen said, knowing that it didn't matter in the least that he had absolutely no memory of Fiona Bradshaw. "So it's her daughter."

"And to think," Geraldine said angrily, pushing the poker through the coals, "that I supported that girl when she opened her salon. I paid good money for a manicure, and I wasn't well out the door when one of my nails smudged. I should have gone back."

Stephen felt the conversation slipping away from him. "Are you sure it's her? Did her mother tell you?"

Geraldine snorted. "Of course she didn't tell me — she didn't come near me. Too ashamed of what her brazen daughter has done, no doubt. Maureen Hardiman told me, delighted to have a bit of scandal to report, as usual. Naturally, I let on I knew already."

"Good for you." Stephen's fingers crept back towards the keyboard — the first Scrabble game in ages that he was showing any signs of winning.

"Small slip of a thing," Geraldine said, settling onto the couch and picking up the remote control. "Don't know what he sees in her. Dyed hair, of course, like her mother. Can you see Hannah ever having to dye her hair?" She pressed a button on the remote and the television flicked on. "Oh, not that fellow again — he's always on the *Late Late*. Must have written a book."

"Mm-hmm." Stephen typed in *cousin* as quietly as he could, and his score jumped to 176.

"I'll have to tell her," Geraldine said, still watching the television.

Stephen swung towards her again. "Tell who? Hannah?"

"Of course Hannah. She'll have to hear it from me."

"Why? Won't that only upset her?"

Geraldine looked at him incredulously. "Stephen, do you really think she wouldn't find out? In a place the size of Clongarvin it'll be all over town in no time. I'd prefer she heard it from me than from some gossip like Maureen Hardiman."

Hannah's father returned to his Scrabble game. He'd long since given up trying to understand the workings of his wife's mind. Far easier to figure out what to do with a Q, a B, three Es and a couple of Ps.

Vintage was Clongarvin's first wine bar. It was all dark wood, subdued lighting and low couches arranged around candlelit tables, not at all what Adam was used to when he went out for a drink.

He sat alone on a stool by the counter, having failed to persuade Hannah to accompany him. He hadn't pressed her too hard: maybe a night of doing nothing more strenuous than lying in bubbly water was what she needed this weekend. And going out on his own had never bothered him. Clongarvin being the size it was, and this being Saturday night, he was reasonably sure of bumping into someone he knew before long.

In the meantime he was content to drink his Guinness — thankfully, the stock wasn't limited to wine — and watch the woman who'd caught his attention pretty much as soon as he'd walked in.

She was the only female member of the group of four musicians who were performing on the small, slightly raised area — you could hardly call it a stage — in a corner of the room, diagonally across from where he sat.

It wasn't that she was beautiful — no, he really couldn't call her that. There was certainly something striking about the neat pointed features, but she wasn't beautiful. Her hair, some pale colour he couldn't determine, was pulled off her face by a wide black hairband and captured into some kind of low ponytail. No tendril escaped — there was nothing to suggest the length or the texture of it.

Her eyes were hidden behind a pair of small, perfectly round dark-rimmed glasses. From this distance he couldn't be sure, but he thought her hands were broad, the knuckles jutting sharply from her splayed fingers as they travelled along the keys of her instrument, some kind of long silver flute that flared gently at the tip.

She was dressed entirely in black. A high-necked blouse fell in sharp pleats to her waist, where it was gathered into a wide belt made of some shiny material. A long, loose skirt stopped just short of her ankles, meeting a pair of black boots with pointed toes. The

59

whole of her body was covered, apart from her hands and face. There was no clue to the shape that lay beneath the stiff folds of her top, or the drapes below.

Not beautiful, no, not in the least pretty. Unsmiling, wholly focused on the music they played. She sat hunched in her seat, her chair set back a fraction from her companions, the suggestion given that she was trying to distance herself from the whole affair.

And yet Adam watched her. What drew him to examine that frowning pale face, to wonder what colour the eyes were behind their glass barriers, to imagine undoing the ponytail, peeling off the black hairband and watching the pale hair tumble downwards?

The other three musicians were casually dressed in white shirts and chinos. One played a keyboard, the other two had instruments that looked familiar to Adam, but his musically ignorant eye couldn't positively identify them. The enormous version of a violin could be either a cello or a double bass, and the fourth was possibly a saxophone, but he wasn't laying any bets.

He enjoyed the sound they produced. They played old favourites like "You Go To My Head" and "Blue Moon" and "These Foolish Things", and popular songs from the musicals, like "On The Street Where You Live" and "I Feel Pretty", and a few Beatles numbers and a couple of movie themes — and the treatment they gave each tune, the subtle rhythms they introduced, made them fresh and lively and interesting. It was music you couldn't help tapping a foot along to.

The female musician seemed unaware of her surroundings. The buzz of chatter in the wine bar didn't appear to bother her; she didn't react to the smatter of applause at the end of each piece. She flicked the pages on the stand in front of her and glanced now and again at one or other of her fellow musicians as they moved on to another tune, but she was removed somehow from the warm, busy room.

"Adam, over here." A couple he knew were gesturing to him from the far end of the counter. He took his drink and joined them, and the next time he looked towards the musicians' platform, half an hour later, all that remained were two music stands and three chairs, on one of which was perched an empty half-pint glass.

"Leah Bradshaw," her mother said. "Fiona's daughter. She opened a beauty salon on Russell Street a few years back. Not much of a place, if you ask me."

"I know it," Hannah said bleakly. "I was there."

"Small skinny thing," Geraldine said. "Her figure isn't half as nice as yours." She stopped. "You were there? When?"

"Oh . . . months ago, I don't remember exactly."

She remembered exactly. Eight months ago, early summer, when Patrick's back had been stiff after digging up the hedge.

"Do you know her?" Geraldine asked. "Did you get something done there?"

"No . . . I bought a voucher for a massage. A present for someone."

A back massage, Hannah had said. *A gift*. She remembered Leah Bradshaw, remembered recognising her vaguely from school, but they'd have been in different years.

"I can't for the life of me see why he'd prefer her," Geraldine said. "Even if you are my daughter, there's no comparison. Some men need their heads examined."

Some men obviously preferred their women blonde and petite, with the kind of boyish figure — small breasts, slim hips — that Hannah had always envied. Nails short and beautifully shaped, painted pale pink, as Leah had written *back massage* on the gift voucher, coloured lavender like the walls of the reception area, and taken Hannah's sixty euro.

"You're better off without him," her mother said, "although I know that's cold comfort now, love."

I like the colour of your hair, she'd said to Hannah. *Very rich, and a lovely shine to it.*

"Her mother plays bridge with me," Geraldine said. "Fiona Bradshaw — I don't think you know her. Not someone you'd warm to, bit of a cold fish."

See you again, she'd said, as Hannah had walked out the door. *Thanks a lot, take care.*

"I felt I should tell you," Geraldine said. "I didn't want you hearing it from someone else. You didn't mind me saying it?"

Had Patrick known her already? Had Hannah innocently bought him forty-five minutes alone with his other woman? Had they laughed about that as Leah massaged his naked, oiled skin, her slender body leaning over his? Or had they bothered with the

62

massage at all? Maybe they'd found something more interesting to do with one another.

Or — worse, much worse — had Hannah introduced them? Had she been the one who'd brought them together? Didn't bear thinking about.

"Are you still there?" her mother asked.

"Yes," Hannah answered. "Still here." Standing in the middle of the car park, feeling miserable, but still there.

"You don't mind that I told you? You're not cross with me?"

"No, of course not . . . Look," she said, "I have to go. I'll talk to you tomorrow."

Leah Bradshaw. Was it better to have a name and a face? Did it make it any easier? Or was it worse to know exactly who Patrick had left her for? She flipped her phone closed and slid it into her pocket, then grabbed the shopping trolley again and pushed it towards the yellow van. What did any of it matter, when he was still gone and she was still alone?

As she unloaded the trolley, piling bags into the back of the van, a man passed her wearing a navy jacket and a dark green woolly hat. A rucksack that looked heavy was hanging off one shoulder. "Hello," he said. "Nice evening."

"Hi."

He seemed vaguely familiar. He unlocked a nearby taxi and slung his rucksack onto the back seat before getting in himself. He must have given her a lift somewhere, not that she got taxis too often.

As she negotiated the little van out of the car park a few minutes later, she turned abruptly back in the direction of the town and drove through emptying early-evening streets until she came to Indulgence. She pulled into a space across the road and sat, engine idling.

She studied the prettily painted frontage. The downstairs windows were dark, the salon closed at this hour. On the first floor a light shone faintly from one of the two tall, narrow windows.

Were they inside now? Was she cooking dinner for him — or were they sprawled in front of a television, the way she and Patrick used to do? Was she telling him about her day while he poured her a glass of wine?

The street was quiet, most workers at home and cosying up for the night. Hannah glanced around, saw a few scattered pedestrians, a man dismounting from a bicycle, a dog sniffing at a lamppost. Nobody taking any notice at all of the little yellow van.

She could lob a rock through the downstairs window and drive off quickly. The thought came out of nowhere, filling her with a shocked thrill. She could get a can of black paint and fling it at the pretty lavender walls. She could —

A nearby door opened: a man and a boy appeared on the path and walked in the direction of the van. The man smiled briefly at Hannah as they passed.

What was she doing? What was she thinking? Was she completely mad? She put the van into gear and drove off quickly, her blood racing. She didn't stop until she got home.

February

"I want to really pamper her this year." Geraldine's hand hovered over the plate of assorted biscuits. She shouldn't — a biscuit was the last thing her mid-section needed — but Lent wasn't far away and she'd have to do without them then. "God knows, she could use a treat."

"What about a voucher? You can't go wrong."

"Ah no, not a voucher." Geraldine selected a pink wafer — not her favourite, but practically no calories apparently. "Stephen thinks we should pay for someone to paint the outside of her house. I know it could badly do with it, but where's the pampering in that?"

"Mmm — and anyway, who would you get to do outdoor painting in February?" Alice watched a woman wheel a buggy along the rows of shoes and boots. "What age is she going to be?"

"Thirty-three, can you believe it?" Geraldine finished the wafer and took a shortbread finger. A finger couldn't hurt, even if it was loaded with butter. "I never thought she'd get to that age and not be married. What age was Ellen?"

"Twenty-eight."

"There you go. And she has three now."

"That's right." Ellen was Tom and Alice's only child, living for the past decade in Australia. "Wish we saw more of them."

The customer picked up a black patent boot, and Alice put down her cup. "I'll go."

The shop was quiet in February, the winter buying mostly over, too early for anyone to want sandals, no big occasions coming up that would call for new shoes.

Except Valentine's Day, on Saturday week. A couple of men had bought vouchers in the past few days, and some women had come in looking at heels. Geraldine would get her usual card and box of Thornton's, provided she made some reference to the fourteenth at least twice over the coming week.

"Are you doing anything for Valentine's Day?" she asked when Alice returned, having sold the marked-down boots and a pair of half-price slippers.

Alice considered. "Cooking very romantic pork chops, probably. You?"

"Bacon and cabbage, our usual Saturday dinner." Geraldine gathered up the plate of biscuits and the two empty cups. "And maybe I'll make a rhubarb tart, if there's any around."

"Very romantic."

In the small kitchen she rinsed the cups and left them on the draining-board, and slid the biscuits back into their tin as her thoughts returned to her daughter. Hannah had been flown to Paris for her birthday last year, didn't know a thing about it until they'd arrived at the airport. Patrick had pretended he was picking someone up — his brother, was it? Some relation anyway.

Geraldine had been charmed when she'd heard — it had sounded so romantic. By then, of course, she and Stephen had had several weeks to get used to the fact that their daughter was living with a man who wasn't her husband. It had been a different story when Hannah had told them Patrick was moving in.

You haven't known him a wet week, Geraldine had protested.

Three months, Hannah had said. *I know it seems soon, but it's what we both want. And with Annie being transferred to Cork, the timing is perfect.*

Annie had moved into Hannah's spare room three weeks after Hannah had bought the house, and she'd been with her ever since. She was the perfect tenant, paying her rent on time each month and going home to her family in Sligo every weekend. And now she was being transferred, and Patrick, whom Geraldine still regarded as Hannah's new boyfriend, was to be her replacement.

It's still so soon, though, Geraldine had insisted. *Couldn't you get another tenant, just for a few more months even?*

But Hannah had been determined, and Patrick had moved in. And despite her parents' misgivings, it had seemed to be working out. Geraldine remembered the phone call from Charles de Gaulle airport, how happy Hannah had sounded. She'd been convinced they'd come back engaged, but that hadn't happened. And look at them now.

She sighed as she replaced the lid on the biscuit tin. Just as well Hannah was worn out these days, with no time to brood. Up in the middle of the night to bake, bake, bake, and then standing behind that counter all day long. Thankfully things were going well so far: she was doing a reasonable trade and she seemed to be enjoying it — at least, that was what she told them. But she looked so tired and lost whenever Geraldine met her. Of course, her heart was still broken.

Geraldine knew what her daughter needed for her birthday — she'd known as soon as Hannah had signed her name on the lease, as soon as she'd finally committed to opening her own business. And much as Geraldine hated presenting her only child with a cheque on her birthday, that was what she and Stephen had to do.

She washed her hands and walked back out to the shop. She'd talk to Stephen this evening, decide how much they'd give. He'd be happy, always the practical one.

And tomorrow she'd parcel up the nice pink sling-backs that Alice would let her have for forty euro. Whatever else, a girl needed shoes on her birthday.

"I have a proposition for you."

Hannah eyed him warily. "Go on."

"Don't look so suspicious. This could be mutually beneficial."

"Go on."

"Well, you know Nora's coming home next week, for a while anyway."

"Yes?" Hannah's guarded expression slid up a notch.

"And you still haven't got around to advertising for a tenant, although you're probably living off beans on —"

"No," Hannah said quickly. "No. I'm sorry Adam, but it wouldn't work. We . . . might fall out over something, and things could get messy, and . . . Look, she's your sister, but I really don't know Nora all that well — I mean we're very different, and you'd be caught in the middle, and —"

"Hang on a sec," Adam said. "What do you think I'm suggesting?"

"That Nora moves in with me. And while in theory the idea is fine, I just think —"

"Stop talking," he said.

Hannah stopped.

"I meant," he said, "that I let my place to Nora and I move in with you. Me. Adam."

"Oh." She sipped her red wine. "Right. You and me. Sharing my house."

"Just for a while obviously," he said, his eyes on her face, "until you get your head together, and see where you're going with the business."

"Right."

"You know you need someone to share the bills, even though you keep putting it off."

"I know."

"And I thought you'd rather someone you know."

"I would."

"And if Nora decides to stay in Ireland she'll find a place of her own — this would just be a stop-gap for her, a few weeks maybe."

"Right." Hannah nodded. "Uh-huh. Yes."

Adam smiled. "You look like a rat caught in the headlights."

"Don't you mean a rabbit?"

"Whatever it is, you look like it. You don't have to decide right now, obviously — and we won't fall out if you don't fancy the idea, although I might sulk for a few days. But while you're mulling it over, consider this: I never leave the toilet seat up, I always squeeze the toothpaste from the bottom, and I only drink from the carton when nobody's watching."

Hannah grinned.

"Oh, and I'm a happy drunk."

"That's true."

"And I can fix your computer when it breaks down."

"You do that already."

"Yes, but . . . I'd be on the spot. Instant repairs."

Hannah laughed. "I'll bear that in mind. And I presume Kirby would be part of the package."

"God, yeah — he'd have to be. But he's house-trained, obviously. And he loves you."

"And I love him too. But he sheds."

"Only a small bit." Then, seeing her expression, he added, "OK, a big bit. But we can confine him to wherever you say."

"He wouldn't be allowed in the kitchen, ever. He could lose me my accreditation."

"Fair enough."

"Or upstairs. Or on my couch — he has yours destroyed. And he'd have to sleep in the shed."

"Fine."

It just might work. And it would certainly ease her financial worries. She squeezed Adam's hand. "I know you're only doing this for me, and I appreciate it."

"Are you kidding? The alternative is to share my flat with Nora — no thanks." Adam lifted his glass. "Anyway, enough of that. What do you think of this place?"

"It's great — just what Clongarvin needs." Hannah placed her glass on the low table in front of the couch and studied the band in the corner. "I like the funky music too, really fits in. She looks a bit schoolmarmish though, doesn't she?"

"Who?"

"The one with the clarinet. All that black, and the hair scraped back. And the professor specs."

Adam studied the clarinet player. "Can't say I noticed."

"And look at the frown on her. I wouldn't like to get on her wrong side."

"That's probably because she's concentrating."

"Mmm. The guy with the double bass looks foreign. Anyway, where were we?"

"We were just about to plan your birthday."

She groaned. "God, I was hoping you'd forget. Let's plan nothing, please — I really don't feel like celebrating this one."

"All the more reason. And sorry, but you have no choice. How about dinner on me, anywhere you fancy that won't bankrupt me?"

She picked up her glass again. "Honestly, Adam, I'd rather not."

73

Sorry about this, Patrick had said, *there's no one else free to collect him. We'll still be in time for dinner, I promise*. And he'd dropped her at the arrivals door and gone to find a parking space. And even when she couldn't see a flight from London on the board, it hadn't clicked. She'd just thought his brother had got the time wrong and they'd be there all night, waiting for him to arrive, and her birthday dinner would be ruined.

And then Patrick had reappeared, pulling her weekend bag on wheels behind him. *Tell you what*, he'd said, smiling at her astonishment, *let's go to Paris instead*.

"Anyway," she said to Adam, "my birthday's on a Tuesday this year, so I'll be having my usual early night."

"We could wait till Saturday to go out."

She shook her head. "Let's just leave it. Really."

"OK, I'll get you a surprise instead. What colour scarf have you not got?"

She smiled. "Green. Not that awful touristy green, a nice sage. Go to Benetton and ask them." She paused, and then added, "Yes, I would like you to move in. You and Kirby."

"What?"

"I would, definitely."

"No, that was too quick. Why don't you sleep on it?"

"Don't need to. As long as you pay your rent on time, split the bills and replace everything you break. And never, ever drink from the carton."

"You're totally sure about this?"

"Totally. I know you well enough to kick you out if you drive me mad."

"That's true." He clinked his glass against hers. "It's a deal." He thought. "How would Thursday suit for me to move in?"

"Thursday's fine. Call into the shop in the meantime and I'll give you keys."

Her tenant problem solved, just like that. She wished everything was so easily fixed.

The buzzer sounded, its harshness making Patrick wince as always. A second later he heard Leah speaking softly on the intercom in the hall.

A second later: "She's here."

"Right," he called. "I'm on the way."

He looked in the mirror and tweaked the knot of his tie and ran a hand over his hair. It wasn't his first meeting with Leah's mother. He'd been introduced to Fiona Bradshaw around two years ago at an art auction, and since then their paths had crossed occasionally at various functions. They'd nodded at one another, shared the odd brief group conversation.

Her photo appeared quite regularly in the newspaper's social pages. She'd been featured once, about a year ago, in connection with her job as environmental officer with the local council.

Patrick had the impression of a cool, poised woman, at ease in social situations, well able to hold her own, if not exactly someone he'd seek out for a friendly chat. And now their personal lives were about to intersect, and he wondered what lay ahead. If Leah's reports of her mother's feelings about their relationship were to be believed — and he had no reason to doubt them — the future looked interesting.

The fact that Fiona wasn't exactly over the moon about Leah's pregnancy was unfortunate, but not unexpected — and in truth, remembering his own dismay when Leah had told him, Patrick could hardly blame the woman. But they were all civilised adults, and he presumed they'd manage to get beyond it. For his part he'd be charming and pleasant, and hope for the best.

He smoothed his hair again and left the bedroom, at precisely the same moment that Leah opened the front door to her mother.

"Mum." It wasn't an embrace, more a brief connection, Leah's lips barely touching her mother's cheek. Fiona was taller than her daughter by about six inches. Her glance met Patrick's as Leah drew back.

"So," she said. No hand outstretched.

"You know Patrick," Leah said, and he smiled and kept his own hands by his sides, and received a cool nod.

"We've met," Fiona began unbuttoning her fawn coat, "here and there." She wore a grey cardigan and skirt. Her dark red hair gleamed, her lipstick a precise match. She smelt of marzipan. The tips of her long nails were white. A jewel flashed on her left hand as she gave Patrick her coat. "Thank you."

"We're having fish pie," Leah said, walking ahead of them into the apartment's tiny sitting room. "It won't be long."

She was nervous. She'd snapped at Patrick earlier over nothing — he always left his shoes in the hall — and she'd spent the past few evenings poring over her cookbooks, deciding on and rejecting any number of dishes. Patrick had had the sense not to argue, to pretend to weigh up the advantages of fish over chicken, to consider the wisdom of serving asparagus in February.

In the sitting room he poured drinks. Gin and bitter lemon for Fiona, iced tea for Leah, single malt for himself. He poked the fire and added a couple of briquettes. Then Leah left the room to check the fish pie and boil the water for the asparagus, and he sat across the fireplace from Fiona.

"Chilly tonight." He stretched his feet towards the blaze, itching to kick off the shoes he'd put on just minutes before.

Fiona sipped her gin and kept her eyes on the fire. "It is."

He became aware of the clock ticking on the mantelpiece. He put down his drink and crossed to the CD player. "Any preference for music?"

She didn't look in his direction. "I have no idea what you have."

"Right." He selected one of Leah's Lyle Lovett CDs and slipped it into the drive. "Let's take a chance on this one then."

The door opened and Leah reappeared. Her face, he noticed for the first time, was slightly puffy. "Five minutes."

Lyle Lovett strummed his guitar and began singing about a porch, and Leah threw Patrick an exasperated glance before turning to her mother. "Are you warm enough?"

Patrick thought about the meals around Geraldine and Stephen's kitchen table. The roast chickens fragrant with thyme and lemon, the rich casseroles, Stephen's tangy, oozing blue cheese burgers. The mismatched crockery, the casual, relaxed conversation. Something Hannah had baked — raspberry roulade, apple strudel, sour cream coffee cake — usually rounding off the meal.

He became aware that Leah was glaring at him, and realised he'd missed something. "Sorry?"

"I said your father goes on a cruise every winter."

"Oh . . . yes. Yes, he does."

They'd joked about bringing his father and Fiona together. "He's sailing around Greece at the moment." Since he'd been widowed, more than twenty years earlier, Bill Dunne's tastes had run to women considerably younger than fifty-eight, and substantially less uptight than Fiona Bradshaw. He'd run a mile.

"Mum's been on cruises, haven't you?"

"Oh, yes? Where have you been?"

Leah leapt up. "Sorry — I forgot something." She practically ran from the room. Patrick took a deep swig of his whiskey, welcoming its oaky burn.

"I don't approve of all this," Fiona said suddenly. Her voice was completely neutral. She might have been listing the countries she'd visited from her cruise ship.

"I gathered that," Patrick replied evenly. May as well give as good as he got. "I presume Leah explained that the baby wasn't planned."

"She did — which in my opinion makes it worse." She'd hardly touched her drink. "You're hardly teenagers."

"No."

"And now my daughter is accidentally pregnant by a man who until a month ago was living with another woman."

"Yes." What else was there to say? He drank more whiskey. "That's true." He hesitated. "Not that it changes the way I feel about Leah." *Not that it's any of your damn business.*

Fiona didn't respond.

Patrick got to his feet again. "Another drink?" When she shook her head he crossed to the cabinet where the bottles were kept and refilled his own glass. A buzz might help him keep his cool — and as long as she regarded him as a philandering bastard, he might as well be an alcoholic too.

Leah reappeared just then. "OK, it's all ready. Bring your drinks."

Patrick watched Fiona leave the room, feeling that the battle lines had been well and truly drawn. Still, what could she do, other than rant at him whenever she got the chance? He followed her into the kitchen-cum-dining room, steeling himself against the next hour or so.

Every day she was learning more and making fewer mistakes. Through trial and error she'd whittled down her original fifteen recipes to ten, ditching some, replacing others, substituting ingredients here and there, experimenting when she had the time. The apple and cinnamon hadn't worked, the honey and sesame had morphed into ginger and sesame, the poppy seed and key lime had been a slow starter but now sold steadily — especially, for some peculiar reason, on Mondays.

She didn't dare open without a good supply of at least two chocolate varieties. She'd learnt to bag the leftovers in threes rather than sixes, and she'd introduced a special-offer variety each day. Thanks to Adam, she'd discovered an American website that sold discounted cupcake paraphernalia — themed paper cases, toppings, decorations — and she'd set up an account with them.

And she very quickly realised that mopping the floor at ten to five was practically a guarantee that she'd have a flurry of last-minute customers.

She was constantly tired. She dragged herself out of bed at three o'clock each morning and baked and iced and decorated solidly till just after half past eight, when she loaded the yellow van and drove to the shop. She fell into bed each evening to sleep soundly — no more dreams — until the alarm beeped her awake again.

And on Sundays she regularly slept till midday, sometimes even later — a phenomenon that hadn't occurred since she was fourteen.

She'd lost track of her TV programmes; she hadn't checked her emails in ages. She couldn't remember the last time she'd opened a book or a newspaper.

She'd forgotten what a social life was. In the month since Cupcakes on the Corner had opened, her only outings had been to work each day, and a weekly dash that took in the cash-and-carry and the nearest supermarket, until Adam had finally persuaded her to visit the new wine bar with him a couple of weeks ago.

And while she'd enjoyed the buzz in Vintage, the feeling that she was out for the evening, she relished even more her precious Saturday nights at home, when she could laze around the house or soak in the bath for as long as she wanted instead of rushing off to bed.

She had a few regular customers already. The secretary from the office block up the road who came in every Friday around eleven with the same order: "One coffee cream, one vanilla chocolate, three peanut butter and four chocolate coconut." The young man in a grey suit who called every other morning for two of whatever was on special offer. One of Hannah's old teachers, Mrs O'Neill, who dropped in on Saturdays for a bag of leftovers for the three grandchildren who visited her every Sunday afternoon.

A young woman had come in one day who looked familiar, but Hannah hadn't placed her until the woman had smiled and said, *Hey, I know you. You used to babysit me and my sister Claire.* She was Una Connolly, and she worked three afternoons a week in Clongarvin's library, down the hill from Cupcakes on the Corner. She'd taken to calling at least once a week since then. She'd told Hannah that Claire waitressed in the town's only Chinese restaurant. *She has a little boy,*

Una had said. *Jason, he's four. We're all mad about him.*

And every week Hannah made a little money. Not much left over once the bills had been paid, hardly enough to justify all her slaving, but it was *her* money, from *her* efforts, and it felt good.

And now she'd almost made it to her second month, and Adam had moved in four days before, and had taken possession of the second biggest bedroom. Kirby's basket had been moved into the shed and he'd sniffed his way around the garden and made the acquaintance of next door's cat — who'd marked her territory with a swipe at Kirby's nose.

And so far the new arrangement looked like it just might work out.

Adam was still in bed when Hannah left for work in the mornings, and in the evenings they often ate together. He'd taken to trying dishes from her *Meals in Minutes* cookbook, and she was touched by his efforts, even if they were more enthusiastic than accomplished.

You don't have to cook for me, she'd protested.

Don't worry, he'd assured her, *it won't last.*

Her parents approved wholeheartedly of her new tenant. Hannah was quite sure that her mother at least lived in the fervent hope that she and Adam would one day walk down the aisle together — and if it kept Geraldine happy, who was Hannah to argue?

And today, the tenth of February, was her thirty-third birthday, and her feelings about this particular date were mixed, to say the least.

There was the memory of last year, of course. Boarding the Aer Lingus flight to Paris, still unable to believe what Patrick had arranged. Sharing a bottle of red wine in a tiny late-night bar, eating thick slices of rustic bread topped with peppery salami and gloriously pungent cheese. Dipping the crusts into the bowl of buttery, garlicky juice in which Patrick's *moules* had been served. Not mentioning that he'd packed the wrong shoes for her burgundy dress, and not nearly enough woollens for the sub-zero temperatures, not caring that the shower in their hotel ensuite trickled tepidly. They'd huddled together under blankets that smelt of grass, and listened to the pipes clanking, and a woman holding a one-sided shrill conversation somewhere, and the faint horns and sirens and shouts in the street far below their two narrow, shuttered windows.

She blocked out the image of the Parisian bedroom — the flowers on the wallpaper had been blue! — and thought again about Adam sharing her house. Of all the people she could have picked to be her tenant, Adam would have been her unhesitating first choice.

The trouble was, she didn't want a tenant, or housemate, or whatever you wanted to call it. She wanted to share her home, and her life, with a romantic partner, like most thirty-three-year-old women. Instead she had her best friend and an overweight black Labrador.

Still, it was better than living alone, wasn't it? Eating a solitary dinner night after night, putting on the telly purely to drown the sound of your fork clinking as you speared a bit of sausage or scooped a mound of beans. Washing up your one plate, your single knife and fork.

Buying a toothbrush you didn't need, because one on its own sticking out of the tumbler on the bathroom shelf was far too pathetic. Switching on the radio just to hear someone else's voice as you cracked your umpteenth egg into flour, butter and sugar —

The shop door opened and she blinked the thoughts away. "I wasn't expecting you."

"It's my lunch hour," Geraldine said, "and I wanted to wish my only child a very happy birthday."

Hannah smiled. "You rang me this morning. You and Dad are coming around for tea later."

"I know, but Adam will be there, and I just wanted to see you on your own and give you this, from both of us." Geraldine reached into her basket and produced an envelope. "Happy birthday, love. It's a cheque, I'm afraid, but we thought it was probably what you needed most right now."

Hannah hugged her mother. "It is — thanks a million."

As she took the envelope, Geraldine lifted a box from the basket. "And this is a little something else, because I couldn't let money be your only present."

Hannah opened the box and pulled out a pink shoe. "Oh, Mam, they're gorgeous — you always know exactly what I like."

As she slipped off one of her black pumps the shop door opened again, making the bell ping loudly. They both turned, Hannah still holding the shoe.

"Hello there." A man came towards them, his eyes darting from one woman to the other. Hannah thought he looked familiar, but couldn't for the life of her think where she'd seen him. He held a sheaf of pages. "I was just wondering if I could leave these on the counter." His accent wasn't Irish.

"What are they?" She dropped the shoe back into its box and he passed her the top page. *Carpenter available*, she read. *Custom-built kitchen and bedroom furniture. All jobs considered. Free quotation, recession-beating prices. Quality guaranteed.* And beneath, in smaller lettering, *John Wyatt*, and a mobile-phone number. She handed the leaflet to Geraldine.

"I'm just trying to spread the word," he said. "Would you mind?"

"Of course not." She took the bundle from him and placed them on the counter. "Are you just starting out?"

He didn't seem young enough to be starting out. He was her age, easily, or a few years older. His hair was cut tight into his head, so short it was hard to determine its colour. His chin was dotted with dark stubble. He reminded her of a PE teacher she'd had in school — Mr Flaherty, was it, or Flannery?

"I've not been long in this area, just a couple of months," he told her, "but I've been a woodworker for quite a while, about fifteen years." He glanced at the pink shoes, still sitting in their box, and Hannah quickly moved them to the shelf behind. He smiled and switched his attention to the cupcake display. "These are interesting — who's the baker?"

"My daughter here," Geraldine said, looking up from the leaflet. "She makes the most wonderful gourmet cupcakes."

"Well," he said, smiling at Hannah, "in that case I shall take two of the . . ." he scanned the coloured labels ". . . vanilla chocolate, please."

"You're not from Ireland, are you?" Geraldine asked, as Hannah pulled on a pair of plastic gloves and put his order into a yellow box.

He shook his head. "Scotland — but my mother comes from Tipperary, so we spent a lot of time here as kids."

"And what's brought you to Clongarvin?" Geraldine didn't see, or chose to ignore, Hannah's frown.

He smiled again, not seeming to mind the interrogation. "Change of scene."

"You like it here?"

"I certainly do. Nice friendly place."

Hannah was terrified the next question was going to be whether his wife liked it. "Three fifty, please," she told him quickly. "I hope you enjoy them — the vanilla chocolate is one of my best sellers."

"Thank you." He took the box and pocketed his change. "And thanks for the advertising."

"No problem."

As he turned away, the rocking chair on the wall caught his eye. "Well — now that's what I call an original design feature."

"It was my grandfather's," Hannah told him. "He made it possible for me to set up this shop, so we thought it would be nice to remember him in some way."

"Good — a bit of family history." He studied the chair, nodding. "Lovely workmanship. And the colour is very . . . eye-catching."

Hannah grinned. "I'm not entirely sure Granddad would approve of his chair being painted blue — or being fixed to the wall, for that matter."

"Och, you might be surprised."

"Hannah has very good taste," Geraldine said. "She has a way with colour — you should see her house."

He caught Hannah's eye, and she saw amusement in his face. "Well, I'd best be off," he said, heading for the door. "Bye for now."

They watched him walk out. "What a nice man," Geraldine said. "And works with his hands — I like that."

Hannah folded the plastic gloves and laid them aside.

"I love the Scottish accent, don't you?" Geraldine said. "It's so soft."

Hannah rearranged the remaining vanilla chocolate cupcakes.

"I think he liked you. I mean, there was no need for him to hang around admiring that rocking chair."

Hannah smiled.

"I wonder if he's married," Geraldine said. "He wasn't wearing a ring, but maybe men don't in Scotland."

"Let me try on these shoes," Hannah said.

The best thing you could say about Clongarvin, Nora Paluzzi decided, was that it wasn't as cold as New York in February. On the other hand, it hadn't stopped raining since she'd arrived, and three days of non-stop driving rain were every bit as bad, in her opinion, as cold that cut right through to your bones.

But at least it wasn't Dunmallon, where her parents had dragged her and Adam every summer, back to the farm where her father had grown up. Dunmallon with its single petrol pump, sub-post office, pathetically stocked supermarket and scatter of pubs, one more dreary than the next. God, what a hole, everyone knowing everyone else's business, or letting on they did. Everyone looked for at mass on Sunday, and woe betide you if you were missing without good reason. Ma and Da delighted to be back there now, God help them.

At least Clongarvin had some semblance of life about it, however parochial. The clothes in the few boutiques weren't bad, even if they cost three times what you'd pay in New York. There was a halfway decent deli — although again the prices had shocked her — and the two-screen cinema (two whole screens!) was actually showing movies from just six months ago.

Not that she intended to make Clongarvin her home for any length of time — perish the thought. But it would do while she caught her breath and planned her next move. And it might be fun to look up some of the old gang from school — Francine, Jojo, Leah, Dee — in the unlikely event that anyone was still living here.

She walked into Adam's tiny kitchen, which smelt of dog. The whole damn place smelt of dog — what had possessed him to get a huge Lab in this tiny apartment? She took the box of Cheerios from the shelf above the refrigerator — the fridge, the fridge — and pulled out a handful. She shouldn't eat, with Hannah's dinner just over an hour away, but her body clock was still all screwed up from the trip, so mealtimes were either forgotten or totally confused, and she was starving right now.

As she crunched, the calendar on the wall caught her eye. Valentine's Day tomorrow — big freaking deal. She was finished with love and romance: been there, done that, got the divorces to prove it.

Mind you, she was a damn sight better off now than before she'd met her exes, neither of whom could live with the knowledge that everyone fooled around in New York. Nora only wanted a bit of fun on the side — where was the harm in that? But the professor had run for the hills before the ink was dry on the marriage licence, and Dr Paluzzi couldn't hack it either, couldn't turn a blind eye, more fool him. At least they both had lots of cash — and Nora had enjoyed her share from the first divorce, and was looking forward to the next.

She wondered about the men of Clongarvin. She wondered if she'd find what she wanted among them while she was here. Just because she was done with love didn't mean she was done with men — far from it.

She closed the Cheerios box and replaced it on the shelf. She left the kitchen and went into the doggy-smelling bedroom to make herself pretty for dinner.

"Does he look like you?"

Patrick shook his head. "Not in the least. He's shorter and balder, and his eyes are blue."

"And you said he's younger."

"Yeah, by three years."

Leah's hand rested on his thigh as he drove, her fingers stroking absently. He enjoyed how tactile she was — presumably from force of habit, since her job involved so much physical interaction.

"I'm dying to meet this brother of yours," she said. "The first of your family."

"That's right."

The surprise trip had been more awkward to arrange than last year's. Getting time off for Hannah had been easy — a phone call to Joseph Finnegan at the bakery, whom Patrick knew well, and it had been sorted. With Leah, he'd had to plan his strategy more carefully.

The reason for his brother's imaginary visit home from London became a cousin's imaginary fortieth birthday celebrations in Offaly the following day, to which he and Leah had also been invited. "They want us there by lunchtime," Patrick had told her, "so you'll have to take the whole day off. I've booked us into the local hotel for the Saturday night."

He was assuming the discovery that they were headed to Paris as opposed to Offaly would banish any annoyance Leah might feel at having been duped into thinking she was going to meet some of Patrick's family. She'd met none of them so far, since Patrick's father had had the temerity to leave for his Greek islands cruise just before Patrick and Leah had become an official couple. Hopefully she wouldn't mind that the Offaly celebrations existed only in Patrick's imagination, and that any family introductions would have to wait a little longer.

Presumably she'd be pleased with the hotel he'd found for them on the Internet, which had better live up to its impressive description. No way could he risk ending up in a dump like last year's — Hannah might overlook faulty plumbing and erratic heating, but Leah liked her comforts. Patrick had paid considerably more this time round, and he expected to be well rewarded.

"What time did you say his plane is in?"

"Ten to eight."

Interesting how easily both women believed his lies. Hannah, of course, had had no reason to doubt him — until Leah, he'd covered his tracks well, been discreet on the few occasions he'd wandered. But Leah, who'd been party to his deceiving Hannah, who'd seen him covering his tracks and telling his half-truths, was still happily trusting him. Interesting, how easy it was.

Interesting, too, how intoxicating deceit could be. Until Leah had managed to get pregnant and Patrick's cover had been forcibly blown, the excitement of having both women, each so different from the other, had been wonderful. Sex, regardless of who he was with, had never been so fulfilling.

And if Leah hadn't got pregnant, who knew how long the situation might have gone on, despite her constant urging him to tell Hannah, to leave Hannah? *Soon*, he'd said, *when the time is right*, knowing, even as he spoke, that he was repeating the mantra of so many men — and indeed, women — before him. Knowing that he would happily have lived with the situation long term. What man wouldn't, for Christ's sake? And was it really so bad, trying to keep them both happy for as long as he could?

He couldn't believe it when Leah had dropped her bombshell. *I'm sorry darling*, she'd whispered, clinging to him. *Don't be angry, it was nobody's fault.* Naturally, after that everything had changed, and Hannah, unfortunately, had suffered in the fallout — something Patrick had never intended to happen.

He couldn't imagine being a father. He'd never envied friends with children, never wondered when his turn would come. Hannah had dropped hints now and again — inevitable, maybe, when they were living together, and she'd been in her thirties by the time they'd become a couple — but Patrick had managed each time to postpone what he'd regarded as the inevitable. *Some day*, he'd said, *when we're both ready. When the time is right.*

He pulled in by the arrivals building. "Why don't you go in," he said, "and I'll find a parking space? Won't be long." Ignoring, as he spoke, the faint echo of his identical words a year ago.

He watched Leah walk towards the automatic doors. Her waist had begun to thicken — and hadn't her hips got slightly wider? She'd also started to develop the tiniest suggestion of a double chin, and her ankles weren't quite as slender as before. She was still beautiful, of course. He wondered what other changes were in store, what pregnancy would do to her body as the months went on.

He found a parking space and unloaded the case he'd packed the previous night while Leah was in the bath. The thought occurred to him as he made his way back towards arrivals that maybe he should have chosen another destination: Leah might not be too pleased if she ever discovered that she was following so closely in Hannah's footsteps. But it had to be Paris for Valentine's Day, didn't it? Women expected Paris.

And technically, of course, Hannah's trip had been for her birthday rather than for Valentine's Day, even if the two dates were so close together. But Leah might not see it like that.

The doors to the arrivals hall slid open and he walked through. Too late to change anything now — and, anyway, the past was in the past. He watched Leah's expression as he approached her, smiling.

"Tell you what," he said. "Let's go to Paris instead."

"Another slice?"

Nora shook her head. "Not for me, thanks." One slice of decidedly unexciting shop-bought quiche was more than enough. She picked up an oven chip — talk about ruining a potato — and slid her glass towards Adam. "I'll have a top-up though." Eighteen euro she'd paid for the wine, and it was just about drinkable. Eight dollars would get you a decent Chablis in New York.

Adam filled her glass. "So how're you settling in? Anything you can't find in the apartment?"

"Just the Jacuzzi," she told him. "And the pool. But I'm sure they're there somewhere."

He grinned. "You're not in Amerikay now. None of that posh rubbish in Clongarvin."

"Don't I know it." She smiled so they'd think she was joking. "I'd forgotten how much it rains here too."

"So what d'you think you'll do?" Hannah asked. "Are you moving back to Ireland?"

"Not sure yet," Nora replied, wishing they'd all stop asking. "I'm considering my options."

It still amused her, how her brother and Hannah Robinson had hung around together for as long as she could remember and had never, as far as she knew — and she was pretty sure she'd know — had any kind of a romantic fling with each other, never even a wham-bam-thank-you-ma'am night after a couple of drinks too many.

And now here was Adam, moving in with Hannah right after her big relationship bust-up. Was he secretly hoping to be her rebound guy? Had the thought of getting together really never occurred to either of them? Weird. Definitely weird.

And then there was the whole cupcake-shop business. It might work in New York — it *did* work in New York — but who opened a shop that sold nothing but cupcakes in a small Irish town in the middle of a serious recession? And Hannah baking everything herself, getting up in the middle of the night, according to Adam — was she nuts? Nobody could keep that up for long.

She and Hannah had never hung around together at school. For one thing, they were a year apart — but even if the two of them had sat beside one another for five solid years of secondary school, Nora was willing to bet that they'd hardly have known each other's last names at the end of it. They were fundamentally different; they operated on completely disparate levels.

Nora wondered idly what Hannah's ex was like. She'd never come across Patrick Dunne — their paths hadn't crossed before she'd left for the States. Adam had said something about him being involved with the local newspaper, but she knew nothing else about the man, apart from the fact that he'd apparently done the dirty on Hannah.

Of course neither of their break-ups, hers or Hannah's, had been mentioned over the quiche. Nora certainly didn't feel like talking about Jackson Paluzzi, and Hannah was probably just as anxious to put the newspaper man behind her.

Nora looked without appetite at the cheese selection Adam was putting on the table — insipid white Cheddar, blue that wasn't half blue enough, Camembert that looked too firm to have been out of the fridge for long — and thought with yearning of chunks of Monterey Jack scattered with toasted pecans, melting slices of Swiss draped over prosciutto, Neufchâtel spread thickly on a warm bagel, scamorza drizzled with olive oil and sprinkled with black pepper.

"So," Hannah said, cutting into the Cheddar, "do you see a big change in Clongarvin?"

Nora pretended to consider. "I suppose so . . . yeah, quite a few changes." Which, of course, was a lie — apart from the odd unfamiliar building and a scatter of boarded-up premises, the place was depressingly pretty much as she'd left it more than a decade ago. She remembered how impatient she'd felt then, how desperate she'd been to finish school and get on a plane — any plane — and leave behind the same old faces, the boringly familiar cafes and shops and narrow streets.

And now she'd had enough of small talk with her brother's friend. She drained her glass and got to her feet. "Thanks a lot, you two — I guess my body clock is still screwed up. I better leave before I fall asleep on the table."

"No coffee?" Adam asked, and Nora, imagining the instant horror she'd probably be served, shook her head.

"Drop by any time," Hannah told her, "now that you know the way."

"Thanks, I might just do that." Both of them knowing she wouldn't be dropping by. How ridiculous were social conventions?

Adam walked her back to his apartment. The earlier rain had cleared, leaving the air damp and clean.

"I was thinking today, I must look up some of the old gang," Nora said as they skirted the puddles. "That's if they're still around."

"Like who?"

"Like Francine Kelly, or Jojo Fitzpatrick. Or Leah Bradshaw."

Adam shrugged. "Can't say I remember any of them."

Nora grinned. "If Francine heard you — she fancied you like mad for ages."

"Did she? You might have told me. Any idea what you want to do otherwise?"

"You mean a job?"

"I suppose I do."

She shrugged. "Don't really need one, bro — the advantages of alimony."

"I know, but don't you want something to keep you from being bored while you're here?"

"Yeah, maybe. Depends what's available, I suppose." In the States she'd worked behind the scenes in a radio station, and before that she'd divided her time between PR and various jobs with fashion magazines. She was adaptable, if not exactly qualified. "I get the impression work is fairly thin on the ground here right now."

"Depends what you're willing to do," Adam told her. "If you don't set your sights too high you'll probably pick up something. Hannah was talking about taking on a part-timer in the shop."

"No, thanks," Nora said swiftly. "Not my scene." She could think of few less appealing prospects than standing behind the counter in a cupcake shop. "I'd rather something a bit more . . . challenging." Glamorous was what she meant, but he'd probably laugh.

They reached the apartment block. Adam hugged her. "Night, sleep well."

"I intend to. Talk tomorrow." She turned towards the door.

"Hey, speaking of tomorrow," Adam said. "Want to come out for a drink? Can't leave you all on your own on Valentine's night."

She smiled. "Yeah, sure — why not? Gimme a call."

"And do me a favour," he said.

"Yeah?"

"Lose the Yankee accent."

She laughed. "I'll do my best. See you." She turned the key in the lock and went inside, checking her watch and realising that she was in time for *Grey's Anatomy*.

Hannah weighed flour and sugar and added them to the bowl of the food processor. Get as much done as you can the night before, ease the pressure when you stumble, half asleep, into the kitchen at three in the morning.

Once she woke up a bit though, once she got into the routine of mixing and chopping and stirring and icing, she had to admit that it wasn't so terrible being up when the rest of the country was asleep. There was something peaceful about moving around the warm kitchen, radio playing softly so Adam wouldn't be disturbed, surrounded by the scents of new sponge and vanilla and roasting nuts.

Not that she wouldn't choose to be tucked up in bed, given the option, but someone had to produce the hundred and forty-four cupcakes — and until her fairy godmother appeared and waved a wand, that someone was going to be her. She opened the fridge and took out butter and eggs and left them on the worktop. She filled the cups of four muffin trays with pink paper cases decorated with red and white hearts.

Adam was in his room directly overhead, working to meet a deadline. Neil Young drifted faintly downwards.

Kirby was in the sitting room, not yet put out for the night.

And not once, not even for a second, did she dwell on the fact that tomorrow was Valentine's Day, and that whoever bought one or more of her special sweetheart cupcakes (strawberry centre, white chocolate icing, sugar-paste heart on top) would in all likelihood be spending Valentine's Day with someone they loved.

She didn't think about last year's Valentine's Day or the man who would be spending it with someone else this year.

No, not for a second did any of that cross her mind. She didn't torture herself thinking about how they might spend the day. She didn't remember the breakfast of warm croissants and *chocolat chaud* in bed last year, the film in the darkened French cinema that evening, the shared bath afterwards.

And while she wasn't recalling any of that, Neil Young was telling her that only love could break her heart. What, he asked, if her world should fall apart?

She tipped what was left of Nora's wine into her glass and concentrated on how over-made-up Adam's sister had been, how bored she'd seemed all evening, how ridiculous her American accent sounded. How relieved Hannah had been when she'd left.

Much safer to keep on thinking about Nora, as she assembled strawberries and chocolate chunks and little pink sugar-paste hearts in bowls on the worktop.

And when she'd finally made all the preparations she could, she took off her apron and filled the kettle for her hotwater bottle. Then she went into the sitting room and sat on the floor beside Kirby, who was slumped beside the radiator, his head resting on his paws. She bent and put her arms around his warm neck and buried her face in his smooth black coat, and listened to the soft thump of his tail on the carpet.

"Quiet tonight," Adam said. "Thought you'd be busier, with the night that's in it."

The barman nodded. "All the loving couples are out to dinner," he said. "Be in later, I'd say."

"Right." Adam pocketed his change and turned his attention to the female musician. Tonight her hair was completely hidden, swathed in some kind of black turban. Below it she wore a black turtleneck jumper and a pair of straight black tailored trousers over shiny black ankle boots. Her legs were thin, her knees pressed together. Her feet were slightly parted, toes turned inwards.

She made eye contact with nobody, as far as Adam could see from where he sat, apart from the keyboard player, who stood more or less in her line of vision. She didn't smile between numbers. Occasionally she pushed her small round glasses further up her nose. During the more lively tunes one of her feet tapped along sporadically. Her back was hunched a little. Now and again a frown creased the skin between her eyes.

She was his own age, or close enough. As far as he could make out she wore no rings — did musicians take rings off before they played? Her fingers flew over the keys of her instrument — what had Hannah called it? A clarinet. The keys of her clarinet. The backs of her hands might be freckled, but from this distance, and in this light, it was hard to be sure.

Adam couldn't for the life of him figure out why she fascinated him. She didn't remotely resemble any of his previous girlfriends. There was nothing he could put a finger on, nothing charming about her. Nothing he could point to and say —

"Hey."

He spun round to see Nora walking towards him. "There you are. What'll you have?"

"I might chance a vodka martini, if they can manage it." Nora glanced idly around. "Nice little place. About time Clongarvin got a wine bar. Let's grab a couch while we can." Her gaze fell on the musicians in the corner. "Get the secret agent with the clarinet," she said.

Alice bundled the envelopes together and brought them into the kitchen. Two for Tom, the gas bill and a bank statement. Three for her — a Visa bill, a postcard from Sheila in the Canaries and one with a catering-company logo in the top corner that she vaguely recognised.

She laid the envelopes on the table before fishing Tom's boiled egg out of the simmering water and setting it into one of the yellow pottery eggcups with chicken feet that Ellen had given them years ago as an anniversary present.

She put the butter dish into the microwave and cut two slices of brown bread. She dropped three teabags into the teapot, waited for the kettle to click off and made the tea. She took marmalade and milk from the fridge and went to the kitchen door and called, "Tom?"

She sat at the table and turned the postcard over. *Having a lovely time,* Sheila had written *Very warm. Bit of a trek to the beach so we're staying put by the pool. See you soon.* The picture was of a platter of seafood on a blue and white checked tablecloth.

She opened the envelope from the catering company. Its director turned out to be a woman she knew slightly from meetings of local businesswomen that took place each month, but that Alice attended sporadically. Alice was invited to purchase tickets for a dinner-dance that was being organised to raise funds for a dialysis machine for Clongarvin's hospital. *I'm sure you'll want to support this very worthy cause,* the director had written, *and if you can rally your friends too, so much the better.* The event was scheduled for a date in late March, and would be held in a local hotel. *Sponsorship is generously being provided by various local businesses, which means that all proceeds on the night will go directly towards the cost of this vital machine,* Alice read. There would be a champagne reception before the meal, and lots of spot prizes throughout the evening.

A champagne reception — and no doubt plenty of sponsored wine with the dinner, and more alcohol available at the bar afterwards. Alice heard Tom's footsteps on the stairs and pushed letter and envelope under the others.

"Morning, love," she said. He'd never been at his best in the first few hours of the day — that was nothing new.

"Morning." He sat and topped his egg. He never shaved till after breakfast. She hated the stubble: it made his face seem dirty.

"It's nice out today," she said. They had to have a bit of chat at the table — she couldn't sit there in silence, even if Tom's end of the conversation was mostly grunts at this hour. "The forecast says no rain, so I'm going to chance putting out the clothes before we head off."

She wouldn't say anything about the dinner-dance. She'd have to support it — she'd buy two tickets and ask Geraldine if she and Stephen would go instead. She'd say Tom wasn't feeling the best, a bit run down at the moment. She'd be quite happy to pay: she'd call it an early Easter present.

He eyed the salt cellar on her side of the table and she passed it over to him. A bottle of wine every night, par for the course now. And more often than not, a gin and tonic before dinner for him too. The other evening he'd gone to answer the phone and she'd taken a sip of the gin and tonic. It had been hard to taste the tonic.

And he snored every night — when had that started? He snored, and his breath was sour in the morning when she smelt it.

"You're not eating," he said, and she picked up her knife and began to butter her toast.

"Miles away," she said, smiling.

You wouldn't call the trip a disaster exactly, but it hadn't gone quite as Patrick had hoped. It had begun on the flight to Paris, when Leah's asthma had acted up slightly.

"Did you pack an inhaler?" she'd asked him, and of course he hadn't. It hadn't occurred to him because she hadn't had an attack in months, not since shortly after they'd met. So their first hour in Paris had been spent finding an all-night pharmacy and trying to explain about the pregnancy, and about the medication her doctor had recommended in the event of an attack. Hardly the most romantic of starts.

The hotel was a disappointment too — further from the centre than Patrick had understood, and distinctly lacking in friendliness. They'd made the best of it, of course. They'd taken advantage of the large Jacuzzi bath, and they'd ordered breakfast in bed from the unsmiling concierge, and Leah had bought horrendously overpriced but wonderfully saucy underwear in the small, dangerous gift shop.

The weather was very cold, which he'd been expecting from the previous year. He'd packed plenty of woollens, and they made frequent stops for *chocolat chaud* during the day, but Leah still shivered violently after just a few minutes outdoors. Patrick made a mental note to go south for any future winter breaks.

The restaurant they picked for dinner on Valentine's night was unremarkable. Leah's *pot-au-feu* was fatty and he counted three mussels in his *bouillabaisse*. The violinist who wandered among the tables stared openly at Leah's breasts as he played, making her uncomfortable. Patrick consoled himself with the thought that only he was aware of the silk and lace confections that lay underneath the black wool dress, and only he would have the pleasure of removing them later.

In the plane on the way home her hand stole under his blanket, but for once her touch had no effect. "Never mind," she said, taking out her magazine, but Patrick did mind. He minded that he'd spent far too much on a mediocre few days. He minded that her mother despised him. He minded how terrifying he found the notion that in four months or so he'd be a father.

"I'm just tired," he told her, and closed his eyes.

"Hello again."

He wore a pale blue denim shirt under a rust-coloured V-necked jumper. She decided the almost-shaved head suited him. His eyes were halfway between blue and green. She was glad her mother wasn't there to see him turn up again, to put two and two together and come up with eighteen.

"I called to say thank you," he said. "I got a phone call yesterday from someone who'd picked up one of my leaflets here."

Hannah smiled. "Well, I'm glad to have been of assistance." She still thought she'd seen him somewhere else, and she still couldn't remember where.

"You certainly were of assistance. And while I'm here," he said, scanning the samples on the stand, "let me take some more of these delicious cupcakes off your hands."

"You mustn't feel obliged to keep buying them," she said. "Really, you don't have to." If her mother heard her . . .

"Not at all — they're a lot cheaper than taking out an ad."

"I suppose they are." She liked the dimple in his left cheek when he smiled. "In that case, what can I get you?"

He selected three, and watched as she arranged them in a box. "Do you really make them all yourself?"

"I certainly do. I have it down to a fine art."

"I'll say — you must have tons of energy."

She laughed. "More like gallons of coffee — and the knowledge that if I don't bake them, I'll have nothing to sell."

"Aye, that would do it." He took his wallet from his jeans pocket. "I see you don't have your trusty assistant with you today."

"You mean my mother — no, she was just passing by that day. She has her own job. But I am going to take on someone part time, when I can get around to it." She handed him the box and took his tenner. "Whereabouts in Scotland are you from?"

"A wee island called Bute, off the west coast," he told her. "I dare say you'll not have heard of it."

"No." She wondered what had brought him to Ireland. He'd mentioned his mother was Irish — maybe he was simply exploring his roots. Or maybe he'd met an Irish girl in Scotland and followed her back here. She counted out his change. "Thanks a lot, enjoy them."

"I will." He tucked his wallet away and put out his hand. "We've not been properly introduced. You know I'm John Wyatt, and I think your mum mentioned your name, but I'm afraid I've forgotten it."

"Hannah Robinson," she said. His hand was warm. "Nice to meet you."

When he'd gone she checked the time. Ten past four — still most of an hour to go. She must get some music for the shop. Even a little radio would do to kill the awful silence between customers.

And she must definitely take on a part-timer. Now that Adam was helping out financially, she could manage to pay someone for a couple of hours, two or three mornings a week. The bliss of being able to walk out at ten and just sit somewhere with a coffee, or wander through the shops, or down by the river. A chance to do nothing, that was all she wanted.

Having Adam move into the house had definitely been a good idea. Since he worked from home a lot of the time, he was still making dinner for both of them most evenings. The fact that cooking was not his forte was easily cancelled out by the pleasure of getting a meal served up to her, not to mention having someone to eat it with.

She could do without Kirby's coarse black hairs that seemed to settle on every surface in his vicinity, and the doggy smell that lingered in the sitting room even after she'd used the fabric spray. But it was a small price to pay, a minor downside to a mostly successful arrangement.

Almost six weeks on from Patrick's departure and the world was still turning, just as it always had. Hannah hadn't laid eyes on him since the day she'd opened Cupcakes on the Corner, which was hardly surprising, given that she'd had exactly one night out since then and that most of her time awake was spent standing behind a counter, or churning out more cupcakes at home.

She still missed him, of course, but the intensity was fading. She still woke lonely, but even that wasn't as piercing as it had been. She was surviving, and she had the shop to thank mostly for that.

She'd survived Valentine's Day. Business had been brisker than usual, and the pink-tissue-wrapped sweetheart cupcakes had sold well. She'd gone home afterwards and resisted Adam's efforts to drag her out with him and Nora.

She'd had a bath, her Saturday-night treat, and afterwards she'd put on pyjamas, sat in front of the fire that Adam had lit earlier and watched the first three episodes of Adam's box set of *The Office*, and shared a bag of Aged White Cheddar Kettle Chips with Kirby. Not exactly the Valentine's night of her dreams, but perfectly enjoyable.

The shop door opened and one of her regulars walked in.

"Hi," Hannah said. "I've been wanting to have a word with you."

"Good news," Geraldine said. "We're going to a dinner-dance."

"A dinner-dance?" Stephen eyed her over his glasses. "How exactly is that good news?"

"Well, for one thing it's for a very worthy cause — a dialysis machine for the hospital."

"Which is good news for dialysis patients." He poured sauce over his chicken breast. "I'm waiting to hear how it's good for me."

Geraldine spooned cabbage onto their plates. "It's good because we got the tickets for free."

"So we personally are not, in fact, helping to provide the hospital with a dialysis machine."

"Well, no — but that's beside the point. Have you enough mash?"

"Yes thanks. So who's giving us this wonderful treat?"

"Don't be sarcastic. Alice bought the tickets. She got a letter about it and felt obliged to buy tickets, but apparently Tom isn't feeling up to it, so she asked if we'd go instead."

Stephen frowned. "Tom isn't feeling up to it? Since when?" He reached for the butter dish.

"I've already added butter to those potatoes. That's what Alice told me. Apparently he's run down. She's going to put him on a tonic."

"He didn't look run down to me today. He hasn't been off sick for as long as I can remember. He's as healthy as I am."

"Well, that's what I thought too, but I didn't like to contradict her. Maybe he's just putting on a brave front." She sprinkled black pepper on her chicken.

"Maybe he just doesn't want to go, more like it. When's it on?"

"Not for ages — the end of March, the last Thursday, I think." She refilled their water glasses. "I'll drop your dinner jacket into the cleaner's tomorrow."

She set down the jug. "Stephen, don't say anything to Tom — there might be another reason that Alice isn't saying."

"Like what?"

"I don't know — maybe they're going through a bad patch or something. I just think it might be better if you said nothing."

Stephen sighed heavily and added a wedge of butter to his mash, and Geraldine decided that it might be wise to let it pass.

PA required, Nora read. *Experienced, flexible, highly organised & efficient individual with an excellent attitude to work and the ability to adapt and work under pressure.*

Nothing about qualifications. She read on.

Responsibilities will include diary management, compiling PowerPoint presentations, organising travel, accommodation and meetings, providing PA support at senior management level.

Piece of cake — apart from the PowerPoint presentations, which Adam could coach her in. She skimmed down to *Professional Qualifications* and read *Leaving Cert* and *Secretarial Qualification*. Was that it? She had the Leaving Cert, and the secretarial qualification could be arranged with a phone call to Sonia at one of the fashion magazines. A letter on headed paper from New York would surely do the trick with the hicks of Clongarvin.

No mention of what kind of company it was, not that it bothered her. Not when she was doing this purely for

110

laughs, not when she could leave any time she felt like it. She'd apply to the box number, see what it threw up.

"Here we go."

The taxi driver pulled up to the kerb. Nora folded the newspaper and looked in amusement at the lavender walls, the pink window boxes filled with the little vividly coloured flowers — something beginning with C, she thought — that everyone seemed to grow in Ireland in February. Indulgence, the ornate gold letters spelt over the window. Pure Leah Bradshaw, as girly as ever.

"How much?" He mightn't be bad without that horrendous woolly hat. Probably hiding a bald patch. Sexy green eyes though, and decent enough teeth.

"Four thirty, thanks."

Nora pulled out a note and checked that it was a fiver. "Keep the change."

"Thanks a lot."

Nice music too — she was partial to a bit of Miles Davis. But of course a taxi driver didn't interest her. She stood on the path and rang the bell outside the salon, and smoothed her leather jacket as she waited.

"Surprise," she said when the door was opened.

Leah's eyes widened. "Nora O'Connor? Is that you?" She stepped forward and put her cheek against Nora's. "Bloody hell, you look fantastic. It's been years."

"I'm here for a massage," Nora told her. "I booked under Jackie Collins."

Leah laughed. "That was you? I should have known." She stepped back into the hallway and held the door open.

"Come in. How did you find me?"

Nora walked past her, taking in the deep blue carpet, the white reception desk, the framed certificate on the wall behind. "You're kidding, aren't you? This is Clongarvin."

Leah Bradshaw had put on weight. Her face was heavier. Hard to see her figure with the loose flowery thing she wore, but her ankles had thickened too. Maybe she had kids now. No ring on the wedding finger though.

"Come on." Leah walked ahead of Nora down the narrow corridor that led off the hall. "We have lots to catch up on."

"We certainly do."

Nora was led into a small treatment room that contained a massage table, a trolley piled with various bottles and pots, a hi-fi system on a shelf and a single chair. "You can strip down to panties and lie under the towel," Leah said. "I'll be right back."

"Hey, no need to disappear — I'm not shy." Nora unbuttoned her jacket and slipped out of it. The room was warm and scented. Some elevator music wafted softly through the hi-fi speakers. "Nothing under here that you haven't seen plenty of times."

She was aware of her still firm body as she undressed — and conscious, as she listened to Leah's voice, while she laid her clothes on the spindly-legged turquoise chair and unhooked her Agent Provocateur bra, that her school friend was checking out the full breasts, flat stomach, firm thighs.

Jackson Paluzzi's obsession with his wife's figure — he'd happily paid for the personal trainer, the yoga and Pilates classes, the regular spa treatments — had served some purpose. And his first anniversary present of a boob job hadn't hurt either.

"Right, let me have it." She swung her legs onto the massage table and rolled onto her stomach, aware that her thong made it quite clear that Nora Paluzzi didn't have an ounce of cellulite. "I like it good and deep — as the actress said to the bishop."

She closed her eyes and prepared for an hour of gossip and pampering.

John Wyatt took his saxophone from its case and thought about the treacle-haired woman behind the counter of the shop that sold nothing but cupcakes. "Hannah." He said the name out loud, liking the soft roundness of it. It suited her.

The lie about his sweet tooth was forgivable. How else was he going to get to know her? She was never at Vintage on Saturday nights, or anywhere else he'd been to. And Patsy at the woodwork store was delighted to take the cupcakes off his hands, so he was making someone happy, which surely cancelled out the lie.

He was lonely, and it had been quite a while. Hannah Robinson was friendly, and the only ring she wore was on the middle finger of her right hand. Enough grounds for asking her out? Maybe he should bide his time, get to know her a bit more.

Or maybe he should go for it, take a chance. Not much to lose if she turned him down. A minor embarrassment, a small disappointment. Easy enough not to put himself in the way of meeting her again.

He opened the sheet music and began to play around with "Penny Lane" for Saturday night.

She turned the key again and pumped the accelerator. The little yellow van shuddered, coughed and went silent. Hannah groaned and leant her head against the steering-wheel. This was all she needed after a slow day, a thumping headache and a big wash on the line that Adam had probably forgotten to take in when the rain had finally come at four o'clock, the one time she'd been too busy to phone him.

It was still lashing now, but at least the thunder and lightning had stopped. She'd always been terrified of lightning — it had taken all of her resolve not to close the shop and hide in the back until it had passed. And now the van had broken down, and who knew how much it would cost to get fixed?

She pulled out the keys and grabbed her satchel and umbrella and stepped into the rain. She'd hail a taxi and go home — in this rain, and with her busy schedule, waiting for a bus wasn't an option — and she'd get Adam to phone his mechanic friend, and hopefully this wouldn't be a major disaster.

Her shoes were completely sodden by the time a taxi pulled up. She closed her umbrella and opened the door.

"Can you come around the corner? I have some trays to unload from my van."

The driver looked familiar. "Sure — hop in and I'll drive you."

"Thanks."

He helped her shift the wooden trays from the van to the back of the taxi. Hannah gave her address and sank gratefully into the passenger seat, closing her eyes. A hot bath when she got home, even if she couldn't spare more than ten minutes in it. Adam would have grilled some sausages and mashed a couple of spuds, hopefully. And two Disprin might shift this damn headache.

"Your van break down?"

"Yeah," she said, without opening her eyes. "Trust it to be raining."

"Sod's law," he said, and she nodded. The music was pleasant, something mellow and jazzy. She opened her eyes and stole a look in the driver's direction. He wasn't wearing the woolly hat, but she was pretty sure it was him.

She remembered him driving her to the restaurant the night Patrick had broken up with her, and home again later that evening, with her parents in the car. Funny how seldom she took a taxi, and she'd got the same driver three times in a row. Clongarvin wasn't that small, was it?

His hair was muddy blond, and curled around the edge of his collar. His left hand rested on the gear stick as he negotiated Clongarvin's rush-hour traffic. He wore a green jumper. She couldn't be sure from this angle, but she thought his eyes were green too.

He caught her glance and threw her a smile. "Thought you'd nodded off."

"Nearly."

Nice even teeth. She turned to the window and noticed that the rain had finally stopped and been replaced by a pale lemon sun that was doing its best to shine.

March

"Did you know that Leah is the woman Hannah's ex left her for?"

Adam poured boiling water into the mugs. "I heard something."

"Does Hannah know?"

"Yes." He handed her a mug. "Nora, it's in the past — leave it alone. Hannah's moved on." He offered her a biscuit but she waved the packet away. "She's doing fine now."

She sipped her coffee and grimaced. "What's the deal with you two?" she asked. "You and Hannah, how come you never got together?"

Adam bit into his custard cream. "You're such a drama queen. You know quite well Hannah and I are just friends. It is possible, believe it or not."

"Right." She tapped a nail against the side of her mug. "Do you remember Leah?"

"Not really. She was one of the princesses you hung around with, that's about it."

"Leah was the small dark one. She's the small blonde one now."

Adam shook his head. "Nope. Nothing. Did she fancy me too?"

Nora laughed. "Oh no, Leah was immune to your charms. She went for the studs."

"Thanks."

Hannah had told him about calling into Leah's salon and getting the gift voucher for Patrick. *I probably brought them together*, she'd said, trying to smile. *Isn't that a good one?*

"I got a massage from her the other day," Nora said. "Wasn't the best I've ever had, but it wasn't bad."

"You don't say."

"Stop looking like that. I didn't know about Hannah till after I went. And, like you say, it's all in the past, and nothing to do with me."

"Yeah . . . so you two had a good gossip?"

"Of course we did. I had to find out what everyone else was doing. Get this — Jojo married a widower with six kids."

Adam took another biscuit. "Fascinating. I just can't believe it. Good old Jojo."

"Shut up." Nora pulled an envelope out of her bag. "Here's the real reason I came round — have a look at what I got in the post this morning."

Adam took the envelope. "What is it?"

"Read it."

He pulled out the single sheet and scanned it. He looked back at Nora. "You're joking."

She giggled. "Isn't it a scream? Talk about a small world, even for Clongarvin."

He stared at her. "You're not going to go?"

She took back the letter and folded it. "Of course I am. The first job I apply for and I'm called for interview. You should be pleased. And why the heck shouldn't I go?"

"Because you'd be working for him."

"So? Just because he did the dirty on Hannah, who I hardly know, I'm not allowed to work for him?"

Adam frowned. "Well, no, but —"

"Look," Nora said, "I might not even get the job. But if I do, well, like you keep telling me, Hannah's moved on. Right?"

"Are you going to tell Leah about this?"

Nora paused. "No. Why should I? She said nothing when I told her I was looking for work, although she must have known lover-boy was in the market for a PA. Anyway, she'll find out soon enough if I get the job."

"Jesus." Adam lifted his mug. "I'll never figure women out."

He wouldn't mention it to Hannah. It might come to nothing. On the other hand, if Patrick Dunne decided to take Nora on as his PA, it might be awkward explaining to Hannah why he'd kept quiet about his sister applying for the job. He sighed.

"Hey, bro," Nora said, putting a hand on his arm, "I didn't tell you anything, OK? Wouldn't want you getting into trouble with Hannah. You know nothing about this job interview. Right?"

Adam nodded slowly. "Right."

He might never figure her out, but she had him completely sussed.

As Geraldine slid the grill pan towards her and lifted the lamb cutlets onto the warmed plates she heard her husband's key in the lock. After thirty-five years of marriage, their timing was impeccable. "Yoo-hoo," she called, and a second later Stephen's head appeared. "Just in time," she said. "I'm dishing up."

"Smells good. Won't be long."

He thumped up the stairs and she uncorked the red wine that they'd opened the night before, then emptied what was left into the two glasses on the table. She drained the broccoli and transferred the potatoes from the steamer to a bowl. She turned the oven down to low so the apple crumble would keep warm.

She pictured the kind of meal Stephen would serve up if their working hours were reversed and he was the one who got home earlier. On the very odd occasions he'd cooked dinner in the past he'd taken several hours and used more saucepans than she'd thought they possessed. He wasn't a bad cook, the end results were generally very palatable, but for the time and effort involved she could have cooked for the week. Just as well she was always home ahead of him.

"Guess what," she said, when they were sitting opposite each other, he having splashed his face and exchanged his work shirt and shoes for sweatshirt and slippers. "Alice and Tom are coming to that dinner-dance after all."

"I know," he said. "Miraculous recovery."

"Tom mentioned it to you?"

"He asked if you and me wanted to go. I told him we already had tickets."

Geraldine looked sharply at him. "You didn't say Alice gave them to us, did you?"

122

"No — I said as far as I knew you'd got them from someone who'd bought them and couldn't go."

"Good."

Alice had been strange, that was the only word for it. *You won't believe,* she'd said to Geraldine, *but wasn't Tom asked to buy tickets to that dinner-dance by one of his patients, so it looks like we're going along, after all.*

There'd been an expression on her face that Geraldine couldn't put a name to, a smile that wasn't a smile, and she didn't meet Geraldine's eye as she spoke.

Of course Geraldine hadn't asked how Tom was feeling — clearly that story hadn't been true. Just as well she'd told Stephen to say nothing to Tom at the dental clinic. There was something going on between Alice and her husband, but whatever it was, Alice wasn't saying.

Geraldine had offered to pay for her and Stephen's tickets, but Alice firmly refused. *They were a present,* she'd said. *I wouldn't hear of it.* So now they were all going, the four of them.

They hadn't often gone out together in the past, even though she and Alice got on fine in the shop, and Tom and Stephen would go for a drink after work every now and again.

Alice and Tom were older than Stephen and Geraldine — at almost sixty, Alice was around seven years older than Geraldine, and Tom had celebrated his sixtieth well over a year ago — but that in itself wouldn't have stopped them meeting up socially.

Maybe it was the fact that they worked side by side every day.

We can share a taxi, Geraldine had suggested, and Alice had agreed. So on the last Thursday in March they were all dressing up and heading off to the Dunmurray Arms Hotel for a night out that probably none of them wanted.

Stephen hated having to wear his dinner jacket, and only danced when it was completely unavoidable. Geraldine would miss *Dexter*, and she didn't fancy having to get up for work after a late night. And Alice and Tom had whatever was going on between them, so they were probably looking forward to it with even less enthusiasm.

But it was for a good cause, so that was that.

And who knew? They might even enjoy it. She had that navy dress she'd worn only once, to Aoife's cocktail party last autumn. Hopefully she'd still fit into it, with everything else feeling a little snug these days. She'd cut out all treats till the dinner-dance — Lent was next week anyway — and maybe desserts too.

"I saw that Leah Bradshaw today," she told Stephen. "She walked past the shop, all done up."

Fiona Bradshaw was still avoiding her at bridge, and Geraldine was pretending not to notice. All a bit awkward really, but she had no intention of giving up her weekly game, and it wasn't as if she and Fiona had ever been close in the past.

"I phoned Hannah at lunchtime," she said, "to see how Una got on."

"Oh yes?"

"She did fine, apparently. Hannah will stay with her this week, to make sure she learns the ropes, and then she'll let her off on her own next week."

"Good."

Geraldine vaguely remembered the Connolly girls, for whom Hannah had babysat in her teens. The parents still lived across the park in Larch Crescent, although the father rarely left the house — Parkinson's or MS he had — and the mother was a bit odd, would say hello to you one day and ignore you the next.

Claire, the older girl, had had a baby a few years back. Geraldine recalled the minor scandal it had caused, remembered seeing Claire and a boy — the father, she presumed — pushing a pram, both looking like children themselves.

But Claire was always pleasant, would smile when she met you, not like her mother. And Una, the younger sister, was a nice little thing too. Hannah seemed happy with her choice of assistant.

"It'll be great for her to have a bit of time off," Geraldine said. "Take some of the pressure off her."

"Certainly will. Did she mention the van, how it's running now?"

"I forgot to ask. She would have said if it was still acting up."

"Hope it wasn't a bad buy."

They'd got it cheap from one of Stephen's patients who had a small garage out in the country. Patrick had arranged for the yellow spray painting, and the fitting of the wooden brackets in the back to hold Hannah's trays in place.

They ate apple crumble — Geraldine allowed herself a small portion, now that it was made — and in due course the dishes were washed up, the fire was lit and the television switched on. Stephen played Scrabble against a virtual opponent on the computer, and the evening passed in the same way that most of their evenings did.

And when she went upstairs, Geraldine slipped the navy dress out of the dry cleaner's plastic sleeve and tried it on in the bathroom, and decided that desserts were definitely out for at least the next three weeks.

"Nora O'Connor is back in town."

It was something to say, another sentence to cut through the disapproving silence that rushed to fill any gap in their lunchtime conversation these days.

"Who's Nora O'Connor?" Fiona wasn't happy with her tagliatelle today — too much sauce — which didn't help.

"You remember Nora — we hung around together at school. She was often in the house. She went to the States straight after doing the Leaving. She hasn't been back since — or rather, she's been back the odd time just to visit her parents . . . You don't remember her?"

"Can't say I do. So she's home for good?"

"Her marriage just broke up." As soon as the words were out Leah regretted them. "She's thinking of staying in Clongarvin for a while," she added hurriedly. "She might try for a job here. I said I'd keep an eye out."

126

Leah hadn't told Nora that Patrick was looking for a PA. She had instinctively kept quiet about it. Nora O'Connor had looked after herself in America. Her skin was clear, her body toned and smooth. Leah, remembering Nora's teenage single-mindedness when it came to getting a boyfriend, had decided there was no point in inviting trouble.

Not that she didn't have complete trust in Patrick — those people who said if a man is unfaithful once he'll do it again didn't have a clue what they were talking about. *You're the one*, he'd told her. *You're my soul-mate. I need you like I need food.* It wasn't Patrick she didn't trust, it was Nora O'Connor.

Fiona pushed her half-eaten lunch aside. "Your face is puffy," she said to her daughter. "It'll get worse. I went the same way as you."

"My ankles are swollen too," Leah said, grateful that her mother was at least acknowledging the pregnancy. "And I'm getting heartburn a lot." *And I've gone up a bra size and I can't close the zip on my jeans, and for the past fortnight I haven't been able to keep my hands off Patrick. And my breasts have become incredibly sensitive — he only has to look at them.* She felt a ribbon of desire flutter through her, and took a hasty mouthful of lasagne. *Not the time, not the place — and certainly not the company — for such confidences.*

"What's going to happen to the salon when you have to stop working?" Fiona asked abruptly.

"I'll get someone to keep it ticking over until I can go back," Leah answered. "Just for a month or so."

"Can you afford to pay someone?"

"Oh, yes," Leah said. "Part time, anyway."

Preferably someone who'd work for peanuts and hopefully not lose all of Leah's remaining customers. The salon hadn't been doing much more than ticking over for some time now, but there was no need to admit that here.

"And who'll look after the baby when you go back?"

Leah decided that a joke about Fiona taking on the role of childminder wouldn't go down too well. "We'll find someone," she said. "There are plenty of young girls who'd welcome the job, I'm sure. And I'll just be upstairs."

Fiona raised her hand and immediately a waiter appeared. Leah's mother had always been good at attracting the attention of waiting staff. "I'll take an espresso," she told the waiter. "And kindly let the chef know that my tagliatelle had far too much sauce."

The waiter took her plate, murmuring apologetically and glancing at Leah.

"Nothing more for me, thanks," she told him, laying down her fork. She and Patrick often ate here when neither of them felt like cooking in the evening. The food was good and not too pricey, the chef first-generation Italian. You'd think Fiona would have kept her mouth shut, allowed them one little slip-up.

"Seen any good films lately?" she asked. "Any new books?" Stick to the safe topics.

Fiona shrugged. "A couple of interesting Booker nominations," she said. "I'll pass them on. Nothing worth mentioning at the cinema — I lasted twenty minutes at the one that got the Oscar for best director. Can't imagine why, complete rubbish."

She didn't acknowledge the waiter as he put her coffee in front of her. "So," she said, dropping a sugar lump into the tiny cup, "have you any plans to marry this man?" Looking impassively at Leah, as if she'd asked her for the time.

The heady smell of the coffee wafted towards Leah. She resisted an impulse to fan it away as she searched for the least incendiary answer. "We're taking things slowly," she said eventually. "One step at a time." Under the table she crossed her ankles.

"Slowly?" Fiona's eyebrows raised. "You're with him a wet week and you're pregnant."

"You know very well," Leah said tightly, "that we didn't mean it to happen." She pressed her feet together. "And I'd hardly call ten months a wet week," she added — and immediately realised her mistake.

Fiona frowned. "Ten months? You told me you met him in October."

Leah forced herself not to look away. "We met last May, actually. I didn't feel it was something you needed to know."

"So you lied to me. I see." Her mother sipped coffee. "Your little affair was going on for — what? — eight months or thereabouts. You were the mistress all that time, with him going home to Hannah Robinson every night." She dabbed her mouth. "No wonder you were so evasive any time I asked if you'd met anyone new."

"I couldn't say anything — how could I?" Leah asked angrily. "It's not exactly something you share with your mother." She wished she'd ordered green tea, something to do with her hands, but it was too late. All she wanted now was to leave.

"I wonder how long it would have taken him to finish with her if you hadn't got pregnant," Fiona said then in the same bland voice, her eyes on Leah's swollen, blotchy face.

Leah scanned the room for their waiter, and of course, didn't find him. "I need to get back," she said, her voice quivering. She rummaged in her bag.

"There's no need for you to be like that," Fiona said. "I know I sound unsympathetic —"

"You sound bitchy." Leah found her purse and pulled it out. She'd just called her mother a bitch. Her hands shook as she pulled at the clasp.

"I'm only telling it like it is." Fiona reached across the table and grasped Leah's hand. "How do you know he'd ever have left her? He might only have been —"

"He *loves* me," Leah said, a little too loudly. A couple of heads at the nearest table swung in their direction. "We love each other," she said quietly, forcefully, pulling her hand from her mother's grip. "He left Hannah, he's with me now, and we're having your first grandchild, whether you like it or not. Nothing you can say will change that."

She pulled a twenty-euro note from her purse, but Fiona waved it away impatiently. "I'll pay — you paid last time. I'm only looking out for you, I'm only trying to make you see —"

130

But Leah was gone, hurrying past the tables towards the door, the money fluttering onto the white tablecloth.

Fiona watched her only child rushing away from her. Then she lifted her cup and finished her espresso.

"Remember to take off the gloves when you're handling cash. Did I show you where the spares are in the back?"

Una nodded. "You did, yeah."

"Not that you'll need them, but just for future reference. Oh, and if anyone looks for the lemon and lime, make sure you mention that they're made with organic fruit."

"OK."

"And don't forget to mention the nuts if anyone goes for the chocolate peanut butter or the coffee pecan. I know it's on the sign, but I always say it, just to be on the safe side."

"Right."

"And will you make a note if anyone looks for a variety that's not here? Tell them we rotate the stock, but that you'll let the baker know what they were asking for."

"OK." Una smiled.

Hannah stopped. "Am I fussing too much?"

"Ah no, you're just making sure I get it right — but you've already used up ten minutes of your two hours."

"Right, I'm off." Hannah walked towards the door. "You have my mobile number."

"I have."

"Don't be afraid to use it for any reason — I won't be far."

"OK. See you later."

Ridiculous, how reluctant she was to leave Cupcakes on the Corner in anyone else's hands. Una was well able, and she had a lovely manner with the customers — after just a few days she was as confident as Hannah behind the counter. What was the worst that could happen?

And straight away her imagination supplied all the options. An armed robbery — someone who'd taken note of the cash drawer and come back to help himself. Someone might be watching the shop now, seeing a young girl left in charge. Or a fire in the laundrette next door — how ancient are those machines? Imagine the state of the wiring, a disaster waiting to happen. Or a burst pipe, water cascading down the walls, ceiling collapsing —

With a major effort of will, she kept walking in the direction of the coffee shop where she'd arranged to meet Adam. She pushed the door open and there he was.

"Welcome to the world." His cup was half empty.

Hannah perched on a chair opposite him. "I shouldn't be here."

He laughed. "You're feeling guilty for deserting your ship. For leaving your baby with a stranger."

"Don't make fun — what if something goes wrong? What if there's a — a burst pipe or something?"

132

"A burst pipe — Jesus wept."

"Well, a robbery then."

"A robbery." To the waitress who'd appeared, Adam said, "A pot of strong tea for my friend here please, and a couple of horse tranquillisers."

"Very funny. This is my livelihood I've just left a twenty-year-old in charge of." She looked at the waitress. "Don't mind him, just a tea please."

"You said Una was well able," Adam pointed out.

"She is — when I'm standing beside her."

"And how will she be less able when you're not there? She can still put cupcakes in a box and tot up the bill, can't she?"

"Yeah, I know . . ." Hannah unbuttoned her jacket slowly.

"She can still take money and make change."

"I know, I know. You're right."

"And I assume she has your number in case anything does come up."

"Yes, of course she has. Everything's under control." She took off the jacket and laid it on the chair beside her. "Any chance of a packet of salt and vinegar crisps with that tea?" Since she'd become the proprietor of a shop that sold nothing but confectionery, Hannah had developed a craving for all things savoury.

As Adam walked towards the counter she took her phone out of her bag, checked again that it was on and charged up, and set it beside her on the table.

Just in case.

★ ★ ★

133

"Now Geraldine," Maureen Hardiman said, lowering her voice and leaning in, "there's something I think you should know, and I'd rather you heard it from me."

Bridge was over for the night, and they'd been shepherded into Aoife's kitchen for tea and nibbles — Aoife didn't like getting crumbs on her Axminster. Geraldine's heart sank. She armed herself with a chocolate macaroon from a nearby plate, stifling the voice that reminded her of the snug-fitting navy dress. "What is it?" No point in saying she'd rather not know: with Maureen that wasn't an option. And anyway, she did want to know, whatever it was.

"Well, of course," Maureen went on, brushing cake crumbs from her green cardigan, "it shouldn't make much difference really. I mean, things have moved on, haven't they?"

Geraldine noted with satisfaction that Maureen's broken veins were especially vivid in the fluorescent light of Aoife's kitchen. "What is it?" she asked again, staring pointedly at Maureen's roots, which were overdue a touch-up by at least a fortnight.

"It's just," Maureen said, patting her hair and glancing around at the little knots of women, "I saw Leah Bradshaw this afternoon."

Geraldine bit into the macaroon and chewed. Fiona Bradshaw was safely across the room.

"And I'd *swear*," Maureen said, lowering her voice a notch further, almost mouthing silently now, "that that girl is expecting. She has all the signs of it, her face is swelled up, and she was wearing —"

134

"You don't say," said Geraldine briskly. "Isn't that lovely? Fiona must be thrilled." She put down the macaroon that had suddenly begun to taste of aeroboard.

Maureen's eager face fell slightly. "Yes, I'm sure she is," she said, "but poor Hannah will be very upset, I'd say."

"Oh no, not at all," Geraldine said. "Didn't I mention? She has a lovely new man, a master carpenter from Scotland. He's totally smitten — and he's loaded, from what Hannah tells me." She lowered her voice to match Maureen's. "Now don't tell anyone this, Hannah would kill me, but he owns an island. Quite a substantial one, apparently."

"Oh." Maureen took a second slice of Aoife's Victoria sponge from a nearby plate. "Oh, isn't that great. Oh, I'm delighted to hear that."

Maureen might easily be mistaken — what had she to go on but a puffy face and some baggy clothes? Didn't all the young ones wear baggy clothes these days? And, anyway, what difference could it make to Hannah now?

Geraldine would say nothing to her. There might not be a grain of truth in it.

"You have jam on your chin, dear," she told Maureen, a little too loudly.

She was in black again. The same long skirt, he thought, that she'd been wearing the first time he'd seen her. A long-sleeved black top that showed a couple of inches, no more, of her throat. Flat black shoes, black tights. Her pale hair gathered up and caught high on the back of her head.

She played with the same ferocious concentration, barely looking up from the music on the stand in front of her, not acknowledging in any way the scatter of applause between numbers. He wondered what her smile looked like, what it might do to her face.

Small Change they were called, according to the barman. *Know anything about them?* Adam had asked, but the barman didn't. And here came Nora, threading through the knots of drinkers towards him, wearing a tight-fitting neon green top he hadn't seen before and a pair of loose, faded jeans.

"Hi there," she said, kissing his cheek. "Oh, nice aftershave." She turned to the barman as he placed Adam's pint in front of him. "Martini, very dry." She perched on a stool beside Adam. "I have news," she said. "I got that job."

"You did?" Her eyes were dramatic, all dark and long-lashed. Her hair was loose and smelt of coconut. "The one with the paper?"

She grinned. "Yeah. The one with the paper."

He was better-looking than she'd been expecting. She'd assumed that any man who'd go for nice-but-boring Hannah Robinson couldn't be up to much, so Patrick Dunne had come as a pleasant surprise.

Lovely to meet you, she said, when they were introduced. Gripping his hand firmly, meeting the dark brown eyes. Reacting to a handsome man the way she always reacted, with undiluted charm. *So you're looking for a new PA.*

She'd blagged her way through the interview. She'd skirted round her lack of qualifications, she'd deflected questions with more questions, she'd made him laugh more than once. She'd pulled out all the stops to make him feel that she was the PA he wanted, that what she lacked in credentials would be more than made up for with enthusiasm and initiative, and it had worked.

But of course she'd known it would work. Nora O'Connor had always known what men wanted.

"Leah wasn't exactly over the moon when I told her — probably thinks I'll seduce Patrick." She laughed. "As if." The barman put her drink in front of her and she flashed him a smile before turning back to Adam. "She's pregnant, by the way."

Adam stared at her.

"Told me the other day, when she was giving me the massage. Don't know if you want to say anything to Hannah."

"She told you she's pregnant?"

"Yeah — she's due in June."

He shook his head slowly. "Unbelievable." He lifted his pint. "Say nothing to Hannah when you meet her."

"Wouldn't dream of it."

"Hang on a minute," he said then, slipping abruptly off his stool and making his way across the room. The music had finished, the musicians packing up. The woman was turning away as Adam approached.

"Excuse me," he said, and the man pressing switches on the keyboard lifted his head.

"I just wanted a quick word with —"

He indicated the woman who was threading her way rapidly around the low tables, moving towards the back of the pub. Without giving the man a chance to respond, Adam hurried after her.

"Excuse me," he said again, more loudly, but the chatter must have kept his voice from reaching her because she kept moving, seemingly unaware that she was being followed. Just before she got to a blue door which led, he presumed, to some kind of rear exit, he caught up with her.

"Excuse me —"

She stopped then and turned, a quick swing of her head, and even in the dim lighting, Adam could see the dark flush that spread rapidly upwards and covered the pointed, elfin face. She was almost exactly his height. She clutched her clarinet to her chest. "Yes?" Her voice was wary. She regarded him as if he was about to attack her.

He had absolutely no idea what to say. The impulse that had pulled him towards her hadn't supplied him with words. He hunted for something, anything, to break the silence between them. "Sorry to bother you," he began, and stopped, completely out of inspiration.

The flush deepened on her cheeks. Tiny dark freckles were scattered across her nose. Her free hand felt for the door handle behind her. She blinked rapidly behind her little round glasses as she waited for him to continue.

And finally, when she must surely have been on the point of turning away, Adam thought of something. "Er . . . I just wondered — er — what the title of that last piece was."

" 'I've Got A Crush On You'," she said all in a rush, in a breathy, whispery voice that he almost didn't hear.

"I really like your music," Adam said, but she was gone, vanished abruptly through the blue door, leaving behind a faint powdery, flowery scent. Adam stood there for a second or two, and then he walked back slowly to where Nora sat.

She eyed him curiously. "What was that all about? What did you want with the sinister woman?"

Adam leant against the counter and picked up his drink. "I thought I knew her," he said. "I thought she was somebody's sister, but I was wrong."

I've Got A Crush On You. He wasn't superstitious, he didn't believe in signs. There was no significance to be attached to the title of a song — it had no bearing on anything.

The way she'd blushed when he'd spoken to her. The frightened look she'd given him, the tense set of her body, as if she expected him to pounce at any minute.

Her hair was paler in colour than straw. Her lips were too thin and her nose was too pointed, and she never smiled and the glasses hid what might be her best feature. She had large hands and feet.

But she lost herself in the music when she played. And the thought of unpinning her hair, of taking off her glasses and looking into her eyes, of putting his palm against her pale face — the thought of all that was inexplicably tempting.

I've got a crush on you, sweetie-pie.

"I have a new PA," Patrick announced, undoing his tie.

"I heard," Leah answered. "I know her. We were at school together."

"You were?" He looked at her, surprised. "She never mentioned that."

Sorry to drop by unannounced, but I had to tell you, Nora had said, in her yellow wrap top that was probably cashmere, her black skirt and oh-so-soft black boots. *You'll never guess,* she'd said, standing in the doorway of Indulgence, and straightaway Leah had guessed.

Haven't a clue, she'd said, heart sinking.

"Hello again," John Wyatt said.

Hannah turned. "Oh," she said quickly, "hi there, I was just —"

"You're cleaning up?" He glanced at the clock on the wall. "You finish at five?"

"No, no — I mean yes, I do finish at five, but it's not quite that yet." She propped the mop against the back wall and began to peel off her rubber gloves. "Actually, it's part of my cunning plan — start to wash the floor and customers come in. Works every time."

The dimple appeared in his cheek. "In that case I'd hate to disappoint you. I'll take a couple of whatever's good. You choose."

140

"No preferences?" Sliding a tray towards her, reaching for a chocolate lime.

"Not really." It wasn't a lie: he was immune to them all. "How do you resist them, surrounded all day?"

She laughed. "Believe me, if you spent as long as I do baking them, you'd soon lose the taste." She closed the lid of the little yellow box. "Sometimes I think if I never see another cupcake it'll be fine."

"Do you never get a break?"

She passed the box across the counter to him. "Funny you should ask. I've just taken someone on who does a couple of hours three mornings a week. It's heaven."

He passed her a five-euro note. "And what about evenings?" he asked. "Do you ever get a free one of those?"

Hannah looked at him.

"I thought," he went on — he had to go on, because she had made no response — "you might like to meet up for a drink, or . . . whatever, really."

He knew instinctively that she was going to turn him down. Was sure, all at once, that she wasn't interested — or that she was with someone who hadn't given her a ring.

She held his money, decidedly uncomfortable. "Actually —"

Yes, she was turning him down. He wished himself anywhere but where he was.

"I'm really sorry," she said slowly, "but I've . . . recently broken up with someone, and I don't think —"

"That's fine," he said, smiling to show he didn't mind in the least. "Just a thought, no harm done."

"Sorry," she said again, pulling out the drawer and rummaging to get his change. "If the timing was different, or —"

"Really, it's fine." He took the money and pocketed it. "You need time to recover. I understand perfectly."

"Thank you," she said, "for . . . being so nice about it." She gave a tiny smile. "If it wasn't such a cliché, I'd say it's not you, it's me."

He lifted a hand. "No problem. Be seeing you."

That was that. He wouldn't be seeing her again. The four steps to the door seemed to take forever.

When she got the answering machine for the third time, Fiona knew her daughter was avoiding her.

You've reached Indulgence, Leah said in her salon voice. *Sorry we can't come to the phone at this time, but if you leave your name and number we'll return your call at our earliest convenience.*

Fiona waited for the beep, and then said, "Leah, it's me. Please get in touch." She paused. "There's no need for us to fall out. Give me a ring when you get this message."

She hung up and walked to the window and looked out at the long, narrow back lawn that her neighbour's fourteen-year-old son mowed every fortnight in return for twenty euro. Fiona remembered when a youngster would have cut a neighbour's grass for nothing, but that time was long gone.

She leant against the window-sill and thought of how her plans for Leah were all going terribly wrong, and she wondered bitterly about the unfairness of it.

Look at the salon she'd financed when Leah hadn't two cents to rub together, fresh out of beauty school and no notion what to do next. Hadn't Fiona sorted her out? Hadn't Leah been happy to take her mother's money? How many mothers would have done as much and asked nothing in return?

Look at the men she'd had in mind for Leah — sons of friends, with qualifications and good jobs and excellent prospects. The efforts she'd made to introduce Leah to them. The few dates that had come out of such meetings, the hopes Fiona always had, and then, a week or a month later, Leah saying it hadn't worked out. But someone would have turned up eventually, Fiona was certain.

And now look at her daughter. Pregnant and unmarried, living with a man who'd been happy to string her along for months, who might never have left his other woman if Leah hadn't been careless enough to get caught.

A man who'd made small-talk with Fiona whenever they'd met socially, all the time running around with her daughter on the quiet. Who looked at Fiona defiantly now, not a scrap of shame for having behaved despicably. Proud, probably, of his bastard on the way.

And Leah, looking at her mother as if she hated her, after all Fiona's efforts. Screening her phone calls because Fiona showed concern, because she said what she was thinking, instead of smiling and pretending she was pleased with how things had worked out.

The salon would inevitably suffer with the disruption, Leah's whole future uncertain now, because who knew how long this man would stay with her, how long before his attention was caught by another pretty blonde? How was Fiona to remain silent? What mother could?

History was repeating itself in a horribly ironic way, with her own daughter playing the part of the other woman. Leah was inflicting the hurt now that had been visited on Fiona thirty years ago, the bitterness and shock of it every bit as vivid today as they had been then.

I'm sorry, he'd said, as Fiona had stood dumbfounded, the tea-towel still in her hand. *I didn't mean it to happen, it just did.* Leah sitting on the kitchen floor, banging a wooden spoon on the tiles. *I'm so sorry.*

Fiona's heart thudding in her chest, a prickle of cold sweat on her forehead. Bending to pick up her daughter, needing something to hold on to. *How long?* All she could manage to say, with her throat closing up and her abdomen clenched so tightly she could hardly breathe. *How long?* Her legs beginning suddenly to tremble, forcing her to put Leah down again in case they both crashed to the floor.

The desolation after he'd gone, the chasm he'd left behind. The torture of having to face him when he called to see Leah. The shell forming around her so that after a while it became — not easy, never easy, but not quite so impossible to smile and pretend that he hadn't destroyed her heart.

And worst of all, on hearing of his aneurysm less than a year later, the fresh grief, the hurt on hurt that had almost caused a complete breakdown. No satisfaction, no sense of justice being done, none of that.

She'd stayed away from his funeral, not trusting herself to come face to face with the woman who'd caused it all. It had taken her five years to visit his grave, to stand in front of his headstone and read his name in the granite, and realise that she felt nothing any more, nothing at all.

She sighed impatiently, not seeing the long strip of lawn beyond the window, the neat shrubs running along either side. Wasn't she entitled to be angry now? Wouldn't any woman in her position, with her history?

She turned from the window and went to run a bath, and to pour a large gin and bitter lemon to accompany it.

"Something happened today," Hannah said.

"What?"

Adam was poaching eggs to sit on top of their smoked haddock. Smoked fish had never done much for Hannah — and she certainly wouldn't have chosen eggs as an accompaniment — but she was starving, and not about to quibble when it was being served up to her.

"Someone asked me out," she said.

"Who?"

"A man — he's been into the shop a few times. You don't know him. A carpenter."

"I see." Adam cracked the second egg and dropped it carefully into the swirling water. "And he's asked you out."

"Yes."

"And you said?"

"No."

Adam lowered the heat under the saucepan. "You turned him down?"

"I did." Hannah set the table with cutlery and glasses. "The problem is . . . I'm wondering now if I did the right thing."

Adam lifted out the eggs and laid them on the fish. He brought the plates to the table. "You are? What's he like?"

"Nice." She poured water into their glasses. "He seems nice," she said, "what little I know of him." She picked up her fork. "Thanks — this looks interesting."

Adam poked his egg with a fork and dipped bread into the pool of yolk. "But you're not sure that you're ready."

"Yes. I mean no, I'm not sure."

"I wouldn't worry. If he's keen he'll be in again."

"Maybe . . . if I haven't scared him off."

Adam grinned. "Ah, men aren't that easily scared. Nobody would ever get together if they were."

Hannah cut a corner off her fish. "When he asked me out I sort of . . . froze. I wasn't expecting it, and my instinct was to say no without really thinking about it."

"Right."

"I know I have to move on, I do realise I can't lock myself away . . ." She sighed. "Oh, enough about me. What about you? You haven't been on a date in ages."

Adam shrugged. "What can I say? It just hasn't happened."

"And what about Nora? Has she put her eye on anyone?" From what Hannah remembered, Nora wasn't one to stay on her own for long.

"Not that she's told me." Adam paused. "Actually, Han, speaking of Nora, there's something I'd better tell you, before you hear it from someone else."

Hannah's fork stilled. "What?"

"Ah, it's nothing really." Drawing more bread through his egg yolk, mopping up the yellow gloop. "It's just that she's got a job — with the newspaper."

Hannah stared. "Nora's got a job with the paper? Doing what?"

He chewed his eggy bread. "She's going to be Patrick's PA, if you can believe it. She starts on Monday."

"Oh." Hannah sipped water. "That's weird." She cut a piece of egg white. "Not that it makes any . . ." She poked at the yolk. "But it is a bit weird though, isn't it?"

"It's nothing," Adam said. "She probably won't last longer than a week. Anyway, what do you care? I just didn't want you hearing it by chance, that's all."

"Thanks."

Hannah wondered what had happened Patrick's last PA, super-efficient Andrea with her peanut allergy and her English husband and her son in the army. Andrea who never forgot a meeting or missed an appointment, Andrea who set up golf tournaments and organised business lunches — and had reminded Patrick, probably, when Hannah's birthday was approaching.

And now Andrea was gone, for whatever reason, and Patrick had taken on Nora O'Connor, who'd presumably remind him when Leah Bradshaw's birthday was drawing near. Nora would organise his schedule and arrange his day and book his flights when he travelled. Nora would spend a lot of every day in his company.

"She knows who he is, right?" she asked Adam.

"Yeah. She's friendly with Leah — they used to hang around together at school."

"I remember. So Leah got her the job."

"Yeah, maybe . . . I'm not sure." Adam looked uncomfortable. "Han, you know what Nora's like. It probably never crossed her mind that it might be a bit . . . awkward."

Like hell it didn't. Hannah smiled across the table at him. "She's right, why should it be awkward? It's all in the past now. It really doesn't bother me."

She looked down at the remains of her dinner. Smoked fish definitely did nothing for her.

Maybe Alice was the only one who noticed. It wasn't as if he was falling around the place, and he hadn't thrown up or disgraced himself in any way. He was slurring his words a bit, certainly, and his eyes were bloodshot. He looked like someone who'd had a few too many, and he

148

was louder than usual, monopolising the conversation, like he always did after too much alcohol.

But maybe it was more obvious to her; maybe it didn't really bother anyone else. And so what, anyway, if he'd overdone it a bit? They were out for the night, weren't they? They were helping a good cause, and it wasn't doing anyone any harm. And there were plenty of others who'd had more than a few — you only had to look around to see that.

It was useless. The knot in her stomach wouldn't budge. Her armpits felt horribly damp, her hands kept making fists. She wanted to go home — she wanted them both home and out of sight — before everyone started talking about Tom Joyce, who was making a bit of a fool of himself at the charity dinner-dance.

The band switched to a slow waltz and Stephen extended a hand to her. "Come on," he said, pulling her up. He wasn't a hundred per cent sober either, she told herself — he didn't volunteer to dance when he was — but he was still well able to hold his own, and Geraldine didn't seem in the least concerned about him.

Alice tried to will her tension away as she let Stephen lead her around the stifling, perfumed room. "Isn't it hot?" she said, but he wasn't listening, his head tilted towards a neighbouring couple, the man saying something that made him smile.

I'm worried about Tom's drinking, she wanted to say to him. *Maybe you could have a word*. But of course she kept quiet. Tom would hit the roof — and it wouldn't be fair to Stephen, who was more a work colleague and a casual friend than someone you could expect to get involved in something like that.

There was nobody she could talk to. Not Tom's family, such as they were — a priest brother in Colombia, a pair of sisters, one married, one separated, both living in England, a ninety-two-year-old uncle in a nursing home at the other side of the country whom they visited a handful of times a year.

Alice wasn't close to either of her own siblings, not in that way. And of course she wouldn't dream of mentioning anything to Ellen — what could their daughter do, so far away, except worry about her father?

At half past twelve Alice told Geraldine she had a headache, and Geraldine immediately said, "I'll get Reception to call us a taxi," so Alice suspected that she'd been wanting to go home too. The taxi arrived remarkably quickly — they were still gathering coats and bags when the porter came and found them.

Tom stumbled, getting into the back, and Stephen put a hand on his arm and said, "Easy there, fellow," and Alice's face burnt in the darkness. She sat between Tom and Stephen, and before they were through the gates of the hotel Tom's head had drooped towards her shoulder. She prayed he wouldn't snore.

Geraldine turned in her seat. "The dinner was nice, I must say."

"My beef was tough," Stephen said.

"How long till we have to get up for work?" Alice asked, so neither of them would look for Tom's opinion of the beef.

They both groaned, and Geraldine said, "Oh, don't think about that."

Tom's mood would be black in the morning. Alice dreaded the drive into work. He usually dropped her, since the shoe shop was on the way to the dental clinic, and it made more sense than to take the two cars. She made her own way home, relishing the half-hour walk after her day in the shop; unless the weather was very bad, in which case she took a lift from Geraldine.

"That's nice music," Geraldine was saying to the driver.

"It's Herbie Hancock," he told her. "One of my favourites."

"Do you play yourself?"

"I do, a bit."

Tom's head was heavy on Alice's shoulder. She shifted slightly, and Stephen immediately moved to allow her more room. "I'm fine," she said quickly. Here was the roundabout. Up the hill and two more left turns and they were home.

She dug her elbow into Tom's side when the car stopped, and he snuffled awake. "Money for the taxi," she hissed — she had only a fifty-euro note in her wallet — but Geraldine said, "Alice, forget it — we'll sort it out tomorrow." Stephen walked around the car and opened the back door and shepherded Tom out onto the path.

"Maybe he needn't bother coming in tomorrow," he said to Alice in a low voice, as she climbed out after Tom. "Let him sleep on. We can manage."

Alice dug into her bag and fished out the door key, and grabbed Tom's arm as he lurched towards her. "We'll see — thanks very much," she said to Stephen, as she steered Tom towards the house.

"Will I go to the door with you?"

"No, we're fine. You head off."

Tom leant heavily against her as she walked as quickly as she could up the driveway, which had never seemed so long. The taxi sat there idling, long after Stephen had got back inside. She willed them to go, to stop watching Alice Joyce supporting her drunk husband.

Lying alone in bed later — she hadn't been able to get Tom past the living-room couch, so she'd pulled off his shoes and lifted up his legs and left him there — she imagined the conversation in the taxi after they'd been dropped. About how Tom had been lashing it back, about poor Alice having to put up with that. Maybe a remark about a dentist needing a clear head and a steady hand.

Or certainly they'd be thinking it, even if it was left unsaid.

She'd leave him there in the morning: she wouldn't even try to wake him. She'd phone Stephen and ask him to say Tom wasn't well. She turned onto her side and read 1:14 on the clock. She closed her eyes and tried to sleep.

Leah couldn't sleep. If it wasn't the constant urge to pee, it was the horrible acidic lurch of heartburn that had her lying awake next to Patrick at almost three in the morning.

And if it was neither of those, it was Nora O'Connor. Oh, it was stupid to think Patrick was going to be seduced by the first attractive woman who looked at him, or flirted with him. It was stupid and insecure, and she despised herself for thinking it.

She was pregnant with his child; he'd left his long-term partner to be with her. She was pretty and confident and independent. He loved her, and she satisfied him in bed, she was sure of it. What possible reason would he have for straying?

Except that he'd done it to Hannah. He'd been with her for more than a year, he'd been living in her house, and then he'd met Leah and that had been that. And Nora was very, very good at attracting a man. And she'd be working closely with Patrick, every day probably. She thought about Nora's lean, well-kept body, her sexy lingerie.

So you were at school together, Patrick had said. *In the same class?*

Yes, but I hadn't seen her in years until the other day, Leah had told him. *We were never that close really. And she went straight to the States after school and lost touch with everyone. She was married twice; neither of them lasted.*

She should have said something to him when Nora had told her she was job-hunting. She should have realised that there was a possibility Nora would apply when she saw the ad for the PA. She should have said, *If you see an application from Nora Paluzzi or Nora*

O'Connor, dump it. I know her, I was at school with her, and she's hopeless. She's been sacked from every job she ever got, and now she's back here looking for work. Don't touch her with a barge pole.

And Patrick would have believed her, and thrown Nora's application into the bin. She should have said something, but she hadn't.

She turned towards Patrick. Maybe sex would put her to sleep. She reached across and put her lips to the side of his neck, to the spot he liked. She opened her mouth and pressed her tongue to his skin. She bit the flesh gently, her hand moving slowly down his chest, past his stomach, her fingers burrowing into the coarse hair below.

He stirred. "Hey," he whispered thickly, "can't sleep?"

She moved closer and took his nipple into her mouth and sucked. He groaned sleepily and reached for her hips, and pulled her against him.

He loved her. There was nothing to worry about.

Adam slept on his stomach, as he always did, legs splayed, arms flung out, duvet falling sideways off the bed.

He dreamt about her. He dreamt about her pale hair flying around her head as she played her clarinet on a much bigger stage, all by herself. He sat in the empty auditorium and listened to her. She wore red, a long dress that flowed around her and pooled at her feet. And when she finished he stood and walked towards her, and she put down her clarinet and smiled and opened her arms to him, hair streaming around her pale, pale face.

"Thank you," he said, climbing the steps and pulling her towards him, hands sinking into her hair as his mouth found hers, as his tongue eased her thin lips apart.

John Wyatt sprinkled brown sugar and splashed milk onto his porridge, and ate it standing by the window as he always did in the morning. He liked that his third-floor flat had a view of Clongarvin's main street, even if the traffic at night had taken some getting used to after the peace of Kerrycroy, the tiny coastal village where he'd spent most of his life. Now that he was sleeping through the night again, he was able to appreciate his central location, his bird's-eye view of the comings and goings of Clongarvin's residents, especially first thing in the morning.

Today was Friday: he should finish the kitchen cabinets for Carlton Road by lunchtime, if he put his mind to it, and then he'd head across town to check out a new enquiry. He was lucky to have anyone showing any interest, with the recession as bad as it was. Hopefully he'd manage to keep body and soul together until he'd built up enough of a business to relax a bit.

The gigs helped, of course — and that was thanks to Wally, whose cousin Patsy worked in the woodwork store where John bought most of his supplies. Funny how things worked out: a chance remark one day about the fact that he played the sax, and Patsy was saying, *Oh you should meet my cousins, they're in a band*; and before you knew it John was practising with Small Change, and then they were playing in the newly opened Vintage every Saturday night, which helped with the rent on this place and on the tiny workshop he'd found by the river.

He took another spoonful of porridge and watched the early-morning bustle in the street below. A man sprinted towards a red van that was causing an obstruction, waving apologetically at the driver in the car behind it before climbing in and moving off. A woman in a green jacket walked slowly past a shoe-shop window, contrasting with the hurried pace of most of the other pedestrians. A bus pulled into a stop, engine chugging as the straggle of waiting passengers disappeared inside.

I'm leaving, he'd told Lara, and she'd shown no surprise. The only surprise, maybe, that he'd waited so long. Nineteen years in a marriage that should never have taken place, that had been entered into when they were both too young to listen to anyone's advice.

And eight months after the wedding, when both of them had already realised their mistake, Danielle had turned them into a family — Lara unknowingly pregnant as they'd walked down the aisle — and there was no leaving then, no grounds for walking out, because lack of love wasn't enough, was it, when a child was part of the picture?

No animosity on either part, no harsh words, no bitter quarrelling between them. But no romantic love either, the initial fierce blaze extinguishing itself almost as quickly as it had ignited, leaving behind a friendship, you could call it, but without any deep warmth or feeling. Nothing to have you rushing home in the evenings, nothing to have you aching for the other's touch. They tolerated each other amicably, was the best you could say.

And occasionally, when loneliness caused him to reach out to her in the night, she responded, but it was an empty, mechanical coupling that left him more bereft, if anything.

Danielle helped. The poor girl had held them together for years. It had been harder, much harder, to tell her. *Your mother and I are separating*, John had said. *Nothing has happened, we haven't fallen out, there's nobody else involved. We just feel there's no point in staying together any more.*

Now that I'm moving out, you mean, Danielle had replied. Her expression had been difficult to read, her feelings kept to herself, as they always had been, even when she was a young child.

We've decided it's best, John had told her. *I'm going to Ireland for a while — I think a change of scene might be good. I'll be back as often as I can to see you.*

It was OK, he told himself. With Danielle starting college in Edinburgh there would have been a parting anyway; they'd have been separated for weeks at a time.

It's a change, he'd said, *that's all. You're still as important to both of us as you always were.*

They'd still meet, either in Edinburgh or at his parents' house on Bute whenever both of them could make it back there. They'd be like so many other separated families across the world, living under different roofs most of the time, seeing each other when they could.

But of course something had been lost between father and daughter, something John had sacrificed by choosing to leave the family home, and he mourned it bitterly. Danielle had always been closer to Lara — he supposed it was inevitable with mothers and daughters.

He'd gone back twice. He'd met Danielle as planned and they'd spent Boxing Day together at his parents' house. Danielle had talked quite cheerfully about college; she seemed to be enjoying it. She'd cut her hair, which John had privately regretted, and she'd grown thinner, which he didn't approve of either. He'd teased her about boyfriends, and she'd laughed and given nothing away, as ever. They'd had a good day.

But all the same something was lost, and they both knew it. *You might come to Ireland in the spring*, he'd said to her. *I'm in a nice little town — you could stay a week in the holidays*. And Danielle had said maybe, but nothing had been fixed, and no more had been said.

A couple walked hand in hand down the street, a rolled-up newspaper tucked under the strap of the man's briefcase, an umbrella swinging from the woman's free hand. It was hard to be sure from this distance, but John put them in their twenties.

Hannah Robinson was in her late twenties, or maybe her early thirties. Her skin was beautifully fresh, like a young girl's, but her body was all womanly curves, the same solid build as her mother. Her breath smelt of mints, and her hair was dark and wavy.

158

He'd asked her out too soon. He should have dropped into the shop a few more times, maybe worked the music into a conversation. He could have mentioned the gig in Vintage and suggested casually that she drop in some Saturday night. He'd been too impatient, and she'd turned him down.

But at least he knew she was unattached, even if she wasn't over her ex. Unless, of course, the ex was someone she'd made up to let him down gently. All the games . . . he'd forgotten the games. He had no time for games.

He finished his porridge and left his bowl in the sink, on top of last night's dinner dishes. He brushed his teeth and grabbed his keys. He left the small flat and took the stairs two at a time, as he always did.

Busy. Keep busy.

Alice stood at the sink and waited for her toast to pop up. She didn't feel a bit like eating — she'd got three hours' sleep at the very most; breakfast wasn't high on her list of priorities — but she'd need something inside her if she was to put down a morning's work.

She'd been surprised to hear Tom going upstairs a while earlier — if he was only using the loo he could have stayed downstairs. But then she realised he was probably making straight for their bedroom, to climb between the sheets that would still be warm after her. He couldn't have slept well on the couch, no matter how much alcohol he'd put away.

But then she heard his step on the stairs again — and a minute later the kitchen door opened and he walked in, fully dressed. His face was deathly pale and he looked exhausted, but he'd shaved and put on a tie.

"You're not going to work, are you?" she said, before she could stop herself.

He pulled out a chair and sat heavily. "Of course I am," he said. "Is there tea in the pot?"

She put out a cup and poured for him. "Will I boil an egg?"

He shook his head.

"Toast? Cereal?"

"No, I won't have anything."

Underneath his eyes there were heavy pouches. She supposed they must have been there for a while, but this was the first time she'd taken notice of them. He'd cut himself shaving, just once, to the left of his Adam's apple. A scrap of toilet paper was red in the centre.

"I can drive, if you like," Alice said. "I could leave the car at the clinic and walk back to the shop." She'd be late, but she could phone Geraldine on the way to let her know. Geraldine had often opened up — she had her own set of keys.

"I'm fine," he said. "I've slept it off." He poured milk into his cup and drank thirstily. "I overdid it a bit last night," he said.

Alice made no response. She couldn't contradict him, but this wasn't the time to talk about it. "I was thinking we might go out for dinner this evening," she said. "I could meet you in town. We could go to Giovanni's, save the cooking."

He probably wouldn't feel like drinking this evening. They could have a quiet chat maybe, in neutral surroundings. She topped up his cup.

"I don't think I'd be up to going out," he said, watching the tea flow into his cup. "I'll get a takeaway if you don't feel like cooking."

"It doesn't matter," she said. "Just a thought."

The early-morning air was sliced with frost. The car was cold. Tom turned the heating on full and the fan whirred loudly, drowning the radio. Alice pulled her coat tightly around her and clicked her seatbelt into place, and rubbed her hands together. She kept forgetting her gloves, in the drawer of the hallstand. She should leave them out where she'd see them.

Tom reversed out of the driveway, too fast it seemed to Alice, but again she held her tongue. The road glittered, and the paths on either side were full of children and mothers on their way to school. They turned onto Carbert Road, and Alice made a list in her head for a lunchtime shop: milk, toothpaste, washing-up liquid, eggs, nail-varnish remover. Something else she couldn't think of.

"Do you need anything?" she asked Tom. "I have to go to Dunnes at lunchtime."

"No," he said, and just then she remembered: batteries for the remote control.

The air in the car got marginally warmer, and Alice turned the heater down a couple of notches. On the radio, which was now audible, someone was saying, ". . . causing a tailback from the Red Cow roundabout."

161

She was glad they didn't have a long commute every morning. On a quiet day the drive to the shop took ten minutes, and even in the heaviest traffic it was still well under half an hour.

Afterwards, trying to remember the sequence of events — because she kept trying to remember, she couldn't stop trying to remember — all she could see was the colour of his jacket. All that was there, when she sent her mind back to the minutes leading up to the accident, was the small bright blue patch of his jacket, the flash of bright blue that was suddenly there — suddenly, sickeningly, *there* in front of the car, and she shouted something — Tom's name? Something else? — and she was thrust against her seatbelt, she felt the tug of the strap across her body, the nylon taut against the side of her neck, her hands flying out to smack against the dashboard, the blue gone, no more blue now, and the thump as she was flung back against her seat, as the car skidded to a stop, swerving in an arc across the road, *no, no, no, no, no, no, no, no, no, no, no,* her voice unable to stop repeating it, *no, no, no,* her fists beating against her thighs, *no,* her head shaking from side to side, *no, no,* pulling at her seatbelt, struggling to get it off, *no,* and someone screaming and screaming, and people running and shouting and crying, and still repeating *no, no, no,* the blue hidden now behind all the other colours, the reds and the purples and the browns, *no, no,* and at some stage the new, shrill scream of a siren, and doors opening and closing, and her door opening, and someone unbuckling her seatbelt

162

and someone slapping her face, slapping it hard, the new shock jolting her into silence, her screaming stopped, her mouth gaping dumbly, her whole body shaking violently as she was helped from the car, guided towards the open doors of an ambulance, clutching at the hands that supported her, a blanket wrapped around her, the smell of wool and antiseptic as she was hoisted up into the ambulance, and all the time the screaming, someone screaming, voices shouting —

— and stretching her arms towards Tom, the blanket dropping off her shoulders as he put something, the end of a stick, a pipe, into his mouth, Tom's face so white, the man beside him laying a dark blue arm on Tom's shoulders as Tom's cheeks puffed out and turned pink, as he took the stick from his mouth and the man took the stick from Tom and looked at it, his arm still on Tom's shoulders, his fingers curved around them, and everything was sharp and hard, and a man was talking to her, she could see his mouth moving but the words made no sound, as the blanket was wrapped around her again, as she was eased down onto the trolley in the ambulance, as her handbag appeared on the floor beside her, and when she looked towards Tom again he was gone, and she wanted to ask for him, she wanted to call out for him but the words made no sound —

— and afterwards, she had no idea how long afterwards, the curly-headed guard at the station put a blue and white mug of too hot, too sweet tea on the table in front of her — her lashes stiff with salt, her eyes hot and stinging, the ball of her sodden tissues lying

163

next to the mug, her skirt creased — and then he sat on the wooden bench beside her and said quietly, "Now Alice, there's something I have to tell you."

And as he spoke, as he told her, her face crumpled and the screams and the tears began all over again.

Geraldine unlocked the grille and slid it upwards into its casing. She opened the shop door and stepped in, inhaling the robust, leathery scent. She locked the door again and walked through to the rear of the shop, where she hung her coat on the back of the door and stowed her handbag in the small green press that held the accounts ledgers and the petty-cash box.

She filled the kettle and plugged it in, and lifted the two red mugs from their hooks. The mugs said Oxo in fat white letters. She took the milk carton from the tiny fridge and sniffed it. She dropped teabags into the mugs and added half a spoonful of sugar to hers before she remembered she'd given it up for Lent. She took out the teabag and poured the sugar into the sink.

She switched on Alice's transistor and let the ads wash over her as the kettle began to sing. She didn't care for the local radio station, but Alice liked it. At a minute to nine, she went out to the shop and unlocked the front door, and wheeled out the display of boots on sale. She went back and poured boiling water into her mug, adding milk as the newscaster reported on the latest political scandal, and the shelving of plans for a new motorway in the west,

164

and the protests over the cancellation of another flight out of Shannon airport, and Carbert Road in Clongarvin being closed following a traffic accident. That would be what was delaying Alice.

At ten past nine she called Alice's mobile and got her voicemail. "I presume you're stuck in traffic," she said. "No rush — it's quiet here. See you in a while."

At twenty past nine, when there was still no reply from Alice's phone, she called the house. Maybe they'd both slept it out after last night, or maybe Alice's mobile was stuck in her handbag, out of hearing.

But the phone rang and rang, and she finally hung up.

At half past nine she phoned the dental clinic. "Is Tom there?" she asked Suzie, the receptionist.

"No — Stephen says he's not coming in," Suzie told her.

"Has he phoned? Or Alice?"

"No, I've heard nothing."

"Will you put me through to Stephen?"

Stephen had heard nothing either. "He's sleeping it off, I'd say. I've asked Suzie to cancel his appointments for the day."

"There's no sign of Alice either though — and she'd definitely let me know if she wasn't coming."

"Right . . . I suppose you'll just have to wait. She'll be in touch eventually."

At a quarter to ten Geraldine phoned Hannah, who told her that Una Connolly's four-year-old nephew had been knocked down on his way to school. "I'm waiting to hear how he is," Hannah said. "Una just rang me on her way to the hospital."

"Oh Lord, the poor little thing."

"Why were you ringing me?"

"Alice never showed up for work," Geraldine said, "and Tom isn't at the clinic. I can't contact her on her mobile or at home."

"They could be stuck in traffic. Maybe the accident caused a hold-up."

"But Alice would let me know. It's not like her at all."

"Her battery could be gone."

"Mmm." But Geraldine was anxious.

The main item on the ten o'clock news was an accident on Carbert Road in Clongarvin, in which a young boy had been knocked down and fatally injured.

Alice couldn't stop crying. She leant her elbows on the table and buried her face in her hands and sobbed loudly, the tea forgotten. "Oh God," she wept, thinking of the small blue boy flying upwards. "Oh Jesus, God, oh God almighty."

And some time after that, with the tears finally over and her throat aching and her eyes burning and her head throbbing, Tom walked into the room, chalk-faced, and said quietly, not meeting her eye, "We can go home now."

And all Alice could think was how desperately she wanted to hit him.

★ ★ ★

Nora strolled along the rails of clothes, running a hand over the different fabrics, occasionally pulling something out to have a closer look.

"Can I help you at all?"

She smiled at the assistant, who could lose half a stone, easily. "Not really, thanks — just looking."

She wasn't just looking: she knew exactly what she wanted. In the dressing room she removed her top and jeans and tried her selection on, turning to see as much as possible in the floor-length mirror. She got dressed again and walked to the checkout desk with a purple high-waisted skirt, a fitted cream top, a black wool wraparound dress and a deep crimson jacket.

"Hang on to these," she told the assistant. "I need to pick up some lingerie."

A basque maybe, she hadn't bought a new one in ages. Stockings, of course, and suspenders. A cream bra for under the top, one that gave serious cleavage. French knickers. A couple of lace thongs.

And it was so satisfying, as the assistant folded her purchases and wrapped them in tissue, as Nora slid her credit card across the counter, to remind herself that Jackson Paluzzi was paying for lingerie that some other man, with any luck, would get a lot of pleasure from.

Not that she had any specific man in mind, of course. But with her new job, and meeting all those newspaper employees, somebody was bound to come along.

And if he happened to be out of bounds, well, so much the better. The last thing she needed was another husband.

"What d'you fancy?"

Leah, full of heartburn, didn't fancy anything. She looked for the least offensive dish on the menu. "The poached salmon."

"Me too."

Patrick closed his menu as Leah stifled a yawn and eased her swollen feet one by one from her stilettos. She'd barely made it from the car to the table in them. "No sauce on mine," she told the waiter as he took their order.

What she wouldn't give to be stretched on the couch in front of the telly, a cushion under her back. What she wouldn't give for a foot massage — except that Patrick wasn't talented in that department. His attempts at massage left her more frustrated than relieved.

He reached across the table and covered her hand. "Good day?"

She pushed her hair out of her eyes with the other hand. It needed a cut, but she hadn't the energy. "Fine. You?"

"The usual." He filled their water glasses. "Did you hear about the accident on Carbert Road?"

"I did. Horrible."

His wine arrived, and her apple juice. She was sick to death of apple juice. She hoped to God he wouldn't say cheers.

He lifted his glass towards her. "Cheers."

Irritation flooded through her. She knew it was her hormones gone haywire, but the knowledge didn't stop her wanting to wipe the smug look off his face, whatever it took.

She looked for a way to rattle him, and found it. "By the way," she said, "did I mention that your new PA is Adam O'Connor's sister?"

Patrick lowered his glass. "You don't say."

"Twin sister, actually." She watched him assimilate the knowledge that he'd just employed the sister of his ex's best friend. "Not that it matters," she added, daring him to contradict her. "I mean, now that you and Hannah are history."

He shrugged. "Of course not. Why would it? I'm just surprised, that's all." He lifted his glass again. "Mind you, she did say she came from around here, so I suppose it shouldn't surprise me if I know someone belonging to her, in a place this size."

"I'd be a bit careful all the same, if I were you," Leah said. "She probably tells Adam everything — you know how twins are."

Patrick smiled, his equilibrium restored. "I hardly think Adam would be interested in the comings and goings of a newspaper office."

"Probably not." Leah sipped apple juice. "They've moved in together — did you know that?"

"Who?"

"Adam and Hannah — he's moved into her house." She laughed lightly. "I assume it's just to help her out financially."

He studied her. "I would imagine so."

"On the other hand," Leah said, "I wonder if he was just waiting for you and her to break up."

Patrick sipped his wine. "And I wonder," he said mildly, "why you're being such a bitch."

Leah looked innocently at him. "I have no idea what you mean," she said. "I'm just making small-talk."

And for the next forty minutes, while they played with their food and made more small-talk, he didn't take her hand again or touch her foot with his under the table.

"He was only four," Hannah said. "He was in Junior Infants. His mother was taking him to school."

"The driver was breathalysed?"

"Tom . . . yes, he failed. They'd been out the night before, with Mam and Dad, and apparently he was quite drunk going home." She sighed. "He works with Dad. You would have met them, him and Alice. They would have been at Mam and Dad's twenty-fifth anniversary party."

"Alice? Doesn't she own the shoe shop?"

"Yeah. She's in an awful way. She was in the car with Tom when it happened. They were going to work."

Adam ran his socked feet absently along Kirby's back. The dog, sprawled on the carpet in front of the couch, grunted happily.

"Mam was in the shop on her own all day," Hannah said. "Alice didn't contact her till the afternoon — they were in the police station all morning."

"Was the husband kept in after failing the breath test?"

"No — he was released on some kind of bail. I can't remember what it's called."

They sipped their coffee in silence. The rain lashed against the window, the first proper storm Hannah could remember so far this year. She imagined the little boy's parents listening to the same lashing rain, the same howling wind.

Or maybe they didn't hear it. Maybe they were beyond hearing it.

"Una was so upset when she rang me, poor thing. Imagine, she was apologising for missing work. I told her to take as long as she needed."

"What did you say he was? Her nephew?"

Hannah nodded. "Her sister Claire's son. He was the first grandchild, on both sides — they all doted on him, apparently."

She remembered Claire as a youngster, all wiry and long-legged, mad into sports, couldn't care less about clothes or boys or anything unless it involved a field and a ball. But it was Claire, and not prettier, quieter Una, who'd got pregnant at seventeen, just a few years after Hannah had given up babysitting. Everyone had been convinced that the boy, the father, was surely going to disappear, like so many before him, and that Claire's parents would be saddled with the child's upbringing.

But Dave, the father, hadn't done what everyone expected. He'd stayed around, eventually managing to provide a home for his small family. Hannah had lost touch with the girls by this time, but Una had brought her up to date.

Dave's a house painter — he works with his cousins. He and Claire rent a house in Springwood Gardens. It's really quite ordinary, but Dave has it looking lovely. He's got an eye for colour. You should see Jason's bedroom — it's brilliant. The kind of room every boy would love.

She'd taken out her wallet and shown Hannah a photo of a round-faced, earnest little boy with an unevenly cut fringe and the full Cupid's bow lips of the very young.

He's a bit older than that now, this was taken last summer. His hair is getting darker too. Claire hates that. She wants him to stay blond.

He's gorgeous, Hannah had said, and Una had smiled.

Isn't he? He's spoilt rotten, but he's not a bit cheeky.

And now he was dead, and his hair would never get darker. Hannah cradled her coffee mug and leant against Adam's shoulder. "God, I can't imagine what his mother is going through right now. Life's so unfair, isn't it?"

"Sure is."

"Anything funny on telly?"

They searched around and eventually found *Curb Your Enthusiasm*, and sat watching as Larry got into an argument in an ice-cream shop, but for once Hannah found it all terribly pointless.

"He ran out in front of the car," Tom said. "There was no way I could avoid him."

172

It was the first thing he'd said to her, after the silent drive home in the taxi, he in the front seat, Alice behind. She'd refused the guard's offer to drive them, their car out of bounds until after it had been fully examined. They were not going to arrive home in a squad car. Not that, on top of everything else.

The music in the taxi had nearly driven her mad; she'd never gone in for the sound of trumpets. She'd sat back and stared out the window, her hands cradling her bag, and she thought about nothing, only how the music was driving her mad. But she hadn't said anything, hadn't asked the driver to turn it down or switch it off.

They'd let themselves into the house and Alice had gone straight into the kitchen and filled the kettle, even though tea was the last thing she wanted. What she wanted, the only thing she wanted, was to turn the clock back seven hours, to unravel the day and start again.

Tom had gone upstairs and she'd let him. She hadn't called him when the kettle boiled and she made tea. He hadn't appeared by the time Geraldine showed up an hour later in response to Alice's call, the shoe shop closed early for the day.

And only when Geraldine had left, and the sky was almost completely dark, did Alice hear his footsteps on the stairs. She picked up the tea-towel as the kitchen door opened and he walked in.

"He ran out in front of the car," he said immediately, his voice low and broken. "There was no way I could

173

avoid him. It happened in a second, there was nothing I could do."

Alice finished drying the two cups she and Geraldine had used. She put away the banana bread that neither of them had touched. She kept her back to him as she took potatoes from the vegetable rack and brought them to the sink.

"You saw it too," he said. "You saw how he ran out. You were there too."

Alice began to peel the potatoes, noticing with some surprise that her hands were shaking.

"Alice," he said, "didn't you? Didn't you see how he ran out?"

She faced him then, a half-peeled potato in her hand. "You shouldn't have been driving," she said, trying not to make the words too loud. "You should have let me drive." A wobble on the last word that made her stop and take a breath. "You were drunk last night and you were still under the influence this morning, and a little boy —"

Her voice cracked, and she turned back to the sink and tried to finish peeling the potato, but she could hardly see it for the tears. Where were they all coming from? Wasn't there a limit to how many you could produce?

"I felt OK," Tom said. "I didn't feel that I couldn't drive."

Alice wiped a sleeve across her face and went on peeling.

"I'm sorry," he said. "If you knew how bad I feel —"

174

She whirled then, the potato flying from her hand and thumping onto the floor between them, skidding across to rest by the fridge. "*You* feel bad? You didn't lose a son today, did you?" The words bursting out of her, flying from her mouth. "You have no idea how those people feel, no *idea*, because you're too busy feeling sorry for yourself." She clamped her mouth shut. She crossed the room and grabbed the potato, her heart thudding, the breath gasping out of her nose in sobs.

She heard, or sensed, Tom leaving the kitchen. She dropped the potato and the peeler into the sink and held on tightly to the edge, trying to calm herself.

A file will be sent to the DPP, the curly-haired guard had told her. *Because your husband failed two breathalyser tests he will be charged today with drunken driving. As this is his first offence, we can release him on station bail, and he'll be summoned in due course, probably in a few months, to appear at the district court and be formally charged with whatever the DPP decides.*

And what then? Alice had asked, her hands twisted together around the fresh tissues he'd given her. Terrified of his answer, and terrified of not knowing his answer.

He'll be summoned to the circuit court for trial. That'll take another few months, probably in the autumn some time. He'd seen the next question in her face, and added, *Sentencing will depend on the charge, and on how the case goes in court — it's impossible to anticipate the outcome at this stage.*

175

But he could go to prison?

The guard had met her terrified eyes calmly. Her situation was probably nothing to him. He probably hated Tom, another drunk driver who'd mown down and killed a little child. *He could go to prison, yes. Quite possibly.*

After a while Alice prised her hands from the edge of the sink. She went to the press and took down a can of beans. She opened the can and spooned the beans straight into her mouth, standing by the window, looking out into the blackness and seeing nothing except the little flying blue boy, whose life they had ended.

April

The church was as packed as Hannah had seen it. It might have been Christmas Day, or Easter Sunday maybe. Most of the pews were full, people shuffling along to make room for still more. The atmosphere was thick with the smell of damp clothes and waxy flowers and furniture polish.

The little white coffin sat in front of the altar, a single wreath laid on top, spelling out *Jason* in red carnations. Someone was playing the organ, a tune that sounded familiar to her.

Cupcakes on the Corner was closed, the first time in its twelve weeks of existence that she'd closed it outside normal working hours. *Back at one*, she'd written on the sign she'd stuck to the door. Two hours off to mourn Una's nephew, Claire's son.

"God, it's warm."

Beside Hannah, Geraldine fanned herself with a hymn booklet. The shoe shop was closed, too, had remained closed since Friday, three days ago. *Closed until further notice* was what Geraldine had written on the sign that went up on the door, the day after the accident. *God knows when she'll be able to reopen,*

Geraldine had told Hannah after she'd seen Alice. *She's in an awful state.*

There was a rustle among the congregation and Hannah looked up to see a priest walking to the altar. She got to her feet with everyone else. The priest told them in a soft voice that they were about to take part in the Mass of the Angels. He said that he had baptised Jason, that he had met him often in the Junior Infant class when he visited the school. He remembered Jason's cheerfulness and love of drawing pictures, and he said a terrible cross had been given to Jason's loving family.

Somewhere behind Hannah a woman was sobbing bitterly. Feet shuffled, people coughed and sneezed and blew noses and cleared throats, and a woman cried her way through the Mass of the Angels.

A choir from Jason's school sang "He's Got The Whole World In His Hands" at the offertory. A teenage girl played Eric Clapton's "Tears In Heaven" on the violin while everyone filed up to communion. Jason's aunt Una walked to the altar and struggled through a terribly maudlin poem about little angels that caused a renewed rustling and sniffling.

And then the mass was over, and they all got to their feet again and shuffled towards the top of the church to pay their respects to the bereaved family. When she eventually reached the front pew, Hannah took Claire's limp hand in hers and said, "Claire, it's Hannah Robinson, I'm so sorry," and the girl looked emptily back at her and nodded, and the man beside her, who

Hannah assumed was Jason's father, shook with sobs, head bowed, as she pressed his hand.

She sympathised with Claire and Una's mother, dry-eyed and haggard, and shook hands with the next two people whom she took to be Jason's other grandparents, and a couple of red-eyed teenage girls who might have been Jason's aunts. She hugged Una, weeping at the end of the pew, and she shook hands with Claire and Una's father in his wheel-chair in the aisle.

On her way back down the church Hannah saw her mother with an arm around the shoulders of the woman who was still crying helplessly, and she realised it was Alice.

She had been a PA for three hours and twenty-seven minutes. She'd made coffee for her new boss (strong, black, two sugars) and met some of the journalists and secretaries who worked for the newspaper, none of whose names she remembered now. She was given a desk in a kind of anteroom outside Patrick's office and shown by one of the other females (Audrey? Andrea?) where Patrick's filing cabinet was, and how he liked his files to be organised.

She'd been introduced to the diary in which she was to record Patrick's schedule, and she'd been shown the database of contacts she'd need when arranging meetings, making hotel reservations and the like.

She'd been brought to the staffroom where they could make coffee or tea and eat lunch; the toilets had been pointed out to her on the way, and the password to access the newspaper's computers had been divulged.

An email address had been assigned to her. She'd had her photo taken for an identity card, and she'd been given forms to fill in, looking for tax numbers that meant nothing to her — Adam would help there.

On her desk were a dark green phone, a computer, an intercom pod, a spiral-bound notebook, the hard-backed diary and a selection of pens. In the top desk drawer she found a stapler and a half-full packet of staples, a solar-powered calculator, a bottle of Tippex, a box of paper clips, a pair of scissors, a roll of Sellotape, a safety pin, a box of rubber bands, a three-pack of highlighter markers with one missing, and two unpared yellow pencils with pink rubber tips.

Behind her desk there was a wooden cabinet on which sat a coffee-maker, coffee and filters, a bowl of sugar lumps and six mugs, with a bundle of spoons poking from one. Presumably if Nora wanted coffee for herself she'd have to go hunting for milk.

Nobody had complimented the black wraparound dress or the crimson jacket. Patrick's eyes had flicked over her, but he had made no comment. He'd disappeared at ten — "Off to meet a colleague, back later" — and she hadn't seen him since. She hoped nobody would come looking for him, as she'd forgotten to ask him where he'd be or what "later" meant. She hadn't thought to get his mobile number, which surely his PA should have.

Nobody had rung. For three hours and twenty-seven minutes the green phone had sat silently on her desk, except for when she'd phoned Adam.

What's happening? he'd asked, and she'd told him not much, and they'd arranged to go for a drink that evening.

She debated ringing Leah, and decided against it. Leah was being cool, no doubt about it. She needed to get used to the idea that Nora was working with her partner, that was all. Give her a week or two.

She wondered if Leah's pregnancy had been deliberate or accidental. Had Leah engineered it so Patrick would leave Hannah? And what would Hannah make of this news, coming so hot on the heels of his leaving her? She wondered without much interest if Adam had told Hannah about the baby yet.

"I'm bored," she said aloud, to the empty room. She leafed through the diary, reading past entries in some other woman's handwriting. She got up and opened the door of Patrick's office and wandered in. If he came back she'd say she was looking for anything that needed filing.

His office smelt of his aftershave, which she found a bit heady. An orange scarf dangled from a coat-stand in one corner, and a black umbrella. A silver-framed photo of Leah and himself in what looked like a hotel lobby stood on his desk — she wondered if Hannah had occupied the silver frame originally. A jumble of papers was scattered across the walnut surface — she had no notion of sorting them.

His first-floor window overlooked the street. Not much doing out there, as usual. She wondered if her impulse to leave the US had been a bit premature. Of course, now that she had her green card she could go back any time. Maybe she'd try the west coast next. LA might be interesting, or San Francisco.

She checked her watch: a quarter to one. Nobody had mentioned lunchtime so she assumed it was up to her when she took it. She wasn't particularly hungry, but it would be something to do. She left Patrick's office and ripped a page from the spiral-bound notebook. She wrote *Gone to lunch — Nora* and left it on his leather swivel chair. He might miss it on the desk, with all those papers.

She took her bag and jacket from her desk drawer — no coat-stand for the PA — and walked headlong into Patrick as she turned the corner for the lifts.

"Oops." He caught her arms to steady her. "Had enough already?"

Nora smiled. "I thought I'd go to lunch, since there wasn't a lot to do."

"Good idea." He turned towards his office. "Hang on a minute and I'll join you — I was going to take you out anyway, for your first day."

"Lovely."

As she waited she pulled out her lipstick and her handbag mirror. That was more like it, a decent lunch with a good-looking man across the table. She was glad now she'd chosen the wraparound. He'd enjoy a bit of cleavage when she leant across to tell him what she and Leah had got up to as teenagers. He'd enjoy that too —

she'd spice it up a bit for him. And if he told Leah afterwards, what could she say? Wasn't Nora only having a laugh, sharing a few harmless memories with him?

She tucked her lipstick back as he reappeared. Yes, things were definitely looking up.

"She's riddled with guilt, poor thing," Geraldine said. "She says she'll be into work tomorrow, but I can't see her being able. I told her I'd open up and she could play it by ear."

Hannah sipped her tea and made no reply.

"And that poor girl at the church, the mother," Geraldine said. "She was just broken-hearted. I don't think she knew what was going on." She shook her head. "It's just terrible, the whole business, isn't it?"

"Yes."

"There was no sign of Tom when I dropped Alice home after the funeral. He's probably ashamed to face anyone. God, imagine being responsible for the death of a child. It doesn't bear thinking about."

Hannah nodded.

"I knew he liked a drink, but I never would have taken him for a drinker — not a serious drinker, I mean. He was definitely a bit under the weather at the dinner-dance, but you'd think by the next morning it would have worn off, wouldn't you?"

"Mmm."

"He's taken leave from the dental clinic. They're looking for someone to replace him for a few weeks. Alice says he'll have to go to court. That'll be awful, for both of them."

185

"It will, awful."

Geraldine paused and studied her daughter. "Are you alright, love? You seem a bit quiet. Are you upset about the funeral?"

"Sorry," Hannah said. "It's not the funeral — I mean, of course that's terrible, but that's not what's bothering me right now." She lifted her cup and drank again.

"What is it, love?"

"I saw Leah Bradshaw today," Hannah said quietly.

Geraldine said nothing.

"I think . . . at least, I'm pretty sure that she's pregnant."

"Oh, love," Geraldine said, putting a hand on Hannah's arm. "Oh, I'm so sorry."

"It's OK," Hannah said quickly. "I'm fine really. I just got . . . a bit of a land, I suppose."

It had taken her a minute, on her way back to the shop from the funeral, to recognise the slight blonde-haired woman across the street. She'd glanced at her and then away — and something, some flash of memory, had made her look back. And there she was, the woman Patrick had left her for. Standing at the edge of the path, scanning the oncoming traffic.

And as Hannah stared, her anger so palpable she could taste it, willing the other woman to see her, on the point of storming across the road and slapping her, Leah raised her arm to signal to an approaching taxi.

And the movement had stretched the fabric of her jacket against her body and clearly outlined the swelling underneath her bust.

186

Hannah watched, dumbfounded, as Leah got into the taxi and disappeared. *Pregnant*, Hannah thought. *She's pregnant with his child.*

"It's just so soon," she said to Geraldine. "It seems so quick." Reaching for a ginger nut, cracking it in two. "Doesn't it?"

I'm not ready to be a father, Patrick had said every time the subject had come up. *We're in no hurry, are we?* And Hannah had accepted it: no point in arguing if it wasn't what he wanted. So they'd taken precautions, and no babies had happened, and she'd waited for him to be ready.

"She must have been pregnant when . . . he was still with me," she said, tapping the half-biscuit against the side of her cup. She raised her head to look at her mother's face. "Do you think it was an accident?" she asked, knowing it was wishful thinking, not wanting to accept that Patrick had wanted children after all, just not with her.

"Well . . ." began Geraldine.

"Doesn't matter," Hannah broke in. "No point in ifs and buts. It was just a shock, that's all."

"I know, love," Geraldine said softly. "Of course it was." She took a ginger nut. "I'm supposed to be off these for Lent but, really, what's the point?" She dunked it in her tea. "Where did you say Adam was gone?"

Hannah cradled her cup. "Out for a drink with Nora. It was her first day at work today."

"Oh, was it? I didn't know she'd got a job. Where is she working?"

And just like that, they were back to Patrick.

Wally slapped John on the back. "Hey, Johnny. Fancy meeting you here."

"Hello there. What'll you have?"

"Fizzy water, ta."

"Working tonight?"

Wally nodded. "Probably be quiet, but I'll do a few hours."

Monday nights at Vintage were very different from Saturdays. At almost ten o'clock, barely a dozen drinkers were about, soft piped music replacing the Saturday-night band.

The barman returned with their drinks. "Thanks, Neil," Wally said, lifting his glass towards John. "*Sláinte*."

They sometimes ran into one another on Mondays. John had developed the habit of dropping in for a pint or two on his way home from the rented workshop, just down the road. He liked the quietness of Monday nights, liked the chance to kick back and do nothing for an hour or so. And Wally, whose work brought him all over Clongarvin, sometimes found his way to Vintage on Mondays too.

We could use a saxophonist, Wally had said when he'd rung John, his cousin Patsy having passed on the number of the carpenter musician from Scotland. *That's if you're any good, of course.*

No sign of a smile in his voice, so John couldn't tell if he was joking. *I'm not bad*, he'd replied. *No complaints so far.*

Why don't you come round when we're rehearsing?
Wally had suggested. *Try out a few pieces with us, see
how it goes.*

So he'd gone to Wally's house and met the three of
them, and they'd played together for an hour or so. The
pieces were popular ones John knew well, and he soon
adapted his playing to suit their quirky style. He knew
he fitted in well, so he wasn't surprised when Wally, the
unspoken leader of the outfit, invited him to join them.

*We play here and there, wherever we can pick up a
gig,* he told John. *As it stands, we've got no regular slot,
but there's a wine bar just about to open down by the
river and I've heard that the owner wants some live
jazz, so I'm going to have a word with him.*

Carlos, the Portuguese double bassist, had heavily
accented and quite broken English, and Wally's sister
Vivienne, who played the clarinet, was so shy she barely
spoke, so it was Wally whom John felt he knew best
after almost two months of playing with them.

"Well —" Wally drained his water and stood "— that
taxi won't drive itself. See you Wednesday." Wednesday
was rehearsal night, usually held in Wally's house.

"Good luck now." John raised his pint and drank,
and wondered, as he often did, what Danielle was
doing right then in Edinburgh.

"Hannah saw that Leah Bradshaw today," Geraldine
said.

Stephen tried in vain to remember who Leah
Bradshaw was. "Really?"

Geraldine stirred her tea. "It appears," she said, "that she's pregnant. Can you believe it?"

"That's a surprise." Leah Bradshaw. The name rang a faint bell, but that was it. Stephen waited for more clues.

"Maureen Hardiman mentioned something a couple of weeks ago, but you never know with her if there's any truth to it."

"I know."

"You'd think they could have waited. You'd think they would have had some consideration for Hannah."

Ah, yes, that Leah Bradshaw. Stephen raised his cup. "Was she very upset?"

"What do you think? Of course she was upset. She pretended she wasn't, but it was obvious." Geraldine sighed. "I wish she'd meet someone else. There must be loads of nice men out there, but she hardly ever goes out."

"She's trying to get a business off the ground," Stephen pointed out. "That doesn't leave a lot of time to socialise."

"I know, I know — especially now with that awful accident, and Una gone again."

"But she'll be back in a few days, surely?"

Geraldine lifted her shoulders. "Who knows what'll happen now? That whole family must be devastated."

They drank in silence for a while. It was twenty past eleven, and they were having their usual night-time cup of tea before going upstairs to bed.

"We were talking at work today," Stephen said after a minute.

There were four male dentists working in the clinic — three now, without Tom. Geraldine had met them all. The other two were in their thirties, both with young families. Tom had started the clinic more than twenty years before, with another man who had since died. Stephen had worked there for a decade. The two younger men had joined in the last five years.

"About Tom," Stephen added. He lifted the spoon in the sugar bowl and let the sugar spill off it.

"Oh, yes?"

"We were thinking that he doesn't have that long left to work," Stephen said, digging the spoon in again.

Geraldine stared. "What do you mean, he doesn't have that long left? Tom is barely sixty."

"He'll be sixty-two next birthday," Stephen said. "He could take early retirement now if he wanted."

Geraldine frowned. "Early retirement? Has he ever talked about it?"

"Well, no, but that doesn't mean —"

"I wish you'd stop playing with that sugar," Geraldine said. "I can't see Tom wanting that at all: he's much too active to give up work. What would he do with himself all day?"

Stephen lifted the teapot and refilled their cups. "Well, maybe after what's happened, he might change his mind."

Geraldine's hand, reaching for the milk jug, stilled. "After what's happened? Stephen, you're not going to hound him out, are you? Have you forgotten that it was Tom who started the clinic? He got you in there, for God's sake."

191

He put his hands up. "Of course I haven't forgotten. It's not entirely up to me — I'm just one voice in there."

"You're the senior voice. You and Tom are the seniors. The others haven't been there long enough to be having that kind of discussion."

"Look, it wasn't an official discussion — it wasn't anything like that. The subject just came up casually over lunch, that's all."

"It was an *accident*," Geraldine said angrily, "and he'll be well punished for it. The man could go to jail, for heaven's sake."

"I know he could."

"We're his friends. He'll need us to be there for him."

"I know," Stephen repeated. "We will be there for him."

"So there'll be no more talk of him having to leave work?"

"Geraldine, I told you it wasn't like that."

"But if the subject comes up again, you'll defend him?"

"Yes."

Geraldine reached for a biscuit.

"I thought you'd given them up for Lent," Stephen said.

"Oh, who cares about bloody Lent?" Geraldine snapped. "There are more important things than *Lent*!"

She dropped the biscuit and put her head into her hands. Stephen reached across the table and stroked her arm.

"Sorry," he said.

"No, I'm sorry," she said, and he could hear the tears in her voice. "I'm not cross with you, it's just . . . What a horrible thing to happen. It's just horrible."

"It is," Stephen said, squeezing her arm gently. "It really is horrible."

They sat opposite each other, the tea cooling in their cups, the clock on the wall every now and then giving a soft electronic whirr.

Patrick lay back in the hot, scented water and closed his eyes.

We had this password, Nora had said, leaning across the table towards him, *for when we fancied a boy.*

Waiting for Patrick to ask, so of course he'd asked.

It was "climax", she said, watching his face. *If one of us worked it into a sentence, the other knew to lay off whoever it was, or else.*

The dress she wore crossed over her breasts, and when she leant towards him, it revealed quite a substantial amount of them. She'd caught him looking once, more than once. It didn't seem to bother her.

Did you ever fall out over boys? he'd asked.

It was just talk — there was no harm in it. It was just harmless talk about two schoolgirls and what they might have got up to.

Nora had grinned. *A few times we shared, if he was too good to resist*, she'd said. *Not at the same time, of course.* Smiling, poking her fork into the pasta she'd barely touched. *Although there was this one guy . . .*

193

Trailing off then, laughing. *Leah would kill me*, she'd said. *She'd have my guts for garters.*

Go on, Patrick had said. *Your secret's safe with me. I won't tell.*

She'd put a finger to the side of her mouth, pretending to consider. *Well*, she'd said, *let's just say he got a very tasty, um, sandwich one night. We were all a bit drunk . . . but it was great fun.*

Twirling a fork through her pasta, smiling. *He was older, he knew a thing or two about keeping us happy.* Bringing her fork to her lips, sliding it out slowly. *Oh, my.*

Patrick lay in the warm water and pictured two teenage girls peeling off their school clothes — unknotting ties, unbuttoning white shirts, stepping out of pleated skirts. Teasing him, giggling as they undressed. Lying on a bed, or on a floor maybe — yes, let's put them on the floor, in front of a log fire, with their firm bodies and their white lacy panties.

He was an older man, someone Patrick's own age, probably. Watching as they had fun with each other before taking off his own clothes and joining them.

He knew a thing or two about keeping us happy. Oh, my.

He lifted himself quickly from the bath and patted himself dry. He walked naked into the bedroom.

Leah looked up from her book and glanced at his erection. "Oh God," she said. "Sorry Patrick, not tonight. I'm totally bushed."

★   ★   ★

194

Hannah lifted her glass and sipped. The Spanish wine had a creamy taste that hinted at apples. "Mmm, this is a good one, must remember it."

"Now aren't you glad you came out?"

"You didn't give me a lot of choice."

But she *was* glad, happy to escape her gloomy thoughts for a couple of hours. Here in this dimly lit wine bar it was easier to push ex-boyfriends out of your head, to stop endlessly calculating, counting back the months to figure out when he might have made a baby with another woman.

She raised her glass again. "To happy times," she said, "that are just around the corner."

"I'll drink to that."

As their glasses clinked, a movement caught her eye and she turned to see three men and one woman assembling on the little stage, setting up instruments, settling into their seats. "Hey, I forgot about the music."

She watched them preparing, leaning across to talk to one another. She saw the woman in black taking a seat, bending forward to set pages on the stand in front of her. The keyboard player, his back to her, sorting wires and pressing switches, the enormous double bass being positioned on its stand. The man with the closely shaven head raising the saxophone to his —

"I don't believe it," she said softly, lowering her glass.

"What?"

"The man on the far side, with the sax."

"What about him?"

"He's the man who asked me out — John Wyatt. He's John Wyatt. Remember I told you, and I said no." He hadn't been back to Cupcakes on the Corner, almost three weeks now without a sign of him, and she kept telling herself she was relieved. Of course, she hadn't mentioned his invitation to her mother, who would have been dismayed at Hannah's refusal. She could just hear Geraldine telling her that the best way to forget Patrick Dunne was to replace him.

"I thought you said he was a *carpenter*," Adam said. "Not a musician."

"Well, he was a carpenter — I mean he is. I had no idea he did this too."

She was sure he'd never mentioned playing a musical instrument. But they'd spoken so little — two or three times altogether, a few minutes at the most. She knew virtually nothing about him. She remembered thinking he looked familiar, the first time he'd come into the shop, and now she realised it was because she'd seen him here.

She sipped her drink. The band played "Round Midnight" and "Moonglow" and "At Last", the slow old tunes wafting over her, perfectly suited to the intimate candlelit surroundings.

He wore a white shirt open at the neck, its sleeves rolled to the elbows. He looked relaxed as he played, perfectly at ease with his instrument. She loved the idea of a man who could make music. Patrick hadn't even been able to sing, much less play an instrument.

She drained her glass and turned to Adam. "Same again?" She hadn't been going to stay long: she'd been planning an early night or, at least, not too late a night. But what was the rush, with a Sunday lie-in to look forward to?

It had been so long since she'd had a night out — another drink wouldn't hurt.

They had two more. By the time the music stopped, Hannah's head was buzzing pleasantly. "He's coming this way," she said, as John approached the counter, in conversation with the man who'd been playing the keyboard.

"Say hello," Adam ordered.

"Hello there," she called immediately, and they both looked across.

"Well." John smiled as he came over. "Hello to you. Still selling your cupcakes?"

"Of course."

She'd forgotten how attractive his accent was. He showed no embarrassment; there was no awkwardness meeting him again. She introduced him to Adam. "He's a carpenter in real life," she said.

The men shook hands, and then John turned to indicate his companion. "Wally O'Toole."

"Hi," he said.

"Hey," Hannah exclaimed. "I know you — you drive a taxi, don't you?"

She hadn't even looked at him up to this, too preoccupied with her discovery of John in the band to notice anyone else.

He grinned. "Sure do. Presume you got your van fixed."

"Oh yes — you brought me home that day."

He was definitely Irish, no trace of a foreign accent there. He had a nice smile with very even teeth, and tousled muddy blond hair. She was surprised that he remembered the van breaking down.

"Hannah sells cupcakes," John said, his eyes on her. "She makes them herself."

"Cupcakes," Wally repeated. "They're some kind of fancy buns, are they?"

Hannah laughed. "That's exactly what they are. Cupcakes is just a more sexy name."

"Well, I'm all for sexy buns. Can't have too many of those."

John turned towards the counter and signalled to the barman. He pointed at Hannah's wine glass questioningly but she shook her head. She didn't fancy ruining her one day off with a hangover.

"What's your shop called?" Wally asked.

"Cupcakes on the Corner," she told him. "It's written on the side of the van."

"Is it yellow too?"

"It is, actually."

"That's good," he said. "Yellow's a good colour for a cupcake shop."

"I like your music," Adam was saying to John. "A nice mix of instruments." He glanced around. "The other two aren't joining you?"

"No," John said. "Carlos goes straight home to his new wife, and Vivienne isn't really into socialising afterwards."

Wally drained his sparkling water in one long swallow. "And you'll have to excuse me — she'll be waiting for me to drive her home. Nice to meet you both. Johnny, see you next week." And he was gone, weaving his way through the tables towards the rear of the pub.

John turned back to Hannah. "So what do you think of our music?"

"I love it — I had no idea you were a musician." She'd been too hasty, turning him down. He really was quite good-looking. She wondered if he'd ask her out again. Maybe she should take the initiative — but even as the thought occurred, she knew she'd never have the courage. She'd never had that confidence around men, could never imagine putting herself into the vulnerable position of asking someone out and risking rejection.

Just like she'd rejected John Wyatt. She watched him chatting with Adam, one hand braced against the bar, the other holding his drink. Maybe it wasn't too late: maybe she could try to encourage him again.

"I've always wanted to play a musical instrument," she remarked during a break in their conversation. "Anything really, I wouldn't mind." Which wasn't true at all, of course — the thought of playing an instrument had never, as far as she could remember, crossed her mind. She'd never pressed the keys of a piano, or plucked a guitar string, or put a tin whistle to her lips. But he wasn't to know that.

"You should take lessons," he said. "Vivienne's a music teacher."

"Is she?" Adam asked. "Where does she teach?"

"Oh, just in her own home, as far as I know," John told him. "She's quite reserved, doesn't give much information away. In fact, I think it was Wally who told me she was a teacher, not her."

"She looks a bit fierce," Hannah said. "I'm not sure I'd want her teaching me anything."

John laughed. "I can't think of anyone less fierce than Vivienne — she's as timid as a deer. And she's a beautifully sensitive player, totally focused."

"I might take lessons myself," Adam said. "I fancy the clarinet."

Hannah groaned. "Oh God — as long as you practise in the shed." She turned to John. "Adam is my tenant," she explained. "We've known each other forever." Was that making it plain enough that they weren't romantically involved?

"And your shop is going well?" John asked. Giving no sign at all that the status of Hannah's relationship with Adam was of the slightest interest to him.

"Fine," she said. "It's still hard work, some weeks better than others, but I'm still there, and managing to pay the bills, just about."

"Well done," he said. "That's pretty good going, these days."

"How did you get to be in the band?" Adam asked him.

John told them about Patsy in the woodwork store, who'd put him in touch with Wally. "I was lucky — it's a good group. We play well together, and everyone gets along."

Yes, she had definitely been too hasty. He was probably exactly what she needed to help her forget about Patrick Dunne.

200

The lights went up in the bar just then, and she looked at Adam. "Will we hit the road?"

He drained his pint and grabbed his jacket. "We'll see you again," he said to John. "We're in here a fair bit."

"No doubt."

"And if you ever need a cupcake," Hannah added, "you know where I am."

That was as much as she could do to try to reopen the door she'd shut in his face a few weeks ago. He might or he might not be willing to try again, but at least she could encourage him a little.

"Safe home," he answered, lifting a hand to her.

She wondered if he watched them walking out.

Nothing had changed. Everything had changed.

In the days after the accident they had breakfast together in the mornings. Tom got up and shaved and dressed himself, as if he was going to work.

But they met in the kitchen, having spent the night in different bedrooms.

Ah, don't, he'd said, when she'd taken her nightdress from under her pillow, her toothbrush from the ensuite bathroom. *Ah, Alice, why are you doing this? Ah, don't do this.*

But she'd been raw. She'd been angry and heartbroken and still full of tears, and she hadn't answered him, just gathered up her slippers and her book and her clothes for the morning and walked out, across the landing to the bedroom they still called Ellen's, although it was years since their daughter had slept there. Now when Ellen came home, she and Lenny and the children stayed in Lenny's mother's house across town, which had four bedrooms and just one elderly woman living in it.

She'd lain awake in Ellen's bed, afraid to close her eyes, afraid of the pictures that might appear. In the morning she'd got up at twenty to eight like she always did on a work day. She'd gone downstairs and put rashers and tomatoes under the grill, like she did every Saturday, and when they were cooked Tom had come in, and they'd sat down and eaten breakfast.

Neither of them had mentioned what had happened the day before. Alice had said she was leaving the shop closed, and he hadn't responded. She'd made some remark about the weather, and he'd asked about his blue shirt, and Alice had asked if he wanted more tea and he'd held out his cup.

She'd gone back to the shoe shop on the Tuesday, the day after the funeral, and four days after the accident. That morning, Tom didn't appear for breakfast, and she didn't call him. It was a relief to have somewhere to go, something to set the alarm for. Not that she needed the alarm, not that she'd had a decent night's sleep since it had happened.

And once she got to the shop she realised that nothing was the same.

She watched the faces of people coming in, looked for a sign that they knew. Waited for their revulsion to show, waited for them to spit in her face and call her a murderer — because wasn't she as guilty as Tom, when you thought about it? Shouldn't she have driven,

202

shouldn't she have insisted, knowing the state he was in?

Geraldine was her saviour. Geraldine made no mention of the accident. Geraldine chatted about everything else, and smiled at the customers when Alice couldn't. Geraldine took no notice when Alice was snappish. Geraldine followed her into the back when Alice disappeared, and held her while Alice wept, and told Alice that she couldn't have done anything, she could have done nothing at all.

When Alice got home in the evenings Tom was there, reading the newspaper or watching one of his quiz shows on television. He liked Anne Robinson and *University Challenge*, but he wasn't a big fan of *Countdown*. This would be the first time they'd meet in the day, since he didn't get up now before she left the house.

There was never a bottle of wine on the dinner table. The water jug was all there was, with a couple of lemon slices floating on top. Tom was still drinking, though. She smelt it sometimes on his breath, but she said nothing, and she didn't bother looking for bottles. What was the point?

She still cooked their dinner, although he was the one with the free time now, but he'd always been hopeless in the kitchen so she didn't push it. God knows what he'd serve up.

They made small-talk now, across the table in the evenings. Alice would tell him about Geraldine's ten-euro win on a scratchcard, about the launderette next to Hannah's shop going out of business. The weather might be mentioned, the days getting nice and long now. He'd say if he was out of shaving foam, or if next door's dog had got into the back garden again. She'd offer more potatoes, another spoon of rice pudding.

She never asked him about his day. No mention was made, by either of them, of him returning to work. Geraldine had told her they'd got a temporary replacement at the dental clinic, but Alice didn't pass this information on at home. She had no idea whether Tom was in touch with Stephen, or with either of his other colleagues. Some instinct stopped her talking about it. He'd go back when he was ready. He couldn't stay at home for ever.

They had a visit from a guard Tom knew, whose teeth he looked after. *Your solicitor will be working away on your behalf*, he said. *Keep the spirits up, keep busy, that's the thing. I'll keep you posted on any developments from our end*, he said, and Alice thanked him and cut more coffee cake.

She found it amazing that Tom hadn't lost his licence. The car had been returned to them a couple of days after the accident, and no mention had been made of taking Tom's licence away. He'd killed a child and failed a breath test, and he was still legally entitled to get behind the wheel of a car and drive.

But he didn't drive. It had been Alice who'd taken his car to the garage to have the dent in the bumper straightened. She hated doing it — her fingers were white on the wheel, her body clenched so tightly she could hardly breathe — but the sight of the dent had been unbearable to her. Tom hadn't gone near his car since then. It sat in the driveway, ignored by both of them.

She had no idea what Tom did all day. She didn't know what time he got up, or how long he stayed in his pyjamas. He didn't have to go out for the paper: they had it delivered. She was pretty sure he hadn't been near a golf course, even with the nice mild weather they'd been having lately.

But he did go out, because he bought whiskey. Alice found the first bottles by accident, searching in the bin for a receipt she'd thrown away. They'd been pushed right to the bottom, three empty Powers Gold Label bottles. She'd taken them out and brought them to the recycling bins at the roundabout, ten minutes' walk away. She kept an eye out for others, and whenever she found them she recycled them.

No mention was made of it.

She'd decided to say nothing to Ellen. What would be the point of worrying her, so far away? Ellen would probably feel she should come home, which Alice dreaded. Imagine their daughter seeing Tom in this state, imagine her walking into this nightmare. Time enough to tell her when things began to happen, when telling became unavoidable, as it surely must do.

So when Alice wrote her weekly letter — they only phoned on special occasions — she made no mention of a dead child. She didn't talk about a court case, she didn't bring up the failed breathalyser test.

Not much news since my last letter, she'd written. *Nothing much happens in Clongarvin.* She made a brief mention of the dinner-dance; it was something to say. She told Ellen about the sale in the shoe shop. *Flying off the shelves*, she wrote. *Geraldine and I are worn out.* She described a top she'd bought, she asked about the children. *Dad is working hard as usual*, she wrote. *He sends his love.*

She was convinced that Tom would be sent to jail. Why would anyone let him off, after what he'd done? Even if he hadn't meant to do it, he'd still got behind the wheel of the car of his own accord. She was a driver, she could have driven: that would probably be mentioned in court. She could have prevented it, if she'd driven the car that morning instead of Tom.

The taxi driver from the night before could be traced: he could be asked to give evidence about Tom's condition. Not that they needed evidence, with the breathalyser results. It was an open and shut case — wasn't that what they called them? And Tom would have to be punished for what he'd done.

She hadn't moved back into their bedroom. With every night she passed on the other side of the landing, it became more of an impossibility. She discovered that she liked the compactness of the single bed, after years of sharing a king-size. She was beginning to forget what it felt like to have another body lying beside you at night, to have someone else's odour mixing with yours in the morning.

She used a hot-water bottle in place of Tom's warmth. She left the window open more than he would have liked. One night she left the curtains open too, and stared out at a scatter of stars till morning. She slept little, some nights not at all, but during the days she seemed full of restless energy.

Tom's name hadn't been mentioned in the newspaper reports of the accident, but she thought word must be getting around. The phone rarely rang at home now: she hadn't heard since the accident from the few women who'd normally ring her for a chat — and she hadn't the courage to ring any of them, in case they hung up.

Despite her initial fears, there hadn't been any negative reaction in the shop — nobody had accused her of anything to her face — but lately sales were down. Of course, they'd slowed in the past few months with the recession, like sales in every shop, but now it seemed quieter than ever. She prayed she was imagining it, that people hadn't turned their backs on her because of what had happened.

She thought about the boy's parents. They filled her head as she climbed the stepladder to take down a shoebox, as she peeled carrots, as she brushed her teeth. She thought about the grief Tom had visited on them. She imagined the mother taking little clothes off the line, knowing there was nobody left to wear them. She thought about a football lying forgotten under a bush, the father remembering the last time they'd kicked it around the garden together.

They filled her head, these two people. She'd never seen them — she'd been in no state to sympathise at the funeral, even if she'd felt she had any right to shake their hands. She didn't know a thing about them, apart from their names, and the fact that they'd once had a little child.

And she knew where they lived.

Springwood Gardens, the death notice said. No house number, no name. Alice knew roughly where Springwood Gardens was, in behind the town hall, part of the jumble of housing estates that had been built over the last twenty years, when the Celtic Tiger had been roaring and builders had been booming.

Beloved only son, the notice said, *of David and Claire*.

O'Brien was the surname. Jason O'Brien was the boy Tom had killed. It shouldn't be too hard to find David O'Brien in Springwood Gardens. There couldn't be too many David O'Briens around. If there was confusion she could say she had a mass card to deliver.

She folded the death notice and put it back into her bag. She took an onion from the vegetable rack and began to peel it.

Vivienne. He loved the name. He was reasonably sure he'd liked it before he knew it was hers, but now he loved it. It suited her perfectly, so soft and feminine. Vivienne the clarinet player.

He'd been thrown by the other musician saying he was driving her home after the gig on Saturday night. What did that mean? Were they an item? Was her home his home too — or did they just live in the same direction, so it made sense for them to travel to the wine bar together?

208

Adam had no way of knowing — so he decided to assume she was single, and proceed with his new plan.

Sooner or later, it had to happen.

After several Friday nights of successfully managing to ignore the events that had taken place in the lives of their daughters, matters between Fiona Bradshaw and Geraldine Robinson finally bubbled to the surface — in Maureen Hardiman's home, of all places.

The bridge itself took place in the drawing room. Maureen called it the drawing room, but as far as Geraldine could see it was identical in both size and layout to her own sitting room. Typical Maureen, putting on airs, with her collection of spindly-legged two-seaters that really only seated two very good friends comfortably — what was wrong with fold-up chairs? — and the ridiculous little tables that barely held their cards and score sheets, never mind a handbag.

There was nothing disastrous *per se* about Fiona and Geraldine meeting up. Hadn't they been in the same room several times since Patrick's defection? Hadn't they even sat opposite each other for a set time each evening? They were both mature women; they could handle a sensitive situation with the dignity and tact it required. There was no reason for any loss of face, or sharp words of any kind. No blame whatsoever need be attached to either party, for indeed both women were entirely blameless.

Geraldine took her seat opposite her partner as usual at the start of the evening, and play commenced. In due

209

course a new game was announced, and the partners who were moving found their new positions, and began again. The cards were dealt, the usual discussions ensued. Games were won and lost, scores were entered; the evening wore on.

As usual, Geraldine and Fiona eventually found themselves playing against one another. At no time over the course of that particular bridge game did Geraldine address Fiona directly, or vice versa, unless communication was strictly necessary. The two women's eyes never met, their hands remained resolutely apart, despite the limited space on Maureen's tables. So far, so normal.

Such a shame then, after successfully negotiating their way through most of the evening, after keeping to separate sides of the room during the ensuing tea and nibbles, that Geraldine happened to overhear a chance remark in Maureen's hall, when the gathered assembly were manoeuvring themselves into coats and retrieving umbrellas. When, in fact, all danger of a contretemps of any kind between the two women might have been assumed to have passed.

"Fiona," Dolores Mulcair was heard to say, in her unmistakably strident tones, "I hear that your Leah is expecting."

In the act of buttoning her coat, Geraldine froze.

"Yes," Fiona replied, "in June."

Geraldine turned slowly and faced her enemy, and discovered Fiona to be looking directly across the hall at her, even while Dolores was congratulating her loudly, even as Maureen Hardiman was saying triumphantly, "I knew it!"

210

And if she'd seen the slightest hint of remorse, the tiniest sign of regret in Fiona's face, Geraldine might possibly have found it in her heart to say nothing, and to let the moment pass. Sadly, she saw nothing of the sort as she gazed across the hall. Fiona simply stared back impassively.

So Geraldine smiled. "That was quick," she said loudly, over the buzz of conversation — every bit as loudly as Dolores. "Weren't you saying just at Christmas, Fiona, that you wished Leah would find some nice man?"

Fiona frowned. "No, I —"

"Oh, yes, I definitely remember you saying that," Geraldine continued, "and now she's due in June, which means she got pregnant . . ." pretending to calculate, aware that the conversations had trailed off around them ". . . way back in September, it must have been. Imagine that — she was pregnant all the time. Now don't you tell me," she went on, wagging a finger at Fiona, "that you had no idea, you dark horse."

A dead silence. Eyes swivelling from Geraldine to Fiona. Fiona's expression unchanged, apart from a slight flush in her cheeks. She opened her mouth, and closed it again. Geraldine waited.

"So who's the lucky man?" someone asked finally, into the silence.

"Yes, Fiona," Geraldine said, the smile rigid on her face, "who is the mystery man that nobody knew about?"

Fiona met her gaze squarely. What else could she do?

"Patrick Dunne is his name," she said evenly, "as you well know, Geraldine."

A collective indrawn breath. Eyes back on Geraldine now, waiting for her reaction. They all knew Patrick had been with Hannah: hadn't Geraldine often mentioned him, saying how good he was to her daughter? Hadn't she expressed her hope to quite a few of them that he'd propose at Christmas? And now they all knew that it was never going to happen, that he'd moved on to Leah Bradshaw, who was pregnant with his child.

Geraldine turned without another word and opened Maureen's teak door. She stepped into the damp night air and closed the door on the silence, and walked on shaking legs to where she'd parked the car.

Already she regretted it. It had been irresistible, baiting Fiona like that. It had been so satisfying to wipe the smug expression off her face. But now they'd look at Geraldine in pity, and they'd be careful not to mention Hannah. And of course, Fiona and herself would be watched furtively any time they came face to face in the future.

Still, it was out in the open, no more avoiding to be done now, no more wondering when everyone would find out. She and Fiona would carry on as usual, she supposed. They'd be polite and cool, and never, ever friendly. And, of course, the other women would be sensitive to Geraldine's situation, and Leah's pregnancy wouldn't be discussed in front of her, which was a blessing.

She started the engine and drove home, trying to remember if there was any custard. She could do with a bowl of custard — which was perfectly allowable as long as you made it with skimmed milk.

The intercom buzzed. Nora dropped the emery board and pressed the *receive* button. "Yes?"

"Can you come in?"

She heard the words in stereo as usual. Patrick's actual voice on the other side of the door behind her was almost as audible as the more mechanical words that issued through the machine. She'd pointed out to him that he only had to raise his voice slightly to call her into his office and thereby do away with the need for the intercom altogether, but he'd laughed.

"On the way," she replied.

She released the button and got up, taking her pad and biro from the desk, smoothing her purple skirt, checking that the seams in the back of her stay-ups were straight.

He sprawled in his chair, hair tousled, tie askew. She crossed to the window, dropping her pad and pen on his desk as she passed. She slid the window open, aware of his eyes on her as she leant against the sill and reached upwards.

"Stuffy in here," she said. "You need air-conditioning."

He smiled as she picked up her pad. "Like I keep telling you, you're not in New York now."

"Don't I know it." She hitched up her skirt a fraction and perched on the side of his desk. "Am I taking a letter, sir?"

Ten days down, she was reasonably sure she wouldn't spend the rest of her life — or even the rest of this year — working for the *Clongarvin Voice*. But it would do to pass the time for a while — and really, apart from the lack of any trace of glamour, she had no serious objections to the job.

The paper was a weekly, which meant their only really busy day was Thursday, and even that had been easy enough last week, with the others still regarding her as the new girl who wasn't expected to know her way around yet. Patrick's schedule wasn't too hectic most of the time, which suited her just fine — and compared to some of the scumbags she'd come across in New York, he was pretty much the ideal boss.

He fancied her, of course. Men were rubbish at hiding that. He couldn't keep his eyes off her chest, he watched her mouth when she talked, he probably lusted after her rear view when she walked away from him. And of course she fuelled the attraction, enjoying the attention of a good-looking man while well able to keep him at a distance.

The clothes she wore to work were carefully chosen to tease, to give just enough away without being too revealing. Her skirts were figure-hugging, but long enough to look suitable for the office. Her tops showed cleavage, but not too much — unless she leant in and allowed a better view. Her blouses weren't exactly sheer, but sufficiently fine to hint at what lay beneath. She kept a bottle of perfume in her desk drawer.

She knew, as she scribbled down his words, that he was looking at her. Slouched in his chair, he was taking

214

her in. Maybe even fantasising a little. She felt his eyes on her body as she half sat on the corner of his desk. She could have sat in the visitor's chair: they both knew that, but he hadn't suggested it. This position was more interesting, for both of them.

"That's it," he said, as she finished. "Will you get that out before lunchtime?"

"Of course." She closed the pad and slid off his desk. "How's Leah? I haven't seen her in a while."

She'd sent a text a few evenings ago, just to say hello and see the reaction. Leah's reply, when it came, had been brief: *Up to my eyes, hope all's well. Must meet up soon.*

"She's fine," Patrick replied. "A bit tired, naturally."

"Naturally . . . When's she finishing up?"

"Oh, not for another month or so." He smiled, his eyes straying to the neckline of her pale grey top. "No maternity leave when you work for yourself."

"No, that's true." She pushed her hair behind her shoulders. "Well, I'd better get back to work."

"What about lunch?" he said, as she reached the door. "Have you plans?"

She turned, her face full of regret. "Actually, I have, sorry. Some other time."

She had no plans, of course. But it was fun to keep him at a distance — until he was gagging for it.

Always such fun, the foreplay.

Una came back to work on the Monday following Jason's funeral.

215

Hannah took in the pale face, the determined smile. "Are you sure you're ready for this? You can have longer."

Una shook her head. "Thanks, but I need to get back to some kind of a routine." She hesitated. "And I think Claire and Dave would like to be alone for a while — they've been surrounded by people since —" She broke off, pulling a tissue from her bag and pressing it to her eyes. "God, sorry — I'm not going to do this all morning, I promise."

"Go in and put the kettle on," Hannah told her, "and make yourself a cuppa. I'm afraid there's only UHT milk."

But Una pushed the tissue back into her bag and began to unbutton her jacket. "No, I'm OK, honestly. Just give me something to do, and then you head off."

Hannah glanced around the shop. "Well, I didn't get a chance to sweep the floor this morning," she lied, "so you could do that."

Una hung her jacket and got the broom from the back room. "They're devastated," she said, as Hannah began to untie her apron. "Completely broken-hearted, the two of them." She pushed the broom around the clean floor. "Dave told me Claire cries all night, just lies in bed all curled up and cries." She gathered up nothing in the dustpan while Hannah took her jacket from the back. "She sits in Jason's bedroom for hours in the day. Dave can't go in there — he says he just can't bring himself."

Hannah made no move to put on her jacket. "Listen," she said, "there's nothing I have to do in town today. Why don't I stay around here? Why don't the two of us —"

Una straightened up, holding the empty dustpan. "No, no, don't do that — if you stay here I'll just feel useless. I'll be fine, honest." She paused. "I hope that doesn't sound like I'm trying to get rid of you."

"Yes, it does, and I'm highly offended. You're sure you'll be OK?"

Una nodded. "I'm sure. See you at twelve."

"Ring me if you need to."

So Hannah left the shop, for once not relishing her two hours of freedom. As she walked down the street a taxi passed, the driver lifting a hand in greeting. Hannah waved back, not recognising him until he'd passed. Wally, minus the woolly cap. She hoped he'd put it away till next winter.

She turned a corner and saw with a sinking heart that Nora O'Connor was walking rapidly in her direction, too close for Hannah to pretend not to have seen her and duck into the nearest shop.

"Hi there," Nora said as she approached. "I was just on my way to you, actually."

Dark green skirt that hugged her hips and fishtailed out beneath. Black fitted jacket over snow white blouse. Black boots, snug on her calves.

Dressing up for Patrick Dunne. The thought popped, completely unbidden, into Hannah's head. She wished she was wearing something slightly more fashionable than her old blue top and grey trousers. "Did you want me for something?"

Adam never talked about his sister's job at the newspaper. When Hannah had given in to her curiosity and asked him how it was going, he'd told her that Nora hadn't said much one way or another. Hannah couldn't imagine that working for the *Clongarvin Voice* held too many attractions for Nora O'Connor — apart from its editor maybe.

"I wanted to pick up some of your little cupcakes for a meeting," Nora said. "Thought they'd add a nice fancy note."

"Oh . . ." Hannah immediately felt ashamed. Why should she assume that Nora would make a play for Patrick? Who was she to judge Adam's sister — whom she hardly knew, after all? "That's nice of you. Una is in the shop, she'll look after you."

"Yes, Adam mentioned you'd taken on an assistant. Business must be going well."

"Not bad," Hannah said. "It's hard work, but it's keeping me solvent — more or less." She began to edge away. "Well, I'd better . . ."

"Me too — catch you later." And Nora was gone, leaving a whirl of something that smelt expensive after her. Off to buy cupcakes for a meeting that in all likelihood Patrick would attend. Hannah wondered if he'd notice them, if he'd recognise them as hers. Surely he'd remember her cupcakes, after all the sample recipes she'd presented him with once she'd made up her mind about opening the shop.

They hadn't met since the first day she'd opened, but she'd seen him a few times over the past couple of months. Across the aisles in a supermarket as she stood in the queue with her trolley. Sitting in the front seat of a taxi once, thankfully not looking in her direction. Flicking the pages of a magazine in the window of his regular barber's as he waited for the hot-towel shave that was his weekly treat to himself. And once with his arm curved around Leah Bradshaw's waist as he shepherded her across the street. Hannah couldn't be sure if they had spotted her and chosen to avoid a meeting. Probably, and quite understandably, she supposed — but it had hurt nonetheless.

She still felt a lurch when she saw him. She still loved the look of him, the dark hair, forever in need of a tidy-up, the deep brown eyes, the stubble that crept back a couple of hours after he'd shaved. The tallness of him, the solidity of his body. She remembered his smell, the musk of his aftershave, the sharp tang of his sweat.

She turned another corner and realised she was on the block where Alice's shoe shop was. Might as well check out the new stock — not that she could afford a pair of tights, let alone shoes, but a look wouldn't hurt.

A sign on the window read *Everything 10% off.* Another read *All stock reduced.* Geraldine sat alone on a stool to the rear, reading a magazine. She looked up as Hannah walked in. "Hello, love — nothing wrong?"

"No — I'm just at a loose end. Una came back this morning."

"Oh, how is the poor girl?"

"Very upset, of course, but I think it'll do her good to be back at work." Hannah looked around. "It's quiet here, isn't it?"

Geraldine closed the magazine. "There's been nobody in yet today."

"Nobody at all? Even just looking?"

The shelves were filled with brightly coloured shoes and sandals. There was an assortment of boots labelled *Final Reductions — up to 70% off*. There were two rows of slippers and a selection of sports shoes.

Geraldine sighed. "Since the accident, since we reopened, things have really slowed down. It wasn't that noticeable at first, we were blaming the recession, but the more it goes on . . ." She shook her head. "I just don't know."

Hannah stared at her. "You think it's to do with what happened? You think people are avoiding the shop?"

Geraldine lifted her shoulders. "I really don't know what to think, love — but in a place the size of Clongarvin, things don't take long to get around."

"Where's Alice?"

"Gone to the cash-and-carry, and to do a few other jobs. There's no need for the two of us here."

"I suppose not . . . How is she?"

Geraldine considered. "Well, she's improved a bit since she came back, and she's doing her best to put a good face on it, but she looks terribly worn out — she must be worried sick about what's ahead of them. I've tried inviting them round to dinner, but she keeps making excuses."

"What about Tom?"

"He seems to have gone to ground — Alice changes the subject whenever I ask her about him, and Stephen says he's made no effort to contact the clinic about

220

going back to work." She closed her magazine and stood up. "Will you have tea?"

"Only if you're making it."

The shop door opened as Geraldine reappeared, and Hannah drifted over to the shelves and picked up a red peep-toe sandal with a woven wedge sole, and tried on a lime green stiletto that would probably look a lot better below Nora O'Connor's slender ankles.

"You'll come for lunch on Sunday, won't you?" Geraldine asked when the other woman had left, empty-handed. "I'm doing lamb."

"I'll be there."

Sunday was Easter Sunday. Last year, she and Patrick had spent Easter in a small house on Achill Island. They'd driven up early on Good Friday and stayed till Easter Monday evening. By prior agreement, he'd given her a gold-wrapped Lindt chocolate rabbit, and she'd given him a sixpack of Walkers cheese and onion crisps. They'd eaten Easter Sunday lunch in the local hotel and walked it off on the beach afterwards.

"When do you expect Alice back?" she asked as they were drinking their tea.

"Not for another hour, I'd say. It was after ten when she left." Geraldine paused. "Anyone nice into the shop?"

"Not really. No one out of the ordinary."

Hannah knew she was thinking about John Wyatt. She wondered if he was travelling to Scotland for Easter. If not, they could well have been spending Easter Sunday together, or part of it at least. He hadn't been back to Cupcakes on the Corner since they'd met in Vintage. Of course it didn't matter — she hardly knew him — but still it irked, this feeling that she'd been hasty, that she'd thrown something away without considering its worth. Maybe she'd visit Vintage again some time with Adam.

When she got back to the shop, Una reported that a woman had bought two dozen cupcakes, and asked for a written receipt.

"Auburn hair, well dressed, American accent?"

"Yes. You know her?"

"I know her."

Two dozen cupcakes, easily their biggest order to date. It occurred to her suddenly that Patrick might specifically have asked his PA to shop at Cupcakes on the Corner. Salving his conscience maybe, by throwing some business her way? Not that it mattered a damn whose decision it had been — an order was an order, wherever it came from.

Still.

"I've invited my mother for lunch on Sunday," Leah said. "I couldn't leave her on her own at Easter."

"Fine," Patrick answered, thinking about the way his PA's fingers trailed across the skin of her throat as she spoke on the phone. Back and forth, back and forth, across that smooth, polished-looking skin.

"Will you pick up some Rennies on your way home?" Leah asked him. "The original ones."

"No problem."

He bet she wore stockings, with lacy tops that clung to her thighs. An inch or so of tanned bare skin above, before the other lace began.

"What time will you be home?" Leah asked.

"Around six, I'd say. Maybe a bit later."

He wondered again if she'd had a job done on her breasts. She certainly took every opportunity to show them off. Not that he was complaining. He wondered if you'd be able to tell by touching them.

"I'm doing lasagne," Leah said.

"Lovely."

After he'd hung up, Patrick sat for a few minutes behind his walnut desk. Then he pressed the intercom and said, "Can you come in?"

There was always a letter that needed to be written, if you thought about it for long enough.

The woman in the church shop opened the ledger and thumbed through the pages till she got to the current one. "For the living or the deceased?"

"Deceased," Alice said.

"What name?"

"Jason O'Brien."

"Oh, that little boy," the woman said, writing in the ledger. "Tragic. That driver should be strung up."

"Yes." Alice chose a mass card from the selection presented to her. It showed Jesus holding a lamb in one hand and a shepherd's crook in the other.

"Shared or full mass?" the woman asked.

"Full."

"Seven euro that'll be, so." She detached a receipt and handed it to Alice. "Thank you kindly," she said, as Alice handed her a ten-euro note.

It took her less than fifteen minutes to drive to Springwood. She pulled into the kerb on the first road of the estate — Springwood Park — and opened the mass card and wrote *Jason O'Brien* on the empty line, and *Alice* in the space for her name. She slipped the card back into its envelope and returned it to her pocket.

She got out of the car and locked it, and looked around. Springwood was a mix of terraced and semi-detached houses with low iron railings, and in some cases hedging as well, separating the narrow front lawns. Some residents had replaced the grass with cement or paving to create a driveway; others had bordered the lawn with flowerbeds. A few were terribly neglected — she guessed they were rented — but most were fairly well cared-for.

The front doors were painted red or black or navy or yellow, coloured-glass inserts in a few, a large brass frog's head knocker on one. Lace curtains or no curtains or Venetian blinds. A tawny cat washed its face on a gate pillar and ignored her. A battered man's brown shoe lay on its side by another gate. *For sale* and a mobile-phone number on a cardboard sign stuck in the rear window of a black 2006 Micra.

"I'm looking for the O'Briens," she told a woman with long blonde hair who turned out of a gate and came towards her, but the woman shook her head.

"They're in Springwood Gardens," Alice said, "David O'Brien," but the woman said, "Sorry" in a foreign accent and walked on.

"The O'Briens," she said to a man walking a small black and white dog. "Springwood Gardens." The dog sniffed at her shoes, his tail wagging.

"Dave and Claire, the ones who lost their little boy?" he asked, and Alice nodded, heart thudding.

"I have a mass card," she said, but he'd already turned away from her to gesture up the road.

"Second next turn left is Springwood Gardens," he said. "They're on the right, about halfway down."

"You wouldn't know the number?"

He shook his head. "Anyone will tell you," he said. "Ask anyone."

But when she took the second left turn there was no one to ask, except two small boys around seven or eight, sitting on the edge of the path eating Taytos, a grubby white football trapped between the feet of one.

"Do you know where the O'Briens live?" Alice asked, and they stared at her, still crunching. She didn't want to say where the little boy was killed. "Dave and Claire O'Brien?"

One of the boys took his hand out of his crisps packet and pointed. "That house," he said, "with the flowers," and Alice followed his finger and saw the red bunch of wilting roses tied to the gatepost with a faded white ribbon.

"Thank you," she said, crossing the road, feeling their heads turning to watch her as she approached the gate. There was a plastic-covered note attached to the bouquet. Alice bent and read *To Jason, all our love forever, the McCarthys* in a child's careful script.

She straightened and regarded the house. It looked much like its neighbours, the middle one in a terrace of five. The lawn was neatly mown, the flowerbed studded with hard-pruned rose bushes. The windows were bare except for an upstairs one whose curtains were closed. The front door was dark green with a brass thirty-seven on it.

She walked up the cement path, pulling the mass card from her pocket. She pushed it quickly through the letter-box and walked away, out the gate and back onto the path, past the two boys who were still eating crisps.

"Are you alright?" Geraldine asked her, back in the shop. "You're very pale."

"I'm fine."

"Did you get everything you wanted? Did you get the sleeping pills?"

"Yes . . . I'll make us a cuppa."

She filled the kettle, seeing the wilted roses tied to the gate, the carefully pruned rose bushes in the garden, the green door with thirty-seven in brass screwed onto it. She'd felt resistance as she'd pushed the card through, a draught excluder on the other side probably. She hadn't waited to hear the card falling onto the floor.

She thought about the mother picking it up, taking out the card and reading *Alice*. Showing it to the father, who'd shake his head when she asked if he knew anyone called Alice.

She'd found four empty whiskey bottles pushed to the bottom of the bin two evenings ago. She'd pulled them out and brought them to the recycling station.

She'd lied to Geraldine about going to the doctor to get sleeping pills. It was the first time she'd lied to Geraldine.

Adam typed *clarinet* and pressed *search*. After a few seconds the screen changed, and he read *2,234 results*. He scrolled slowly through clarinet mouthpieces and sheet music for clarinets and clarinet cases, and the odd actual clarinet. He went back to the home page and typed *clarinet instrument* and searched again, and this time eleven results showed up.

He studied a silver clarinet that was being sold by george4234. The price quoted was forty pounds, which was considerably lower than the ones he'd seen attached to clarinets in Clongarvin's one and only musical-instrument store, and george4234 was in the United Kingdom, which seemed close enough. There was a bid of forty-two pounds on the clarinet. Adam typed in a bid of forty-four and pressed *enter*.

Not an eBay member yet? the screen asked. *Register here.* He chose a user ID and a password and filled in all the boxes with the information required for him to get his hands on a clarinet for forty-four pounds.

However shy she was, a music teacher could hardly refuse a would-be eager pupil. If she said she was fully booked, he'd ask to be put on a waiting list. He'd tell her that he'd just bought a clarinet and he was desperate to play it and she'd been recommended to him. It wasn't a complete lie — John Wyatt had called her a beautifully sensitive player, which was surely a recommendation. He'd also said she was as timid as a deer, which Adam liked.

He'd be patient. He'd be gentle and non-threatening, and he'd gain her trust, however long it took.

And who knew? He might even learn to play the clarinet.

In number thirty-seven Springwood Gardens a woman sits on a single bed, on top of a Spiderman duvet. The curtains in the room are drawn, although the day is barely halfway through. Enough light filters through the unlined fabric — zoo animals on a yellow background — to pick out the small white wardrobe and matching chest of drawers, the red wooden toy chest, the shelf full of *Mr Men* and *Dr Seuss* and *Thomas the Tank Engine* books. The row of small footwear — his white runners, his red wellies, his blue slippers — underneath.

The woman sees none of these. She sees him soaring on a swing, shouting, *Higher! Higher!* and laughing delightedly as she pushes him. She sees him squatting on sand, filling a bucket as the tip of his tongue pokes from his mouth, his blue togs slipping down in the back to show an inch of his bottom.

She sees his cheeks puff as he blows out four candles on a blue and white cake, a dribble of saliva plopping onto the icing.

She feels his hand slipping out of hers as he runs onto the road because he's just seen Paul on the other side. She feels the terror, she sees the car, she hears the scream bursting out of her as he flies into the air.

Higher! Higher!

He is all she sees now.

Adam produced a Smarties egg from behind his back and held it out to her. "Happy Easter."

"Ta."

"Where's mine?"

"Hang on." She opened the press under the sink and took out a similar-sized cardboard box. "There you go."

"Oh good, mint Aero."

"Of course mint Aero — don't I always get you that?"

They made coffee and settled at the kitchen table. "So," she said, peeling the gold paper from her egg, "when are you off?"

Adam and Nora were travelling the fifty miles to their parents' house for Easter Sunday lunch.

"I'm collecting Nora in an hour." He broke a curved slab from his egg. "I suppose I should be working up an appetite."

"Me too." Hannah dipped a shard into her coffee mug. "We'll just have half now."

"Listen," he said then, his mouth full of chocolate, "I think I want to tell you something."

"What?"

He licked the tips of his fingers one by one. "I've just bought a clarinet."

Hannah turned to him, the melting chocolate halfway to her mouth. "What?"

"I said —"

"A real clarinet that you play?"

"Yes, a real clarinet. I bought it on eBay. It should be arriving in the next few days."

Hannah laughed. "I don't believe it. Why did you do that? You're about as musical as an elephant."

"Thank you." He crunched chocolate loudly. "I'll have you know I'm going to take lessons."

"You're going to take *lessons?* And where are you going to find a clarinet player?"

"Actually," he said, dipping a shard into his coffee, not looking at her, "I've found one. The woman in the wine bar. You know, in the band. She gives lessons."

Hannah put down her mug. "Look at me," she demanded.

Adam turned an innocent face towards her. "What? It's no big mystery — I've decided I'd like to learn to play the clarinet, and there just so happens —"

"You fancy her. You fancy the fierce woman."

Adam attempted to look affronted. "Of course I don't. Why would you think that? I just want to learn —"

"Your face is going red," Hannah said. "You do fancy her."

"I don't know what you —"

"You bought a clarinet because you fancy her, and you're going to pretend you want to play it."

"I won't be pretending," he protested. "I think it might be . . . interesting, learning to play a musical instrument."

"You haven't a note in your head."

"That's got nothing to do with —"

"I bet you didn't even know what a clarinet was until you started fancying her. I bet you thought it was a flute or something."

"Of course I knew what a clarinet was," he said. "As a matter of fact, I'm familiar with all the woodwind instruments."

"Woodwind instruments," Hannah said triumphantly. "You've been swotting up so you'll sound as if you know about them in case she asks you."

He stopped. "Damn," he said then. "You're good."

"So you do fancy her."

"Yes," he said, replacing his remaining half-egg in its cardboard box. "I do. I'm not sure how it happened, but I find myself quite . . . taken with this woman." He got up and took his mug to the sink. "And, just for the record, she's not a bit fierce."

Hannah stood too, brushing chocolate crumbs from her clothes. "Well, I have to say I think it's terribly romantic, buying a clarinet just to get to know someone. Terribly foolish, of course, and extremely wasteful, but very romantic." She put her mug in the sink. "So when do the lessons begin?"

"Er, here's the thing about that." He ran water. "She hasn't actually agreed to teach me yet. But that's only because I haven't actually asked her."

Hannah stared at him. "You haven't asked her yet?"

"Well, I thought I should get the clarinet first."

"Yes, but what if she says no? What if you have to have some kind of musical qualification or something before she'll take you on?"

Adam looked at her in dismay. "I never thought of that."

"What did you pay for it?"

"Forty-eight pounds. I had to bid a bit." He grinned. "Still cheaper than dinner for two."

Hannah picked up the tea-towel. "But could you not have tried asking her out? It might have been slightly less trouble than buying a clarinet on eBay." She giggled.

"Go on, laugh. For your information, she's pretty shy. I think she'd run a mile if I asked her out just like that."

Hannah looked fondly at him. "Have you ever actually spoken to this woman?"

"Very briefly — I asked her the name of a piece they played one evening, and I think I nearly gave her a heart attack."

"So in fact you don't even know if she's single."

"Well, not exactly —"

"She could be married. She could have half a dozen kids."

232

Adam threw her a pained look. "I've decided to assume otherwise, until I know for sure."

"I see." Hannah dried a mug. "I have to say, though, she's nothing at all like the ones you usually go for."

"I know." He smiled as he lifted the second mug from the water. "Maybe I've been going for the wrong ones."

"Maybe we both have," she said thoughtfully.

Alice gave him new pyjamas, handing them across the table when they'd finished breakfast. Sunday was the only day they had breakfast together now.

"Happy Easter," she said. "It's just pyjamas. You needed a new pair anyway."

His hand trembled slightly as he took the brown-wrapped package. "I got you nothing," he said. "I'm sorry." Other years she'd been given chocolate eggs, Terry's or Toblerone.

"It doesn't matter."

She should tell him to pull himself together. She should be trying to get help for him, urging him to talk to their doctor maybe about his drinking. But the rage was still there, keeping her immobile. The rage had made her buy the pyjamas, knowing she would get nothing in return. Another little portion of guilt for him to carry around.

He'd stopped shaving every day: now it was two or three times a week. He looked worse after he shaved, his chin littered with cuts. No way could he do any dental work with those shaking hands. She'd stopped going into his bedroom — his bedroom now, not theirs any more — apart from once a fortnight when she took the old sheets off his bed and put clean ones on. The room smelt of whiskey, although he was keeping it fairly clean.

"I'm going to eleven mass," she told him.

"Are you?"

She didn't think he'd been to mass since the accident, unless he went during the week when she was out at work.

"I'll go for a walk by the river afterwards," she said. "It's a good day for walking." Sunday mornings they'd often have gone for a walk after mass if the weather was alright.

"That'll be nice," he said. "You'll enjoy that."

"I'm doing lamb chops for dinner," she said. Not the stuffed turkey crown that she usually got at Easter. Chops would do him this year.

"Lovely," he said. "I look forward to that."

Fiona brought a bottle of Glenfiddich for Patrick and a set of bath oils for Leah, and was presented with a string of chunky lilac beads that Leah had bought with Patrick's credit card.

"It's from both of us," she said, as Fiona opened the long grey box. "Happy Easter, Mum."

No hug. They didn't hug each other these days, Patrick noticed.

"Thank you darling," Fiona said, glancing at the beads before snapping the box shut. "They're delightful. And thank you too, Patrick," she added. "It's thoughtful of you both."

234

She was making an effort. Patrick poured her a generous gin, added bitter lemon and a lemon slice. "Cheers," he said, raising his glass. This would be alright. Fiona was getting over her resentment of how he and Leah had got together. Somewhere along the way, she'd got used to the idea of the baby they were having. Maybe she was even beginning to look forward to her first grandchild.

The conversation over the drinks was formal, as he'd expected. They talked about the upcoming budget and the helicopter crash in Donegal, and the changeable weather. Leah asked her mother about the garden, and Fiona talked about kerria and forsythia and pyracantha, and other names that didn't mean a thing to Patrick.

Lunch was chicken, Fiona's meat of choice. Patrick opened a bottle of Sauvignon Blanc from New Zealand that had cost more than thirty euro, and poured a glass for himself and Fiona. They talked about an exhibition in the National Gallery that Fiona had visited on a recent trip to Dublin, and a reiki course Leah was planning to do after the baby arrived. Patrick mentioned an upcoming trip to France, to attend a journalists' convention in Lyon. The main course passed peacefully.

And then, as they were just starting on the crème caramel, Fiona said, "May I ask again if you two have any plans to get married?"

Leah shot Patrick a look — warning? pleading? — before turning to her mother. "It's not something we've talked about."

"I see." Fiona rested her spoon on the side of her plate. "And I take it you're going to continue living here after the baby is born."

"Mum," Leah said quietly.

"We'll find a bigger place when we get the chance," Patrick said quickly. "One thing at a time."

"As I understand it," Fiona said coolly, "you have no property of your own."

"Please Mum," Leah said, "don't ruin this."

"I'm just attempting to establish the facts, darling." Fiona continued to look questioningly at Patrick. "You lived in your parents' house, didn't you, until you moved in with Hannah Robinson?"

"That's true," he said tightly, resisting the impulse to pick up the wine bottle and bring it down on her immaculately coiffed head. "My mother died when I was young, and I lived with my father up to a year and a half ago."

"And then you moved in with Hannah," Fiona said, "and now you've moved in with Leah."

"Mum." Leah's voice held a note of desperation, but her mother didn't even glance in her direction.

"Mrs Bradshaw," Patrick said evenly, "I find your attitude quite offensive, and I suspect it's entirely deliberate."

Fiona smiled. "Oh, don't be silly," she said. "I'm not trying to offend anyone. I'm just concerned about the future upbringing of my grandchild, that's all — and your present circumstances don't seem all that . . . stable to me."

236

Patrick said nothing. A pulse throbbed in his forehead.

Fiona turned to Leah. "Geraldine Robinson put me in a very embarrassing position at bridge last week," she said. "She demanded, in front of everyone, that I name the father of your baby, knowing full well that everyone there knew that Patrick had been with her daughter until recently. Well, you can imagine how that went down, can't you?"

"So you were embarrassed," Patrick said, ignoring Leah's hand on his arm, "and now you're taking it out on us."

Leah stood up abruptly, clumsily. Her face had flushed deeply and her eyes were filled with imminent tears. She turned and left the room.

Patrick watched her go, then forced himself to turn back and meet Fiona's gaze. She was Leah's mother. Like it or not, she was part of Leah's life — and part of his now.

"I'm sorry if you've been put into an awkward position with your friends" — he emphasised the last word slightly, imagining the bridge contingent, delighted to have a bit of a scandal to chew on — "but Leah and I will not be pushed into making any plans simply to spare your blushes. We'll do things in our own time, as we see fit, and I hope you can accept that without causing Leah any more distress."

Fiona held his gaze for what seemed like an awfully long time. Her face was as devoid of expression as ever, and Patrick suddenly wondered if she'd had something done to it to prevent any movement, any alteration of

237

her features that might cause lines to develop. Then she got up and unhooked the strap of her bag from her chair back.

"Thank you for the lunch. I'll see myself out."

She left the room and Patrick made no attempt to follow her. He didn't get up when he heard the raised voices in the hall, he didn't move when the bedroom door was slammed, or when the front door was opened and closed shortly afterwards.

Eventually he poured what remained of the wine into his glass and sipped the tepid liquid unhurriedly while he finished his dessert. Then he got up and began to clear the table.

"And how's the new job going? I wish you'd come out to see us more often."

"I would, Ma, if I could hop on a bus, but you know there's none to Dunmallon, so I have to wait for Adam to take me." Nora shot an apologetic glance at her brother, who glared back. "The job is fine, although I probably won't stay there too long — it's not me, really. I'm trying to decide what my next move should be."

"I hope you're not thinking about going back to America," her mother said quickly. "Daddy and I wouldn't like that at all. Would we?" she demanded, turning to her husband.

"No," he said, through a mouthful of roast potato.

Adam smiled to himself. They probably thought she'd get married again the minute she set foot on American soil.

"You picked up the accent," their father said to Nora.

"I did, didn't I?" Nora helped herself to another spoonful of garden peas. "Ma, this lunch is amazing — I forgot how much I missed your roast lamb."

"Three hours in the oven, a hundred and sixty," her mother said. "Forget twenty minutes to the pound, it'd come out half raw. Three hours, isn't that what I always do?" she asked her husband.

"Three hours," he said, forking up more lamb.

"And Adam, what's your news?" their mother asked. "Any nice young lady?"

"No Ma," Adam said. "I'm between nice young ladies right now. But I'm keeping an eye open."

Every time he met her she asked. He presumed the question was programmed into every woman who gave birth to a son. He debated briefly telling them about the clarinet, but then decided to wait until he'd at least got the lessons set up.

His mother sighed. "I'll never be a grandmother," she said, "with the pair of you. Nora keeps getting divorced, and you're doing nothing at all."

"Ma, you're far too young to be thinking like that," Adam said, trying to calculate his mother's age. Sixty-three, or thereabouts. "There's lots of time."

"There is not lots of time. Everyone your age is married or getting engaged. There'll be nobody left to choose from if you wait much longer."

"True . . . I'll set my mind to it so. Would I put an ad in the paper, d'you think?"

As his mother sighed exasperatedly, Adam wondered what Vivienne's home was like. He imagined a small cottage — a single woman's house, he thought firmly — filled with things made of china, and flowers in vases. Rugs in muted colours on the floors, and maybe a wall hanging of birds that she'd made herself. A small room where she gave her lessons, her clarinet on a polished wooden table next to a music stand. Narrow attic stairs to her bedroom, the bed covered with a white crocheted spread.

"How's Hannah?" his mother asked.

"She's doing OK," he said, relieved at the change of subject. "Kept busy with the shop, which is great."

"We must take a trip up to see it." She turned to her husband. "Mustn't we?"

"Oh we must, some time soon."

A dreadful squawking erupted just then outside the back door, causing them to abandon the roast lamb. They rushed out to find the hysterical chickens being chased joyfully around the yard by Kirby, who'd somehow managed to wriggle free from his rope.

He was reattached more firmly to the yard gate, well out of reach of the fowl, who soon recovered from their fright and began pecking the ground again.

"He's full of energy," their father said, regarding the dog sternly.

"I might take him for a bit of a walk after lunch," Adam replied. "Tire him out."

They went back inside and followed the lamb with tea and fruit cake, and then their father disappeared to watch the second half of the hurling, and Nora and her

240

mother tackled the washing-up while Adam escaped with his dog, and strolled along country roads for an hour.

"God, nothing changes there," Nora said on the way home, Adam negotiating the car between the potholes that lined the laneway to their parents' house.

"No, but it suits them." He longed suddenly for that life, the comfortable coexistence with the person you chose, and who chose you.

Nora yawned. The boredom of it though. Miles from anywhere, nothing going on. "I'd slit my wrists. You can have my cake," she added. "I'm watching my fabulous figure." Ma never let anyone leave without a generous slab of fruit cake.

Adam hadn't mentioned the clarinet to Nora. He could imagine her reaction. It was a daft thing to do — he knew exactly how daft it was. But there was the hope within him that this daft action, this illogical plan of his would lead him to where he wanted to be.

Next Saturday night he'd approach Vivienne. His clarinet should have arrived by then and everything would be in place. He'd intercept her on her way to the back door and ask if he might please have a word. He would make every effort not to sound like a crazed stalker.

She couldn't possibly turn him down. He was only looking for music lessons. Where was the harm in that?

May

Alice pulled in three doors up on the other side of the street. There was no sign of the two little boys from the last day, but the flowers were still there, withered now but still hanging by their white ribbon from the gatepost of number thirty-seven. And the curtains were still closed in the upstairs room.

There was no car directly outside the house, but maybe the father was gone to work in it, or the mother. Would they be back at work, three weeks after their child had been buried?

Alice knew little about them. The accident wasn't discussed in the shoe shop. All Alice knew was that Hannah used to babysit the two sisters when they were young, the mother and the aunt, and the aunt worked for Hannah now.

She wondered were Jason's parents married, or had they got around to that. She guessed they hadn't been married when Jason had come along four years earlier. The sister saying the poem on the altar had looked in her teens still, and the mother couldn't be much older. She might have been still at school when she'd found herself expecting.

Two girls in blue school uniforms walked past the car, one pressing the keys of a mobile phone, both heads bent over it. A small dog pattered across the road in front of Alice, sniffing at something on the edge of the far path, lifting a leg briefly against a streetlight and then trotting away rapidly.

A car drove past, coming up behind her unnoticed, making her start. Someone cycled by, whistling. It began to drizzle, settling silently on the windscreen. A man came out of the house beside number thirty-seven and walked past it buttoning his coat, not glancing at the flowers as far as Alice could see.

She sat for fifty minutes, a magazine open on her lap in case anyone looked at her, in case anyone approached her to know what she was doing there, but nobody did. The dark green front door of number thirty-seven remained closed. Nobody came or went from the house. She thought she saw a movement once, in the uncurtained upstairs window, but it might have been her imagination, or a trick of the light.

At twenty to four she started the car and drove back into town.

He passed the yellow-fronted shop on the opposite side of the street. He walked half a block and then he turned back, crossing the road when he saw a gap in the traffic. He pushed the shop door open and walked in.

The woman behind the counter wasn't Hannah. It threw him for a second, he hadn't been expecting that.

"Hi," she said, smiling.

She was younger, hardly out of her teens. Her skin was pale, her hair tied back. She wore the same apron he'd seen on Hannah, with wide white and navy stripes overlaid with a yellow smiling sun. Her lipstick was too light pink against her pale face. Her eyes were washed-out green.

"Hi there," he said, glancing at the displays under the counter. "I'll take a couple of cupcakes — you can choose."

"No preferences?" she asked. "With or without nuts? Chocolate chip?"

"Not fussed," he said. "They're all good."

"That's true." She selected a peanut butter and a rum and raisin and put them into a small box.

"Hannah not around today?" he asked, as he handed her a fiver.

"She's gone out for a bit — she'll be back at noon."

He remembered, then, her saying that she'd taken on someone part time. "Tell her Scottish John was in, would you? Just to say hello. Sorry I missed her."

"I will. Thanks now."

"See you."

At the woodwork store he handed over the two cupcakes, and was thanked and scolded in equal measure by Patsy, who was trying, as ever, to lose weight. "You're the devil, John Wyatt, you know that?"

Hannah hadn't been back to Vintage for the past two Saturdays. She'd seemed pleased to see him the last time — she'd made a point of letting him know that she and her companion, whose name John had forgotten, were just friends. But she hadn't been back. Wouldn't she have shown up again if she'd been at all interested?

She might come this weekend, if the part-time girl remembered to pass on his message. If she thought he still wanted to keep up the contact, she just might be there.

The dark brown UPS truck stopped outside the house and Adam watched a man in a brown uniform get out, slide open a side door and lift out a package that didn't look long enough to house a clarinet. He thought maybe it wasn't for him, it was a delivery for a different house, but then the man turned in the driveway and walked up the path.

Adam waited until the doorbell rang. He walked downstairs and opened the front door. "Morning."

"How do." The man looked at the label on the brown package. "Adam O'Connor?"

"That's me." The man handed him the clipboard and he signed along the dotted line. "Thanks."

He brought the package into the sitting room, where Kirby was dozing. "Look what I got," he said, tearing off the plain brown paper to reveal a black case. He opened it and saw that it was lined with dark blue velvet, and that the clarinet was in three silver pieces inside. When he finally figured out how they slotted together he put the mouthpiece between his lips and blew.

A low sound squawked out, like the honk of a seal. Kirby pricked his ears.

Adam pressed a key and blew again, more forcefully, and this time he produced a noise altogether more high-pitched, but equally tuneless.

Kirby lifted his head and regarded Adam, ears still cocked.

Adam moved jerkily along the keys, pressing and blowing, honking and squeaking in equal measure. Midway through this performance, Kirby shuffled to his feet and padded to the sitting-room door. He sat looking pointedly at it.

In less than a minute Adam was completely out of breath. He lowered the clarinet and waited for the feeling of light-headedness to pass. "It's OK," he told Kirby, "I won't be doing any more of that for a while."

He had a long way to go. Maybe he should have started with a tin whistle.

"I'm worried about Alice," Geraldine said, folding her glasses.

Stephen entered *biscuit* using a triple-word square and his total shot up to 215. "You're worried? Why?"

"She's not herself." Geraldine slid the glasses into their soft tartan case. "She seems to have no interest in the shop any more. Last week we made less than five hundred — I don't ever remember a week that bad — and it didn't seem to knock a feather out of her."

Stephen tried to find a word that contained L, X and two As, and preferably ended in T. "Don't forget, we are in a recession. All businesses are suffering."

Geraldine unplugged the television. "It's not that, though — this is different. I'm really wondering if there's some kind of boycott going on."

Stephen gave up and tagged AXL onto the E of *fable*, which only earned him eleven points. "Hardly a boycott. Surely everyone appreciates that the accident wasn't Alice's fault — what would be the point in taking it out on her?"

Geraldine bundled the newspaper sections on the coffee-table into a neat pile. "You'd be surprised. I'd swear Sheila Barrett crossed the street when she spotted me yesterday — she never misses the new stock, and there hasn't been a sign of her lately." She straightened the rug in front of the fire with her foot. "And another thing — Alice has started disappearing in the middle of the day."

"Disappearing?"

"Well, she doesn't say where she's going, just that she has things to do, very vague. She was gone for over two hours yesterday. Normally she just does the weekly run to the cash-and-carry, or takes half an hour around the town now and again."

"She's got a lot on her mind," Stephen said, eyeing the *excel* his virtual opponent, Stanley, had just entered.

"She certainly has — half the time she doesn't seem to hear me when I talk to her." Geraldine walked to the door with her newspaper bundle. "Will I make tea for you?"

"I might be another while," Stephen said, determined not to let Stanley, described only as adept, beat him. "Have your own, and I'll be up when I finish this."

250

In the kitchen Geraldine poured water into the kettle and put a teabag into her cup. No point in a pot if it was only her. She took one ginger nut from the pack and left the rest in the press.

If you need to cut my hours that's OK, she'd said to Alice. *Just while things are slow.* She and Stephen would manage fine — if she had no income at all, they'd manage on what he made. But Alice had shaken her head and said, *Ah no, I wouldn't do that.*

She must be losing money now, must be out of pocket. Ridiculous for Geraldine to be there all the time, when some days only half a dozen customers came in and others they didn't sell a single pair of shoes.

How's Tom doing? she'd asked, a couple of times since the accident, and Alice had said, *He's fine* or *Bearing up* in the kind of tight voice that had kept Geraldine from saying any more.

Come to lunch on Sunday, she'd suggested more than once, *you and Tom. I'm doing a nice bit of pork.* But Alice had shaken her head and said, *Thanks Geraldine, but I think we won't*, and Geraldine had eventually given up.

The kettle boiled and she made tea and brought it upstairs with her biscuit. Just as well she had William Trevor to take her mind off things.

"That's it — she's getting up," Hannah said. "Move."

Adam slipped off his stool and threaded his way swiftly through the tables of drinkers. He reached the back door as Vivienne approached, clarinet clutched to her chest. Tonight she wore a long black dress with sleeves to her elbows, and black suede ankle boots.

It was now or never. "Excuse me," Adam said, smiling.

At least, he hoped it was coming out as a smile.

Vivienne stopped, the colour flooding into her cheeks. No sign of recognition — she might not remember him approaching her before. Adam stood between her and the door. There was nowhere for her to go — unless she bolted back the way she'd come.

"Sorry to bother you," he said, "but I wanted to say I really admire your clarinet playing."

She blinked and pushed her glasses up her nose, the tiniest of smiles flitting for an instant across her flushed face. "Thanks," she said quickly, her eyes darting to the door behind him.

"I believe," he hurried on, "that you give lessons, and as I've recently come into possession of a clarinet, I was wondering if you would —"

"No," she said then, shaking her head rapidly. "Sorry." Pushing her glasses up again, looking beyond him to her escape route. "I don't."

"Pardon?" She couldn't be turning him down out of hand. "But I was told that you give music lessons, and I would really love —"

"I don't teach adults," she said. "Children, I just teach children." Her voice was low, and he strained to hear it. She looked more pointedly at the blue door. The blush was receding, leaving her face blotchy. She was blinking rapidly behind her round glasses.

252

Children. The one thing he hadn't anticipated, that at thirty-one he'd be too old. It was a blow, but Adam held his ground. "Well, would you consider making an exception?" he asked. "I don't know any other clarinet teacher, you see, and I'd really like to learn. And I promise I'm as ignorant as any child."

But she shook her head again. "Just children," she repeated. "I'm sorry." She shifted the position of her clarinet slightly and took a step towards the door.

"Please," Adam said, nothing left to lose. "I've just bought it, you see, and if you don't teach me it'll sit in my house gathering dust, and nobody will ever get to play it. It'll be a terrible waste of a clarinet. You don't want that, do you?"

She was clearly uncomfortable. She opened her mouth and closed it again. She'd run out of ways to tell him no. He could feel her anxiety, her whole body tense with it, but his determination drove him on. Out of the corner of his eye he spotted the keyboard player approaching.

He decided to make one last attempt. "How about you just try me out for two or three lessons, and if you're not happy then, you can send me on my way and I'll never bother you again? Would you consider that? Please? Just a few lessons?"

She sighed then, a frown creasing the skin above the bridge of her glasses. "Half eight on a Thursday," she said, her eyes fixed on the blue door.

"Sorry?" Her sudden surrender caught him unawares.

"Half eight on a Thursday," she repeated, in precisely the same resigned tone.

253

"OK. Great." Adam stepped aside at last and pushed the door open for her. "Where do I go?"

She moved towards the blue door, close enough for him to smell the lemony scent that rose from her tightly bunched hair. "Ten Fortfield Avenue."

"And your name?" he asked, wanting to hear her say it.

"Vivienne O'Toole." Over her shoulder as she disappeared.

The keyboard player arrived and Adam held the door open, struggling to remember his surname — was it O'Toole too?

"Thanks, mate." Nodding at Adam but not recognising him, by the look of it. No curiosity evident, no suspicion as to what Adam might have been saying to Vivienne. Surely a husband or partner would want to know.

"Great gig tonight," Adam told him, and the man thanked him again as he walked through the blue doorway.

She hadn't asked Adam's name. She didn't want to teach him; he'd bullied her into it. She was more comfortable, probably, in the uncritical presence of children. Chances were, she was dreading next Thursday already.

But she'd agreed, and in five days Adam was going to see her house and be in her company for at least an hour. He was going to be her very first adult pupil.

And he was finally going to discover whether she was single or not.

254

Ten Fortfield Avenue. Vivienne O'Toole. Baby steps, he thought, still hardly understanding what drove him on, but knowing he wanted to persevere. Baby steps, and lots of patience.

As he walked back to the bar he noticed that the Scotsman was talking to Hannah.

"Well," she said, as they walked home later.

"Well yourself," Adam said. "You first."

Hannah smiled. "I'm meeting him for coffee on Wednesday morning. I decided I'm tired of being a hermit."

"Good for you." They turned onto the bridge.

"And you?"

Adam ran his hand along the smooth, cold surface of the metal rail. "Get this — she teaches children, not adults."

"Oh." She threw him a sympathetic look. "Oh Adam, that's too bad — and after buying the clarinet as well. You'll just have to find another teacher."

"Actually I won't — she's agreed to take me on. She tried her best to turn me down, but I nagged a bit."

Hannah laughed. "Are you serious? You're going to a children's music teacher?"

"I am."

"You do realise that she'll probably have you playing 'Baa Baa Black Sheep'?"

Adam regarded her sternly. "We may well begin with that, yes. But I'm confident that I'll progress to more adult material in due course."

Hannah tucked her arm into his. "Of course you will. You'll be giving recitals by Christmas."

"Very funny." They turned off the bridge. "But now that you mention it, maybe I could do a bit of busking."

"Why not? You could be like that fellow in the KitKat ad — remember? Everyone throws money at him the minute he stops playing. You could make a fortune."

"Ha ha." After a pause, he added, "What was the keyboard player's surname, can you remember?"

"Who? Oh, the taxi driver. Wally something. What about him?"

"Well, the night we met him he said he was driving her home."

"Did he? I don't remember."

"So they might be together."

"Mmm . . . Or he might just be doing her a favour. Maybe they live near each other."

"She's O'Toole, but I can't remember what his surname is."

"Tell you what," she said, "until we know for sure, let's not dwell on it. Let's plan your career as a busker instead."

They walked on, both in high good humour. Both hopeful of happy outcomes.

He was buried in a family plot, the granite headstone already covered with O'Brien names dating back to 1939. Alice hadn't known where to look, had walked along the gravel paths searching for freshly dug graves. In the end Jason's was easily identifiable by the wreath spelling his name in red flowers that she remembered seeing in the church on top of his white coffin.

It lay now on the mounded earth, flanked by two fat creamy white candles that burnt in glass jars. A wooden cross was stuck into the ground just in front of the headstone, with a small photo in an oval brass frame attached to the top, and a little metal plaque underneath that read simply *Jason O'Brien 2005–2009*.

Alice laid her flowers next to the red wreath, no card attached. She said an Our Father and a Hail Mary and a Glory Be, her eyes on the little photo. His smile was wide. His teeth were tiny and perfect. He had a chubby, baby face. She said an Act of Contrition, her lips moving silently.

She went home then and put on the dinner for Tom, who'd fallen asleep in front of the fire again.

"So," Nora said after they'd ordered, after their menus had been replaced with her martini and Leah's tonic water. "How are things?"

The puffiness she'd seen in Leah's face the last time they'd met was more pronounced, the earlier suggestion of a double chin now a distinct reality. Leah was still attractive — or rather the echo of her attractiveness was still there in the dark brown eyes, the regular nose, the full lips. But the overall effect was blurred now, as if her original elfin prettiness had been diluted. Little wonder that Patrick's thoughts were straying.

Leah sipped her tonic water. "Just wish it was over at this stage. I am so sick of being bloody pregnant."

"How long more?" The martini was ice cold and delicious. Nora pulled one of the olives from its cocktail stick with her teeth.

"Four weeks, about. Seems like for ever."

Nora smiled. "Poor you. Soon be over."

Leah grimaced. "Yeah — and then I'll be up to my neck in Pampers while Patrick swans out to work every day."

"Ah, he'll help though, when he's around." But Nora couldn't see Patrick holding a baby with any degree of comfort, let alone changing a nappy.

Leah nodded glumly. "Hope so. This baby . . ." she hesitated ". . . well, it wasn't exactly his idea. I mean," she added hastily, "he's thrilled, of course, but . . ."

The baby hadn't exactly been Patrick's idea: what a surprise. "He'll rise to the challenge," Nora said. "Just wait and see. As soon as he sets eyes on it."

"Of course he will." Leah looked far from convinced. "Anyway," she said, shifting her position, adjusting her weight on the chair, "enough about me. How's the job going? Patrick tells me you're settling in well."

A new note of horribly false brightness in her voice — but as far as Nora could tell, nothing more. No hint of suspicion, no sign of jealousy.

They hadn't met since Nora had begun working for Patrick, more than a month ago now. The occasional text had been exchanged, each mentioning vaguely a future lunch date, but until the previous evening nothing had been arranged. And then, out of the blue, a

258

text from Leah: *Lunch 2moro? My treat.* And here they were.

"The job is fine," Nora said. She hadn't missed Leah's look when she'd walked in, the envious glance her lilac wool top, silver grey pencil skirt and black stilettos had earned. "Nothing I can't handle."

She wouldn't mention Patrick directly. She was still feeling her way towards the reason for today's lunch. "The people are nice. A few of us went out for a drink the other night."

She'd spent the first twenty minutes trying to escape from Evan in Accounts who clearly fancied his chances. In the end she'd gone to the toilet and joined another group when she'd got back, where the talk was of babies and teething and weaning. She'd excused herself after ten minutes, pleading stomach cramps. Back at the flat she'd watched an episode of *Law & Order* she'd seen six months ago in the States.

"It's interesting, working for a newspaper. I haven't done it before."

"And you'll stay in Clongarvin?" Leah looked up as the waiter put her plain pasta in front of her.

"For the moment," Nora replied, spearing a cube of feta from her Greek salad. "I'll have another of these," she told the waiter, holding up her martini glass. "I'll do the drinks bill," she said to Leah, "since you're not having any."

"Don't be silly," Leah said. "You can pay next time. We mustn't let it go so long before we do it again."

"Absolutely not," Nora replied.

259

Leah envied her: that much was obvious. She probably wasn't entirely happy still about Patrick being in close proximity with Nora, whose looks and figure were so much more attractive than her own right now. But as far as Nora could see, Leah's only motive for inviting her out to lunch today was because she needed someone to talk to — or possibly, Leah being Leah, she might have decided that by keeping Nora close it would make it more difficult for anything to happen between her and Patrick.

She had no idea, none at all, that she was too late. Shame, really.

Why don't you lock the door? he'd said, as soon as she'd walked in.

Why don't I leave it open? she'd replied.

Not surprised, not in the least, by his suggestion. It was what she'd known would happen, very soon after she'd started to work for him. Sooner even, his eyes lingering on her crossed thighs, on the V of her top, at the interview. His hand holding hers a second too long as he'd thanked her for coming, as he'd promised to be in touch. She'd thought then, *You're up for it.* They were always so obvious.

Leave it open then, he'd said. Watching her as she'd crossed the room that smelt of the drinks he'd had at his three-hour lunch. Better sober up before he went home to Leah. Nora hadn't minded that he was tipsy, it usually added to the fun. Got rid of the inhibitions.

Come in for a minute, he'd said, as he'd passed her desk on his way back, walking none too steadily, and she'd known.

260

She'd made her way unhurriedly around the desk to where he was slouched in his big leather chair. She'd swivelled the chair around to face her.

"Are you ready for this?" she'd asked softly.

"Take your knickers off," he'd replied thickly.

She'd stood in front of him and opened the buttons of her blouse one by one, taking her time. She'd reached behind and unhooked her bra. She'd released her breasts from their cups, all the time looking at his face. She'd hoicked up her skirt and eased her underpants slowly over her hips. She'd let them drop to the floor, and stepped out of them.

"Now me," he'd said, and she'd undone the button of his trousers and slid down the zip and reached inside before straddling him in her lace-topped stockings, in her black stilettos, in her bunched-up skirt and open blouse.

No need to talk, both of them knowing the rules. His mouth had found her nipple, she'd guided him into her with his office door unlocked, anyone liable to knock and walk in without waiting for a response, as she'd seen people do plenty of times, as she did herself all the time. His huge hands on her bare buttocks, her hands in his hair, watching people passing in the street below.

Moving against each other, the leather chair creaking in rhythm, anyone liable to walk in, her excitement mounting as he gripped her buttocks, as she bent her head and found his mouth and took his tongue between her teeth, as he moaned, as she lifted her head again, drawing breath sharply, and arched against him —

Yes, much too late for Leah to be taking her out to lunch, to be buying her a Greek salad and two martinis.

Fiona Bradshaw took particular care with her preparations. She stroked on liquid eyeliner, resting her elbow on the dressing-table to keep her hand steady. She blended cream shadow carefully and dotted concealer under her eyes. She brushed on powder and blotted two coats of lipstick with a tissue.

She dressed in linen, a suit of duck-egg blue that Leah said was the perfect shade for her colouring. She added pearls at her throat and in her ears. She replaced her everyday gold watch with the white gold one that had a diamond in place of the number twelve. She slipped her feet into new dove grey suede shoes, sprayed scent at her wrists, neck and cleavage.

Imagine her disappointment then, when she walked into Frances Mitchell's sitting room looking as good as she could possibly look, and saw Frances' daughter Cathy sitting with Geraldine Robinson's usual partner.

A wasted effort. Geraldine was too embarrassed, probably, to face her after the showdown two weeks before. No bridge game last week because of Easter, plenty of time for Fiona to plan her outfit — and all for nothing.

No mention was made, during the game or over the coffee and cakes afterwards, of Leah's pregnancy. Nobody asked Fiona how her daughter was doing; nobody wanted to know what baby names were being considered. Nobody at all, thanks to Geraldine

262

Robinson, was wondering how Fiona felt about becoming a grandmother for the first time.

She helped herself to a sliver of Frances' chocolate rum cake, smiling at Aoife's account of her niece's honeymoon in Mauritius, admiring the bracelet Maureen's husband had given her for her birthday. Accepting the compliments on her own appearance graciously. Showing no sign at all of her resentment, giving no indication that she'd even noticed their lack of curiosity.

Keeping up appearances. Which, of course, was what it was all about.

"She hasn't gone back to work yet," Una said. "Dave is doing a few bits and pieces, but Claire's still not ready. And with the month's mind coming up next week, that'll bring her right back down again."

Hannah slipped off her plastic gloves. "They're keeping her job open?"

"For the moment, yeah, but for how long? You couldn't blame them if they gave it away — they can't wait forever."

Hannah took her phone from the shelf behind the counter and slotted it into its pocket in her bag. "Maybe when the month's mind is behind her . . ."

"Maybe." Una watched as Hannah slung the bag onto her shoulder. "So what have you to do this morning?"

"I'm meeting someone for coffee," Hannah said feeling, to her great surprise, a rising warmth in her face. "Just a friend," she added, ducking her head and rummaging in her bag.

"The friend who called in here one day?" Una asked, smiling. "The nice man from Scotland who was really disappointed when you weren't here?"

Hannah laughed. "Mind your own business. See you later."

The café was dotted with people. John sat at a table by the far wall reading the *Irish Times*, a blue mug in front of him.

"Hello," she said. Her stomach was fluttering ridiculously. "I hope I'm not late."

For her first date with Patrick they'd gone to the theatre. They'd watched *The Faith Healer*, he'd taken her hand and tucked it around his arm as they reclaimed their seats after the interval, and the tips of her fingers had tingled with pins and needles for the last twenty minutes. She'd rested her calf against his and hoped to God her breath wouldn't be stale by the end of the evening. The following morning, kneading dough in Finnegan's bakery, she couldn't remember how the play had ended.

She ordered cappuccino and John got a top-up for his tea. He wore a faded blue sweatshirt that looked very soft. His nails were bitten, his fingers slender for a man. Musician's fingers, Hannah thought, seeing him sitting with the other band members, playing his saxophone.

He told her he'd come to Ireland after walking away from his marriage. He spoke of his wife without bitterness, he mentioned a divorce pending. He told her about a daughter studying law in Edinburgh University.

He asked her about the cupcake shop, how it had started, if she'd always been interested in baking. He moved his hands as he talked. He smiled a lot. His teeth were even, and cream-coloured.

Hannah spoke briefly of Patrick, but didn't explain how they'd broken up, made no mention of Leah. She talked about Adam moving in with her to help with the bills after Patrick had left, and his twin sister Nora, home from America after her second divorce.

She told him about Kirby the black Labrador who shed hairs everywhere. She described the awful armchair Adam had brought home from the charity shop to protect Hannah's red couch from the black hairs.

She spoke of her dentist father, and her mother working in the shoe shop. She drank a second cappuccino. He ordered a black coffee. And by the time she thought to check her watch, her two hours off had ended twelve minutes earlier.

Number Ten Fortfield Avenue wasn't in the least what Adam had been expecting. Instead of a cosy cottage for one he found a two-storey red-brick semi attached to its identical opposite number in an area of Clongarvin he knew only slightly, never having had much occasion to visit it.

Fortfield Avenue was one of several similar roads in the neighbourhood — Fortfield Park, Fortfield Drive — all lined with red-brick houses, most of them semi-detached, all two-storey.

Vivienne's house looked big for a woman on her own. Adam locked his car and slipped the keys into his pocket, gripping the clarinet case firmly. Here we go, he told himself. Time to find out, once and for all, if there's a man in her life. He walked up the short paved path, noting the dark green six-year-old Corolla parked on the gravel beside it, and pressed the white button on the uPVC door frame.

A loud, harsh buzz sounded from within, causing a little brown bird perched on a nearby cable to flutter away. When nothing further happened for almost a minute, Adam began to wonder if he had the right house. She had said number ten, hadn't she? He lifted his hand to press the bell again, but lowered it when he heard someone approaching. The door was opened, not by a man at all.

"Yes?"

Adam offered his most charming smile. "Good evening," he said. "I've come for a music lesson."

"Yes," the woman repeated. Unmoving. Unsmiling. A pair of what looked like gardening gloves in the hand that hung by her side.

"With Vivienne," Adam added. Maybe the house was full of music teachers. Maybe he'd come to the smallest music school in Ireland.

"You know she only takes children," the woman said. "Up to twelve. No adults."

266

"Right." Adam shifted his clarinet. "She did mention that, yes, but after some discussion she agreed to try me out . . . to give me a few lessons," he amended hastily.

"Yes."

Mouth set in a thin, disapproving line. Clearly not impressed with Vivienne's first grown-up pupil. Adam put her somewhere in her late fifties or sixties, with short, silvering hair pulled off her face with what looked like a child's hairband. Large fading freckles were scattered across her face. "You'd better come in then."

She stood back not quite far enough, forcing Adam to squeeze past her, holding the clarinet case awkwardly above his head to avoid a collision. The hallway was narrow and dimly lit, and smelt of turnip.

"Wait in there," the woman ordered, and Adam stepped into a room that contained a green tweed couch covered with clear plastic and two matching armchairs similarly protected. A portable television was perched on a high stool in the corner, to the left of the small fireplace in front of which dried plants were arranged in a tall glass vase.

As the woman disappeared Adam became conscious of piano music coming from somewhere in the house, a classical piece that meant nothing to him. He wondered again if the house contained more than one music teacher.

He sat in one of the green tweed armchairs, plastic crackling loudly as it accepted his weight, and let the distant notes wash over him as he checked out his surroundings. The carpet was biscuit-coloured with maroon swivels, the walls were papered with embossed cream. A painting of men pulling a curragh up onto a beach hung over the fireplace. Adam spotted photos in frames on the mantelpiece. He crackled to his feet and walked across to study them.

There was Vivienne, maybe ten years old, standing solemnly by a five-bar gate, hair twisted into two thick plaits that hung at either side of her bespeckled face. Grey jumper, plaid skirt that stopped above her skinny knees, long white socks, black-laced shoes. A book tucked under one arm. A boy of about the same age was sitting on top of the gate, grinning at the camera in his grey trousers and grey jumper, feet tucked behind the third bar.

And there Vivienne was again, early twenties he guessed, mortar board topping her tied-back hair, sitting formally in blouse and skirt, hands resting in her lap, one holding a rolled-up piece of paper. No glasses this time, her blue-grey eyes looking somewhere to the right of the camera, the smallest hint of a smile on her unpainted lips.

As he moved to the next photo — a black-and-white family group — he heard footsteps in the hall. He turned just in time to see a boy of about twelve passing the doorway, a booklet of some sort under his arm. The front door opened and closed, and then Vivienne appeared, two red spots in her cheeks. "This way," she said, and promptly disappeared.

Adam grabbed his clarinet case and followed her into the hall, in time to see her vanish through a doorway further down. The second room was smaller than the first, and held only a piano with a long stool beneath, a small folding table, a wooden kitchen chair and a music stand.

"There's a cat on the piano," Adam said, standing in the doorway.

An enormous marmalade cat was sprawled along the top, staring fixedly at Adam with its yellow-green eyes. As he watched, it gave a languid flick to the tip of the tail that dangled down to one side.

Vivienne was riffling through a bundle of papers on the table, her back to the door. "He likes music," she murmured, without turning around. "But if you'd rather . . ."

"No, no," Adam answered. "It can — I mean, he can stay. I don't mind."

Cats did nothing for him; he felt no affinity with them whatsoever. Give him a dog any day. On the other hand he had no serious objections, as long as they kept a reasonable distance from him. He hoped fervently that the current one would respect his boundaries.

That unblinking stare was unnerving though. Adam shifted his attention to the window next to the piano, and saw the woman who'd shown him in. She was kneeling on a green pad beside a flowerbed, a pale blue basin on the ground next to her, a supermarket plastic bag covering her hair. The gardening gloves were back on her hands.

"Is that your mother?" Adam asked. "In the garden."

"Yes," Vivienne replied shortly. She wore a dark grey cardigan over a black top and black trousers. Her hair was pinned up tightly on the back of her head.

She lived with her mother. No sign yet of anyone else. She wasn't wearing a ring. Adam's hopes rose a notch.

"Sit down," she said softly, still not looking in his direction. She added something under her breath that he didn't catch.

"Pardon?"

"Eighteen," Vivienne repeated, selecting another sheet and scanning it. "Euro. For the lesson. Per lesson."

"Oh." Adam hadn't given a thought to the cost. Eighteen euro seemed reasonable to him; he must be getting the child's rate. "That's fine. Should I take the stool or the chair?"

His voice sounded too loud. The room smelt faintly of mints, with a musty undertone that he guessed was coming from the cat.

Vivienne lifted her head then and regarded him, her cheeks deeply flushed now. "Chair," she said, the faintest suggestion of surprise in her voice. "The stool is for the piano."

"Oh . . . right. Of course. Silly me."

He crossed the room and took his seat, feeling the cat's stare following him all the way. Outside the window the woman got awkwardly to her feet, crossed the lawn with her basin and upended it into a round green container. On the way back to the flowerbed she glared into the room, and Adam hastily shifted his gaze.

Vivienne placed a sheet of music on the stand. Adam read "Mary Had A Little Lamb", and imagined what Hannah would say.

270

"Jacket," Vivienne murmured, pulling the long stool out from under the piano and sitting on it. She was about three feet diagonally across from Adam, with the music stand between them. "You need to take your jacket off."

"Right." He placed the clarinet case on the floor, shrugged off his leather jacket and hung it over the back of the chair. "I've a lot to learn." He smiled, rolling up his shirt sleeves.

Vivienne made no response.

"I heard someone playing the piano," Adam said, just to put something into the silence, "while I was waiting." He picked up the clarinet case and opened it.

Vivienne reached an arm across and turned over the front page of the sheet music.

"Was that you?" he asked, determined to have some kind of conversation as he slotted the pieces of his instrument together. "Were you playing the piano earlier?"

"No," she murmured, her eyes on his hands. "That was a pupil."

"Oh? You teach piano too?"

"I *only* teach piano," she said, the colour rising in her face again.

"You only teach piano?" Adam stared at her. "But you're teaching me the clarinet."

She lifted her eyes and met his. "I said no," she reminded him, her voice holding a hint of impatience now. "I tried to say no. You kept asking." She was clearly ill at ease, her hands pressed now between her knees, her shoulders hunched.

"Sorry," Adam said. "It's just that, er, I've always wanted to play the clarinet, and I assumed, since you played it . . ."

She only taught piano. She only taught piano to children. He tried to feel remorseful — he'd badgered her into it, he hadn't allowed her to refuse him — but his delight at being so close to her, at having her all to himself, didn't allow for remorse.

"Sorry," he repeated. "I'll behave, I promise. I'll be a model student."

She didn't smile, but her expression relaxed slightly as she gave him a tiny nod before turning to look at the sheet music again. He wondered how many lessons it would take for her to be at ease in his company.

"We'll begin with the scales," she said, "and move on to this simple tune" — indicating the opened booklet — "which you can practise at home for the next time."

The next time. She was almost close enough for him to reach out and touch her face, to take off her glasses and unpin her hair. He smelt mints again, and the musty animal scent. Close up, he realised that her face was covered with pale freckles that blended into one another.

"What's the cat's name?"

"Pumpkin," Vivienne answered, looking pointedly at the sheet music. "So we'll start with the positioning of your fingers."

"Mine's Adam," he told her, as he raised the clarinet. "My name, I mean. I don't think I mentioned it before."

272

Another tiny nod. Clearly, the name of her only adult pupil wasn't of great interest to Vivienne O'Toole.

"That month's mind is on Sunday," Alice said. "I'm going to go."

She hadn't mentioned the funeral to him. Of course he'd have known it was happening, but she'd slipped out of the house that morning and said nothing. She'd walked to the church, still afraid to get behind the wheel of a car, any car, and Geraldine had ended up driving her home, such a state she'd been in.

Tom had been nowhere in sight when they'd reached the house, so Alice guessed he'd fled upstairs when he'd spotted Geraldine's car. No comment had been made about her red eyes at the dinner table later that evening, which she'd been glad about.

But now she was annoyed at his lack of involvement. How could he just detach himself when he'd been the cause of it all? "I think you should go," Alice said. "It would be the right thing to do, to go to the month's mind."

He went out walking the odd evening, when it was dark enough to pass unnoticed on the street. Alice would smell the alcohol when he got back. He'd choose pubs they'd never visited probably, in parts of Clongarvin where they knew nobody. She wondered if he ever walked in the vicinity of Springwood Gardens, ever called into a pub that the mother or father might have visited.

He made no response now, no comment about attending the month's mind, and Alice felt her anger

273

rising. "You can't avoid people forever," she said sharply. "You can't just stop everything because of what happened."

Tom put his knife and fork down on his plate. "I can't go to that month's mind," he said. "I just can't. You can't expect me to."

"You have to face up to things," Alice persisted. "You have to move on, like I'm trying to do."

"How can I move on," he said, "when I don't know if I'm going to jail or not? You're expecting too much of me."

"Well, I know one thing," she said, the irritation scratching inside her. "Drink isn't going to help. Drink is what caused all this."

He pushed his chair back abruptly and walked towards the door.

"Well, finish your dinner anyway," Alice said. A sausage and a half, and two bits of white pudding, still lay on his plate. "You can eat your dinner without anyone seeing you."

He left the room without answering and she listened to his steps on the stairs. She laid her cutlery down and put her head into her hands. After a while she took the two plates and scraped the food into the bin.

At nine o'clock precisely, as Adam was still trying to grasp the concept of breathing from his abdomen — how was that possible, when your breath went in and out of your lungs? — the door was pushed open and Vivienne's mother, whom Adam hadn't noticed leaving the garden, walked in with a small tray that held a glass of milk and a plate of biscuits.

"Break," Vivienne said, taking the tray. No attempt at introductions was made. The older woman didn't look in his direction.

Adam got to his feet and put out his hand as the woman turned to go. "Adam O'Connor," he said clearly. "Delighted to meet you, Mrs O'Toole."

For a second he thought she was going to ignore him and keep going, but after the briefest of pauses she offered him her hand. "We're not used to catering for adults," she said flatly. "I only have Jammie Dodgers."

"They'll do fine," Adam assured her. "I wasn't expecting anything at all."

She looked scandalised. "We always do a break," she told him. "The children find the hour too long."

"I can understand that," Adam said gravely. "Thanks very much."

She left the room without another word. Adam turned back to Vivienne, who had set the tray on the window-sill. She held the glass of milk out to him. He took it, and accepted a Jammie Dodger when it was offered. "Thanks."

He never drank milk on its own — it affected his sinuses — but he suspected a refusal would cause more discomfiture. He wondered if he could find a way to give it to the cat, who was watching the proceedings intently from above.

"Have you been teaching long?" Vivienne hadn't taken a biscuit. The three Jammie Dodgers were clearly all his.

"Eight years," she said. "You'll need to practise your abdominal breathing at home. Every morning and evening."

"I will," he promised. "And how long have you been playing the piano?"

She shifted on her stool. Personal questions were clearly a problem. "Eighteen years," she said, examining a speck on her cardigan sleeve.

"Wow, that's —"

"Twelve years the clarinet and oboe," she went on, as if he hadn't interrupted. "Eleven years the violin. Six years the saxophone."

Adam looked at her in amazement. "You play all those instruments?"

Vivienne nodded and looked pointedly at his glass, and Adam drained it — no hope at all of palming it off — and finished his biscuit.

"Now," she said, turning back to the music stand, and Adam brushed Jammie Dodger crumbs from his shirt and lifted the clarinet again.

Take me to a hotel, Nora had said. *I want to do it on a queen-sized bed.* So he had.

It hadn't been hard to organise. Nora had booked the hotel room in Galway for one night in her name, paying in advance with Patrick's company card. In the morning she'd called in sick and taken the bus to Galway. She'd booked in at noon and gone upstairs.

He'd arrived at one and walked past the reception desk, briefcase in hand, business-suited, attracting no attention at all when he'd taken the lift to the third floor and knocked on the door of room number 324.

They'd ordered a room-service lunch. They'd run a bath. They'd left at five and driven the hour back to Clongarvin.

We must do it again, she'd said, squeezing his thigh in the car before getting out. *You're full of energy.*

You're not so bad yourself, he'd said, glancing around before slipping a hand under her skirt.

Next time she might bring him to Adam's flat, make him pass within three blocks of Indulgence to get there. Nothing like a bit of danger to keep things interesting.

Hannah wiped her hands on her apron and walked through to the sitting room, where Kirby was curled in his charity-shop chair. She stood for a minute, listening.

"What do you think, Kirby?" she asked. "Is our boy showing promise?"

The dog lifted his head and thumped his tail against the side of the awful grey and blue check upholstery as the first two lines of "Mary Had A Little Lamb" floated down from upstairs for the umpteenth time.

Hannah settled on the couch and reached for the remote control, humming along.

I can't, she'd said, when John had suggested dinner some evening. *Saturday night is my only free one, and you're playing in the wine bar then.*

I'm not on till nine, he'd said. *We could get an early bird — which, of course, would suit a cheap Scotsman perfectly. Would seven o'clock give you enough time to get home from work and out again?*

He was different from Patrick in every way, which could only be a good thing. It wasn't too soon, was it, more than four months now since Patrick had walked out? She wasn't rebounding, was she?

Seven would be lovely, she'd said. *How do you feel about Indian?*

He made her laugh. He listened when she spoke — he wasn't only waiting for her to finish so he could say something else. He smelt of soap, nothing fancy. She liked the clothes he wore. She liked his shoes.

Adam walked into the sitting room as the closing credits of *Coronation Street* were rolling.

"I heard you practising," she said, switching off the television. "Very promising."

"Do you know how to breathe through your abdomen?"

"No."

"That's what I have to do, apparently. Look —" he placed the flat of his hand below his waistline"— you have to feel the breath coming from down here." He inhaled. "I think I'm getting it."

Hannah smiled. "That's good. Your teacher and her mother will be so proud. Have you discovered yet if she's single?"

"Not exactly — I couldn't very well come out and ask her — but the signs are hopeful."

"Are you coming to Vintage tomorrow night?"

"I thought you were going out to dinner."

278

"I am, but I'll be in after. Will I meet you there, nine-ish?"

"You will." He picked up the remote control and sat back on the couch. "I might ask Nora along."

"Fine."

Adam scanned the Aertel screen, humming. After a few seconds Hannah recognised an out-of-tune version of "I've Got A Crush On You".

Alice hadn't planned to go to the cemetery after the month's mind mass. She'd sat a few rows back from the front of the church and recited the prayers, stood and knelt when everyone else did. She watched the parents and their families, the father's head bent, the mother's blonde hair tied in a low ponytail. She'd stayed in her seat while people came up to them afterwards and whispered, and hugged the mother, some of them.

Alice waited until they filed down the aisle past her pew, the father's hand cradling the mother's elbow. So thin, she looked, the mother. So pale. So empty.

And afterwards Alice had got into the car to go home, and somehow she'd found herself at the cemetery.

They stood around the grave, ten of them. Four older people, one of the men in a wheelchair. The grandparents, she guessed. The mother's sister, who'd gone to the altar at the funeral and read a poem, dressed today in a grey jacket and denim skirt. A young man with a shaved head, two other teenage girls. A small enough family, the newest member wiped out now. The red wreath that spelt his name had been removed from in front of the wooden cross.

Alice stood three graves away and kept her eyes on the headstone in front of her in case they turned around. There was a murmur from them that she couldn't make out. It didn't sound regular enough to be praying, but she couldn't be sure.

They turned away eventually, walking past the spot where Alice stood. She glanced around and made brief eye contact with one of the older women, and smiled sympathetically. Her smile wasn't returned, and for a second Alice thought, *She knows who I am*.

But there was no shock of recognition in the woman's face, no expression of anything but grief, and Alice realised that the woman was simply too caught up in it to respond to a stranger's smile.

Back home she stuffed a chicken and roasted potatoes with garlic and rosemary, and mashed carrots and parsnips. At dinner Tom didn't ask about the month's mind mass, and she didn't mention it, or her trip to the cemetery.

"Business is not going well," she said, as he cut into his chicken. "I'm going to have to reduce Geraldine's hours, just temporarily till things pick up."

Even if the slow-down in business was to do with the accident as much as with the recession, surely it wouldn't last. Surely the memory of it would fade, and customers would return in time. She used to love running her shop — it was all she'd ever wanted to do.

"I'm sorry to hear that," Tom said. "I didn't realise things were that bad." He was still on full pay from the clinic, extended leave they were calling it, but that couldn't go on much longer.

"I'd like you to think about going back to work," she said. "It's not good to be staying out so long. You're only making it harder for yourself in the long run." And you need to stop drinking, she wanted to add, but held her peace this time.

He chewed his chicken and she waited for his response, and it was quite a few seconds before it became clear to her that none was coming.

They met at the restaurant. He'd offered to pick her up but Hannah had refused. "It's only a ten-minute walk," she'd said. "I need the exercise."

The weather was good. The warming air smelt like the beginning of summer. Hannah sprayed on a flowery scent and chose a grey dress with tiny pale blue polka dots whose folds played down her curves. She realised she was happy. She smiled at people who came towards her, and most returned her smile.

"You look sunny," John said. He was waiting outside, leaning against the restaurant wall, hands in the pockets of the chinos he wore when he was performing.

Hannah laughed. "I think that sounds like a compliment." She looked at the sky. "D'you think we've any hope of a summer this year?"

"Absolutely." He held the door open and she walked ahead of him. "By September we'll be wishing for a drop of rain."

They weren't the only early-bird diners. Waiters scurried around, depositing baskets of poppadums and dishes of chutney, uncorking bottles of wine, whisking away the remains of meals. As they were shown to a table, Hannah remembered her last meal out, the night Patrick had dropped his bombshell and she'd taken a taxi alone to the restaurant. Trying her best, as each course was set before her, not to bury her face in her hands and howl.

"Your friend who plays the keyboards," she said.

"Wally."

"Yes, Wally. I've been in his taxi a few times. He's with the girl who plays the clarinet, isn't he?"

John smiled. "No — they're brother and sister."

"Oh — my mistake. I assumed, when he mentioned he was driving her home that time . . ." Brother and sister. Adam would be pleased.

"Fancy some wine?" John was scanning the list.

Hannah smiled and reached for her menu. "Why not? You choose — I'm not fussy."

He was good company, as she'd known he would be. He described the village where he'd grown up, and she saw the narrow shingle beach, the whitewashed houses cradling the shoreline, the fishing-boats moored along the pier, the lobster pots bobbing on the water. He told her about his parents, his fisherman father battling arthritis as fiercely as he battled the elements, his volunteer meals-on-wheels driver mother whose apple jelly was a consistent winner at the annual fête.

Hannah told him about her grandfather. "He was the one who got me interested in baking. He taught me how to make rock buns and almond cookies when I was

282

eight. He got me my first apron and electric mixer. His father was a baker, but I never knew him."

"Wasn't it frightening," he asked, "opening your own shop, all by yourself?"

"Terrifying, and in the middle of a recession too. I'm sure people thought I needed my head examined." She smoothed a small crease in the tablecloth. "Even with Granddad's legacy, which helped a lot, there was still a fair bit of expense involved, and I also have a mortgage to pay, and all the other bills that go along with a house. My parents didn't say it, but I know they were worried I'd go belly up in a week."

"It's their job," he smiled, "to worry about you."

"I suppose so. Luckily I've proved them wrong and I'm still here — if not exactly raking it in." Their waiter brought poppadums, and she reached for one. "And I haven't collapsed from exhaustion — not yet, anyway."

When the wine arrived. John filled their glasses and lifted his. "I have every faith in you. This time next year you'll be counting the profits, mark my words."

Hannah touched her glass against his. "I'll drink to that."

Her mother's perfume, these days, smelt terribly cloying to Leah. In the past few weeks she'd completely lost her taste for anything sweet — developing instead a craving for salt and vinegar Pringles sprinkled with soy sauce — so it was hardly surprising that Fiona's heady almondy scent made her want very much to gag.

"Thank you," she said, when her mother handed her a jar of verbena hand cream, knowing that it was the nearest Fiona would come to an apology.

They hadn't spoken since the disastrous lunch on Easter Sunday, when Fiona had practically called Patrick a gigolo — not until Fiona had rung the other night and suggested she call in for a short visit on her way home from bridge, using exactly the same tone of voice she always did, as if they hadn't parted in anger almost three weeks earlier. And Leah, caught unaware, had found herself agreeing.

Patrick wasn't there. Leah had suggested he make himself scarce, and he'd been happy to oblige. When the baby came, he and Fiona could make their peace. When Fiona realised that Patrick was as committed to parenthood as Leah was, she couldn't object to him any more, and a silent truce would come into force. It had to.

In the meantime, Leah would have to be the buffer. "Coffee?" she asked her mother. "Or tea? Earl Grey?" She was determined to keep this meeting neutral, had resolved to be polite and hospitable, and no more.

Patrick hadn't once referred to Fiona's implied accusations: no mention had been made of the Easter Sunday encounter. That day he'd left the apartment without coming into the bedroom where Leah lay. She'd heard the front door closing softly, and she'd turned her face to the wall. She hadn't heard him return — she'd woken much later to the sound of the television, and walked out to find him asleep on the

284

couch, his jacket still on, the remains of a pizza in a box on the floor beside him.

"Your cot is still in the attic," Fiona was saying, "and I think a playpen. Of course, you may prefer to buy new ones."

She was trying, as much as Fiona could try. Leah should meet her halfway — she'd probably need her mother around when the baby arrived. Need, not want.

"Thank you," she said, in the same neutral tone. "I'll think about it. Did you say tea or coffee?"

She and Patrick had made love twice in the past fortnight, both times at her instigation. Patrick hadn't looked for it. He hadn't once turned to her in bed, hadn't woken her up in the middle of the night the way he used to.

It was the baby, of course. He was wary of doing anything that might harm the baby; that was all. Once the baby arrived things would sort themselves out.

"Have you seen much of Nora O'Connor?" Fiona asked, as Leah began to lay out cups and saucers.

"A little."

Nora had called by the salon out of the blue a few days earlier. She'd brought a toy white rabbit and a bottle of jasmine-scented bath salts. "How're you feeling?" she'd asked, leaning against the door jamb in her cream linen cardigan and blue linen trousers. "We must do lunch again," she'd said. "My treat this time. When you get a chance."

Leah hadn't asked Nora about her job. She'd shifted her weight and told Nora she had a customer waiting. "I'll give you a call," she'd said. "Thanks for these."

She'd text Nora at some stage and they'd go to lunch, and Leah would hope, as she'd been hoping now for weeks, that Nora would look past Patrick for a diversion. That Patrick wouldn't consider being unfaithful, even if Nora did set her sights on him.

"You look tired," Fiona said. "Are you getting enough sleep?"

Three weeks, give or take, and Leah and Patrick would be parents. He hadn't once asked about names, even though she'd left the book where he couldn't miss it. He never wondered aloud if they'd have a boy or a girl, hadn't once asked her which she'd prefer. He'd gone along to the classes when she'd asked him and taken part like all the other expectant fathers, but he never mentioned the baby the rest of the time, ever.

Surely when it arrived he'd change. Surely he'd take one look at his son or daughter and fall in love.

"I think I'm having a girl," Leah said suddenly, wanting someone to share it with, and only having her mother. "I just have this feeling."

Fiona regarded her above the rim of her cup. "A girl," she said, without expression. "You could be right — although I was convinced you were going to be a boy."

Leah squeezed lemon into her tea. "How did you feel," she asked then, "when you saw me? How did you and Dad feel?"

Fiona lowered her cup. "We were happy to have a healthy baby, of course," she answered placidly. "Just like you will be."

Just like you will be. As if Leah had made this baby all on her own. She hoisted herself from the chair. "I need the toilet," she told her mother, and walked heavily from the room.

He'd mastered "Mary Had A Little Lamb" and "Sur Le Pont d'Avignon". He'd eaten the Jammie Dodgers when they'd appeared for a second time, and drunk the milk — and suffered the consequences the following day. He'd attempted small-talk with Vivienne's mother when she'd appeared — admiring the garden, remarking on the fine weather they'd been enjoying — even though the older woman was clearly suspicious of him. (And who could blame her? If ever someone's motives were suspect, Adam's were.)

He'd even reached out to pat the giant marmalade cat, which seemed to live on the piano — but to his relief it had shrunk away from him, and Vivienne had said quickly, "He's shy around strangers."

I wonder where he gets it from, Adam had thought.

Any attempt at personal conversation on his part brought a fresh flood of colour to her face — if she could have shrunk away from him as the cat had, Adam suspected she would. So he stuck to questions that related to the pieces they were looking at, and he did his best to be patient and bide his time.

But all the same he was inching towards her, absorbing a fraction more about her with each visit. She had a habit of rubbing her middle finger as she listened to his efforts, and closing her eyes briefly now and again. Her teeth weren't quite straight, and not perfectly white. She never wore jewellery. Her ears, unusually small, had never been pierced.

Her clothes were modest and unremarkable, and all dark colours, black and grey and navy mostly. Her hair was always pinned up, never loose. Her breath always smelt minty. She used no makeup, as far as his untutored male eye could tell.

Her feet were long, her calves — what he could see of them — slender. He was reminded of a scene from *The Piano* when Harvey Keitel had lain on the floor and poked a finger through a hole in Holly Hunter's stocking as she played. Vivienne's eyes were fringed with surprisingly long pale lashes.

And now, during their third lesson, Adam decided the time had come to risk tiptoeing a little further towards her. He waited until her mother had delivered the usual tray — tiny Iced Gem biscuits tonight, which he'd last eaten more than twenty years ago — and left them alone again.

"How did you get involved with the band?" he asked. A musical question: she could hardly object.

She blinked rapidly twice, a nervous gesture he'd noticed before. He wanted to reach out and touch her arm and tell her everything was going to be alright, and not to be afraid.

"My brother," she said quickly, bending to riffle through the pages of sheet music for a new piece for him.

Adam bit the pastel pink swirl off an Iced Gem. "He's a member?"

She nodded. "Keyboards."

288

"I see." Adam crunched his biscuit. Wally the taxi driver, who drove her home after the gigs. Imagine admitting that he knew all that already, that his friend had pumped the saxophonist for information about her. Imagine her reaction if he said that.

"And your brother only plays one instrument? That's a bit lazy, isn't it?"

She looked up, the tiniest of smiles flashing across her features. "He can play the guitar too. And the flute."

"That's better," he said. "So you're a musical family."

A short nod as she pulled a sheet from the bundle and placed it on the stand. Beethoven, Adam read. Bit of a step up from "Mary Had A Little Lamb". Hannah would be pleased.

"What's the name of the band?" Another question he knew the answer to.

"Small Change."

"And how long —"

"We'll try Beethoven next, a lullaby," she said. "When you've finished."

Adam drained his milk and returned the glass to the tray. "What's your brother's name?"

Vivienne shifted on her stool, her smile gone. For a second Adam thought she wasn't going to reply, and then she said, "Walter. Wally."

"And he's a full-time musician?" Aware that he was pushing, but reluctant to return to the formality of the lesson just yet.

"No — he drives a taxi." She looked pointedly at his clarinet, lying on the floor by his chair, and Adam picked it up. "Beethoven," she said again, turning towards the stand, and Adam put the mouthpiece to his lips and awaited further instruction.

And then she said, keeping her eyes fixed on the sheet music, "You're improving a bit." The familiar flush reappearing, drifting slowly up her cheeks. "With the clarinet."

It wasn't much — it was hardly anything. She probably said that to all her pupils to keep them trying. Silly, really, the effect it had on him.

When the woman came out of the house Alice nearly missed her, pressing buttons on the car radio in an effort to find something less depressing than *Liveline*. As she settled on a classical-music station she raised her head, and a movement, some flash of colour, caught her eye on the other side of the road. She turned and saw the woman walking away, head lowered, shoulders hunched, hands thrust into the pockets of a green jacket.

Alice grabbed her bag and got out, no thought in her head but to follow. She locked the car and walked after the woman, suddenly aware of her quickening heartbeat, her dry mouth.

She was far enough behind not to be able to hear the sound of the other shoes hitting the path, but her own footfalls sounded grotesquely loud on the quiet afternoon street. She wished for a pair of sneakers, which she hadn't owned in more than forty years.

290

After crossing a few intersections and turning a few corners the woman reached a bus stop and stood beside the shelter, ignoring the wooden bench on which an elderly man sat, his hands wrapped around the knobbly handle of a wooden stick. The woman's gaze was on the ground in front of her as she waited silently, hands still deep in her pockets.

Alice approached, slowing her pace. No plan, no clue what to do. She hadn't given a thought to anything beyond sitting outside Jason's house.

She stopped a foot or so from the woman and rummaged in her bag. She didn't know how much the bus cost, or where it would take her if she got on. She never travelled by bus. She had an idea that you had to have exact change, so she emptied coins from her purse into her palm and calculated that they came to roughly two euro. Surely that would be enough.

She closed her bag and hung it on her shoulder, and turned her head slowly towards the mother, who was still staring fixedly at the ground. She looked tightly clenched, standing there. Alice could see the shape her fist made in the nearside pocket. The thin strap of a small brown bag crossed her body from her left shoulder to her right hip. Her blonde hair was pulled back into a blue rubber band.

"Excuse me," Alice said, and the mother's head turned slowly towards her, unsmiling, pale. "I wonder," Alice said, struggling with an unexpected lump in her throat, "if you know when the bus is due?"

The mother didn't speak immediately, nothing in her face registered that she'd even heard the question.

Then, as Alice was about to repeat it, she said, in a low voice, "Ten past," and turned away again.

"Thanks."

Alice swallowed the lump in her throat, kept swallowing until it eased. The man on the bench pulled a hanky from his pocket and blew his nose noisily. A younger man approached the bus stop and passed the two women to sit down, rattling change in his pocket, tapping one shoe on the ground, presumably in accompaniment to whatever was coming out of the earphones he wore. A woman arrived from the opposite direction, pulling a smallish suitcase on wheels. A siren sounded faintly in the distance.

Alice was acutely aware of the mother's presence, so close she could have reached out and taken her arm, and told her how terribly, terribly —

The bus rounded a corner just then, slowing as it approached. The two men got up, the older man pulling himself slowly to his feet, knuckles white around his stick. Alice opened her hand and looked at the scatter of coins as the others moved forward.

A man and a woman got off the bus, and the elderly man grasped the pole and levered himself stiffly up the steps. The others followed and Alice moved after them and put a foot on the bottom step.

And then she stopped.

When he'd dealt with the others, when they'd moved down the bus, the driver looked questioningly at Alice. She looked back at him, frozen. What was she doing?

She took her foot off the step. "Sorry," she said. She turned and walked rapidly back in the direction she'd come from. She heard the bus engine revving as the driver pulled away, and she kept her eyes on the path ahead, stumbling a little now and again in her rush.

As she approached the car she lifted her bag to rummage for her keys, and the coins in her hand tumbled onto the road. Without stopping to gather them up, she opened the car and got in, and pulled her phone from her bag.

Not going to make it back, see you tomorrow, she texted Geraldine. She drove slowly out of the estate and through streets full of people, past shops and parks and schools. On the far side of town she pulled into a small car park attached to a church she'd never been inside. She switched off the engine and sat there, watching the few who came and went from the church.

Seeing, each time she closed her eyes, the empty, dead face of the mother.

Eventually she started the car again and drove home through the streets, more clogged now with workers freed from offices and shops.

In the kitchen she fried onions and browned mince. She stirred in stock and tomato purée, she shook in frozen peas and added salt and black pepper before lowering the heat and letting it bubble gently. She peeled potatoes and cut them into chunks. She poured boiling water on top of them and simmered them until they softened.

As the dinner cooked, the kitchen filling slowly with steam, she stood at the window looking out at the garden, at the lawn spotted with dandelions, the flowerbeds that were more weeds than flowers. The shed that needed staining, the mint that was running riot in the herb box.

She opened the cutlery drawer and took out her daughter's last letter, and she read again the news of kindergarten graduations and birthday parties, and a camping trip to the mountains. She looked at the photos Ellen had sent, of grandchildren Alice hardly knew jumping into swimming-pools, eating pizza, laughing for the camera. Healthy-looking and tanned, with such white teeth. She longed to be there with Ellen, to leave this hellish place behind.

When the shepherd's pie was ready she spooned a serving onto a dinner plate. She put it on a tray with a glass of water, a butter dish and the smaller of their two salt cellars. Then she picked up the tray and brought it upstairs to her husband, who had taken to going to his bed some time in the afternoon and not leaving it again till the following morning.

"Guess what," Adam said. "Nora has a man."

"Really?" Hannah closed the door of the washing-machine and straightened. "What's he like?"

Adam draped his jacket over a kitchen chair. "Dunno, didn't meet him."

"So how do you know she has one?"

Adam hesitated. "I think she was hiding him."

Hannah stared at him. "Hiding him? What do you mean?"

"Well, I'm pretty sure someone was there." He filled the kettle. "Nora couldn't wait to get rid of me. She said I should have phoned before coming over —"

"I told you —"

"— and said she hadn't time to make coffee because she was getting ready to go out, but she was definitely cagey. Barely let me get the books I wanted before shoving me out the door."

Hannah turned the dial and switched on the machine. "So you've no proof anyone was there?"

"No, but I know when she's hiding something." He took mugs from the press. "I'd bet anything there was a man."

"But why would she hide him?" Hannah began to lay out her usual baking paraphernalia. "I mean, it's not as if she's forbidden to have men in your flat."

"Dunno." Adam spooned coffee into the mugs. "Maybe he's married."

Hannah took eggs from the fridge. "Married?"

"Hey, I could be wrong," Adam said, handing her a mug. "Forget I spoke, there might have been nobody there."

Hannah sipped her coffee and made no reply.

Adam stirred sugar into his mug. "Anyway, when are you meeting lover-boy again?"

"Saturday. I told him I'd be in the wine bar."

"Good."

"And he's cooking dinner for me on Sunday night."

"Is he now?"

"He is . . . Wish you had some news yourself though."

Adam sighed. "Me too. I'm getting nowhere with her. She's so shy . . . and her mother seems convinced

I'm going to corrupt her daughter if she takes her eye off the ball. She's always peering in at us from the garden when she's not looking daggers at me at break time."

"And feeding you kiddie biscuits."

He smiled. "Actually I'd forgotten how much I like Iced Gems." He turned towards the door. "And now you must excuse me — as long as I'm still taking music lessons, I'd better practise my Beethoven."

"Now that's a sentence I never thought I'd hear you say. You have half an hour before I go to bed."

"Plenty," he called back. "Night-night. See you tomorrow."

Hannah took butter from the fridge, her smile fading.

"Jesus," Patrick said, "that was a bit close."

Nora ran a fingernail along his back. "Imagine his face if he'd walked in and found you in his bed."

Patrick laughed shortly. "Actually, he's really not my type." He winced. "Hey, easy with the claws — no marks, remember?"

"I thought you said Leah wasn't interested." Continuing her slow trail down his spine. "So she won't see any marks if she's not coming near your naked body, will she?" Bending and nipping his shoulder hard with her teeth.

He jerked out of her reach. "Cut it out — we can't take chances like that." He rolled over, pinning her beneath him and trapping her arms. "We can still have our fun — we just need to be careful not to get caught."

She smiled. "But, darling, the risk of getting caught is where all the fun comes in."

June

"I can't get hold of Tom," Stephen said.

"Weren't you going to ring him?"

"I tried, and I got Suzie to try, several times — his mobile is switched off, and the landline just rings out."

"Can't you leave a message?"

"No — there's no answering-machine on the house phone."

Geraldine shook her head. "It's like he's trying to hide. Any time I enquire after him Alice says he's fine, or bearing up, and that's it. I can't very well ask her if he's planning to go back to work any time soon."

Stephen pushed his plate aside. "No . . . but it's been nearly ten weeks now. The clinic can't keep paying him indefinitely for not showing up."

Geraldine set her fork down. "Stephen, I don't know what I'd have done if it had happened to you."

"Don't think like that. I'll have to call around there and have a chat with him."

"It seems like you will," Geraldine said, stacking the plates and bringing them to the sink. "Should I mention anything to Alice, do you think?"

Her hours had been cut. Now she didn't go to work till two, and then held the fort on her own usually, Alice disappearing most afternoons without explanation.

"No," Stephen said slowly, getting up. "Best say nothing to Alice." He took the salt and pepper cellars back to the shelf above the fridge. "Tom might do a runner if he thinks I'm coming."

"Oh, you don't think he would, do you?" Geraldine spooned ice-cream into dishes. "Poor Tom. Poor Alice."

Stephen thought, but didn't say, *At least they're both alive*.

"I'm trying to get my daughter to come over for a visit," John said, "as soon as she gets holidays at the end of the month."

"That's nice," Hannah said, putting a hand over her glass as he lifted the brandy bottle. "Better not, thanks, with my early start. You said she's in college?"

John topped up his own glass. "Yes, in Edinburgh. She's just finishing first-year law."

"And she's been to Ireland before?"

"Yes. We often came here to visit my mother's family in Tipperary when Danielle was growing up. But she hasn't been over in years, and it would be her first time in Clongarvin."

Hannah took a tiny sip of her remaining brandy. "Well, I must say that dinner was most impressive."

"So," he smiled, "my cooking hasn't scared you off."

"Not in the least — I love spare ribs. You're a far better cook than I am."

"Oh, I doubt that very much." He put his glass down on the coffee-table. "But maybe I'll have the chance to compare our cooking skills some time."

"You never know."

He moved closer and bent his head, and put his lips against her throat. "I'm glad I met you," he whispered. "I'm glad you're here."

"Me too." She set her glass down and cradled his head as he moved his lips to the opening in her blouse. She leant back and pulled him down to lie beside her as she began to undo his shirt buttons.

And his mouth, when it finally found hers, tasted of brandy.

Vivienne was not herself.

"You're not yourself," her mother told her at the dinner-table. "You never say no to apple sponge. It's not a bit like you."

"I'm not hungry," Vivienne replied.

"That's what I mean," her mother said. "It's not like you not to be hungry."

"You're miles away," her brother Wally said, when he called around as usual for Saturday tea with his sister and mother. "You haven't heard a word I've said, have you?"

"She's not herself," their mother told him.

"You forgot to give him the new piece last week," Robbie O'Donnell's mother told her on Tuesday. "You were going to give him that new Debussy piece to practise, and you forgot."

"She's not herself these days," Vivienne's mother said to Mrs O'Donnell as she showed them out. "It's not a bit like her to forget something like that."

"Maybe she needs a tonic," Mrs O'Donnell said. "Maybe she's coming down with something."

"When can I stop having piano lessons?" Robbie asked, and his mother shushed him and pushed him ahead of her out the front door.

Vivienne bought a lipstick. It was called Candy Floss and it cost her €8.99. She had no idea if this was expensive, as lipsticks went. She brought it home and sat in front of her dressing-table and pulled off the top and ran the colour across her lips. She turned to Pumpkin, who was sitting on the chest of drawers. "What do you think?" she asked him.

He lifted his head and regarded her unblinkingly.

"I'm wearing lipstick," she told him, and he purred gently.

She studied her face in the mirror. She took off her glasses and peered at her shiny mouth. She made it smile at her, and then the smile vanished abruptly. She rubbed the lipstick off with a tissue and threw the tube into her wastepaper basket.

Ugly, Specky Four Eyes, Freckle-face. The size of those feet, they're gross. What colour is red, Four Eyes? Look at her, she's puce.

Nobody to walk her home from school. Nobody to ring and ask her out. No cards on Valentine's Day, no flowers, ever, for Specky Four Eyes O'Toole. Nothing but music to lose herself in, to block out the cruel voices, to take her away from them all.

304

Music helped her to forget. Music filled her empty spaces. Music was all she needed, until Pumpkin had appeared in the back garden one day six years before, shivering and thin, as unwanted as she had been. Now they had each other. It was enough.

Wasn't it?

"Dinner is on the table," her mother shouted up the stairs.

"Coming," Vivienne called back. She pushed the lipstick deeper into the wastepaper basket. No more of that nonsense. She would be herself again.

She lifted Pumpkin into her arms and left the room, and walked downstairs.

"Can't you stay a bit longer?" he asked. "It's not even nine."

Hannah buttoned her blouse. "Nine is my bedtime, remember? Anyway, the taxi's on the way."

John watched as she slipped her arms into her jacket. "You don't regret what happened?"

She smiled, put a hand to his face. "Of course not."

He kissed her palm. "Good."

It had been different. It had been strange, being with another man after Patrick. But John had been tender, and she'd felt comfortable with him.

Comfortable. Not exactly the word, she imagined, a man would like to hear used to describe his lovemaking.

"What's funny?" he asked.

"Oh, I'm just amused at the way things turn out," Hannah answered. "You never know, do you?"

"No." He started to say something else, but just then a car horn sounded in the street below — and for a second Hannah was back in her bedroom, scattered jewellery at her feet, listening to Patrick telling her he'd fallen in love with someone else.

John crossed to the window and looked down. "That was quick." He came back and took her into his arms.

"I like how you smell," she said against his shoulder. "Nice and soapy."

He laughed. "I'm glad to hear it. I'll walk you down."

"No need," Hannah said, drawing back. "You haven't got shoes on — I'll be fine."

"I'll call you in the morning," he said as she let herself out and hurried down the two flights of stairs to where the taxi waited. She opened the door and slid into the back seat, and gave her address.

"Hi," the driver said, watching her face in the rear-view mirror. "We have to stop meeting like this."

"Oh." Hannah smiled. "I think you must be stalking me."

"Guilty as charged. How's your yellow shop?"

"Still there, thank goodness." She leant back in her seat. "Will you turn up the music a bit?"

"So you don't have to talk to me?" But he raised the volume, and Hannah closed her eyes and let the soft, mellow sound settle around her.

The evening had gone pretty much as she'd imagined it would. They'd both known how it was going to end. She'd sensed John's attraction, and she'd been happy to let it take its natural course. And if the earth hadn't exactly moved, so what? It had been perfectly pleasant, and she was happy with that.

And the earth-moving experiences didn't last anyway. Her first time with Patrick, at the end of their second date, had been intense, her climax leaving her trembling and limp — and look how that had turned out. Maybe the slow burners were better.

She opened her eyes and studied the back of Wally's head. His hair needed a cut. Funny how they kept meeting up. "How long have you been in the band?" she asked him.

"Couple of years," he answered, "give or take. I was the founder member, in fact." There was a short silence, and then he said, "So you and Johnny are an item then?"

"Kind of," Hannah replied, meeting his eyes again in the rear-view mirror.

"He's a good man," Wally said, indicating as he changed gear. "Even if he is from Scotland."

Hannah laughed. "And you're not racist."

His eyes in the mirror crinkled. "Not at all."

When they reached her house she opened her bag. "How much is that?"

He turned to face her. "On the house," he said, "in return for a free fancy bun when I eventually make it into the yellow shop."

"Oh, no, I can't —"

"Oh yes you can," he said. "You're a friend of Johnny's. If it makes you feel better, you can make it two free buns. I've a real sweet tooth."

She smiled. "Well, if you insist — but next time I'm paying, OK?"

"Dead right; I'm not made of money, you know."

She smelt sweet, she smelt of vanilla ice-cream. She reminded him of something in bloom. He remembered her crying that night; he remembered turning on the light for her. How she'd said thank you. How he'd called her back to give her the blue scarf she'd left behind.

So Johnny had got her. Fair play.

At half past ten Fiona ran her usual evening bath, adding plenty of lavender salts. Lying in the scented water she read one chapter of the Gandhi biography and drank a tall glass of warm milk. She towelled herself dry before applying her night-time body lotion.

She cleansed, toned and moisturised her face, applied hand cream and massaged it in. She adjusted her clock radio so the display was turned away from the bed; nothing like watching the time pass to encourage insomnia. She pulled on the white cotton gloves she wore in bed.

And just before she lay back on her down pillows, she felt a sudden impulse to talk to her daughter. She lifted the cordless phone on her bedside table and reached a gloved finger towards the keypad. She hesitated — was it too late? She turned the clock radio back towards her and saw that it was eleven eighteen.

Too late. She replaced the phone. She'd call Leah tomorrow afternoon. They had nothing much to say to each other these days anyway.

Stephen pressed the bell a second time. After several more seconds had passed he stepped back from the door and looked up towards the first-floor windows.

"Tom?" he called. The car was in the driveway. The curtains were drawn back from the upstairs windows. "Tom?"

He put a hand over the side gate, slid the bolt and walked around to the back of the house. He rapped loudly on the door, calling Tom's name again. There was a plastic bag by the wall. Stephen peered in and saw empty bottles with the gold labels of Powers whiskey on them.

He walked back up the side passage, bolting the gate after him. He opened his wallet and found an old receipt. He wrote on the back of it and posted it through the letterbox. He glanced up at the top windows again, then walked down the driveway to his car.

He got in and drove back to the dental clinic.

She should have said something to Patrick before he left for work. She should have mentioned the ache in her back that had woken her a couple of times in the night, sliding dully through her and then easing. She should have said something as he was getting dressed, as she was struggling into the shower, as he was drinking coffee in the kitchen, standing by the window.

As she was dabbing concealer under her eyes, smoothing foundation onto her swollen face.

I have this pain, she should have told him. *It comes now and again, down my back. It's a new pain. It's different.*

But she'd said nothing, because Patrick must be sick of her complaints, tired of hearing about her constipation and her heartburn and her constant need to pee, weary of her indigestion and her nausea and her craving for salt.

So he'd gone to work, kissing her cheek briefly, his aftershave making her want to gag. And that had been three hours ago, and the pain in her back was worse now, much worse, and she'd rung her two afternoon appointments and cancelled them until further notice. And the pain was slicing through her now, easing for a while before coming back and making her gasp with its intensity.

She waited until the latest one had passed and then she picked up the phone and called Patrick's mobile. When it went straight to his voicemail she disconnected and tried again, and when the same thing happened she waited for the beep and then said rapidly, "Patrick, it's me — please ring. It's urgent."

She hung up and tried Nora's mobile, but it rang and rang and remained unanswered. She called Directory Enquiries and got the number of the newspaper offices — the first time she'd needed the main number — and the receptionist told her that Patrick had left for a meeting and no, she didn't know where. Could she give Leah his mobile number?

"I have that," Leah said, "but I can't contact him —
I can't get through to him. Is his PA there?" Surely
Nora would have a number where he could be reached.

"I'm sorry," the receptionist, whom Leah had yet to
meet, replied, "but she called in sick this morning. Can
I take a message at all?"

The pain came again then, and Leah hung up and
bent double, gritting her teeth. When it faded, she
called her mother. "I need you," she said, her eyes
closed. "I think the baby's coming."

As she hung up she felt a warm gush of wetness
between her legs and looked down to see a puddle
seeping into the pale green carpet.

The shoe shop was struggling along, barely solvent.
They kept the sale prices going, lowered the mark-up
on all the new stock coming in, introduced weekly
special offers and with Geraldine's reduced wages they
kept it afloat. Just.

Every afternoon Alice left the shop soon after
Geraldine arrived at two. They had tea together first,
and Alice pretended that everything was still as it
always had been. She let Geraldine know if there were
any deliveries expected and gave an account of any
happenings that morning. She enquired after Hannah's
business and passed on any news that might have come
from Australia. If Geraldine asked, she said Tom was
OK.

And when the mugs were washed and put away she
left, rarely returning before closing time. She'd long
since stopped making up a reason for leaving, and

Geraldine didn't ask any more. At this stage, it would be more unusual if Alice stayed around.

She varied her afternoon routine. Sometimes she went straight to the cemetery; other days she drove directly to Springwood Gardens. She always left the church car park till last, when she'd done the other two.

The flowers were gone from the gate of number thirty-seven. One day she saw Dave mowing the lawn, up and down, up and down. Wearing a dark blue hat with a brim, stopping every now and again to wipe his brow with a bare forearm.

Once Claire came out and walked right past Alice's car, not looking in, no expression on her pale face. Alice sat and watched her in the rear-view mirror until she got smaller and smaller and finally turned a corner.

She thought of them as Claire and Dave now.

The Jason wreath had been replaced by a green plastic rectangular box, about a foot and a half long, in which someone had planted real violas and pansies. It lay where the other had lain, along the top of the grave, just in front of the wooden cross.

She wondered if they were planning to add Jason's name to the big headstone, or if the cross was going to stay. The oval frame of his photo was spotted with tarnish that she couldn't get off, even with Brasso.

She left him flowers, every third day. She signed the cards *A*.

She never went into the church, just sat in the car park outside. A priest came out once and glanced at her car, and Alice was afraid he was going to come over, but then he walked out through the church gates. The following day she sat outside a different church.

She drove home at the same time each day. She made the dinner and took Tom's upstairs to him, and ate hers alone in the kitchen, or sometimes in front of the television if anything interesting was on. She went for a walk after dinner on the fine evenings, the same circular route that took her past the recycling bins and the bus station, down by the river and around by the golf course. It took about an hour and a half — she wasn't a fast walker — and by the time she got back to the house it was usually time for the news.

At half past nine she switched off the television and read her book until she felt sleepy, because there was some comfort in it.

Until one day she got home and opened the front door and saw a brown envelope on the floor, and a scrap of paper lying next to it. She picked up the envelope and saw Tom's name typed on it, and the government harp above it. She tore it open and pulled out the page, and read that Tom Joyce was summoned to appear at the district court on Friday, 14 June, at half past eleven.

She bent and picked up the scrap of paper and saw that it was a receipt from Boots for some toiletries. She turned it over and read, *Tom, please get in touch —* *Stephen.*

"Right," she said aloud, in the empty hallway. She walked to the stairs and sat on the third step, holding the letter and the receipt. After a while she got up and climbed the rest of the stairs to her husband's bedroom. She walked in and crossed to the window. She pulled the curtains apart and shoved the window open.

"Tom, get up," she said, turning to him. "You need to get up now. I have to talk to you."

As Nora pulled on her top she heard a soft beep. She turned to see Patrick switching on his phone.

"Well," she said, "can't wait to get back to the real world, can you?"

"Shit," Patrick said, looking at the screen. "Shit." He jabbed buttons rapidly and raised the phone to his ear.

Nora reached for her skirt. "What's all the —"

"Shh," he said, listening, holding up a palm to Nora. After a few seconds he snapped the phone closed and grabbed his briefcase. "Come on," he said, "we have to go."

"What's the big panic?" Nora asked, zipping up her skirt.

"Leah," he said, already halfway out of the room. "She's having the baby."

"Jesus." Nora stepped into her shoes, grabbed her bag and jacket and hurried after him. "I thought it wasn't due for a fortnight."

He didn't answer, stabbing at the lift button, checking his watch, tucking his shirt into his trousers. "Come on, come on," he muttered.

"Jesus, calm down, would you?" Nora struggled into her jacket. "A few minutes aren't going to make much difference at this stage."

Patrick shot her a look she hadn't seen before, and then he turned back and banged his palm against the lift button. *"Fuck."*

The journey back to Clongarvin was mostly silent. Patrick drove fast, overtaking recklessly, hooting impatiently at anyone who got in his way.

Nora hung on, enjoying the ride. "Is she in the hospital?"

"Yes," he answered shortly.

"What did her message say? How long ago was it?"

He made no response, and Nora gave up. When they approached Clongarvin's outer limits, forty minutes later, Patrick pulled the car over.

Nora looked at him. "I hope you're not expecting me to get out here," she said. "It's miles —"

"Call a taxi," Patrick said, leaning past her and opening her door. "Do it, Nora. I haven't got time to argue." He pulled his wallet from his jacket and shoved a twenty-euro note at her. "Here."

She took the money and got out. "I don't believe —"

But he was gone, screeching towards Clongarvin's maternity hospital.

"Charming," Nora said aloud. She pulled out her phone. "Absolutely bloody charming." She couldn't walk ten yards in these shoes and he knew it. She dialled a number and said, "You couldn't come and pick me up, could you? Long story."

Adam sighed. "Where are you?"

315

Where are you? Leah had said in her second message. *Patrick, please ring me — I need you.* Her voice tight with tension.

And Fiona's message, less than an hour later. Calmer, much calmer. *Patrick, in case you're at all interested, my daughter is having your baby. We're at the hospital.*

And no other messages, just twelve missed calls. Leah, Leah, Leah, Leah, Fiona, Leah, Leah, Fiona, Fiona, Leah, Fiona, Fiona.

He ran through the sliding doors. "Leah Bradshaw," he snapped to the girl behind the glass screen. She tapped her computer and asked if he was a relative.

"I'm the father," he answered through gritted teeth, his gut a tight knot, his shirt stuck to his back, the urge to urinate nagging in his bladder.

Fiona met him at the entrance to the labour ward. The skirt of her navy suit was creased, but otherwise she was as unruffled as ever.

"You have a son," she said, looking at him as if he'd just spat on the ground in front of her. "Congratulations."

John looked at his mobile and read *Danielle*.

"Sorry," he said to Patsy. "Better take this."

"Hi Dad," Danielle said.

"Hey there. What's up?"

"Nothing . . ." Danielle's voice sounded far away. John pressed the phone closer to his ear. "I just got your letter."

316

"Yes?" He preferred writing: he was never good on the phone. "When will I see you?" He'd suggested a week, longer if she wanted. He'd have to invest in a camp bed of some kind, but they'd manage.

"Dad . . . I don't think I'll be coming over. Not this summer," she said.

John transferred the phone to his other ear and moved further from the counter. "You're not coming?"

"No." A short silence, and then she said, "I think I should be here, with Mum."

"I see." He hesitated. "Maybe you could come later in the summer? Don't you have a few months off?" He heard the neediness in his voice, so of course she'd hear it too.

"I think it's better that I stay here," she said, and then he understood. She was choosing, and she'd chosen Lara. She'd taken sides, when he'd thought there was no battle.

"OK, love," he said. "That's no problem. I'll see you next time I'm over. How's everything else?"

When he hung up he turned back to Patsy. "Sorry about that," he said again.

"That's alright dear," Patsy said. "Not bad news, I hope."

"No," he said. "Not bad. Just a change of plans."

"Tell me," she said, putting his purchases into a brown bag, "how's that young lady of yours?" She laughed at the expression on his face. "You needn't look so surprised — why else would you keep buying buns you don't eat?"

John smiled. "No flies on you, Patsy," he said. "She's fine, thanks for asking."

The thought of Hannah lifted his spirits. After so many years he'd almost forgotten the pleasure of affectionate physical intimacy. The warm feel, the scent of a woman's body next to his, the whispered words, the soft sounds of her reaction to his touch —

"Your change, dear," Patsy said. "You're miles away."

"So I had to rescue Nora today," Adam said.

"Rescue her? How?"

"She was stranded on the Galway road. She said she'd had a row with the driver of the car she was in, and she'd made him stop and let her out."

"Whose car? Where was she coming from?"

"She wouldn't tell me. She said it didn't matter, it was over now."

Hannah emptied chopped walnuts from the scales into a bowl. "Shouldn't she have been at work, instead of gallivanting around the place with a mystery man?"

"I didn't ask." He picked a cherry from an open tub. "Nora will do as she pleases, as always."

"That job won't last," Hannah said. "Stop eating those cherries."

"I don't think she cares, to be honest. I wouldn't be surprised if she heads back to the US soon. There's nothing for her in Clongarvin — she's grown out of it."

Hannah said nothing.

"Well, time for my clarinet practice," Adam said, moving towards the door.

"I like that little piece you're learning now."

318

"It's Chopin. I'm getting a musical education, if nothing else."

Left alone, Hannah thought about Nora O'Connor. Clearly she'd got involved with someone she didn't want anyone — or at least Adam — to know about. Someone with a wife, probably, or a partner at least. Someone, maybe, who wouldn't worry too much about being faithful, who wouldn't object if Nora made it plain that she was interested.

Someone like Patrick Dunne, who'd been unfaithful to Hannah, maybe with more than one woman. He'd taken on Nora as his PA and they'd been working closely together for the past few months now.

She measured flour and tipped it into the food processor's bowl. She could be wrong — she hadn't a shred of evidence to point to Patrick. And it was none of her business anyway.

As she weighed sugar, Chopin wafted from upstairs. And a few seconds later, from the sitting room next door, Kirby joined in.

"I'm so sorry," Patrick said. "I honestly didn't think there was a chance anything could happen."

"I know," Leah said.

"If I'd had the smallest idea, of course I'd never have gone to that meeting."

"I know."

"I'd have stayed at home, not gone in at all. You know that, right?"

"Yes."

"You never said anything, you should have said if you weren't feeling well before I left."

"I know. I should."

"But of course I shouldn't have gone off without being contactable, I can see that now. I should have left my phone on."

"Yes."

"At least your mother was here — you weren't on your own."

"No."

"And we have a beautiful son."

"Yes."

Nora had taken the day off. She'd phoned in sick. Patrick was gone to a meeting and couldn't be contacted, and Nora was off sick and not answering her phone. Leah's friend Nora, who couldn't be trusted an inch. Nora who would walk over her own grandmother's corpse to get to a man she fancied.

"Could you get me some tea?" she asked Patrick.

She wanted him gone. She didn't want to look at him.

Geraldine had refilled the teapot twice. She hadn't had to refill the biscuit plate, because it hadn't been touched.

He started drinking, after it happened, Alice had said. *I don't mean one or two, I mean serious drinking. I know he always liked a drink, but this was different. And it was whiskey, which he never used to drink. And lately he's taken to spending most of his time in bed — or whenever I'm in the house anyway.*

320

She hadn't cried. She wasn't crying now. But she looked older, and more tired, than Geraldine ever remembered seeing her.

I did nothing, Alice had told them. *I saw what was happening to him and I did nothing. I said nothing. I was too angry. I thought, if he wants to kill himself, let him. I didn't care — or I told myself I didn't care.*

Her hand had shaken when she'd lifted her cup. The tea had trembled as it had moved towards her mouth.

He's agreed to go to the doctor, she'd said. *I haven't mentioned AA yet, but if he doesn't, I will. And he's going to phone you tomorrow, Stephen. He's going to ask if he can take unpaid leave, until . . .*

She'd faltered then, and Stephen had said quickly, *We'll sort something out Alice, don't worry.*

He's been called to the district court, she'd told them. *On the fourteenth. The solicitor says he'll be formally charged, and then we'll have to wait until the case is heard in the circuit court, another few months.*

Geraldine had pushed the plate of biscuits towards her, but she'd shaken her head. Geraldine had asked her if she'd like apple crumble, left over from their dinner an hour earlier, but she'd said no.

I've been to the little boy's grave, she'd told them. *I brought him flowers. I often visited him.*

And then she'd gone home.

It was his fifth music lesson. They'd spent four hours together so far, and Vivienne remained as out of his reach as ever. Adam was becoming dispirited.

"I like the name Vivienne," he'd said, at the end of the second lesson. That had got no response. When he realised that she answered questions but generally ignored comments, he stuck to questions.

"Is your brother older or younger than you?" he'd asked, during lesson three. "Have you any other siblings?"

"What music do you like to listen to?" End of lesson three.

"How old is the cat?" At the break in lesson four, as he tried not to taste the milk he forced himself to drink.

And at the end of lesson four, in desperation, without thinking: "We'll have to stop meeting like this." She'd blushed deeply at that. He'd kicked himself and retreated hastily.

He felt as if he was maintaining the most delicate kind of balance, tiptoeing towards her until he felt her drawing back, easing off until she relaxed again. Forward and back, in and out, like two dancers at Lannigan's Ball.

Maybe he should just give up, admit defeat. But he couldn't.

And now they were on the fifth lesson, and he wondered how much longer it would be before she kicked him out for asking too many questions, or for not concentrating enough on the music.

This evening she wore a dark blue top and a grey skirt. The top was buttoned almost to her chin, the skirt skimmed her ankles. He wished she wore brighter colours and showed more skin. He wished, just once, she didn't tie up her hair. He wished she still wasn't quite so terrified of him.

"I design websites for a living," he told her as he unzipped his jacket. "Making music is just about as different as you can get from that, I suppose."

"Actually," Vivienne said, "it's not. Music is as logical as computing."

Adam tried not to show any reaction. This was a first: this was the closest they'd come to a real live conversation. He'd made a comment and she'd responded.

"Really?" He was careful to keep the surprise out of his voice. Casual, keep it casual.

"Of course." She rummaged through the bundle of pages on the card table. "Music is the most logical thing there is." She pulled a sheet from the pile and brought it to where he sat. "It's even got its own symbols — look." She pointed at a curved sign that appeared at the start of each set of lines. "See that? Do you remember what it's called?"

"Er —"

"It's a treble clef. I told you it places G above middle C. It always does that, it never changes. And this? Remember?" Indicating a hash symbol, which Adam was pretty sure was called something different here, and whose significance he couldn't for the life of him recall.

"This is a sharp sign," she said, thankfully not waiting for him to admit his ignorance. "It means any note in that position is a semitone above the true pitch. It can't mean anything else, ever."

She was leaning towards him. Their shoulders were almost touching. Her nails were unpainted. He could smell her minty breath, and the powdery scent that reminded him of babies. He could almost feel the warmth of her body.

"And look at that dot," she said. "See where it is? To the right of the note, never to the left. A dot always, always lengthens the note by one half its value. Never one quarter, or one eighth. Always one half."

She wasn't blushing, there was no hint of shyness or embarrassment in her voice. On the contrary, it was filled with a confidence he'd never seen in her before.

"And look, here, the time signature, one number over another. The bottom number always represents the note value of the basic pulse of the music — so here, the four represents the quarter-note. The top number, in this case three, always indicates how many of these note values appear in each measure, or bar. This example announces that each measure is the equivalent length of three crotchets."

"Three-four time," Adam said. "That's a waltz, isn't it?"

Without even trying, he'd stumbled on a way through to her. It was as if he'd cracked a code, or found a key.

"Yes," Vivienne said. "This piece is a waltz. It's Hungarian."

"I have two left feet," Adam said. "Don't ever take me dancing."

And instantly he realised his mistake as Vivienne drew back, the flush rising in her face. "Well," she said, sitting back on her piano stool, the sheet music still clutched in her hand, "so . . . we'll begin."

He'd strayed into the personal, and she'd scurried away from him. But for the first time she'd let her guard down. For a minute or so her awkwardness had vanished, and she'd been herself with him.

He winked at the cat on the piano, who stared back.

Alice toasted bread, that was all. No eggs, no sausages, no pudding. She put out the box of bran flakes but she knew it would be untouched. She took the orange squeezer from the press and put it back again. Just tea and toast.

Tom had gone to the doctor, as he'd promised. Alice had phoned to make an appointment, and the following afternoon Tom had taken a taxi to the surgery, about a mile away. She'd offered to drive him there, but he'd refused. When she got home around six — straight from the shop, no more lost afternoons, no more of that — he was back, sitting at the kitchen table with a cup of instant coffee in front of him.

What did he say? Alice had asked.

He gave me a prescription, Tom told her, *for sleeping pills.*

Alice hadn't known he wasn't sleeping.

And he wants me to go for . . . treatment.

Treatment? But she'd known what it meant.

He's going to try and get me into a treatment centre in Dublin for a few weeks. I told him I'm in court on Friday, so some time after that.

His face, so terribly bleak. His eyes empty of expression. The skin around his mouth puckered, the folds in his cheeks. The dark shadows under his eyes. The gap now between his shirt collar and his neck.

Alice, I'm sorry, he'd said then, in that same hollow voice, but Alice hadn't trusted herself to give a response. She'd turned away from him and begun to get the dinner ready.

And now Friday was here, and Geraldine was doing the full day in the shop. Stephen had offered to come with them to the court but Alice had said no, they'd be fine.

She put a slice of toast on Tom's plate and filled his cup with tea. She picked at her own slice until it was time to go. Fifty minutes it usually took her to drive to Galway, so they were allowing an hour and a half because the courthouse was in the city centre, and traffic might be bad, and Alice wasn't good with the one-way streets.

The day was fine, the sun shining out of an almost completely blue sky. Neither of them commented on the weather as Alice drove off, remembering the last time — was he remembering too? — they were both in a car together. The sky had been blue then too, although it had been much colder. She remembered the whirr of the heater drowning the radio. She remembered turning down the heater and hearing about a long tailback at the Red Cow roundabout, just before —

"Put on the radio, would you?" she asked Tom. "Find something nice. Lyric, maybe."

★ ★ ★

326

Their solicitor was waiting for them in the lobby of the courthouse. He shook hands with Tom, cradling Tom's hand in both his own. He took Alice's arm. "Soon be over," he told them. "Won't last long, just a formality."

They sat on a wooden bench outside the courtroom, waiting to be called. Alice leant against the wall, feeling its coldness through her light grey jacket.

Soon be over. Won't last long.

The bell above the door brought her out from the back.

"Hey," Wally said. "Finally made it."

Hannah smiled. "Hello there." She held up her mug. "I was just having a sneaky cuppa."

"Why be sneaky?" he asked. "It's your shop, you're the boss." He looked around. "Nice little place, nice and yellow." He spotted the rocking chair on the wall and grinned. "I suppose the high chair is for your baby customers."

She tried to look offended and failed. "Actually it belonged to my granddad, whose money helped me set up this place."

He wore a green T-shirt with a cartoon apple on the front, and loose canvas jeans. He was broad like Patrick, but not as tall. Chunky was how she'd describe him.

"I suppose you're here to claim your cupcakes," she said.

He studied the display stand on the counter. "Well, I must confess I am. I told you I have a sweet tooth — and I also happen to know a lady who wouldn't say no to a cupcake."

"You do?"

Of course he was attached. A man with his friendly, easygoing nature wouldn't stay single for long.

"Yes," he said. "Viv, my little sister. She plays in the band — you might have noticed her."

"Yes, the clarinet player. John told me you were brother and sister. She's not a bit like you."

"No, we don't look alike — and she's the quiet one in the family. Shy, really, not good around people. But she's also a much better musician than me."

"She performs every Saturday in front of a crowd — she can't be that shy."

"Yeah . . . the funny thing is, she's fine when she's playing — she's so focused she just blocks everything out. It's when she's one to one with someone she has the problem."

"I see."

She wondered briefly whether to mention Adam and his interest in Vivienne, and decided against it — Adam would kill her.

"So," she reached for a flat yellow box and began to assemble it, "which cupcakes would you like?"

She watched as he bent to inspect the trays under the glass counter. She liked that dark blond hair colour. She wondered when it had last seen a comb. Vivienne looked older than him, but he'd called her his little sister.

"That one," he said, pointing, "and that one."

"A taxi driver who can play keyboards," she said, putting them into the box. "You don't come across one of those every day."

"I'll have you know —" straightening up "— that I play the guitar and the flute too."

She laughed. "Is there no end to your talents?"

He considered, then shook his head. "None, I'm afraid — I'm the original all-rounder."

"Can you bake?"

"Well, no."

"Cook?"

He scratched his head. "Er, not exactly."

"Are you sporty? Artistic? Into DIY?"

He put his hands up. "OK, OK, I can play three instruments not too badly, and I've got a clean driving licence — that's about it. Now give me those cupcakes and let me out of here before you humiliate me further."

Hannah added a third cupcake to the box and handed it to him. "Have a nice day."

"Hey," he protested, "the deal was two."

"You and Vivienne can fight about the third. And if you're happy you can come back and get more — and you're definitely paying next time."

"Done. We're quits, thanks a lot. See you now." He jerked a thumb towards the rocking chair on the wall. "Careful Granddad doesn't take a tumble."

And then he was gone, the bell tinkling behind him.

Hannah leant against the counter and sipped her cooling tea. A few seconds later the door opened again and a woman walked in.

"Nice to see someone looking happy," she said to Hannah.

★ ★ ★

Dave and Claire were in the courtroom.

Alice hadn't expected that, the thought of them coming had never once crossed her mind. The older woman Alice remembered from the cemetery was there too, an arm around Claire's hunched shoulders. They sat on a wooden bench towards the front.

Alice didn't spot them right away. She walked along the central aisle, following the guard who'd ushered them in, her bag clasped tightly in both hands, her heart thudding. She'd never been in a courtroom in her life.

The guard indicated a bench in the front row to Alice and the solicitor, and brought Tom over to the stand — and as Alice was about to sit she saw them, two rows back. She turned abruptly and took a seat across the aisle, aware of their solicitor looking questioningly at her.

Let him think what he liked. She couldn't sit in such close proximity to them, however speedy the process was. She prayed they hadn't noticed her, prayed Claire wouldn't remember the woman who'd spoken to her at the bus stop.

But even away from them she could feel their presence, sensed their eyes on her. Of course they'd know she was the wife — they'd have seen her come in with Tom, who else could she be? Her skin prickled, and she dug her nails into her palms and closed her eyes, and waited for it to be over.

And when, barely five minutes later, Tom was charged with dangerous driving causing death, Alice should have been prepared. She *had* been prepared —

the solicitor had told them that this charge would be the most likely outcome — but as the judge spoke the words out loud, as he told Tom that a trial date would be set and he would be summoned again, this time to the circuit court, Alice stumbled to her feet and hurried back down the aisle and out of the room, a hand pressed to her trembling mouth, oblivious now to who might be looking at her.

In the corridor she pulled a tissue from her bag and wiped her eyes, and blew her nose. She sat on the same bench as before, taking ragged breaths, trying to gather her wits before Tom appeared, knowing she had to be positive for him. When the courtroom door opened she looked up, forcing a smile — and there they were.

Alice ducked her head quickly, but it was too late. She heard the halt in their progress. Her heart sank, and she waited for what she knew was coming.

"That's her. That's his wife."

Claire's voice, it must be. It sounded too young to be the other woman's. Alice kept her head bent, stomach churning.

"You stay away from us." Rising in pitch, thick with anger. "You stop hanging around our house. You stay away from Jason — you don't go near him. You hear me, you creep?"

Alice lifted her head slowly. Claire stood in front of her, hands closed into fists by her sides, her face contorted, the white streaked with red. Her mother and Dave watched silently, their eyes fixed on Alice.

"You hear me?" Claire shouted again.

"I hear you," Alice said softly. "I'm very sorry." Her voice shook. She could feel a pulse beating in her head, the sting of incipient tears.

"Sorry?" The colour darkened in Claire's face. "You're sorry?" Dave put a hand on her arm but she shook it off roughly. "Your husband destroyed us; he destroyed our lives!" Her voice was shrill, her enraged, anguished face close to Alice's now, the spittle flying from her mouth to land on Alice's cheeks. "I hope he's locked up for good — he's a monster!"

"I'm sorry," Alice wept, her hands raised to ward off the blows she was sure were coming, "I'm so sorry."

Claire turned abruptly and stalked away, and the other two followed. They turned a corner and were gone. Alice's shoulders slumped and she bowed her head, pressing the tissue to her eyes again as the courtroom door was pushed open once more.

"Come on," she heard Tom say quietly. "Alice, come on, time to go."

But she didn't lift her head.

"Listen to this," Stephen said. "'Bradshaw-Dunne — On 13 June 2009, to Leah Bradshaw and Patrick Dunne, a son, Reuben William.' "

"What? Show me that."

Stephen passed the paper across the table and Geraldine scanned the notice. "Bradshaw-Dunne — that's Fiona's doing anyway; she'd be into double-barrelled. And what kind of a name is Reuben?"

Stephen sliced the top off his egg. "It's biblical."

332

Geraldine studied the notice. "June the thirteenth, and this is . . ."

"The seventeenth. Thursday was the thirteenth."

"And Fiona was at bridge the night after. She made no mention of it." Geraldine frowned. "That's weird. You'd think she would have been telling everyone."

"Probably didn't want to make a fuss," Stephen said, sprinkling salt, "under the circumstances."

Geraldine tossed the paper aside and went back to her half grapefruit. "Ah, nobody cares about that any more, not now that Hannah's found someone much nicer."

Stephen made no comment. He very much doubted that Geraldine had forgiven Fiona's daughter for breaking up Hannah's previous relationship, but there was nothing to be gained from going into that.

"We're holding interviews today," he said instead, "for Tom's replacement."

"Isn't there someone replacing him already?"

"Yes, but now that he's officially taking unpaid leave, we have to interview. It's a legal thing."

Tom and Alice were travelling to Dublin the following Monday. Alice was accompanying Tom to the treatment centre and leaving him there, and returning home alone. He would be gone for at least a month. Visits, particularly in the first two weeks, were not encouraged.

"She'll find it lonesome on her own," Geraldine said.

"I suppose she will." Stephen finished his egg and pushed back his chair. "Well, I'd better be off." He bent and kissed Geraldine's cheek. "Don't get up," he said, as he always did, and Geraldine, who never got up, went back to the paper and read the birth notice again.

Bradshaw-Dunne. A bit of a mouthful. She'd never seen the point of double-barrelled names. And Reuben sounded too like Ruby for it to sit comfortably on a boy.

June the thirteenth. She worked backwards to September the thirteenth, two weeks before Stephen's fifty-seventh. They'd gone out to dinner for his birthday, the four of them. Hannah and Patrick had given Stephen the box set of Seamus Heaney's poems. Hannah had been full of chat, Geraldine remembered, about her plans to start looking, finally, for a premises. Patrick had mentioned a cruise his father had just booked, around the Greek islands. And all the time . . .

She turned the pages until she found the television listings. Who cared about all that? Ancient history now.

"At least you have your own room," Alice said. "That's good." Not expecting, or receiving, a reply.

Tom laid his case on the bed and walked to the window, and stood with his back to her.

"It's nice and quiet here," Alice said. "Quieter than at home. You'll be able to sleep at night. You mightn't need your tablets."

There was a tree about twenty feet from his window. It looked like some kind of a maple to Alice. They could hear the tiny rustling the leaves made in the light breeze.

"You brought books," she said, "did you?"

"Yes."

"And crosswords? Did you bring the crossword book?"

His shoulders lifted. "I didn't think of it."

"I'll post it to you," she said. "I'll get a few more."

He wore the suit he'd worn to the courthouse. He'd got his hair cut for the court visit. The back of his neck was heartbreaking to her.

"Well," she said briskly, before she made a fool of herself, "I suppose I'd better be off."

Tom didn't move. He gave no indication that he'd even heard her.

"I know it was an accident," Alice said suddenly, the words rushing out of her. "I understand that."

She turned and walked quickly from the small, bare room, narrowly avoiding a collision with the door frame. All down the corridor that smelt of cabbage she waited to hear him calling after her.

She drove the four hours back to Clongarvin without taking a break, the journey as silent as the earlier one had been. As she walked into the house, the phone was ringing.

Alice picked it up and said, "Hello," knowing it would be Tom. Who else would be ringing?

"Mum, how could you not tell me?" Ellen asked.

"I've packed it in," Nora said. "Couldn't hack it, too boring."

"Can't say I'm surprised," Adam answered. "I could never see you as someone's PA. Making coffee and booking hotels, not your style at all."

He didn't bring up the episode on Thursday, didn't ask again how his sister had come to be standing on the side of the road on the outskirts of Clongarvin in the middle of the day. That an illicit relationship of some kind was involved he didn't doubt — but as long as Nora was keeping the details to herself, he wasn't going to waste energy trying to prise them from her.

"So what now?" he asked. "Are you staying put in Clongarvin?"

"Wouldn't think so," she answered. "Nothing for me here really. Don't know what I was thinking about, coming back."

He wondered suddenly if she had any girlfriends. In her emails to him nobody in particular had been mentioned, no name had appeared with any regularity. And here, as far as he knew, Leah was the only one of her old friends she'd looked up, and that hadn't seemed to go anywhere.

Pity, or sympathy, stirred in him. "You know you can stay as long as you like," he said, "in the flat, I mean."

Nora smiled. "Thanks bro," she said. "I appreciate that, but I don't think I'll be bothering you for much longer. I might go back to the States, maybe check out the west coast." She set her glass on the counter and slid off her barstool. "Back in a sec."

When she'd gone Adam directed his attention to the musicians. As usual, Vivienne didn't acknowledge the people around her. She probably had no idea that her only adult pupil had been sitting across the room from her for the past forty minutes.

Tell me about Beethoven, he'd said two nights ago, at his sixth lesson. *Did he really go deaf?*

Why is this note sharp? he'd asked. *What's the significance of that squiggle there? How do I know what key a piece is in?*

And Vivienne had answered his questions easily, and explained about sharps and flats, and had shown him how to identify the key. And then he'd said, in the same casual tone, *I like how your hair smells*, and Vivienne had retreated immediately, as she always did.

And Adam was right back to square one. Unless they spent the rest of their lives talking about music, it didn't look as if there was a hope of him having a future with her.

Hannah had told him about Wally visiting the shop. She said he'd mentioned Vivienne's sweet tooth. Adam had filed the information away without a clue how to use it.

He could imagine Vivienne's reaction if he presented her with a box of cupcakes. *My friend makes them*, he could say, just to take the drama out of it, but still she'd probably faint from mortification, and her mother, followed closely by the giant cat, would in all likelihood be shooing him out the front door with a broom.

He drained his pint gloomily and nodded at the barman for another round. At least he was learning how to play the clarinet — or rather, he was marginally less clueless about it than he'd been six weeks ago. Despite his practising — and of course he'd lost some of his initial enthusiasm — he'd never make a musician, and they both knew it. Surely it was only a matter of

337

time before Vivienne sent him packing. Maybe he should just admit defeat on all fronts and tell her he'd decided to give up the lessons.

"Hi."

He turned to see Hannah dropping her little overnight bag on the ground. She'd taken to going home with John on Saturday night and reappearing on Sunday afternoon.

"Hi yourself. Red or white?"

He was glad she'd found someone to flush Patrick out of her system. Adam had got on well enough with Hannah's ex, like he got on with most people, but the two men had never sought out each other's company. He and Patrick's lives ran along different tracks, leaving them content enough to interact when they came together, but equally happy apart.

"I thought Nora was coming."

"She's in the loo," he told her. "She's given up the job," he added.

Hannah didn't show the surprise he'd been expecting. "Right."

"She's thinking of going back to the US."

Hannah's wine arrived. She swirled the glass but didn't drink. "They had a baby," she said. "Mum rang before I left. A boy."

"Who had a baby?"

"Patrick and Leah," Hannah said. "Patrick's a dad."

No expression in her voice. She might have been reciting a shopping list.

Adam searched for the right response. "I suppose —"

"Hey, nice top," Nora said, reappearing suddenly.
And that was the end of that.

I know it doesn't make an iota of difference to you now, Geraldine had said, *but I just thought I'd mention it, so you knew. They put an ad in the* Irish Times, *if you don't mind.*

A boy, she'd said. A son Patrick had made with Leah, a baby who would grow up to have Patrick's eyes, maybe, or his smile. Who might be good at sports, or writing. Who might love animals, who might travel the world, or follow his father into the newspaper business.

Patrick's son, who might have been her son.

She hadn't expected the news to affect her. She'd known about the pregnancy for months, had long since got over the shock of hearing that. So why this overwhelming bleakness now, at its inevitable outcome? Why the urge to slam the phone down on her mother, to howl at the injustice of it?

I have to go, she'd said to her mother. *I'm meeting Adam, I'm late.*

It was the last thing she wanted, to sit in a crowded wine bar with her social face on, but some instinct had forced her to stick to the plan. She'd packed her clean clothes and her toothbrush, and the various other bits that always travelled with her. She'd washed her hair, she'd dressed in her favourite pink top and the grey pants that she always felt good in, she'd made up her face and sprayed perfume. She'd gone to Vintage and found Adam, and resolved to put the news she'd been told right out of her head.

And in the first minute of talking with Adam, she'd blurted it out.

"You're miles away," John said later. Much later, when they were lying on his bed, his arm across her stomach, the Saturday-night traffic rumbling along the street three floors below.

"Sorry," she said.

"Want to talk about it?"

"Not really . . ." She ran a bare foot along his calf. "I just heard something today that . . . threw me a bit."

He stroked her arm slowly.

"A baby," she said into the silence. "My ex had a baby — or at least, his . . ." She trailed off, feeling the prickle of tears as yet unshed. "Sorry," she said again, turning away from him, completely unable to stop them pouring out.

"It's OK," he said in the morning, when the hour hand of her watch had crawled, finally, to nine, and she could get up. "I understand," he told her, putting out cereal and bread that she knew she wasn't going to eat. "It's too soon," he said, in his boxers and T-shirt, with his unshaven chin and resigned smile. "You need more time."

She wished he wasn't so understanding. She wanted him to be less reasonable, needed him to get angry with her, or at least impatient, so she could feel justified in leaving him. She wanted a reason to let him go, but he gave her none.

340

"I'm sorry," she said again. She stopped herself saying, *It's not you, it's me*, even though it was true. It *was* her: she was being ridiculous and emotional and unfair to him. They'd barely started, and here she was ending it — and for what? For the idea of a baby that would never happen now, for a might-have-been scenario that existed only in her head? Ridiculous.

He didn't offer to walk her downstairs. He made no attempt to kiss her goodbye. He lifted a hand as she walked to the door, smiled and told her to take care.

The taxi she hailed on the street was driven by a man she didn't recognise, who made no attempt to talk as he drove her through the empty Sunday-morning streets. He charged her six euro and she gave him seven. She let herself into the house quietly, in case Adam was still asleep.

She made tea and brought the pot upstairs to her room. She undressed and brushed her teeth and got into bed, feeling the weariness of a wakeful night overtaking her. She drank half a cup of tea, before laying back and closing her eyes.

Two break-ups in six months. She yawned, pulling the duvet to her chin, remembering her anguish when Patrick had left. God, the mess she'd been, in tears at the drop of a hat, any time she was reminded of him.

And then John had shown up, just around the time she was recovering from all that, and she thought, she hoped, that he'd make her happy again.

At least this time there was no heartache, just the sad realisation that she'd made a mistake, that he wasn't the one.

July

Almost half an hour into his seventh music lesson, Adam O'Connor's patience finally ran out. He stopped attempting to play "Five Note Fun" and lowered his clarinet. Vivienne, who'd been pointing at the notes on the sheet music, turned her head towards him, her hand still raised.

"Look," Adam said, "I'm sorry. I can't do this any more."

Vivienne frowned, the blush rising in her face, as usual. "You're doing alright," she said.

"No," Adam answered, laying the clarinet across his lap. "I'm not doing alright. I'm here under false pretences."

Vivienne lowered her hand slowly, her flush deepening. Her eyes were on his face, if not exactly meeting his gaze.

"I never wanted music lessons," Adam said, beginning to twist apart the pieces of his clarinet. "I just wanted to get to know you. You've probably guessed that by now."

Her face was aflame, her gaze dropping to somewhere past his left knee.

Adam slotted the clarinet pieces into the case. "I saw you in Vintage," he said, "and I thought you looked interesting. I didn't know anything about you — I had no idea if you were married or not — but there was just something about you . . . I wanted to meet you and talk to you, see what you were like. So when I heard that you gave music lessons, I bought a clarinet. On eBay."

Vivienne's expression was panic-stricken. Her neck was pink with white blotches. Adam refused to be put off. The words poured out of him. He hadn't rehearsed them, he hadn't planned any of this.

"I bought the clarinet because of you," he said. "It took me ages to put it together when it came — I almost broke it. I'd never considered learning to play any musical instrument before." He smiled briefly as he closed the clarinet case. "Believe me, I know how daft all this sounds, particularly as I'm not the slightest bit musical — as you have of course realised by now."

Vivienne's hands fluttered, a faint gesture of denial. Her mouth opened and closed again. He wondered how much longer he had before she fled from the room.

"You intrigue me," he said, nothing left to lose now. "I've never met anyone like you. I think about you a lot. I wonder what makes you laugh, what you like to eat, whether you're allergic to anything, or if you're into cooking. I just . . . want to get to know you, but you won't let me." He paused, and said, more gently, "I think you're scared of me, but there's no reason to be. I'm not at all scary — ask any of my friends. I'm ordinary and flawed, just like everyone else."

He got to his feet then, holding the case. Vivienne hadn't moved. Her head was slightly bent, her hands clasped in her lap. She was probably willing him to leave.

"Thank you for the lessons," Adam said. "I'm sorry to have wasted your time. Don't get up, I'll see myself out — oh, and . . ." He pulled his wallet from his pocket and took out a twenty-euro note and laid it on the closed piano lid next to the cat, who sniffed at it.

On impulse, Adam slid a business card from his wallet and placed it on top of the money. Something to remember him by, even if it ended up in her bin. Vivienne still didn't move, didn't look in his direction.

"Thank you," Adam said again. "I'll see myself out. Goodbye."

He opened the door and stood back to let in Mrs O'Toole, with her tray of milk and Mikado biscuits, and her astonished expression.

"I know about Nora," Leah said to him at last. Their two-week-old son was cradled in her arms, his tiny pink sucking mouth fixed on her left nipple.

"Hmm?" Patrick turned a page in his book.

"I know about Nora," Leah repeated in the same calm voice, watching him over the curve of Reuben's head. *Reuben, first-born son of Jacob and Leah*, she'd discovered completely by chance on the Internet, and it had seemed too coincidental to ignore.

Patrick looked up. "Nora? What about her?"

Leah watched his innocent face, felt the surprisingly strong tug of her son's mouth.

"What about Nora?" Patrick repeated. "What are you referring to?"

"Patrick," she said calmly, "you know what I'm referring to. I know about you and Nora."

"What are you talking about?" he asked, his book closed, a finger marking his page. "Leah, I honestly don't know what you're —"

"I want you to leave," she cut in quietly, stroking her son's downy head.

"What?" His incredulous expression, all injured innocence. "What the hell do you think happ —"

"Shh," she said. "You'll upset Reuben."

Patrick laid the book on the coffee-table. "Leah," he said urgently, "you've got it all wrong. Nothing happened between me and Nora, I swear —"

"Don't," she said quietly. "Please don't treat me as if I'm stupid."

"I'm not —"

"You slept with her," she said, "probably more than once. You were with her the day Reuben was born."

"Leah —"

"Shh," she said again, easing Reuben gently from her breast, lifting him to rest sleepily on her shoulder, rubbing his back in circles. "You had an affair, like you had an affair with me."

And if, right up to this moment, there had existed within her the most infinitesimal scrap of doubt — despite Nora's abrupt departure from the *Clongarvin Voice*, despite her not having come near Leah since Reuben's birth — if some part of her still refused to accept that it was true, still longed for him to be innocent of any infidelity, she realised at last, as he stood and walked from the room, the splayed book forgotten, that it was all too true indeed.

The decision, when John finally made it, brought relief, and a feeling that it was the right thing to do. Despite his efforts, he'd never really settled in Ireland. The work had been slow in coming, the money never quite enough for him to feel relaxed. He missed the sea, and the familiarity of home, and of course Danielle — most of all Danielle.

In some way, Hannah's departure had brought home to him how much he missed his daughter. He needed to spend time with her now, needed to draw her back to him.

He felt bad about letting Wally and the band down. Wally had been good to him. *I hope you understand*, he'd said, and Wally had assured him — a little too enthusiastically, maybe — that they'd find another saxophonist. *You do what you have to do*, Wally had said. *Good luck, man. Sorry it didn't work out.*

Patsy in the woodwork store had presented him with a Guinness pin and told him to be sure and keep in touch. *All the best now*, she'd said. *We're sorry to lose you.* She hadn't mentioned his young lady, for which he was grateful.

He closed his Irish bank account after his last cheque cleared. He bought a one-way ferry ticket from Larne to Stranraer. He packed his battered van with his tools and his saxophone and his music collection and his clothes. He handed back the keys to his apartment and to the little workshop. His deposits were returned to him.

He drove through Clongarvin for the last time. He passed a yellow-painted shop with Cupcakes on the Corner written in curly blue lettering over the door. In the van he was too high up to see anyone inside, to make out whoever stood behind the counter.

He drove on.

"Where do you keep the cotton buds?" Fiona asked.

"Look how he puts his hand under his cheek," she murmured to Leah as they bent over Reuben's cot. "You used to sleep like that.

"His grasp is so strong," she said when her grandchild's tiny fingers closed around her thumb. "You forget that, how strong their grasp is."

"Should I wash his hair?" Lowering him carefully into the warm water at bath time as Leah looked on. "Where's the shampoo?"

"He has long fingers," she said, watching as Leah towelled his hands dry. "He'll be musical, or artistic."

"Will I put this on him, or should he go straight into pyjamas?" Holding up a yellow babygro for Leah's approval.

And if the phone rang: "You answer that, it's probably a customer. Give Reuben to me." Putting out her arms as Leah got to her feet.

And not once, not a single time in the week since Patrick had left, did Leah's mother say *I told you so.*

For now, that was more than enough.

350

"But she must have said something — she must have made some kind of response."

Adam forked beans onto his toast. "Not a word. She just sat there looking at the floor. Her mother was struck dumb too, when she saw me leaving at half-time. I nearly collided with her on my way out."

"I'm sorry," Hannah said, "but at least you tried. Better to have tried and lost."

"Actually," Adam said, "I think it's 'better to have loved and lost'."

"Is it?" She laid her fork down and mopped tomato sauce with the end of her toast. "What are we like? We're a right pair."

Maybe Nora was right. Maybe we should get together. Doesn't look like we're going to end up with anyone else, does it?"

"Not really." Hannah chewed. "I think you might drive me mad though."

"Probably. Maybe you could join a convent."

"I'll think about it. What about Nora? When's she leaving?"

"End of the week. Her flight goes from Dublin on Saturday morning so she's getting a train up on Friday."

"Will you bring her to the station?"

"I can't — I'm meeting a new client in Athlone. Nora's not bothered; she says she'll get a taxi."

"And what about the ad?"

"It's going into tomorrow's paper."

Adam was staying on in Hannah's house and getting a new tenant for his flat. They'd decided it made more sense that way.

Hannah was thirty-three, Adam almost thirty-two. Most people their age were married, or at least in some kind of committed relationship. In all his dating life Adam had never come close to committing, and now it looked like his fixation on Vivienne was a thing of the past too.

Hannah had just left a man who was kind and intelligent, who turned up when he said he would and treated her right, all because she felt something was missing. What was wrong with them?

"I told Mam about splitting up with John," she said. "And?"

"She was exactly as I expected her to be." She brought their plates to the sink and ran water. "She said I hadn't given him a chance, that I was much too fussy, that I wasn't getting any younger, and how many more men did I think were going to come along? The usual."

"Well, maybe she has a point. Maybe you didn't give him a chance."

Had she given up on John too soon? Could something have developed between them if she hadn't been so hasty? Too late now, she'd never know. "He's gone back to Scotland," she told Adam. "I heard yesterday."

She'd met Wally, rounding a bend in the supermarket, struggling to control the wheels of her trolley.

Oops — he'd moved out of her way, then recognised her. *Steady on there, you're not in the fairground now.* He held a basket. She saw Rice Krispies, frozen pizza and frozen chips.

Sorry, she'd said, *I always seem to get the wonky trolley.*

They'd chatted briefly. She'd asked how the cupcakes had gone down, and laughed at his choice of cereal. He'd promised not to spread the word that she was buying six bottles of wine; she'd protested it was only to get the bulk discount with a coupon she had.

And then he'd said, *I assume you know Johnny's moved back home,* and Hannah's smile had faded, and he'd said quickly, *Sorry, me and my big mouth,* and she'd said, *No, no, it's fine,* but the mood had changed, and he'd said, *Well, I'll let you get off,* and moved away, and Hannah had added toothpaste and macaroni and olives to her trolley, and they hadn't come face to face again.

The trouble was, it *was* fine. She couldn't honestly say she missed John, now that he was gone. She regretted it not working out between them, of course, and she wondered if things might have gone differently in time — but the fact remained that she was fine without him. She missed him a little, like you'd miss the company of anyone you'd got on well with, but that was it.

"What'll you do with the clarinet?" she asked Adam.

"Sell it," he answered. "I'll put an ad on eBay. Easy come, easy go. Might even make a few bob." He opened the sitting-room door and whistled at Kirby. "Come on, you fat lump — time for a walk."

Left alone, Hannah dried the dishes and set out her ingredients as usual. Was this it from now on? Would she and Adam still be sitting down to dinner together in twenty years' time, with the rest of Clongarvin assuming they were a couple living happily ever after? Would she meet Patrick in the street every so often, surrounded by his family, and pretend that her life was just as full?

She sighed and made her way upstairs to bed.

"You're not going to believe it," Geraldine said, barely in the door, her jacket still on.

Stephen lowered the volume on the *Late Late*. "What's that?"

"Patrick Dunne and Leah Bradshaw have split up." She picked up the poker. "Can you credit it, and that little baby just arrived?"

He raised his eyebrows. "You don't say."

"And what's more, I got it from Fiona Bradshaw herself," Geraldine added, thrusting the poker into the centre of the glowing briquettes, collapsing Stephen's carefully constructed pyramid. "She told me in person, made a point of it."

I just thought I'd let you know, Fiona had said. *It didn't work out, and they've decided to separate.* And Geraldine had said, *Thank you for telling me*, because it couldn't have been easy, and they'd nodded at each other and Fiona had drifted away again as Geraldine had reached for one of the shop-bought flapjacks that Dolores Mulcair always tried to pass off as her own.

"That poor little baby," she said, unbuttoning her jacket.

Stephen said nothing.

"It didn't take him long, did it?" Geraldine hung the poker back on its hook. "At least he lasted over a year with Hannah."

"Well, we shouldn't —"

"Oh God," she said then. "I've just thought of something."

"What?"

"He wouldn't try and get back with Hannah, would he?" She looked at Stephen in dismay. "Maybe he already has — maybe that's why Hannah dropped that lovely Scotsman."

"Hang on now," Stephen said, "you're letting your imagination run away with you. We've absolutely no evidence —"

"No, but it would make sense, wouldn't it? There was no reason for Hannah to finish with that nice man, they were getting on so well."

"Geraldine, we don't know that, and people break up all the —"

"Oh God," she said again, dropping onto the couch next to him. "Stephen, she wouldn't be that foolish, would she?"

"No, love," Stephen said patiently, "I really don't think she would."

"Because he'd only turn around in a few months and break her heart all over again."

"That's true."

Geraldine stared into the fire, frowning. "Should I ring her, do you think?"

"No," Stephen said firmly. "Definitely not. We have to let Hannah live her own life."

"Yes," she said, "I suppose you're right."

But the doubt was there all the same, the worry was there. And she knew well that Stephen was worried too, even if he'd never admit it.

"I don't know what I'll do with the pair of you," their mother said crossly. She turned to Wally. "I don't know why you bothered coming for your tea, when all you're doing is pushing it around your plate. And you" — stabbing a finger at Vivienne — "haven't had a proper meal in ages."

"I have," Vivienne said. "I'm just not that hungry today."

"Not for ages," their mother repeated to Wally. "I think she's trying to get that anorexia."

Wally smiled. "Hardly."

He studied his sister, who did seem quieter than usual. It occurred to him that she might be pining for John Wyatt — maybe she'd had a thing for him that nobody had noticed.

"And why aren't you eating?" his mother demanded. "You're hardly watching your figure, are you?"

"God, no." He speared a piece of boiled potato. "Look, I am eating." But the potatoes held no more appeal for him than the poached salmon or buttered carrots — and he certainly wasn't pining for John Wyatt.

356

"We got a temporary replacement for John," he said, to take his mother's mind off their poor appetites, "but we're still looking for a permanent saxophonist. It's either that or force Viv to play two instruments at once."

The ghost of a smile flitted across his sister's face. "Sorry," she said. "Even I can't do that."

He wished again that he could somehow inject some confidence into her. He'd thought being in the band might be good for her, but the experience didn't seem to have had the smallest effect. She played the pieces, but she might as well have been at home in her bedroom for all the attention she paid to her surroundings. She was as shy and withdrawn in company as she'd ever been.

In the car later, on the way to Vintage, he said, "It's a shame John left, isn't it?"

Vivienne nodded. "He was good. It'll be hard to find someone as good."

No sign of discomfiture, no indication that the loss of John mattered beyond its implications for the band. "Anything wrong, Viv?" he asked her. "Anything you want to talk about?"

She turned to him, and he glanced from the road to her face.

"No," she said, after the briefest of pauses. "Nothing at all."

Moving down the columns like she always did, the name caught her eye and stopped her in her tracks.

O'Brien, Jason, she read. *Fifth birthday remembrance. Our darling son, taken from us suddenly on 27 March 2009. Gone but never forgotten.*

She laid down the paper and imagined them sitting around the kitchen table of number thirty-seven. Their families there, of course, to support them. Tea cooling in cups, remembering his last birthday maybe, the four candles on the cake, the party with his little friends gathered around. None of them knowing it was to be his last.

She remembered the face of the mother at the courthouse, the hate plain in her face as she'd looked at Alice. *Your husband destroyed us*, she'd said, her face ugly with hate. *Don't come near us again.*

But Alice had already stopped driving to Springwood Gardens, and she'd given up visiting the cemetery. Now she stayed in the shop with Geraldine in the afternoons, and went home at the usual time.

The house is quiet without you, she'd written to Tom. *I never realised how quiet it is, living on your own. I planted out the hanging baskets. They'll be in full bloom when you get home. I'm thinking of painting the sitting room, maybe cream this time, for a change. I'm a bit tired of the white. What would you think?*

She didn't tell him about Ellen. He didn't need to hear that now.

I can't believe it, Ellen had wept down the phone. *My father drove while he was drunk and killed a child. How could he? How could you have let him? Why didn't you tell me, Ma? Why did I have to hear about it from Cathy O'Regan?*

358

The smallness of Ireland. Someone from Clongarvin working in the courthouse in Galway, some clerk with a sister living in the same neighbourhood as Ellen. A chance remark, a few careless words, and Ellen knew.

Alice had sat on the bottom stair and listened until her daughter had run out of questions. *Listen*, she'd said then, her eyes closed, her words slow and careful. *Listen to me. I've just got back from dropping your father into a treatment centre in Dublin. He'll be there for a month, maybe longer. The accident happened the morning after a night out, and neither of us realised he could still be . . . under the influence. I didn't tell you because, right or wrong, I thought I could spare you all this.*

She'd taken a ragged breath then, and Ellen hadn't jumped into the silence. *We have both gone through hell in the past few months*, Alice had said tightly, *so I need you not to be angry now, because I'm not sure I can take any more* — and her voice had broken then, and she'd bitten her lip and stopped talking, her eyes still squeezed shut.

Oh, Ma, Ellen had said, her voice full of tears, *I'm sorry, I'm not angry; at least, I don't know what I am, it's just . . .*

I know, Alice had whispered, *I know what you mean.*

Ma, I'm coming home, Ellen had said then, *when Dad has to . . . when the case comes to court. You'll need someone with you. I can get a couple of weeks off, and Lenny will hang on to the kids. Let me know when you have a date, and I'll book my flight.*

Alice had opened her mouth to protest — and then she'd shut it again, thinking about having Ellen sitting beside her when Tom was on trial. Her daughter's hand to hold, her child's arm in hers while Jason's parents sat in the same room.

I'll write to Dad, Ellen had said. *I can write to him, can't I?* And Alice had said, *Maybe better to wait till he's home again, and feeling stronger.*

The strawberries will be good this year, she'd written to Tom. *I sprayed the roses, there was a bit of greenfly. I'm afraid the front lawn is full of daisies again, even after that stuff you put down last year. I'm not as good at mowing it as you are, it never looks as good.*

She didn't mention the shop. She didn't tell him what she was planning. Time enough for that.

For sale — wooden clarinet, as new. €45. Location: Ireland. Seller: Adam2401.

He put the cursor on *submit* and pressed the mouse button, and off it went. *That's that*, he thought. *End of story.* He'd given it his best shot and he'd failed.

"What now?" he asked Kirby. "Should I go out and get drunk, and pick up a nice young one? Or should I go through my address book and see if any of my exes are free?"

Kirby grunted, tail swinging lazily.

"You're a great help," Adam told him. He shut down his computer and rummaged in the chest of drawers until he found his togs. A swim would help — a few fast laps up and down the pool should clear his head and banish the gloom. And if that didn't work, he might just consider a few pints later on.

At the sight of him, so wholly unexpected, Hannah's stomach lurched. She straightened slowly, her heart beginning a steady, heavy thudding.

"Hi," Patrick said, smiling. His suit as immaculate as ever. His shirt so white it must have been brand new. "Good morning."

She should probably congratulate him on the baby, but the words refused to come. She could feel the warmth in her face. "Hello."

He looked around. "Hey, I like this," he said. "It's great."

She made no reply.

He moved closer, and she instinctively took a step backwards. If he noticed he made no sign.

"Han," he said, planting his hands on the counter, his expression earnest now, "I need to say something to you." He glanced around the shop. "I know this isn't the ideal place, but —" he gave a small laugh "— to be honest, I wasn't sure you'd agree to meet me anywhere else."

She said nothing. He was still full of easy charm; that hadn't changed.

"You probably want to kill me after what I did to you." His palms went up, his shoulders lifted. "And I can't say I'd blame you. I was a total bastard."

He paused, and still Hannah didn't respond. Her heart thumped steadily. She folded her arms across her chest, willing a customer, or Una, or anyone, to walk in.

Patrick put his hands back onto the counter. "Look," he said, "Han, I think this really isn't the place for what I want to say — someone could come in any minute. Can we meet up, when you're finished?"

She shook her head slowly. "I don't want to meet you," she said, her voice steadier than she'd expected.

"Han," he said earnestly, "I completely understand how you feel. But . . . I really need to talk to you. Please —"

His eyes, such a deep brown you could melt into them. She'd kissed those eyes; she'd gazed into them over a candlelit table.

"Anywhere you like," he said. "Name a time."

She watched his mouth forming the words. She remembered the feel of it on her skin. She knew what it tasted like. "No," she said. "I'd like you to leave now."

"Han, listen to me." He spoke rapidly, leaning towards her, his upper body slanting across the counter. His aftershave wafting over to where she stood. "It's over between me and Leah, it's finished. It was a huge mistake, it should never have happened."

Hannah looked at him, her arms tight across her chest, her heart still thudding, her face too warm.

"She meant nothing to me, nothing," he said. "I was a prize idiot."

How many times had she told him she loved him? How many nights had she lain in his arms, imagining them growing old together, looking forward to all the years in between?

"She gave me the come-on," he said, "and I was stupid enough to fall for it. You must believe me — she

362

meant nothing." He took a deep breath. "Han, it's you, it was always you. You must believe me."

So sincere, looking at her so earnestly. Hannah uncrossed her arms. She planted her hands on the counter and gazed steadily into his eyes. Their faces were inches apart. "And what about Nora?" she asked softly. Her palms damp against the cold glass.

Patrick frowned.

"Leah threw you out, didn't she?" Hannah said. "She found out about Nora and she threw you out." Her legs were trembling but her voice didn't betray her.

"Han, you can't believe —"

"What? I can't believe you'd do it again?" His air of injured innocence was beginning to grate. "The thing I can't believe, Patrick, is that you honestly think I'd have you back."

He reached towards her, and she stepped away quickly. "Don't."

"Han, it's all in the past," he said. "None of them meant a thing, I swear. You were the —"

"Why don't you go?" she said loudly. "Why don't you just turn around now and leave?"

"But you haven't —"

"Patrick," she said coldly, "please leave. I have nothing more to say to you, and there is certainly nothing more you could say that I would want to hear."

He began to move away. "I've sprung it on you," he said. "I can see that. I should have waited, like I was planning to do."

Hannah said nothing.

Patrick reached the door, still looking towards her. "We'll meet up," he said, "when you're ready. When you've had time to think. Give me a call, and we'll talk about it."

She watched his hand reach for the handle. She heard the tinkle of the old-fashioned bell as he pulled the door open. "I love you, Han," he said. "You're the one."

She waited until the door had closed behind him, until he'd disappeared past the window of Cupcakes on the Corner. She leant against the back wall then, taking long, deep breaths, feeling her heartbeat gradually returning to normal.

None of them meant a thing.

She'd been right about Nora, which made two women he'd deceived. Which meant he'd slept with Nora when Leah was pregnant with his child. How many more, she wondered, how many other flings had he enjoyed when he was still with her?

How blind she'd been, how trusting and blind. She remembered how she'd longed to have a baby with him, how she'd brought the subject up more than once. She thought of Leah, left now with a child to raise alone, and shuddered. How easily it could have been her.

She watched the steady flow of people past the window, the odd one glancing in. She looked around the shop — her shop — and she thought of the hours of work that had gone into achieving it, and the slog it still took to keep it afloat. She remembered the uncertainty of her first few weeks, the mistakes she'd made and learnt from.

She pictured Adam draped along the red couch in the evenings, Kirby sprawled on the floor beside him. She thought of how her life was full of possibilities, and that at thirty-three she hadn't used half of them up yet.

The door opened and the bell tinkled as Una walked in. "Well," she said, "you look pleased with yourself."

"The station," Nora said, settling into the passenger seat. "You don't mind me sitting here, do you?"

"Not at all," the driver answered, putting the car in gear and pulling into the stream of traffic.

She'd recognised him as soon as he'd pulled up. She remembered the green eyes. She decided he'd do to restore her bruised ego — not that she'd let that bastard worry her for long.

She could smell her spicy perfume thick in the air, which meant he could too.

"Going far?" he asked.

"Pretty far," she said. "California."

Stretching her legs out, plenty visible in the little grey skirt. Nice and brown too, from the spray she'd treated herself to yesterday. She caught the lightning glance he gave them. Piece of cake, this would be. Good job she'd left herself plenty of time to catch the train.

He stopped at a red light. "Wouldn't mind some Californian sunshine right now."

"Yeah, this weather's crap. I don't know how anyone sticks it." Running a hand absent-mindedly along her thigh as she spoke. The station still a good ten minutes away. Plenty of time.

"You from around here?" he asked.

Nora yawned, stretching her arms above her head, her top rising to show golden midriff. "Born and bred, I'm afraid. But I've lived in the States for years. Just came back for a few months, and now I've had enough. You?"

"Yeah, born here too. Grew up on Fortfield Avenue."

"You've driven me before," she said. "You wore a woolly hat — total fashion disaster."

He laughed. "Hey, gimme a break — it's chilly driving around in winter."

Nora smiled. "I have to say," she said, crossing her legs, causing her skirt to ride up further, "that you're not half bad without the hat."

"Thanks."

"I suppose you have a wife at home."

He changed gear as they approached the roundabout. "Nope. Still footloose and fancy-free."

She waited for him to ask about a husband but he didn't. "Like myself then."

No response — but she'd never objected to a challenge. "Hey," she said, as if she'd just thought of it, "my train isn't for another while. Fancy a coffee or . . . whatever?"

He glanced at her again. "Love to," he said, "but I'm up to my eyes. Sorry." He took the roundabout's second exit, the one that led to the station.

Nora turned to look out the window. "No problem," she said. "Just a thought." Who cared about a taxi driver too dumb to appreciate what was being handed to him on a plate?

He approached the station. He unloaded Nora's case on wheels and pulled up the handle for her. She paid him what he asked for and stalked away.

"Safe trip," she heard him call after her, but she didn't turn back. He'd missed his chance.

Of course he'd been flattered by her offer. What hot-blooded male wouldn't be gratified by a come-on from an attractive woman? And he saw nothing wrong with a bit of afternoon delight, under the right circumstances.

The trouble was, Wally thought as he drove back to the rank, that for some time now his mind had most definitely been elsewhere. And there wasn't a damn thing he could do about it.

"You still have time," Geraldine said. "To change your mind, I mean. Tom isn't home for another couple of weeks; you might have a change of heart between this and then. I won't be a bit put out, really I won't."

"I've no intention of changing my mind." Alice paused. "But maybe you're having second thoughts? Because I can always —"

"Oh no," Geraldine said quickly. "No, no, not at all, I'm happy to take over. It's just . . . I'm afraid you might regret your decision and think it's too late to back out, and I'm just saying I'll understand if you do, that's all."

"Thank you." Alice took a custard cream from the plate between them and laid it on the table by her cup. "I appreciate that."

When the idea had first slipped into her head, as she lay sleepless in her single bed the night after she'd brought Tom to the clinic, Alice's instinct had been to dismiss it. You didn't run away from your problems, you faced them down until you beat them.

But the problem was Jason, and he was dead, and no amount of wishing would change that. So leaving Clongarvin wouldn't be running away from anything, because wherever they went, Jason's death would be there. It would never leave them.

New surroundings might help though. Putting physical distance between them and the nightmare might somehow make it a bit more bearable, might allow them to forgive each other, and themselves. It might make no difference at all, of course, but the possibility was there; the hope was there.

And so Alice had allowed the idea to take root. They couldn't travel outside the country, not with the court case pending, but they could go to Donegal maybe, or west Cork, somewhere nobody knew them or remembered an accident that had happened in March in Clongarvin. Rent a small house somewhere, live simply. Look after each other, like they used to do.

And when she felt the time was right, she'd bring up the subject of early retirement. She couldn't see Tom going back to work, whatever happened at the trial, and he couldn't take unpaid leave for ever. What did the

Americans call it? Closure, that was it. They needed closure. She'd work on him to take early retirement.

They'd have to come back here for the court case, of course. Ellen would be home and they'd need the house so they all had somewhere to stay. So they wouldn't sell up, not yet anyway.

And of course the outcome of the trial would have a bearing on what came next, but they'd deal with that when they had to. They'd deal with the future when they knew what it held for them.

The shop door opened and Geraldine got up. "I'll go."

Business hadn't picked up. There was no need for both of them to be there. It made perfect sense for Geraldine to run the place on her own when Alice left. It would make perfect sense for her to take over the lease completely if Alice never returned to it. Time would tell.

Alice put her untouched custard cream back on the plate. She hadn't much of an appetite lately.

Adam pressed *save* and flipped open his mobile. A number he didn't recognise was displayed.

"Hello?"

No response.

"Hello there," he said. "Can you hear me?"

"I want you to come back." All in a rush, the words running into each other. "I'd like to teach you again."

"Vivienne?"

But of course it was Vivienne. Adam watched goldfish swim across his computer screen. He wondered what it had cost her to pick up the phone and dial the number on his business card — which hadn't, it would seem, ended up in her bin after all.

"Well, the thing is," he said, "I've sold the clarinet. I sold it yesterday, in fact. On eBay."

"Oh."

Silence.

"Hello?" he said again.

"You could try the piano," she said.

"Hey, maybe I could try the piano," he said, at exactly the same time.

Another long pause. He watched the goldfish and tried to summon his thoughts, a slow smile spreading across his face.

"You know," he said then, "that's not a bad idea. I'm not sure that the clarinet was my instrument, actually. I think I'd be more suited to the piano."

Dead silence.

"Are you still there?" he asked.

"You'll need one to practise on," she said. "I could ask my brother if he'll lend you a keyboard. He has some old ones."

Adam's smile broadened. "That certainly sounds like a plan," he said.

A long pause, and then: "Alright."

"Alright?"

"Yes."

"Right then," he said, watching the fish. "The piano it is. Does Thursday still suit you?"

"Yes."

"Same time?"

"Yes."

"Oh, and one more thing," he said, remembering. "Would your mother be terribly offended if I didn't have the milk at break time? Milk . . . gives me a headache."

Another pause. "Alright."

"Right then," he repeated. "I'll see you Thursday."

She hung up without saying goodbye. Adam folded his phone slowly.

She had called him. She had dialled his number and she had asked him to come back. Even when he'd told her about selling the clarinet, she had found another way to get him back.

She wanted him to come back.

"She wants me to come back," he said to Kirby, and the dog's tail wagged lazily. "She misses me. Can't say I blame her really."

Thursday was three days away. He thought about seeing her again in three days, and the delight bubbled up in him.

Hannah didn't recognise her at first. All she saw was another mother with a baby, struggling to manoeuvre the wheels of the buggy over the edge of the path. Two shopping bags hung from the handle. The baby's red face was screwed up with the effort of bawling, its soother dangling from a purple plastic spiral that was pinned to its tiny green jacket.

It wasn't until she had almost reached her that Hannah realised who the mother was. She bent and lifted the front wheels of the buggy onto the path.

Ignoring the mother's thanks, she took the soother and brought it to the baby's mouth. He immediately pursed his lips and drew it in greedily, his blue eyes watching hers as his face calmed.

"Hello," she said softly.

"Thank you," the other woman repeated, and Hannah looked up and saw the slender, drawn face, the red dress that smocked out over the still swollen abdomen, the cropped hair a shade darker now than when she'd sold Hannah the massage voucher. She'd changed a lot since then.

But that was more than a year ago. They'd both changed a lot since then.

Hannah straightened. For a second they looked at each other. Then she turned and walked away.

Bill Dunne had decidedly mixed feelings about being a grandfather. At fifty-eight he was far from ready to embrace the notion of middle age, and he worked determinedly to ensure that he kept any signs of degeneration at bay for as long as possible.

He started every other morning, whatever the weather, with a half-hour run. He drank alcohol with discretion and hadn't smoked since his twenties. He ate fairly healthily — being left a widower with two young sons had encouraged him to upgrade his cooking skills — and every fourth Friday he travelled to a hair salon in Galway for another dark brown rinse.

And having a job that gave him access to plenty of younger, beautiful females went a considerable way towards keeping him young at heart.

372

Bill Dunne had been talented enough, and lucky enough, to have made a better than average living as a freelance fashion photographer for most of his working life. Now he was in the enviable position of being able to pick the jobs he wanted — happily, he was still very much in demand — and reject the others. He worked eight or nine months of the year, and the rest of the time he enjoyed himself, generally in the company of some of the young females he met through his work.

So the notion of suddenly becoming a grandfather, of being thrust into that pipe-and-slippers category, struck him as more than a little premature. Not, of course, that he resented the arrival of Patrick's son into the world — and Reuben looked remarkably and endearingly like Patrick had as a baby — but Bill simply wasn't ready for anyone to call him Granddad. Not now, not yet.

Of course the Dunne name being carried on to the next generation would have been some consolation — except that in this case, it seemed, it wasn't.

"She wants him to be Bradshaw," Patrick had admitted the night before. "Just Bradshaw."

Bill hadn't been told — and hadn't asked — why his son's latest relationship had ended so abruptly, barely a fortnight after the baby's arrival. Given his own healthy libido, he figured it was a safe bet that another woman was involved — and he was hardly qualified to criticise. He privately regretted Patrick's betrayal of Hannah, whom he'd liked, but he figured it was none of his business, so he kept his feelings to himself.

Leah had seemed like a pleasant sort of woman, on the scant occasions they'd met — lunch in her small apartment on Bill's return from his Greek cruise, a Sunday-afternoon stroll through the nearby park, a hospital visit to view his new grandson — but now she was gone too, and so far there was no sign of a successor.

And clearly, whatever had taken place to cause her break-up from Patrick had left her bitter enough not to want their son to carry his father's name.

Would Patrick ever get to know his child in a meaningful way? Would he wander from relationship to relationship, never finding what Bill had had with Patrick's mother, albeit for a shockingly brief dozen years?

And was it really that surprising if at least one of his sons never committed to a woman, given their father's promiscuous lifestyle over the past two decades?

Bill sighed deeply as he ladled his famous chilli into two warmed bowls and brought them through to the sitting room, where his elder son, recently moved back home, sat watching television.

"You're back." Mrs O'Toole regarded Adam flatly.

"I am indeed," he told her cheerily.

"You've no clarinet," she said accusingly, her hand planted on the door jamb.

"No," Adam answered. "I'm switching to the piano. Vivienne thought it might be a good idea." He wondered if she was going to let him in. Maybe she was insulted at having her half-time milk rejected.

"You're switching to the piano," she repeated.

"Yes." He smiled brightly. "If at first you don't succeed, and all that."

She sniffed. "Vivienne tells me you don't drink milk."

"No," Adam said. "I made an effort, because I didn't want to offend you, but it really doesn't agree with me."

"The only other thing I have is dilute orange."

"That would be perfect," Adam said. "I look forward to it."

She stood back then and allowed him into the hall, just as Vivienne and a young boy emerged from the room along the corridor.

"Hello," Adam said, moving towards her, letting the boy past him. "I'm back."

"Yes."

She wore a dark blue dress he hadn't seen before, which ended just above her ankles. Her hair was pinned back from her face with two blue slides. It fell to past her shoulders, and it was wavy. There was a small nervous smile on her pink face. Adam stood in front of her and lifted his hands. "Look," he said, "no clarinet."

"No," she answered, the smile staying put. She turned and walked ahead of him into the room.

The cat sat where it always had, tail twitching as it watched Adam walk in.

"Hello Pumpkin," Adam said. "How've you been?"

"You can sit at the piano," Vivienne said, taking a sheet from the bundle on the table.

He wouldn't admire the dress. He'd pretend he hadn't noticed the new hairstyle, or the unfamiliar perfume. He'd be formal and polite and do nothing to make her feel uncomfortable.

He took off his jacket and slung it across the chair he used to sit on. He took a seat on one side of the long piano stool and waited, his eyes on the black and ivory keys in front of him.

"Would you believe I've never played a note on a piano?" he said.

"What you've learnt so far will help you," Vivienne replied. She sat on the other edge of the stool, leaving a gap of about six inches between them. Adam felt the minuscule shift in atmosphere, heard the small rustle her movements caused. She cleared her throat, a single small cough. He smelt flowers again.

"Thank you for coming back," she said then, so quiet it was almost a whisper.

Adam dared to turn towards her. "Thank you for asking," he said. "I like your hair down, by the way."

"We should start with scales," she said, blushing furiously.

"Scales," Adam said. "Sounds fishy to me, but I'll give it a go."

A sound escaped Vivienne, somewhere between a giggle and a cough. "You should be serious," she said, "or you won't learn anything."

"OK — no more bad jokes." He looked at the keys. "What do I do?"

"Take your hands," she said, "and put them . . ." she moved a fraction closer to him and positioned her fingers ". . . here." Her nails were painted the palest of pinks. "Don't press down, just rest your fingers gently on the keys." The varnish was badly applied, and smudged in several places. "This note is called middle C," she said, indicating. "It's the nearest C to the middle of the piano. When you play in the key of C, C becomes 'doh'. You'll use that key a lot, so try and learn where middle C is."

She slid her hands away to allow his to replace them. Their fingers made the briefest of contact as the switch was made, a feathery touch that caused her to draw back a fraction from the piano. He remembered John saying *as timid as a deer* the night he told them that Vivienne taught music.

"So what now?" he asked.

When she didn't answer he glanced back at her, and her face had changed. "I was bullied," she said in a rush, her eyes firmly on the keys in front of her. "At school, for years. It made me . . . the way I am. It's not you — it has nothing to do with you."

"OK," he said.

It would take time. He might have to invest in a piano at some stage. It might even take a few more instruments, and several lots of lessons.

But they'd get there.

"Now, you really and truly shouldn't have." Geraldine watched in the mirror as Hannah fastened the pearls around her neck. "Darling, it's gorgeous." She turned and hugged her daughter. "I dread to think what you paid."

"That's none of your business," Hannah told her. Much better to let her mother assume that the necklace had cost far more than the thirty-two euro Hannah had paid for it on eBay. Who'd have guessed the bargains to be had on that website, if Adam hadn't taken it into his head one fine day to look for a clarinet? "By the way, Adam's just started taking piano lessons," she said.

Geraldine stared. "Piano? I thought it was the clarinet. Didn't you say he'd bought one?"

"He had, but it wasn't working out so he sold it again. Now he's switched to the piano."

"Funny, I had no idea he was musical," Geraldine said. "He never struck me as someone who was interested in music."

Hannah smiled. "Well, he's very interested now."

"But you don't have a piano," Stephen said. "How's he going to practise?"

"He got the loan of a keyboard," Hannah replied. "His teacher's brother had an old one." She turned back to Geraldine. "So this time next year, he'll be able to play 'Happy Birthday' for you."

Geraldine laughed. "I hope he'll be able to play a lot more than that after a whole year. And, speaking of birthdays, I think it's high time we cut that cake before the candles set it on fire."

"Isn't Alice coming?" Hannah asked. "I thought you were going to invite her."

"I did, but to be honest, I wasn't surprised when she said no. She has a lot on her mind, with Tom coming home in a few days."

"You might as well tell her," Stephen said.

"Tell me what?" Hannah looked from one to the other.

"Alice has asked me to take over as manager in the shop when Tom gets out of the treatment centre," Geraldine told her. "Just temporarily — she's planning to take him away till the case comes to court."

"Take him away? Where?"

Geraldine shook her head. "She's talking vaguely about the coast, but I don't think she cares really. She just wants the two of them to have a change of scene for a while, which isn't a bad idea."

"And what does Tom think?"

"I have no idea — in fact, I don't think she's even mentioned it to him yet. But he'll hardly object to moving out of Clongarvin for a while, after all that's happened."

"Well, no, I suppose not — but what about his job at the clinic?"

Stephen shook his head. "I can't see him coming back to work before the trial — it just doesn't sound like he'd be up to it. And depending on what happens in court . . ." he paused ". . . well, the decision might be out of his hands. Officially he's entitled to six months' unpaid leave, but however long it takes, his job will be there for him if and when he returns — he knows that."

"And what about their house?"

Geraldine shrugged. "Alice was vague. I suppose they might try letting it."

Hannah studied her mother. "And how do you feel about taking over in the shop?"

"To be honest, love, it makes a lot more sense to have just one of us in there these days, it's gone so quiet. I just hope this recession doesn't last much longer or we'll all be twiddling our thumbs." She put her sherry glass on the mantelpiece and turned to the cake. "Now, that's enough of that kind of talk — time to wish me a happy birthday."

She blew out the three candles and they ate cake and drank her health, and then they sat by the window looking out at the endless rain as darkness fell.

Hannah told them that Nora had been in touch with Adam to say she'd found a job in a theatre in LA. "Right up her alley, I'd say." She mentioned that she was considering asking Una to do a couple of full days in the shop, instead of mornings. "It'll give me some free time during the week."

She didn't add that she was thinking of approaching Una's sister Claire, if and when the time came for her to be able to take on a second person to do two more days in the shop, and leave her free to bake at home by day. Claire hadn't gone back to the restaurant where she'd worked before the accident, but maybe in another month or so she might be glad of something part time. It might suit them all, but Hannah wouldn't mention it tonight. Time enough for that.

She told them about the mini cupcakes she'd been asked to provide for a christening. "I'm going to introduce them into the shop, maybe three days a week, see how they sell. They're fiddly, but there's a better mark-up on them." She described a new variety she was trying out. "Pineapple and mango. I'm calling it Tropical Delight."

She made no mention either of Patrick's visit to the shop. She didn't tell them that John had moved back to

Scotland. She said nothing about meeting Leah and her son on the street.

Finally, around ten o'clock, she pulled her phone from her pocket. "I'd better call for a taxi, it's too wet to walk."

Geraldine closed the sitting-room curtains. "It's unbelievable, this weather. Mind you, I don't know why we always expect it to be better in the summer because we haven't had a good one in God knows how long." She turned to the door. "We'll have another cuppa before you go."

They were sipping tea when it happened. The three of them turned towards the curtained window.

Hannah put her cup down. "What was that?"

"It sounded like —" Geraldine began, but Stephen was already halfway to the door, so they followed him out of the house and saw the taxi leaning crookedly against the lamp-post. Roof sign still lit up, engine still running, rain pelting down into the slanted beams of the shining headlights. The road silver with accumulated water. Music still playing faintly from within the taxi.

Hannah ran down the driveway, with Stephen close behind. In the few seconds it took to reach the car she was soaked. She wiped the driver's window with a trembling hand to see inside.

And there was Wally, slumped against the steering-wheel, blood trickling from his temple. He opened his eyes briefly as Stephen shouted at Geraldine to phone for an ambulance, as Hannah wrenched at the crumpled door handle and called his name.

"Hi," he murmured, and his eyes fluttered closed again.

"It's good to be home," Tom said.

He'd lost more weight. His hair needed a cut. His shirt collar was grubby. The dark shadows were still under his eyes, the whites still bloodshot. A mesh of tiny red lines wandered across his cheeks and over his nose. He looked cold.

"I'm glad to have you back," Alice said. "It was . . . quiet without you."

She'd put fresh sheets on his bed the day before, and opened the windows to air the room. She'd hoovered and dusted and polished. She'd filled a vase with cuttings from the shrubbery and put it on the dressing-table, then on the window-sill, and back on the dressing-table.

She'd taken her nightdress from the single room and put it under the pillow on her side of the double bed. She'd placed her slippers on the rug where he'd see them when he walked in. Ten minutes later she'd gone back in and moved nightdress and slippers out again, back to Ellen's room.

"Will you have a bit of lamb casserole?" she asked. "I made it this morning — it won't take long to heat up."

"That'd be grand," he said. He stood in the middle of the kitchen, his suitcase on the floor beside him.

"Tom," she said, and then stopped. He didn't move. "It was my fault too," she said. "I could have driven that day, and I didn't. It wasn't just your fault."

On the last word her voice broke, and he stepped across and put his arms around her. She dropped her head onto his shoulder. "I'm sorry," she wept. "I was horrible to you, and you didn't deserve it." The words she'd wanted to say all afternoon spilling out now.

"Shh," he said, rocking her gently. "Don't feel bad. You don't need to feel bad, Alice love."

"But you didn't mean it," she cried into his shoulder. "You didn't mean what happened."

"No, I didn't. No, I didn't mean it," he said quietly.

"And I treated you like a murderer," she cried. "I acted like you killed that child deliberately."

"Shhh," he said again, rocking her. "Don't cry love, we'll be alright. As long as we have each other, we'll be alright."

It would take time for them to heal; she couldn't expect it to happen all at once. The accident would always be with them, the death of a child forever on their consciences. But standing there in the kitchen, with his arms around her, she began to feel hope.

Tonight she'd feed him and sit by the fire with him afterwards. They might switch on the telly to get the weather forecast, and she'd say something about the fact that they were calling this July the wettest on record. They'd be careful with each other, mindful of what had gone before.

He'd probably comment on the freshly painted walls. They'd look at Ellen's latest photos; she'd tell him the roses seemed to be coming along better now. She might show him the last gas bill, see if he thought they should question it.

She wouldn't ask how the past month had gone. She'd bring him up to date on what had been happening in the neighbourhood, but she wouldn't mention the crash outside Stephen and Geraldine's house the other night. She wouldn't talk about early retirement, or her plans for a move away from Clongarvin. Not this evening, not yet.

And if, when they were putting up the fireguard and locking the front door, he happened to ask if she'd consider moving back into the bedroom, she'd say yes, she'd like that.

"Let's begin by going back over the scales," Vivienne said, "and then we'll move on to the tune."

Adam placed his right hand on the keys.

"No," she said, "your thumb on middle C."

"Middle C, got you. Here?" he asked, sliding everything one space up.

Vivienne sighed. "Did you practise?"

"Of course I did," he said. "I mean, I meant to. It's just that Wally's keyboard is a bit different so it puts me off." He did his best to look ashamed. "Sorry. Maybe you could show me again."

Vivienne placed her fingers on the keys. "This note here is middle C. Remember it's 'doh' in the key of C." She played up the scale, moving her fingers gracefully over the keys, and back down again.

She wore a dark grey trouser suit, and a burgundy ribbon gathered her hair loosely at the nape of her neck. It was all he could do not to drop his head and kiss the pale freckled skin there.

384

"Pay attention," she said softly, and he realised she could see him out of the corner of her eye. He switched his gaze back to the piano and watched her fingers as they moved up and down the scale several more times.

She'd moved in a little from the edge of the stool this evening. Another couple of lessons and their thighs would be almost touching.

"You make it look so easy," he said.

"It is easy," she answered sternly, "if you practise."

"I will," he promised. "Honest. Swear to God. Let me try now."

She wasn't blushing as much. She smiled a little more, even if her smile was still tiny. She looked at his face when she spoke to him. She responded to comments, instead of just answering questions.

It was three weeks to his birthday. It might just be long enough.

My dear Geraldine

Thank you for the lovely card and your very thoughtful gift before we left. It was quite unnecessary, but much appreciated by both of us.

We've found a small house to rent, just outside Clifden. We signed a three-month lease, although the owner was anxious for six, but we persuaded him to give it to us for three. We were very lucky — we only had to do two nights in the bed-and-breakfast. It's a two-bedroom bungalow, quite basically furnished but with lovely sea views. We've taken to going for long walks in the afternoons, weather permitting, and we're both feeling the better for it. Tom is even talking about taking up golf again, which I'm very happy about.

I hope all is well with you and Stephen. I was delighted to hear that Hannah is seeing a new man — she deserves a bit of happiness.

I hope the shop isn't too much for you on your own. If it stays as quiet as it had been before I left, you'll find it easy enough, I suppose. But if it does pick up, remember you have my full permission to take someone on part time. I'll leave it entirely up to you. It's such a relief to know it's in good hands.

Well, I'd better get the dinner on — that sea air certainly gives you an appetite! I'll post this tomorrow on our walk. We'll be going by the village anyway for mandarin oranges — Tom is addicted!

With much love,
Alice

August

"I like to call it saucy salmon pizza," the birthday boy said, bringing out the main course.

"I thought the chicken wings were all we were getting," Hannah said. "I stuffed my face."

"I couldn't help noticing that," Adam answered. "But knowing you as I do, I'm fairly confident that you'll find some space for the pizza."

Hannah turned to Vivienne. "Should I hit him now," she asked, "or wait till he's brought the dessert out?"

Vivienne smiled. "Maybe wait," she said.

"Bloody right," Wally said. "The dessert is what I came for."

And Hannah's smile, when she looked at him, made him want to walk around the table and grab her.

"You and your sweet tooth," she said.

"Me and my sweet tooth," he agreed, and he wondered if she was remembering, like he was, the day he'd walked into her shop to claim his free cupcakes. Knowing then that he wanted her. Knowing before then, long before then.

But in the end, it had taken concussion and a broken wrist to bring them together. It had taken his taxi careening into the streetlight to get her to look at him properly, just before he lost consciousness.

"What have you done with the pizza wheel?" Adam was rummaging in a drawer. "It was always here."

Wally watched as Hannah got up and crossed the room. She wore the blue top she'd been wearing that night — he remembered seeing the lace at her wrists when he'd come to in the ambulance. She'd been sitting on the bench opposite him, her hands at his eye level. He'd travelled cautiously from them to her face.

Did Granddad fall down? he'd asked, and instantly she was crouched at his side, ignoring the ambulance attendant's order to stay where she was.

She put a palm lightly on his chest. *Are you OK?*

You have a yellow shop, he answered, and for some reason this made her eyes fill with tears, and he drifted off again as she raised a blue sleeve to her face.

She was gone the next time he woke, his head thumping, his wrist bandaged and throbbing. He was on a trolley in a tiny cubicle, and he wondered if he'd imagined her earlier.

Was there a girl here before — I mean a woman — with dark hair? he asked a nurse, who was steering an empty wheelchair through the cubicle's narrow doorway.

I didn't see anyone, dear, she answered, pulling his sheet down none too gently.

Hey, watch it, he'd protested weakly, *I'm nearly naked here.* Someone had replaced his clothes with a blue garment that stopped long before his knees began.

390

The nurse didn't bat an eyelid. *Seen it all before, dear. Come along now, we must get that wrist of yours to X-ray and check out that head.*

They'd kept him in overnight because of the concussion, but when he woke the following day his mother and Vivienne appeared at his bedside.

You can come home now, Vivienne said, *after you've eaten your breakfast.*

Wally looked without appetite at the bowl of grey stodge that he presumed was porridge on the table beside him. *How did you know I was here?* he asked them.

One of my music students told me, Vivienne said, her colour rising. *You crashed just outside his friend's parents' house. He called and drove us here last night. We had this exact same conversation then.*

Did we?

But even though he had no memory of meeting them the night before, he remembered Hannah sitting across from him in the ambulance. He remembered the band of blue lace at her wrist, how her eyes had filled with tears as she'd looked at him.

He called into the yellow shop two days later. He pushed the door open with his good hand.

She went delightfully pink when she saw him. *You're OK,* she said. *I rang the hospital yesterday and they'd told me you'd gone home.*

He thrust the bunch of violets across the counter. *This is to say thank you, for looking after me.*

She took the flowers, going slightly pinker. *There was no need,* she said. *I did nothing really. I just went with you in the ambulance.* She hesitated. *It seemed . . . a bit mean to send you off on your own.*

And you got your friend to call to my mother's house.

Well, Adam's learning piano from Vivienne, and I knew she lived with your mother, so I just thought it might be better if someone they knew called to tell them, rather than a guard.

That was good of you.

She smiled. *Actually, as it turns out, I did Adam a big favour. Your mother thinks there's nobody like him now.*

Wally looked at her. *Why would he want my mother to think well of him?*

Because, she said, burying her face in the flowers, *he's got a soft spot for Vivienne.*

Ah. He rubbed a hand across his face. *I see.*

Is your wrist broken? she asked.

'Fraid so — that's the end of my playing the keyboards for a while. Not to mention driving a taxi.

Oh, poor you. How'll you manage?

I'm back in my mother's house till the plaster comes off. I don't have to lift a finger, and my meals are served up to me. He grinned. *It's a tough old world.*

But your car — it must be a write-off.

He shrugged. *Like they say, nobody died. Things'll sort themselves out. They generally do. I had good insurance.*

That's something, I suppose. She paused, then added, going pink again, *You didn't have to, you know.*

I didn't have to what?

Break your wrist. Her face stuck into the flowers again. *To get my attention.*

Wally laughed. *It was a bit extreme, wasn't it?* He rubbed his face again. *The least you could do, really, is go out with me now.*

Hannah put her head to one side. *I suppose I owe you that much.*

She got him, that was the thing. She understood his silly jokes, she forgave his atrocious unpunctuality, she teased his total ignorance of fashion and tolerated his utter uselessness with money. He was himself with her, and she got him.

She called him "sweetheart". Her kiss, when it finally moved from his cheek to his mouth after three dates, was delicious.

And this, Adam's birthday party, was their fifth date. And she was becoming frighteningly important to him.

With an effort he switched his attention to his sister, sitting opposite him. "Alright?" He didn't need to ask. Look at her, blooming after years of crippling unhappiness, when he'd felt powerless to help her, when she'd hardly known how to help herself. Looking so different in the green dress that caught the colour of her eyes.

Blushing deeply in the back seat of their taxi on the way over when Adam's name had been mentioned.

"We're just friends," she'd murmured, turning away from him to look out the window.

"I know that," Wally had answered.

★ ★ ★

The green eye-shadow had been a disaster, and when she'd scrubbed it off with a facecloth — which had taken ages — it had left the skin around her eyes all blotchy. She should have learnt her lesson with the lipstick. And her hair never looked right, no matter how long she left the conditioner in, or how carefully she blow-dried it. Easier to tie it up and forget about it.

Except he'd said he liked it down.

She wasn't a bit sure of the dress. The sales assistant wouldn't leave her alone, went on about Vivienne's figure, which as far as Vivienne could see was nothing to write home about. No bust to speak of, hips hardly there either. Size eight feet, which was mortifying any time she needed shoes.

"And it'll be dead easy to take it up a bit," the girl had said, when it had never occurred to Vivienne to make the dress any shorter. But she'd gone ahead and bought it, and her mother had actually admired it when Vivienne had shown her.

"Nice and bright," she'd said, "smartens you up." Which was really as good as it got from her mother.

And now, halfway through her second glass of wine, the fear of dropping something, or spilling something, didn't seem to matter quite so much any more. And the knot she'd had all day in her stomach had more or less vanished, so she could actually enjoy the food instead of forcing it down.

She supposed she was a bit merry, not used to drinking wine — or any kind of alcohol, for that matter. She suspected that she might feel a little worse for wear in the morning. But who cared, with no music lessons on a Sunday?

She smiled across the table at her only adult pupil, remembering how sick she'd been at the thought of phoning him, how she'd been sure she was actually going to throw up as she'd dialled the number on his business card. How she'd forced herself to stay on the line until he'd answered, how she'd hardly been able to get a word out, so terrified she'd been.

But incredibly, it had worked. He'd agreed to come back. She'd taken the initiative and things had gone the way she'd wanted them to go. And now here she was, on her first ever date at twenty-nine years of age.

"Just a small little dinner, nothing fancy," he'd said. "Wally's coming."

He'd made it as easy as he could; he'd made it impossible for her to say no. Not that she'd wanted to say no.

Not that she hadn't been terrified at the thought of it all the same, even with Wally there. But now that she'd loosened up a bit, she was beginning to see why people went out on dates.

In fact, she was quite prepared to try it again some time.

They ate the salmon pizza, and the raspberry ice-cream that followed. They blew out the thirty-two candles on the giant peanut butter cupcake that Hannah had made. They raised their glasses and wished Adam a happy birthday.

And later, when Wally and Vivienne had left in the taxi, Adam ignored Hannah's mild protest and refilled their glasses.

"We have to toast you," he said, "for being daft enough to open a shop in the middle of a recession."

She smiled wearily, leaning her elbows on the table that was still littered with plates and glasses. "Yes, that was very sensible, wasn't it?"

"And for reaching the seven-month mark, still solvent, and still in one piece."

"Just about."

"And for putting up with me and Kirby for the past six months."

"Yes," she said. "That was very difficult." She lifted her glass. "To us," she said, "who might not have to marry each other after all."

"I'll drink to that."

They finished the wine and cut another two slices from the birthday cupcake. They made a half-hearted attempt at the washing-up and put Kirby out for the night. Hannah closed the windows and Adam bolted the doors.

And then they went upstairs to bed.

Acknowledgements

Thanks to Faith; and all at Hachette; thanks to Aonghus for keeping it in the family; thanks to the Tyrone Guthrie Centre for providing the usual top class hospitality; thanks to Garda John McCabe for his help; thanks to the real Kirby for being a good sport; and thanks to the original Pumpkin for having such a cute name.

ISIS publish a wide range of books in large print, from fiction to biography. Any suggestions for books you would like to see in large print or audio are always welcome. Please send to the Editorial Department at:

ISIS Publishing Limited
7 Centremead
Osney Mead
Oxford OX2 0ES

A full list of titles is available free of charge from:

Ulverscroft Large Print Books Limited

(UK)
The Green
Bradgate Road, Anstey
Leicester LE7 7FU
Tel: (0116) 236 4325

(Australia)
P.O. Box 314
St Leonards
NSW 1590
Tel: (02) 9436 2622

(USA)
P.O. Box 1230
West Seneca
N.Y. 14224-1230
Tel: (716) 674 4270

(Canada)
P.O. Box 80038
Burlington
Ontario L7L 6B1
Tel: (905) 637 8734

(New Zealand)
P.O. Box 456
Feilding
Tel: (06) 323 6828

Details of **ISIS** complete and unabridged audio books are also available from these offices. Alternatively, contact your local library for details of their collection of **ISIS** large print and unabridged audio books.